P9-EDI-342

02692442 9

M

THE EDGE
OF
LIGHT

THE EDGE OF LIGHT

by
Joan Wolf

NAL BOOKS

NAL BOOKS
Published by the Penguin Group
Penguin Books USA Inc., 375 Hudson Street,
New York, New York 10014, U.S.A.
Penguin Books Ltd, 27 Wrights Lane,
London W8 5TZ, England
Penguin Books Australia Ltd, Ringwood,
Victoria, Australia
Penguin Books Canada Ltd, 2801 John Street,
Markham, Ontario, Canada L3R 1B4
Penguin Books (N.Z.) Ltd, 182-190 Wairau Road,
Auckland 10, New Zealand

Penguin Books Ltd, Registered Offices:
Harmondsworth, Middlesex, England

First published by NAL Books, an imprint of Penguin Books USA Inc.
Published simultaneously in Canada.

First Printing, August, 1990
10 9 8 7 6 5 4 3 2 1

Library of Congress Cataloging-in-Publication Data

Wolf, Joan.
    The edge of light / by Joan Wolf.
        p.   cm.
    ISBN 0-453-00738-4
    1. Alfred, King of England, 849-899—Fiction. I. Title.
PS3573.O486E34 1990
813'.54—dc20   89-77094
                                                                                  CIP

Printed in the United States of America
Set in Caledonia
Designed by Nissa Knuth

To Joe
"The wind beneath my wings"

*This must now above all things be said: that I wished to live
honorably and after my life to leave to the men who came after
me my memory in good works.*

—Alfred, King of the West Saxons,
from his translation of Boethius

List of Characters

THE WEST SAXONS

The Royal Family

Ethelwulf, King of Wessex
Judith, Princess of France
Alfred, Prince of Wessex
Ethelbald, Alfred's eldest brother
Ethelbert, Alfred's second brother
Ethelred, Alfred's favorite brother
Ethelswith, Alfred's sister, Queen of Mercia
Cyneburg, Ethelred's wife, Alfred's sister-in-law
Athelwold, Alfred's nephew, son of Athelstan

The Ealdormen of Wessex

Osric, Ealdorman of Hampshire
Ethelwulf, Ealdorman of Berkshire
Ailnoth, Ealdorman of Berkshire
Ethelnoth, Ealdorman of Somersetshire
Ethelm, Ealdorman of Wiltshire
Ceolmund, Ealdorman of Kent
Godfred, Ealdorman of Dorset
Ulfric, Ealdorman of Surrey
Eadred, Ealdorman of Surrey
Odda, Ealdorman of Devon

The Clergy

Eahlstan, Bishop of Sherborne, Alfred's uncle
Swithun, Bishop of Winchester
Ceolnoth, Archbishop of Canterbury
Athelred, Archbishop of Canterbury
Kenwulf, Bishop of Wiltshire
Father Erwald, Alfred's personal priest

Other West Saxons

Edgar, Alfred's companion thane and standard-bearer

Brand, Alfred's companion thane
Roswitha, Alfred's mistress
Godric, reeve of Lambourn manor
Cenwulf, shire thane of Dorset, supporter of Athelwold
Wilfred, one of Alfred's hearthband thanes

The Mercians

Burgred, King of Mercia, Alfred's brother-in-law
Elswyth, Mercian noblewoman
Athulf, Ealdorman of Gaini and Elswyth's brother
Ceolwulf, Elswyth's second brother
Eadburgh, Elswyth's mother
Edred, Ealdorman of the Tomsaetan
Ethelred of Hwicce, friend of Alfred's

The Danes

Ivar the Boneless, leader of the Danish Great Army
Halfdan, co-leader of Danish army
Guthrum, Danish jarl, one of the leaders of the Danish army
Erlend Olafson, nephew of Guthrum
Eline, Erlend's mother
Asmund, Erlend's stepfather
Harald Bjornson, leader of Guthrum's fleet
Ubbe, brother of Ivar the Boneless and Halfdan

PRELUDE

A.D. 856–865

Chapter 1

*T*HE small boy stood in the corner of the room, forgotten for the moment by his father, the king. The thanes who clustered about King Ethelwulf were dour of face and grim of voice, and the word they were constantly using was a word Alfred did not know.

Rebellion.

What did it mean? Alfred melted even deeper into the corner of the king's hall at Southampton Manor and tried to understand what the thanes were saying. His brother Ethelbald was in rebellion; that was clear enough. But what did "rebellion" mean?

For the past year Alfred and his father had been away from Wessex on a pilgrimage to Rome. During that time responsibility for the government had been divided between Alfred's two oldest brothers, Athelstan and Ethelbald. Then, but a few months before, Athelstan had died and Ethelbald had taken the whole kingdom into his own hands.

Now he was in rebellion.

Whatever this "rebellion" was, Alfred thought with a shiver, it could not be good. Not from the looks on the faces of the thanes.

"Prince." It was the familiar voice of one of Ethelwulf's companion thanes. "Come along, lad," the man said now quietly. "The queen is looking for you."

It was a moment before Alfred realized to whom the man was referring. "Oh," he said then, as enlightenment struck, "Judith!"

"Yes, the Lady Judith. She has been asking for you."

"All right," said Alfred, moving out of the shadows of his corner with sudden willingness. Perhaps Judith would know what this "rebellion" meant. "I'll come."

Princess Judith, daughter of Charles the Bald, had been married to Ethelwulf three weeks before in France.

Judith was sixteen years old; Ethelwulf was fifty-three.

"Alfred," Judith said in Frankish as Alfred came though the door of her sleeping room. Not many years separated her from her stepson, and the

3

two had become fast friends during the four-month stay the West Saxons had made at the court of France. In the easy way of children, Alfred had learned to speak simple Frankish and it was he who was tutoring Judith in Saxon. "What is happening?" she asked now, her large brown eyes darker than usual with apprehension.

"I do not know, Judith," Alfred answered, closing the door behind him. "I think my brother Ethelbald has done something bad. The thanes say it is 'rebellion.' " He said the word in Saxon. "Do you know what that means?" he asked.

Judith shook her head. "If you do not know the word, Alfred, then how can I?"

"Oh." He had not thought of that. He crossed the wooden floor and climbed into the room's second chair, which was placed, like Judith's, close to the charcoal brazier. He said, his voice troubled, "It is strange that my other brothers, Ethelbert and Ethelred, are not here to greet us."

Judith sighed with exasperation. "Your West Saxon names! They all sound the same to me!"

Alfred grinned a little. " 'Ethel' means nobly born," he said in explanation, taking obvious pleasure in being able to impart information. "It is a common beginning for the names of West Saxon nobles." He remembered an old grievance, "Of all my brothers, I am the only one not to be called by it. Even my sister is called Ethelswith!"

"You came so long after your brothers and sister," Judith said in her soft voice. "Your father has told me that you are his special gift from God. That is why you have a special name."

Alfred pushed out his lower lip. "I like the name 'Ethelwold,' " he said after a minute.

Judith said firmly, "I like 'Alfred.' "

He looked at her sideways from under long, gold-tipped lashes; then he grinned.

"How old is your brother Ethelbald?" Judith asked next.

The smile disappeared and Alfred looked earnestly at his fingers. "Ethelred is eighteen. Ethelbert is four years older than he, and Ethelbald two years more. That makes him . . ." He frowned in concentration and began to count on his fingers.

"Twenty-four," Judith said finally when it became clear that Alfred had lost his way.

Alfred scowled, furious that he had not been able to do the arithmetic.

At that moment the latch on the door lifted and the door was pushed open. Both Alfred and Judith jumped to their feet as a tall, thin, gray-haired man came into the room.

"My lord," said Judith in a suddenly subdued voice.

"Father!" said Alfred in relief. As soon as Ethelwulf began to cross the floor toward them Alfred asked in Saxon, "What is 'rebellion'?"

"Rebellion," Ethelwulf, King of Wessex, repeated heavily. He turned to Judith and said the word again, in Frankish. Her eyes opened wide with sudden comprehension.

"Sit down, my dear," Ethelwulf said to his wife, speaking in his accented but relatively fluent French. He turned to Alfred. "You may take the floor, my son. My old bones have more need of a chair than do yours."

Alfred subsided with boneless ease onto the fur rug at his father's feet. "What did you say to Judith?" he said to Ethelwulf with the fearless curiosity of an indulged child. "What was that word? What is 'rebellion'?"

Ethelwulf lowered himself into the chair that Alfred had vacated and stretched his long legs before him. " 'Rebellion' is the act of raising an army against one's king," he said, meeting his son's upraised golden eyes. "It appears that your brother Ethelbald, having had a taste of kingship, has decided he does not want to give up the position."

Alfred stared at his father's face. Ethelwulf did not look worried, he thought. He merely looked tired. Whatever it was that Ethelbald was doing, it could not be as bad as Alfred had feared.

Judith was saying, "I am sorry, my lord, to hear this. But one man cannot raise a rebellion alone. Has this son of yours followers?"

"So it would seem," Ethelwulf replied.

"Not Ethelred!" Alfred interjected, in quick defense of his favorite brother.

"No, not Ethelred," his father agreed. "In fact, Ethelred and Ethelbert are awaiting me at Winchester. It appears that Osric, ealdorman of Hampshire, has raised the fyrd in my defense."

There was a moment's silence. Then Judith asked, almost diffidently, "I do not understand your words, my lord. What is the fyrd? What is an ealdorman?"

"An ealdorman is similar to a Frankish count, my dear," Ethelwulf explained. "He is a noble appointed by the king to lead the shire. He is responsible for administering the law in the shire, and he is responsible for defense. The fyrd is the militia that the ealdorman calls up from among the thanes and ceorls of his shire in time of need."

Alfred had been listening to his father's explanation with barely concealed impatience. "Father!" he said as soon as Ethelwulf had finished, "Does Ethelbald have an *army*?"

"Yes, my son," came the sad reply. "I very much fear that he does."

Alfred could feel the muscles in his stomach contract. "What does it all mean?" he almost whispered. "What is going to happen?"

Judith's voice, practical and cool, cut across his. "Who are Ethelbald's followers, my lord? And how many of them are there?"

Alfred's father began to rub the side of his face, a sure sign of distress. "Ethelbald's foster father is my wife's brother, Eahlstan, Bishop of Sherborne. Ethelbald has passed most of his life in the western part of the country, and it is the men from west of the great forest of Selwood who have risen to follow him."

"But the men of the east will stand with you?" Alfred stared at Judith in surprise. He had never heard her sound so . . . authoritative.

"So I understand."

Judith leaned back in her chair. "Well, then, if you have your other sons with you, my lord, and all the shires to the east of this Selwood, it seems to me that Ethelbald's cause will have short shrift."

Alfred saw his father give a quick look in his direction. Then Ethelwulf smiled at Judith. "I am sure it will, my dear," he said in the falsely soothing voice that Alfred knew meant something was being kept from him. "I am sure that it will."

Alfred longed to reach Winchester. His brother Ethelred would be at Winchester, and Ethelred was the person Alfred loved most in the world. He loved his father too, of course, but Ethelred had always been the one to find time for the youngest member of the West Saxon royal family. It was Ethelred who had taught Alfred to ride, who had taught him to shoot his arrow straight and true, who had taught him to hunt. He had even promised that when Alfred returned from Rome, he would teach Alfred to use his sword as well.

Ethelred would not treat him like a baby. Ethelred would tell him what was happening. Ethelred would make him feel safe once again.

The stone walls of Winchester looked much like the Roman walls one saw everywhere in France and Italy, but Alfred found himself looking at the West Saxon capital city with different eyes this day as he rode in through the gate in his father's train. The cities of France and Italy had been far grander than the small market town of Winchester. Alfred had seen the look on Judith's face yesterday when she had first beheld the simple wooden hall that was the king's chief dwelling at Southampton. Southampton was one of the smallest of the West Saxon royal manors; but not even the largest or grandest of them, not even Wilton, remotely resembled the grandeur of the Frankish royal vils.

Alfred's heart lifted when he saw the two figures awaiting them on the steps of the royal hall.

"My brothers!" he said to Judith; but it was at one brother only that he looked.

Ethelbert and Ethelred came to greet their father in proper fashion, and then Ethelwulf presented them to Judith. Their welcome was brief; neither prince spoke Frankish and Judith's Saxon was elementary.

Then Alfred could wait no longer. "Ethelred!" he cried.

The fair-haired young man turned away from Judith and looked at the small boy on the pony. "Alfred!" he said with a laugh, imitating Alfred's distinctive clipped diction. Then Ethelred reached up his arms, plucked his small brother right out of the saddle, and swung him first high in the air and then into his arms for a big bear hug. "How is my favorite little brother?" he asked as he set the child on his feet.

Alfred beamed. "I am your *only* little brother," he retorted, and Ethelred laughed and ruffled his hair.

"That is why you are so precious."

Ethelwulf lifted Judith from her horse. "Come," he said to his sons. "Let us go into the hall."

The great hall of Winchester was fully as large as any king's hall that Alfred had seen in France. The hearthplace in the middle of the floor was so long that there were two fires burning on it, one at each end. The smoke curled upward and went out the open smoke vents in the roof. Carved pillars held up thick cross-beams, and there were doors on either long wall. The wooden walls were hung with brightly colored tapestries, and over the tapestries hung a collection of polished weapons and shields. Benches ringed the room, and the stone floor was covered with fresh-smelling rushes. Several of the flambeaux in the wall sconces were lit.

Perhaps it was not built of stone, Alfred thought loyally as he surveyed the room before him, but it was every bit as grand as Judith's father's palace had been. Best of all, it was home.

Ethelwulf was summoning a serving woman to take Judith to one of the two private sleeping rooms at the far end of the hall, but Judith said, "Alfred will show me."

Alfred was dismayed and looked to his father. He did not want to go with Judith; he wanted to stay here and listen to his father and his brothers talk. But Ethelwulf only said, "I am certain Alfred will be glad to show you, my dear."

Princely courtesy forced Alfred to walk forward to Judith's side and say, "This way, my lady. The room on the left."

It had been his mother's room, and he stopped at the door to stare at the unchanged setting before him. The bed was spread with a beautifully woven cover depicting a golden dragon, the symbol of their house. It had taken his mother over a year to weave that cover; she had done it all herself. The clothes chest was bound with polished brass and the stone floor was covered with the same colorful rugs that had always been there. There was a table with a chest for jewelry, now standing empty. There were two other tables holding oil lamps. Beside each table was a wicker chair, made comfortable with cushions.

"What a lovely room," said Judith. Alfred could clearly hear the surprise in her voice.

"It was my mother's," he said.

A little silence fell. Then Judith said gently, "I hope you do not mind my using it."

He thought about that. "I was surprised when you married my father," he admitted. He added with the brutal candor of childhood, "He is old and you are young."

Judith's lovely face was very still. "The match was made by my father. He deemed it a good idea to ally our two countries in this bitter time of Viking invasion."

"Then you do not mind going away from your home and your people?" Alfred was genuinely curious. When she did not immediately reply, he added, "I would not like it."

"No one asked me if I minded or no," Judith replied at last, and even a seven-year-old could distinguish the bitterness in her voice. A coldness seemed to come across her delicate features. "I am a princess of France; therefore I must marry where I am told. Such is the way of the world."

Alfred was horror-stricken. "You were not asked?"

"Princesses are never asked, Alfred." The coldness had crept into her voice as well.

"What of princes?" With the ruthless egocentricity of childhood, Alfred immediately related her situation to his. "Could I be married like that, away from my family and into a foreign land?" His eyes were huge, his voice appalled.

"No, Alfred." Judith's face softened and she came to put an arm about his shoulders. "Do not concern yourself, my dear. Such a thing could never happen to you. You are a boy. You will have some say in whom you marry."

His eyes searched her face. "Are you sure?"

"I am sure." She smiled.

"But Judith . . ." Now that his own fear had been laid to rest, he could think once more of her. "That is not fair," he said.

"No." The coldness was back in her face and voice. "It is not. But it seems it is only small boys and young girls who feel thus."

He did not know what to say to comfort her. She looked so . . . bleak. "Judith," he said softly, tentatively, "I am very happy that you are to have my mother's room."

Something glinted in her eyes. He hoped, anxiously, that it was not tears. "Thank you, Alfred," she said. "You are a good friend."

He smiled up at her engagingly and offered the biggest treat he could think of. "Perhaps tomorrow you can come hunting with me and Ethelred."

"We shall see," she said. "But I thank you for inviting me."

"If we get to go hunting, that is," he muttered, following her across the floor toward the clothes chest. "Bother Ethelbald and his rebellion!"

Chapter 2

*T*HE talk in the royal hall was only of Ethelbald's rebellion, and soon the ealdormen and chief thanes of the shires east of Selwood began to pour into Winchester in order to take counsel with the king.

Alfred discovered that one of the causes of the rebellion was his father's marriage to Judith.

"But Judith is nice!" Alfred protested to Ethelred when he first learned this upsetting news. "Why should Ethelbald be against her?" He thought of something further. "She is Charlemagne's great-granddaughter, Ethelred. I heard that is partly why Father married her, to link our line to the line of Charlemagne."

"Ethelbald's objection has to do with Judith's being crowned and anointed Queen of Wessex when she married Father," Ethelred explained. "No queen has ever been anointed before, Alfred; not in Wessex and not in the empire. Anointing is for kings, not for queens. In fact, none of the West Saxon thanes is pleased about the anointing. We do not have queens in Wessex. Mother was the king's wife; she was never called queen."

"Judith's mother is called queen," Alfred said.

"That is the way of the Franks. It is not our way."

Alfred brightened. "Perhaps Father can send Judith home. She would like that." He lowered his voice. "I don't think she is very happy here, Ethelred. She doesn't speak our language and she is so far away from her home. . . ."

But Ethelred was shaking his head. "Marriage is for life, Alfred. Father cannot send Judith home."

"Oh."

"Father has sent for Ethelbald to come to Winchester to parley," Ethelred said next.

Alfred was surprised. "Will he come?" he asked after a moment. "Everybody is so angry with him here."

"No one knows what he will do," Ethelred said.

Alfred's fair brows were drawn together. "I cannot remember Ethelbald," he confessed.

"He was at your christening." Ethelred ruffled his little brother's hair. "But I suppose you cannot remember that."

Alfred pulled away from his brother's hand. "Of course I cannot remember that!" He stared at Ethelred in outrage. "I was only a baby!"

"That is true," Ethelred replied gravely. "But that is probably the only time you have ever met Ethelbald. He has always lived with his foster father in the west."

"Ethelred, why did Ethelbald have a foster father?" This was a question that had been puzzling Alfred for several days. "None of the rest of us had a foster father. We all stayed at home with our own father. Why was Ethelbald sent away?"

"When they were children, Athelstan and Ethelbald were at constant odds with each other," Ethelred replied. "Ethelbald resented the fact that Athelstan was Father's heir even though he was not Mother's son but the son of a concubine. Eventually, to keep the peace, Father sent both Athelstan and Ethelbald to be fostered. That is why Ethelbald was reared by Eahlstan."

"Oh." Alfred's next question introduced a new thought, "Does Ethelbald look like me?"

"No. He looks like our grandfather, King Egbert. Father always said that of all his children it was only Ethelbald who had inherited the famous coloring of the West Saxon royal house."

"I look like Mother," Alfred said dismally.

"You are a lucky boy to look like Mother," Ethelred said. "She was a very lovely lady."

"She was a girl."

Ethelred's mouth twitched. "True. But you do not look like a girl, little brother."

"They said in Rome that I looked like a little angel." Alfred sounded utterly disgusted.

Ethelred coughed. "Angels are boys," he said after a minute.

Alfred brightened. "That is true."

"Perhaps you will have a chance to see Ethelbald soon," Ethelred said. "Father has sent a messenger to Sherborne. We must wait for the reply."

The answer came more quickly than anyone had expected. Four days after the king's messenger had departed, Ethelbald himself came riding into Winchester. Alfred had been returning from Mass in the minster when the party from Sherborne arrived, and he saw his brother as Ethelbald dismounted from his great bay stallion in the courtyard.

His first thought was that Ethelbald was big. Bigger than Ethelred. Bigger than Alfred's father. He was bareheaded, with a blue headband holding his shoulder-length hair off his face. And his hair was the color of moonlight.

Alfred watched with pounding heart as his brother, flanked by eight of his thanes, strode up the steps of the royal hall to the great door and disappeared.

Two hours later, the king sent for his three youngest sons and told them of his decision.

"Father, you're mad!" Ethelbert was white with outrage. "You cannot give in to him like this."

"My mind is made up." The king's usually gentle face was set like granite. "I will resign the greater part of Wessex to Ethelbald and take up the rule in Kent."

Alfred looked worriedly from his father's face to his brothers', then back to his father's again.

"Kent and the rest of the shires won for Wessex by our grandfather are but a subkingdom. The rule of Kent is traditionally given to the heir," Ethelbert was saying. "It will be humiliating for you to become a subking under the rule of your own son, Father!"

Ethelwulf closed his eyes for the briefest of seconds. Alfred jumped to his feet and went to the table in the corner to pour his father a cup of mead. There was silence in the room as he carried it carefully across the floor to the king's chair. Ethelwulf smiled at his youngest and accepted the mead.

"Listen, my sons," he said after he had taken a drink from the goblet, and Alfred strained to understand what had caused his father to do such a strange thing as relinquishing his kingdom. "I have been King of Wessex for nigh on eighteen years," Ethelwulf said, "and before that I ruled Kent for my own father. For all those years I have ever done what was best for the kingdom, best for the people. We face now perhaps the greatest threat to civilization ever seen in England. The cruel and pagan Danish hordes sweep down on our coasts and harry our people, as the wolf does the unprotected sheep. It is the time for a young king; it is the time for a warrior. Ethelbald is both those things."

"He is a heartless, ruthless bastard."

Alfred stared in horror at Ethelbert. Even his brother's lips were white-looking.

But Ethelwulf was not angry. "Your brother has ever reminded me of my own father," he said in reply, looking not at his sons but at the golden mead in the gold-engraved cup he held. "He looks like my father, and he is like him in character as well. He was a hard man, Egbert of Wessex, and ruthless. But none can deny that he was a great king."

Alfred could not understand. "But, Father . . . if Ethelbald is bad, how can he be like Grandfather, who was a great king?"

"I have never said Ethelbald is bad, Alfred," Ethelwulf answered. "He is ambitious. So was my father. So was Cerdic, the first king of our line, and Ceawlin, and Ine . . . all the great kings of Wessex." He looked from

Alfred to Ethelbert and then to Ethelred. "Ethelbald is perhaps not the king I would choose if we were at peace. Peace demands virtues he does not possess. But we are not at peace, and I think he is the man to deal with the Danes. He fought with me at Aclea, remember. I have seen Ethelbald in battle, and there can be no doubt that he is a warrior."

Ethelbert made a movement as if he would protest, but the king held up his hand. "I do this for the kingdom," Ethelwulf said. "Remember that, my sons, if ever you come to rule. A true king is one who ever sets the good of the kingdom above his own personal ambition."

"Ethelbald will never do that," said Ethelred bitterly.

Alfred took a step closer to Ethelred and looked, wide-eyed, into his brother's face.

"Perhaps not," Ethelwulf answered his son. "But *I* am yet the sworn and consecrated king, and that is what I intend to do. I will not have this country torn apart by civil war."

"There will be no war, Father." Ethelbert dropped to his knees and clutched his father's arm in his passion. We will drive him out, him and all his west-country followers!" The blue eyes he raised to Ethelwulf were fiercely bright.

"No, Ethelbert." Alfred had never heard his father speak in such a voice. He took another step closer to Ethelred.

"I am determined," the old king continued slowly and with emphasis. "I shall resign the kingdom to Ethelbald. But I have also made an agreement with him that when I die, you are to reign after me in Kent. And if he should die and leave no son old enough to take up the rule, the whole of the kingdom will pass to you. So rest assured, Ethelbert, that I have protected your interests in this matter. Your interests and those of your brothers. The rule of Wessex in this time of peril must never be given into the keeping of a child." Now the king looked from one face to the other, making certain he had their absolute attention. "You are to succeed each other, should the necessity arise," he said. "That I will ask all of you to swear."

Ethelbert slowly straightened to his feet and Alfred saw that his expression had altered. Why, Alfred thought, suddenly enlightened, Ethelbert is afraid for his own inheritance! That is why he is so opposed to giving Ethelbald the rule.

"I see that I cannot dissuade you," Ethelbert said.

"You cannot, my son."

A small silence fell. Alfred lowered his eyes and stared at the brown wool of his tunic. Ethelred placed a warm, reassuring hand upon his shoulder and he heard his father say, "All will be well, my sons. I promise you, all will be well."

The council of West Saxon nobles, the witan, met the following morning at the request of the king. The kings of Wessex had never been autocrats and had always ruled with the guidance of the witan. Yet, as all men knew, some kings were more dominant than others. Ethelwulf had ever been a man willing to submit his plans to the council of ealdormen and thanes and bishops of the West Saxon nobility.

But this day it was Ethelwulf who prevailed.

The reasons were two-fold, as Ethelred tried to explain to Alfred after the meeting of the witan, the witenagemot, had broken up. First, Ethelbald was the prince who was most likely to succeed his father anyway. Athelstan's son was too young, and would be too young for near fifteen more years, to take up the leadership of a country imperiled by the Danes.

Second, many of the thanes present had fought at Aclea. They knew that though the nominal leader of the West Saxon fyrd for that notable victory against the Danes had been Ethelwulf, the true leader had been his son Ethelbald.

And so the West Saxon witan had acquiesced in the request of Ethelwulf to name Ethelbald the new King of Wessex.

There was to be no formal coronation, however. While one anointed king yet lived, the church had refused to anoint another. Ethelbald had not insisted. He had the power; he could wait for the rest.

Instead of a crowning, Ethelwulf had suggested a feast for all the great nobles of the kingdom. "If we do not hold together, then we will fall to the Danes piecemeal," he said to counter the objections from some of his stauncher supporters. "Do you want that?"

No one wanted that, and so the feast went forward. It was held in Winchester two week after the witan, giving time for the king's thanes from west of Selwood to come into the capital.

On the night of the feast, Ethelwulf and Ethelbald shared the honor of the high seat; two kings, the old and the new, presiding over the packed hall and the cautious festivity.

Alfred sat between Judith and Ethelred and listened to the scop singing *The Battle of Deorham*, an ancient battle song of his people.

"Like a great silver eagle, Ceawlin swoops on his foes," the harper chanted, and Alfred's eyes flew to the figure of his eldest brother. Ceawlin, he thought, must have looked like Ethelbald.

His eyes went next to his own slim, childish arms and legs. He would never look like Ethelbald. He had been told too often that he looked like his mother.

Suddenly he saw that Ethelbald was beckoning to him. Alfred scrambled to his feet and went to stand before the high seat. He had not yet done more than exchange a simple greeting with this stranger-brother of his.

"Would you like to bear the mead cup around the hall, youngster?" Ethelbald asked in his deep voice.

Alfred stared up into his brother's eyes. They were not blue in color, nor were they green, he thought, but a mix of the two. There was a fractional pause. Ethelbald was offering him a great honor, but Alfred feared that doing such a service for his brother might be a betrayal of his father.

His father's gentle voice said, "Do as your brother bids you, my son." Alfred turned to find Ethelwulf smiling at him, and then he reached his hands up and took the golden mead cup from Ethelbald. Balancing it carefully, he bore it with solemn-faced grace to the man seated on Ethelbald's left. Slowly Alfred made his way from thane to thane around the hall.

Alfred had almost finished his task when he felt the first pangs of queasiness begin to stir in his stomach. He should not have eaten the spiced meat, he thought with apprehension. He had known he should not, but it had looked so good. . . .

Perhaps if he ignored the sickness it would go away.

He returned the cup to Ethelbald and received a quick, genial smile from his brother's blue-green eyes. He forced a return smile and walked steadily back to his own bench place. Five minutes later he turned to the brother he loved. "Ethelred," he said in a low voice, "I don't feel well. I think I had better go back to the princes' hall."

Ethelred gave him a hard look and said instantly, "I'll go with you."

Alfred nodded and watched as his brother murmured something into their father's ear. Ethelwulf looked sharply at Alfred, then nodded to Ethelred. Alfred's weak stomach was well known to his family.

He was sick in the courtyard, then sick again once they had reached the hall. He felt wretched and weak and horribly inadequate. No one else ever got ill when they ate spiced food. Only him.

He lay down on one of the hall benches and closed his eyes. He was sweating but he felt very cold. "Are you all right?" Ethelred asked.

"Yes." He forced a grin. "I shall be fine, Ethelred. You can go back to the banquet now." His teeth began to chatter.

"You're chilled," Ethelred said and went to fetch another cover. He asked again, after he had piled all his own blankets on Alfred, "Are you sure you will be all right?"

"Quite sure," said Alfred.

"There is a serving man at the door. Send him to the great hall if you need me."

"All right."

After Ethelred had left Alfred opened his eyes and lay still, looking at the fire. The great log was smoldering under a heap of ash. The doors of the hall were all shut fast. It was very quiet.

Ethelred was never sick, Alfred thought. Nor was Ethelbert. And Ethelbald . . . the image of his eldest brother was very clear to Alfred's mind. He would wager that Ethelbald had never been sick a day in his life.

What must it be like, he wondered, to be Ethelbald? To be as tall as a tree and as strong as an ox. To be a warrior all men held in awe. Never to have a doubt, a fear. Ethelbald did not look as if he knew the meaning of the word fear.

Alfred was afraid. He was afraid of being sick. He was afraid of being weak. He was afraid he would never grow to be as strong as his brothers.

Nausea rose again in his throat. He got to his feet and stumbled once more to the door and out into the cold dark air. It was best not to fight the nausea, to get up all that was so upsetting his stomach.

There was a disgusting taste in his mouth and he felt weak in the knees and very chilled when finally he crept back into the hall and into the nest of blankets on his bench.

He wanted his mother. Osburgh had been dead for three years, and in many ways she was but a dim memory, but at times like this he remembered vividly the touch of her hand on his forehead, the sound of her soft voice in his ear. Tears came to his eyes and he set his teeth and forced them down again.

He would not be a baby. He was eight years of age. He would pray to St. Wilfred to make him brave and strong like his brothers. His stomach heaved and he shut his eyes, curled into a small ball, and began to say his prayers.

Chapter 3

*T*WO days after the feast Alfred, along with his father, Judith, and two of his brothers, left Winchester for Kent, where Ethelwulf once more took up the rule he had held for so many years under his own father. The following months went by peaceably enough, although the news from France was distressing. The cities and monasteries of the Seine and the Loire were being burned and plundered by the northmen, and it seemed that Judith's father, Charles the Bald, was helpless to stop the pagan's rampage.

Judith occupied herself that winter with teaching Alfred to read. The Frankish princess had been horrified by the devastation of learning in Wessex, and the burning monasteries in France only spurred her determination to spread the blessing of her own excellent education as best she could. In Alfred she discovered a thirst for learning that not one member of his own family had known existed, and the two young people spent many long winter's afternoons with their heads happily bent side by side over a book.

Spring arrived and the coasts of Sussex and Kent were quiet. No long ships, with their terrifying carved prows and their even more terrifying cargoes of Viking warriors, appeared out of the channel mists to disturb the peace of ceorl, thane, or elderly king.

The coast of western Wessex was not so peaceful. In June Norse raiders from Ireland came up the Bristol Channel, burning and looting. But Ethelbald was at his manor of Wedmore and immediately called up the Somersetshire fyrd to drive the raiders off. They sailed back across the sea to Dublin and were not seen again that year.

Instead, the Danes continued to concentrate their attacks on France. Deserted by most of his nobles, Judith's father was forced to stand by helplessly as the Vikings burned his city of Paris. Of all the glorious churches on the Seine, only four were left standing by summer's end.

Winter came again, the season of safety in Wessex, when the Vikings returned home to their own lands and the snug warmth of their own firesides. With the coming of December, Alfred once more began to spend his afternoons poring over books with Judith.

Ethelred could not understand him.

"Judith makes me feel so stupid," Alfred confessed when his brother expressed astonishment that Alfred was not going hunting yet again. "Do you know she can read Latin and French, and she is teaching me to read Saxon?"

"You are not stupid." Ethelred looked angry. "Why, I remember the time Mother promised a book to the first one of her children who learned to read it, and you, the youngest by far, were the one to win it!"

"I did not learn to read, though." There was color in Alfred's cheeks that had not come from the heat of the fire. "I took the book to one of the monks from the minster and got him to read it to me a dozen times in one afternoon. I learned the words and when to turn the pages." A quick golden glance flicked toward Ethelred's face. "Then I took the book to Mother and recited it by heart. She thought I had read it, but I hadn't."

Ethelred was grinning. "Little devil."

"Judith would never have done that," Alfred said. "Judith would have learned to read the book."

"Judith is a girl. Girls do not have so many claims on their time as boys do," Ethelred answered lightly.

"Judith's father has a palace school, Ethelred." Alfred and his brother were standing together before the hearthplace in the royal hall of Eastdean while their father's thanes gathered their hunting gear in preparation for a day in the forest. "Judith went to school when she was but five," Alfred said. "She says that in France all of the palace children must go to school, must learn to read and write." His small face set. "We should have a palace school in Wessex."

But Ethelred did not agree. "It is enough that a king can write his name, Alfred, so that he can sign royal charters. And every man should know the Latin of the Mass. But I fail to see the necessity of turning all the children of the royal household into clerks."

"Judith says it is the only way to learn wisdom."

" 'Judith says'! You are beginning to sound like Judith's echo, Alfred." Ethelred's brown eyes were bright with annoyance. "Now, are you coming hunting with us today or no?"

Alfred looked at the men behind him, so busy assembling their gear. The household dogs were running around the great room, sniffing among the rushes, excited at the prospect of going out. One of them came over and pushed his head under Alfred's hand. He looked from the hound's head to his brother, and grinned. "I am coming hunting."

"Good lad," said Ethelred, and reached out to ruffle Alfred's bright hair.

In early January Ethelwulf fell ill. At first it did not seem serious, just a chill that would be cured by warmth and bed rest. Then he began to cough and lose weight. In less than a week it became clear that the illness was likely to prove mortal.

The Bishop of Winchester, Ethelwulf's old friend Swithun, came to shrive him. His three youngest sons also gathered around his bedside, and in the presence of Bishop Swithun they promised once again to support and hold to each other for the good of Wessex.

Ethelbald did not come, nor was he sent for.

Ethelwulf died in the small hours of a wild and rainy January morning. As soon as the rain had slowed somewhat, they put his coffin on a wagon. Before and behind the tapestry-draped coffin rode a phalanx of the thanes of Ethelwulf's hearthband. Behind the thanes came a procession of mourners: Judith, Ethelbert and his wife, Ethelred, Alfred. The king's family escorted his body to Winchester, where he had asked to be buried.

Alfred rode beside Ethelred as their horses plodded stoically forward and, like the rest of the funeral party, he huddled in his cloak and under his hood. In order to reach Winchester they had to pass through the Weald, one of England's greatest forests, but even the trees failed to give the riders protection from the driving rain.

His father was dead. He would never see Ethelwulf again, never again hear Ethelwulf call him a gift from God, and smile that warm and loving smile. . . .

Tears welled in Alfred's eyes and mixed with the rain on his cheeks. His head hurt and his stomach churned.

Before him, he saw Judith raise her hand to pull her hood more closely over her head.

What would happen to Judith now that his father was dead? He had heard Ethelbert and Ethelred talking about her the night their father had died. They had said that now her husband was dead, Judith would have to go back to France.

He did not want Judith to go back to France.

He did not want his father to be dead.

A sob rose in his throat and he choked it back down. He would not cry. He was eight years old, almost a man. He would bear his losses like a man. Bravely, like Ethelred.

He wished his head did not hurt so much.

Ethelred endured the wet and the cold in stoic silence and, like Alfred, considered the future.

The death of the gentle Ethelwulf would change little in Wessex. Ethelbald would be formally crowned, and Ethelbert would be named secondarius and take up the rule in Kent in Ethelwulf's stead.

Judith would be sent back to her father in France. Doubtless Charles would have her married off within the year to further some other of his dynastic or financial schemes. Ethelred, who had a kind heart, felt a twinge of pity for the young girl who had been his father's wife. Poor lass. But there was no place for her now in Wessex.

As they were riding in through the gates of Winchester, the rain abruptly ceased. Ethelred turned to Alfred, who had been silent for quite some time, to say something heartening. He stopped when he saw the child's face. "What is wrong?" he asked sharply.

"Ethelred . . ." Alfred's face, the skin of which was always faintly golden even in winter, looked very pale in the gray light. "My head hurts," he said.

Ethelred frowned and leaned over to put a hand on his brother's brow. He was cold, not hot. "Where does it hurt?" he asked.

"Here." Alfred pointed to his forehead.

"You are probably tired," Ethelred said comfortingly. "This has been a difficult journey for you. Once you are warm and fed, you will feel better."

Alfred gave him a shadowy smile, but as he walked beside him to the princes' hall, Ethelred noticed that Alfred held his head very still. Ethelred made him get into bed in one of the hall's private sleeping rooms, where it would be quiet, and told him to rest.

An hour later Alfred was in excruciating pain. Ethelred sat by his bed and held his hand and prayed that he would be all right. "It's as if a hammer is beating and beating and beating . . ." the child whispered. He stared up at his brother and at Judith, who had come to stand beside Ethelred's chair. "Am I going to die?" His eyes were very dark; his eye sockets looked bruised.

"Of course you're not going to die!" Judith was the one to answer. She spoke in Saxon and she sounded appalled. Alfred's heavy, pain-filled eyes turned to Ethelred.

"No, Alfred," he said, and strove to make his voice matter-of-fact and calm. "You are not going to die."

"But when is it going to stop?"

"I don't know. Soon." God, it had to stop soon. "Here," Ethelred said, taking a cold cloth from Judith and holding it to Alfred's forehead. "This will help."

The headache lifted, almost miraculously, an hour later. One minute Alfred was suffering and the next he looked at Ethelred out of dazed and wondering eyes and said, "It is gone."

"Gone?"

"Yes. No more hammering. It's . . . gone."

"Thanks be to God," Ethelred said fervently.

"Yes," said Alfred again. He lifted his head from the pillow as if to test that it no longer hurt, then placed it carefully back. His golden hair spread behind him like a halo.

The door opened and Judith came in, carrying more cloths.

"I'm better, Judith," Alfred said immediately. "The headache is gone."

"Thanks be to God," said Judith, in unconscious echo of Ethelred.

Alfred looked from his father's wife to his brother. "But . . . what caused it? I have never had a pain like that before."

Ethelred reached over and put a large hand on Alfred's small one where it rested on the yellow wool rug that covered the bed. "It is not easy," he said, "being made an orphan." He added very gently, "I will take care of you, little brother. Never fear."

The child's long, gold-tipped lashes fluttered, for a moment, hiding his eyes.

"Are you tired?" Ethelred asked. "Could you sleep for a little?"

Alfred nodded. Ethelred thought he looked very young and very fragile, and he bent over and kissed his little brother's forehead gently, as if his head were as tender as a newborn babe's. Alfred's lashes lifted and he smiled.

"Go to sleep, my dear," Judith said from behind Ethelred, and the lashes lowered once again. Ethelred and Judith looked at each other, then walked together softly out of the room.

Alfred listened to the familiar Latin of the Mass and bent his head so that his hair would swing forward to screen his face. He was standing between Judith and Ethelred, and he did not want them to see that he was crying.

It was wrong of him to be so sad, he thought, desperately trying to stifle the tears. His father was with God. His father was happy. It was selfish of him to be so unhappy. It showed a lack of proper faith.

He bent his head a little further forward. All he could see of Judith beside him was her hand resting on the kneeler before her. On the far side of Judith, unseen at the moment, was Ethelbald.

Ethelbald had been kind to him about his headache. He had even given Alfred one of his own headbands to wear—"to ward off the evil," he had said with a laugh.

Ethelbald was the true king now. A warrior-king, in the great tradition of their house.

But Ethelwulf had had his own kind of greatness, Alfred thought loyally. He would always remember his father's words upon resigning his kingdom to his importunate son: "*A true king is one who ever sets the good of the kingdom above his own personal ambition.*"

The tears threatened again. Never, Alfred thought desolately, never had he felt so alone. Not even when he had been sent to Rome for the first time, at the age of three, a stand-in to fulfill his father's pledge to go on pilgrimage.

Then Ethelred was putting an arm around his shoulder and drawing him nearer. *Do not worry*, his brother's touch seemed to say. *I am here*.

For a moment Alfred leaned gratefully against the hard warmth of Ethelred, and then, resolutely, he straightened away. Ethelred gave him an approving look before both turned once more to the altar where Bishop Swithun was celebrating the funeral mass for their father.

Two days after the funeral, Ethelwulf's will was read before the witan. The witenagemot went on for quite a long time. Alfred sat with Judith in her sleeping chamber, trying to concentrate on a Latin poem and ignore the rumble of male voices from the hall.

Judith was nervous. Alfred could tell from the way she prowled the room; she, who was never restless, today could not seem to remain still.

"What is it, Judith?" he asked finally, when she crossed behind him for the dozenth time in as many minutes.

She halted by the brazier, and he turned to look at her. Her back was to him and her voice was muffled as it came over her shoulder, "I suppose it's just that I am beginning to realize that I must return to France."

"I have been thinking about that," he said, his small face very earnest. "My father has bestowed several manors upon you." Alfred knew this because he had heard a number of West Saxon thanes complaining about the alienation of West Saxon royal property to the Franks. He leaned forward a little. "You can live on your own property here in Wessex, Judith, and I will come and live with you!"

She turned to look at him. "I will have to spend some time with Ethelred, too," he added conscientiously. "He would miss me if I did not."

Tears glinted in Judith's great brown eyes. "Oh, Alfred, I wish we could do that."

"But why could we not do that, Judith? You are a grown-up. You can do as you wish."

Her eyes were luminous with unshed tears. "I am not just any grown-up, my dear. I am a princess of France, and my father will never allow me to remain a widow." She looked down at her slender hands, then linked them together at her waist. "A daughter is a valuable pawn when you are a king." She raised her eyes to Alfred once more. "Look at your own sister, Alfred. Ethelswith is twenty years younger than Burgred of Mercia. Do you think, left to herself, she would have chosen to marry him?"

He stared at her and did not answer.

"God knows whom my father will choose for me next," Judith said bitterly.

Alfred was upset. "I do not think it is fair that girls should have so little say in the matter of whom they are to marry."

Her reply was drowned out by the sudden burst of noise in the hall. The witenagemot apparently was over. Alfred began to gather up his books. He would seek out Ethelred to discover what had happened. Then a knock came at Judith's door.

"Alfred . . ." Judith's face was very pale. "Will you open the door, please?"

He cast her a puzzled look, but went obediently to do as she wished. Outside the door was his brother Ethelbald.

"I have come to see the queen, youngster," Ethelbald said to Alfred in his deep voice.

Alfred turned to Judith. "It is the king, my lady."

"Come in, my lord," Judith replied. Alfred stared at her. She sounded strange.

Ethelbald walked in and the room suddenly shrank. Alfred stared with envy at his brother's wide shoulders. He realized that Ethelbald and Judith were staring at each other, and said, a little uncertainly, "Shall I leave, Judith? Or do you want me to stay?" The glitter in his brother's eyes as he looked at Judith was making Alfred feel apprehensive.

Ethelbald raised an eyebrow at Judith, and she said, "You may go and find Ethelred, Alfred. I know that is what you want to do." She smiled at him and looked a little more like her usual self. He smiled back, picked up his book, and went out the door, leaving Judith alone with Ethelbald.

Chapter 4

*T*HE January afternoon was cold and clear, and when Alfred finally found Ethelred, his elder brother suggested a ride along the Itchen. Alfred was agreeable, and, as he rode alongside Ethelred, his fat short-legged pony jogging to keep up with his brother's bigger horse, he was content to hold back his questions, content simply to enjoy the thin winter sunshine and his brother's companionship, and let Ethelred choose the time to say whatever it was he wanted Alfred to hear.

Ethelred waited until the walls of Winchester were well behind them. Then he said, "Ethelbald is going to marry Judith."

The shock of his brother's words rocked Alfred as forcefully as if the blow had been physical.

"What?"

"I said that Ethelbald is going to marry Judith," Ethelred repeated. "That is what we were discussing at the witenagemot all the morning."

Alfred stared at his brother in stunned surprise. "Ethelbald can't marry Judith," he said. "Judith was married to Father."

"In the normal way of things, you are right," Ethelred said. "The church will not allow a man to marry his stepmother. But the situation here is . . . unusual."

The surprise was beginning to wear off a little, and Alfred considered Ethelred's words. "How is it unusual?" he asked.

"It seems, Alfred, that the marriage between Father and Judith was never consummated."

Alfred stared at Ethelred's profile. "What does 'consummated' mean?"

Ethelred sighed. "I knew you were going to ask that."

"But what does it mean, Ethelred?"

"It means," Ethelred replied carefully, "that Father and Judith did not live together as man and wife."

"Yes, they did," Alfred said, still puzzled.

Ethelred said, even more carefully than before, "They did not sleep together, Alfred. They did not have babies together. They were not like Ethelbert and Ebbe."

23

There was a little silence. "Oh," Alfred said at last.

"You see, little brother," Ethelred went on, "the church has a rule that if a marriage is not consummated then that marriage is not valid. Or at least, so Archbishop Hincmar of Reims, Judith's own metropolitan and an acknowledged authority on canon law, has stated recently. And if Judith was not truly married to Father, then there is nothing to stop her from marrying Ethelbald."

"But does Judith want to marry Ethelbald? Has anyone asked her?"

"That is what Ethelbald was going to do when he went to see her this morning."

"She will have to agree," Alfred said a little belligerently. "I will not allow anyone to make her do what she does not want to do."

Ethelred smiled into Alfred's determined eyes. "Nor will I."

They rode in silence for a few minutes, the only sound the clicking of their horses' hooves on the frozen dirt of the road. Then Alfred said, "If the thanes were not pleased when Father married Judith, why are they willing to see her wedded to Ethelbald?"

"A good question, little brother," Ethelred said approvingly. "It has to do with wanting to keep Judith's bride portion in the hands of the West Saxons. If Judith weds Ethelbald, then the manors left to her by Father will go to her children. If Judith goes back to her father in France, Charles the Bald will doubtless sell the manors to increase his own coffers. No one wants to see either the manors, or West Saxon geld, fall into the hands of the Franks."

Silence fell once again, a longer one than before. Then Alfred said, "Ethelbald is splendid-looking. And he is young. Perhaps Judith will want to marry him."

"I will be very surprised if she does not, Alfred," Ethelred replied. "Ethelbald is not the sort of man women refuse."

Even at eight years of age, Alfred could understand that.

"It would be nice for Judith to stay in Wessex," he said then. "I would miss her if she went back to France."

"There will be an outcry in her own country," Ethelred said. He seemed to be talking more to himself than to Alfred. "She will be marrying without the permission of her father, and Charles the Bald will not be pleased. But we do not think Charles will have the French bishops protest the union. He will not want to alienate Wessex. Or Ethelbald, who, to give him his due, has an excellent record of fighting the Danes."

Alfred did not reply, just looked at his brother and tried to understand what Ethelred was saying.

"To tell the truth, we were all shocked and horrified when Ethelbald proposed the match this morning to the witan," Ethelred said. "It smacks of incest. But when the truth came out about Father's marriage . . . well, it just makes sense, Alfred. The girl is here, she is a royal princess, she has already been crowned and anointed as Wessex' queen, and we will keep the property and money in the country. Ethelbald could not make a better match."

"But," Alfred said in a small voice, "doesn't Ethelbald want Judith for herself?"

Ethelred looked at him. "I am sure he does, Alfred." He smiled. "Judith is very beautiful. How could any man not want her for herself?"

For some reason, Ethelred's answer did not allay Alfred's doubts, but he did not know how to express his feelings. Then Ethelred said, "Let's canter," and Alfred let himself be distracted.

It was when the brothers were returning once more to Winchester that the first pains began in Alfred's head. The late afternoon sun was bright, and as their horses slowed to a walk Alfred felt as if the flashes of light glinting off the river were like spears piercing into his eyes.

"Ethelred," he said, trying to keep the panic from his voice, "I think that pain is starting again in my head."

"Where in your head does it hurt?" Ethelred asked sharply.

"My eyes. And my forehead."

"Give me your reins," Ethelred said. "I'll lead the pony. You just close your eyes and sit quietly. We are almost home."

Alfred gave up his reins and did as he was bidden. But even behind his closed lids, the pain in his eyes was like fire. Soon the shock of his horse's hooves hitting the ground at a simple walk was hurting his head.

"Ethelred," he said desperately as the walls of Winchester loomed on the horizon, "I think I am going to be sick."

"I'll get you off," he heard his brother say, and then Ethelred was standing beside his pony. He felt his brother's big hands on his waist, lifting him effortlessly out of the saddle. As soon as Alfred's feet were on the ground he doubled up and was sick. Ethelred's arm came around him in support.

"I'm sorry," he whispered when he had finally stopped retching.

"Don't be foolish," Ethelred said. He sounded almost angry, but Alfred understood that it was anger born of fear. Alfred was afraid too. He did not think he could bear that pain again.

There was a firestorm going on in his head.

He did not make the hall but was sick again in the courtyard. Then Ethelred lifted him into his arms and carried him into the princes' hall, into the room they both were sharing. Ethelred laid him on the bed and sent for cold cloths.

The agony went on and on. Alfred stiffened his body against it, but nothing he could do seemed to help. Hours passed.

It lifted the way it had lifted the last time, suddenly and absolutely. He looked at his brother and Judith, who had also come to sit by his bed, and said, as he had said once before with the same quiet astonishment, "It's gone."

"Thank God," said Ethelred.

Alfred touched his forehead. "Why am I getting these pains?" he asked, his darkened eyes going from one face to the next, his fingers still on his brow. "Is there something wrong inside my head?"

"No, of course not," Judith answered emphatically. "There is nothing wrong with your brain, Alfred."

"While you were lying here suffering, Alfred, Eahlstan told me that his mother, our grandmother, also had such headaches," Ethelred said.

"Our grandmother?" Alfred's eyes searched his brother's face. "The same thing?"

"So Eahlstan says. It seems they may be hereditary."

"Did our grandmother die from them?"

"No!" Ethelred looked grim. "No, Alfred. Our grandmother died of something quite different. And she lived a long life, too. Long enough to have children and grandchildren both."

It made Alfred feel a little better to think he was not the only person ever to suffer from such terrible headaches. And what Ethelred had said was true. His grandmother had lived to be an old woman. Her life had been normal enough. No one had ever said anything before about her having headaches.

"Does this mean that I will go on having them?" Alfred asked, his eyes clinging to Ethelred's face.

"Certainly not." Ethelred reached out to smooth the hair off Alfred's forehead. "When once we are back to our usual way of life, I'm sure the headaches will go away. It is just that you are upset by Father's death. As soon as Ethelbald is crowned, you and I will return to Eastdean. You will like that, won't you?"

"Yes," said Alfred, but he sounded doubtful. His eyes went to Judith. "Are you going to marry Ethelbald?" he asked Judith.

"Yes." Her brown eyes smiled at him. "I could not refuse the chance of having you for a brother."

A corner of his mouth flipped up.

She leaned down and whispered in his ear, "Ethelbald is certainly a better bargain than Sidroc the Dane."

The other corner of Alfred's mouth curled.

"You need your dogs," said Ethelred, and at that Alfred grinned.

"You West Saxons and your dogs," Judith complained humorously.

"Don't you have dogs in France?" Ethelred asked.

"Certainly we do, but we keep them in the kennel," Judith replied.

"Most West Saxons keep their dogs in the kennel also," Ethelred acknowledged. "It is just my family that likes to keep them in the house."

"Alfred even sleeps with his!" Judith said with a mock shudder.

Alfred laughed delightedly. "They keep me warm," he said. The laugh turned into a yawn.

"You are tired," Ethelred said. "I think it would be best if you got some sleep."

"I'm not tired at all," Alfred said, and yawned again.

Ethelred and Judith laughed and rose from their chairs as one.

"Good night," Ethelred said firmly, and the two of them left the room.

Alfred was asleep almost before the door had closed.

Two weeks later, Ethelbald and Judith were married, and the day after the marriage Ethelbald was formally crowned King of Wessex. Ethelbald granted to Ethelbert the rule as subking of Kent, as he had sworn to do when Ethelwulf abdicated his rights in Wessex to his eldest son, and Ethelbert returned with his family to the southeastern shires to take up his overlordship. Alfred and Ethelred returned with him.

Summer passed and then the autumn. The snows came, piling up on the roofs of the halls, weighing down the trees and clogging the roads. Firewood had to be brought in from the forest on sledges instead of carts. In the week before Lent began, Ethelred took a bride. Her name was Cyneburg, and Alfred liked her well enough. It was important for Ethelred to marry, he knew, as Ethelbert so far had produced only girls, and Ethelbald and Judith as yet had no children at all. The only one of Ethelwulf's sons who had as yet fathered a son was Athelstan, the eldest.

The snows turned to rain. February ebbed away and March blew in. Lent was harder than usual for Alfred this year; he was growing and the Lenten fast left him hungrier than he ever remembered being before. He went to Wilton to celebrate Easter with Ethelbald and Judith, and had a fine few weeks hunting with his brother, the king.

In August there was a small Danish raid near Hythe in Kent, then another one near Maldon. A few houses were looted and burned, and six deaths were reported. Ethelred's wife, Cyneburg, was pregnant, and Ethelred asked Alfred to pray she would give him a son. Ethelbert's most recent child had once more been a girl. It was more than time, Ethelred said, for a boy in the family.

Christmas came, and with it the news that Judith was also with child.

In the midst of Lent, Cyneburg gave birth to a boy, and Ethelred was delighted. Ethelbert was holding Easter at Farnham, and Alfred went to spend the holy season with his brother, as Ethelred was preoccupied with his new role as father and Judith was nearing her own time and not feeling well.

It was while he was at Farnham that the news came of Ethelbald's death.

"It was the red fever," the messenger said grimly. "The king died within forty hours of contracting it."

Alfred knew about the red fever. It was a piteous thing to see. The skin went red and spotty and the fever raged fiercely. Most folk who caught it perished.

Ethelbert, like everyone else at Farnham, was shocked at the news. No one who knew Ethelbald had ever imagined such a thing could befall him. If ever a man looked to flourish for many years, it was he.

"How is the Lady Judith?" Alfred asked.

"She has fallen ill also," came the foreboding reply. "It was the Lady Judith who nursed the king while he lay ill. It seems she too has contracted the fever."

"I want to go to her, Ethelbert," Alfred said. "Poor Judith. She is all alone."

But Ethelbert would not hear of sending his youngest brother into the contagion of Wilton, and Judith was left to suffer alone. Ethelbert had been crowned by the time they learned that though Judith herself would recover, she had lost Ethelbald's child.

It was June before Ethelbert and Ethelred would allow Alfred to go to Wilton to visit Judith. He was grieved to find her pale and drawn-looking and listless. He felt horribly guilty that she had been left to suffer her losses alone, and exerted himself to divert her. But nothing he did seemed to help.

Alfred had been at Wilton for two weeks when the news came that the Danes had attacked Winchester. Alfred listened to the men in the hall and then ran to tell Judith.

She was in the garden, sitting empty-handed on a bench, staring into space. She did that often. Too often. It worried Alfred greatly.

"Judith," he said now as he reached the bench and flung himself down beside her. "A messenger has just ridden in with terrible news. The Danes have attacked Winchester. They brought their ships up the Itchen and sacked the city!"

Her blank gaze transferred itself to his face. Then she roused herself to ask, "Did no one withstand them?"

"Osric called up the fyrd from Hampshire, and Ethelwulf, Ealdorman of Berkshire, did the same. The messenger who came here is asking for men from Wiltshire to assist as well. They are going to try to get back some of the booty before the Danes could finish loading it on their ships." Alfred jumped to his feet again and began to pace up and down in front of Judith. "I wish I could go!"

"No!" That seemed to reach her as nothing else had. "No, Alfred!" she repeated. "You are too young. You do not turn ten until next month." She added, as if repeating a talisman, "You are too young."

"That is what the thanes said," came Alfred's reply. He sounded bitter.

"Where . . ." Judith drew a long breath. "Where," she tried again, "is Ethelbert? Where is . . . the king?"

"In Surrey."

There was a silence. Alfred continued to pace up and down. Judith stared now at her lap. At last she said, very low, "It did not take them long to seize advantage of Ethelbald's death."

Alfred halted. There was a little silence, then he said, "It is true that Ethelbert has not the reputation Ethelbald had as a warrior. And perhaps not the ability. But Ethelbert is no coward, Judith. He will know how to defend Wessex."

"I hope so." Her voice was muffled. Her bent head hid her face.

"Judith . . ." Alfred broached the question he had long been wanting to ask. "Judith, what are you going to do now?"

"I think I must return to France," she answered, her voice still not perfectly clear.

He came to sit beside her once more. "If you do, will your father force you to marry again?"

She shrugged. "I am a woman now, Alfred, not a girl, and I do not care what my father may wish." At last she raised her head to look at him, and her large brown eyes were very somber. "If ever I marry again," she said, "it will be my choice, and no one else's." She sounded as if she were making a vow.

Alfred stared at her. "Did you . . . did you love Ethelbald?" he asked at last in a very small voice.

Her face was oddly still. "Yes. I think I did."

Alfred said, "I think you are right; I think you should go back to France." She turned to him in surprise; she had not expected this reaction from him. "It is too hard for you here in Wessex," he said sadly. "There are too many memories."

"Yes." Quite suddenly her voice shook. "I feel so old, Alfred. I am only eighteen, yet I feel so very old." She squared her shoulders and rose to her feet. "Come," she said, looking down into his upturned face, "let us see what we can learn about Winchester."

The men of Berkshire and Hampshire were successful in retrieving most of the loot the Danes had taken on their surprise raid on Winchester, and this time the Viking ships sailed back down the Itchen with little to show for their trouble.

Ethelbert took up his rule and decided that the old practice of placing Kent and its associated shires under the rule of a secondary king was not a wise one. It encouraged the eastern shires to think themselves apart from Wessex, he said to Ethelred. It would be best for one king to rule over all. However, to compensate Ethelred for the loss of a kingdom, Ethelbert named his brother secondarius, or heir apparent to the throne. As Ethelbert's wife had thus far produced only daughters, it seemed that the kingship would not be passed along through his own descendants.

Judith returned to France, and her father, Charles the Bald, incarcerated her in his palace of Senlis for refusing to marry at his command.

Under Ethelbert, Wessex rested in peace. No Viking ships came along the coasts or up the rivers. The three remaining sons of Ethelwulf lived together in outward harmony. If Ethelred fretted at having lost control of Kent, none knew of it.

In Denmark, Ivar the Boneless and his brother Halfdan, two sons of one of the most famous and fierce Viking pirates known to Europe, Ragnar Lothbrok, began to gather an army. Always before this time, the Viking way in Wessex had been to attack from the sea and then return to the sea. Heretofore a Viking's base had been his ship, and come the autumn, Viking ships had ever turned again toward home. To go a-viking was a seasonal occupation; by winter all sea pirates could count on sitting snug and warm beside their own hearths. But good land in Denmark was growing harder to find, and men returning from the sea were coming back to less and less at home. Men who went a-viking were beginning to want more than mere gold and silver for their booty. They wanted land. Such men as these, thought the sons of Ragnar Lothbrok, would be ripe for joining an army of conquest; an army which would be land-based, not sea-based; an army of permanent occupation. Like the Saxons hundreds of years before, the Danish leaders turned their eyes toward the lush, rich land of England as a likely place of settlement.

When Ethelwulf, King of Wessex, had set forth upon his pilgrimage to Rome in the year 855, he had had five living sons: Athelstan, Ethelbald, Ethelbert, Ethelred, and Alfred. The eldest, Athelstan, had died before Ethelwulf ever set foot again on English soil. When Ethelwulf had asked his sons to swear to succeed each other should the necessity arise, Ethelbald, the new king, had been young and strong and healthy. Then Ethelbald had died of the red fever, leaving the kingdom to the third son, Ethelbert.

In the year 865, ten years after Ethelwulf's pilgrimage, tragedy once again struck the West Saxon royal family. Ethelbert, the reigning king, stepped on a loose nail in the stable at Winchester. It pierced through the sole of his shoe and punctured his foot. In less than a week the young king was dead.

Once again the witan turned to the sons of Ethelwulf to choose their king. Ethelred, who once had had three brothers standing before him in the line of succession for the throne, was the one the witan named. In July he was crowned King of Wessex at the minster in Winchester.

At the crowning ceremony, the new king officially named his brother, Alfred, secondarius, or heir, as his own son was still too young to rule.

In the autumn of 865, the first year of Ethelred's reign, the force that would be known throughout Wessex as the Great Army landed in East Anglia. It was led by the sons of Ragnar Lothbrok and it comprised some seven thousand men. Ivar the Boneless quartered his men upon the country and began to strip East Anglia of its horses. Come the winter, this Danish army would not return home. This time they had come to England to stay.

I

THE STORM GATHERS
A.D. 867–870

Chapter 5

*I*T would storm later. The air was so heavy it seemed difficult to breathe, and the sky had that peculiar light that meant a storm was coming. The horses felt it too. Alfred's chestnut was shying at every stray leaf.

Good, Alfred thought. He loved storms.

Beside him Ethelred said fretfully, "It is too hot to be traveling today."

Alfred turned to his brother. Poor Ethelred, he thought sympathetically. He did look uncomfortably warm. "We should be at Tamworth any moment now," Alfred said.

Ethelred wiped the sweat from his forehead. His fair hair was dark with sweat as well, and his tunic was stained between the shoulder blades. "You don't look hot at all," he said to Alfred. "How do you always manage to look so cool?"

"I don't feel the heat the way you do," Alfred replied. Then, "Cheer up, Ethelred. I see a clearing ahead of us. It must be Tamworth."

"I hope so," Ethelred muttered. He turned in his saddle to look at the thanes who rode behind him on the forest path. They all looked as hot and miserable as he did. He faced forward again and narrowed his eyes to see through the haze. "It is Tamworth," he said. "Thanks be to God."

A few minutes later a guard of mounted thanes was riding toward them up the forest path to escort Ethelred of Wessex and his following into the enclave of Tamworth, the royal center of the English kingdom of Mercia.

Ethelred's sister, Ethelswith, was married to Burgred, King of Mercia, but it was not family matters that had brought Ethelred north this summer. It was the fall of Northumbria to the Danes in the spring that had made a visit to Mercia seem so imperative. Since the time of Ethelred's grandfather, King Egbert, Wessex and Mercia had been allied together in defense. It was time to make certain that such an alliance was still in effect. The Danish army had taken Northumbria with little trouble, chiefly because Northumbria was divided against itself. Ethelred was determined that such a thing would not happen to Wessex and Mercia.

The royal seat of Tamworth was located in a well-protected clearing between the rivers Tane and Trent. In the last century the great Offa had further fortified it by ditches and palisades and a guarded causeway to ford the marsh that protected Tamworth's south. It was over this causeway that Ethelred's party rode now, into the great enclosure of Mercia's royal center.

Alfred had been to Tamworth before, so the sight of the great hall, set high on its built-up earthen platform, did not surprise him. He watched his horse being led off, then followed Ethelred into the guest hall they had been allotted to wash the dust of their journey off before they were taken to meet Burgred.

There was only one private room in the hall and, as Ethelred was traveling without his wife, he offered as usual to share it with Alfred. Ethelred had little care for privacy, but he knew Alfred valued it highly. The two brothers talked easily as they washed and changed into clean shirts and tunics provided by Ethelred's wardrobe thane, Sinulf. The air within the room was sultry and Ethelred immediately began to sweat into his clean clothes.

There was a young Mercian noble waiting for them in the guest hall's main room. "My lord," he said to Ethelred, bowing his raven head in deference, "I am Athulf, Ealdorman of Gaini. I have been sent to escort you to the king."

Alfred and Ethelred exchanged a look of surprise. Ethelred Mucill had been both Ealdorman of Gaini and one of Burgred's chief advisers ever since they both could remember. Where had this youngster come from? Athulf saw the look and explained in a grave voice, "My father died this winter past and the king was good enough to appoint me ealdorman in his stead."

Alfred would never have taken this black-haired, hawk-nosed Mercian to be Ethelred Mucill's son. He looked strong-minded, this Athulf, Alfred thought as he listened to Ethelred's reply. God knew they needed some strong-minded men to advise Burgred. In Alfred's experience, his brother-by-marriage was never one to look a fact in the face.

"Thank you, my lord." The young ealdorman's eyes flicked from Ethelred to Alfred, then back again to Ethelred. "This is my brother, Prince Alfred," Ethelred said promptly. "My secondarius.

The two young men exchanged an amiable if measuring look. Then Athulf said, "If you will come with me, my lords?"

"Bertred?" Ethelred looked around for his treasure thane.

"I am here, my lord." And Bertred stepped forward, carrying the gold-embroidered saddle cloth and gold brooch that were to be Ethelred's guest gifts to his brother-by-marriage.

Ethelred nodded with approval and gestured to the Mercian noble that he was prepared to accompany him. Alfred fell into step beside Ethelred, and Bertred followed with the gifts.

"I am surprised that I have not met you before," Ethelred said to the ealdorman with good humor as they left the guest hall. "I knew your father well."

The Mercian, who could not have been more than two-and-twenty, shrugged. "My father was so busy with affairs of the country, my lord, that it fell to me to deal with the affairs of our manors. I was not often at Tamworth."

Ethelred had evidently had the same thought as Alfred about the young ealdorman's looks, for he said now in his gentle way, "You do not favor your father."

"No." Athulf's voice was a little impatient as he answered the king. Alfred thought that he must have had to answer this comment many times before. "One of my grandmothers was Welsh," Athulf said. "My sister and I favor her. My brother is the one who has the fairness of the Mercians."

"Ah," said Ethelred. Mercia had always shared a border with Wales. Unlike Wessex, however, which had for centuries successfully accommodated and absorbed the Britons within and without its borders, Mercia had ever been at odds with the Britons in Wales. In the last century, Offa had actually built a great dike in order to define that always-hostile Mercian border. Occasionally, however, there was an attempt to patch over the hostility with a marriage. Such, evidently, had been the case with Athulf's grandparents.

"We were much distressed in Mercia to learn of the defeat of Northumbria," Athulf said now abruptly.

"As were we in Wessex," Ethelred replied, his sweaty face grim.

"We heard that two Northumbrian kings and eight ealdormen fell," Alfred said. "Is that true?"

Athulf looked around Ethelred to the smaller, slimmer figure on the king's right. "I fear that it is, my lord." He spoke next to the king. "If the Northumbrians had been able to keep the fight out in the open, they might have had a chance. But once the Danes got within the walls of York, the Northumbrians were like lambs to the slaughter." The Mercian's thin dark face was bleak. "Almost all the fighting stock of the north gone in one afternoon," he said. "It is hard to believe."

There was a small silence. Then, "No one expected the Danes to march north." It was Ethelred speaking now. "Their occupation of York took the Northumbrians by surprise."

Athulf gave the two West Saxons a crooked grin. "That is a true word, my lord. In fact, many of us were fully expecting them to attack Wessex."

"From East Anglia they could have moved anywhere," Alfred replied somberly. "North to Northumbria, inland to Mercia, or southwest to Wessex. The choice was theirs."

"It was the civil strife in Northumbria that attracted them," Ethelred remarked.

"So it would seem." The Mercian rubbed his nose. "Aelle had just deposed Osbert, the king of eighteen years, and Aelle's hold on the rule was not yet secure. To give the Northumbrians their due, they finally did unite to drive out the invaders."

"They could not live together, but they rallied to die together." Alfred's tone was noncommittal.

"The two kings did not actually die together," Athulf said. "Aelle was captured."

Ethelred said, "I did not know that." The look on the young Mercian's face made both brothers slow their steps. The heat of the day had become oppressive. Even Alfred's golden skin was lightly sheened with sweat. "What happened?" Ethelred asked.

"You do not know?"

"I would not be asking if I knew." Ethelred began to pluck at his eyebrow, a sure sign that he was worried.

"Aelle was taken prisoner. Then they . . ." Athulf's voice faded a little and he cleared his throat. He began again. "The Vikings apparently have a traditional way to deal with captured kings. As York burned before his eyes, they took Aelle, and while still he was living, they cut out his ribs and his lungs and spread them like eagle's wings in an offering to their god, Odin." He looked at the two West Saxons. "They call this slaughter the 'blood eagle,' " he said, his face and his voice very grim.

"Dear God in heaven!" Ethelred's brown eyes were dilated in horror.

"May God have mercy on his soul," Athulf said, crossing himself.

"Amen." They had almost come to a halt while they spoke, and now they commenced once again slowly to climb the hill that led to Tamworth's royal hall. "I did not hear aught of this," Ethelred said. His face was streaming with sweat.

"We must withstand them." Alfred's voice was hard and abrupt. "Such barbarians must not be allowed to gain their way in England."

"A true word, my lord," Athulf replied heartily. Then they were before the great door of the royal hall of Tamworth.

Ethelswith of Mercia sat beside her husband the king in the stifling hall and watched her brothers advancing toward her from across the room. Ethelred had put on weight since last she'd seen him, she thought. And he was looking very pale. Ah well, he was approaching thirty; no longer a young man. But not old either, she added quickly, remembering she was but two years behind him. It must be the young men on either side of Ethelred who made him suddenly seem so . . . middle-aged.

Ethelswith's eyes went from Ethelred to Alfred. She had a fondness for her youngest brother and remembered that he would turn eighteen in two days' time. An important birthday. I must give a banquet for him, she thought. Then, with a pang of nostalgia: How much he resembles Mother.

They had reached the high seat and now Burgred rose to welcome his visitors from Wessex. Burgred made Ethelred look young, Ethelswith thought as she watched her brother and her husband going through the ceremonial greeting. Burgred, massive of shoulder and thick of limb, was accepting Ethelred's gift with courtesy. Then he gestured, and one of his own thanes was coming forward with the matched wolfhounds that were his return gift to his brother-by-marriage.

It was Alfred's face that lighted when the dogs were brought forth. He snapped his fingers and the dogs came to him instantly, as dogs always did. He fondled their ears and looked up at Ethelred, his golden eyes alight. "They are beauties, my lord."

Ethelred was too pale, Ethelswith suddenly thought. It must be the heat. She rose from the high seat and said, "You do not look well, brother. Come and sit and I will send for some mead."

Ethelred smiled a little shakily. "It is so hot." Then, as they all began to move toward the chairs that had been set near to the door to catch whatever air was moving, "Young Athulf has just been telling us of Aelle's fate. We had heard nothing of this blood eagle in Wessex."

Ethelswith frowned and set her lips. She did not like to think of what had happened to Aelle. It made her skin crawl. She heard Burgred mumble, "Shocking," and then they had reached the chairs and a serving man was coming with the mead.

Ethelred accepted a cup and drank deeply. A little color seemed to come back to his face. Then he said to Burgred, who had followed his example with the mead, "What does Mercia think the Danes will do next?"

Burgred stretched his neck, as if he found his collar too confining. It was very hot in the hall even with the door open. "My information is that they are still in York," he answered. "Perhaps they will stay there." Burgred took another drink of mead and the sweat stood out on his forehead.

"Alfred does not think so." Ethelred looked from Burgred to his brother, who was sitting in the chair beside him empty-handed, having refused the mead.

"Why not?" Burgred too looked at his young brother-by-marriage.

"They have had too easy a time of it thus far, my lord," Alfred replied to Burgred. His manner was polite, correctly deferential, but he spoke with all the easy confidence of one who is accustomed to having his words heeded. Ethelswith noted that he alone of all the group did not look hot. "Edmund of East Anglia did not resist them," Alfred continued. "Edmund allowed them to winter in his land, to raid his people's horses. Now Northumbria has fallen. I would be greatly surprised if Ivar the Boneless did not try to see what the temper of Mercia and Wessex might be."

In the chair on the other side of her husband, Ethelswith could see Athulf nodding. She knew that the young ealdorman had been telling Burgred much the same thing since news of the Northumbrian defeat had come to them.

"Mercia and Wessex are far stronger than East Anglia and Northumbria," Burgred said. "All of Europe does know that. These Northmen must know it too."

Alfred said, still in that polite, deferential tone, "There has not been a battle of any size in Wessex since my father and my brother Ethelbald beat the Danes at Aclea, and that was sixteen years since, my lord. And Ethelbald is dead. As far as the Danes are concerned, the leaders of Wessex and Mercia are untried in battle." Alfred looked briefly at Ethelswith, then back to Burgred. His clipped voice, though still polite, was yet unmistakably authoritative. "I think they will come against us."

There was a heavy silence. Ethelswith stared consideringly at Alfred's fine-boned face. He was so young, she thought, hardly more than a boy. Ethelred was eleven years his senior, Burgred old enough to be his father. Why should these two older kings listen so seriously to what a boy had to say? Out of the corner of her eye she could see Athulf staring at the slender young prince in slight puzzlement, as though he too were trying to understand this mystery.

"I could be wrong, of course," Alfred said. "But that is what I think."

Ethelred sighed and said gloomily, "I am trying to remember the last time you were wrong."

Burgred grunted. "In any case, it will be well for us to be prepared." He gave Ethelred a sour look. "I do not know about you, brother, but I have no desire to be sacrificed to a Viking god."

Ethelred's returning look was wry. "I can think of ways I would rather pass my time," he said. And Alfred laughed.

The storm that had been building all day broke late in the afternoon, while servants were setting up the trestle tables in the great hall for the evening meal. Alfred and Ethelred were in their room in the guest hall when they heard the first booms of thunder rolling up the valley of the Tane.

Ethelred was lying on the bed in the sweltering room, resting. He put his hands behind his head and said, "Thank God. Now perhaps the heat will break." Lightning flashed. "Close the shutters, will you, Alfred?" he added.

"The room will be hot as fire," Alfred answered, but left off what he was doing to go close and fasten the shutters of the room's single window. Then he turned to look at Ethelred stretched out on the bed. "I cannot find my stomach medicine," he said. "I think I left it in my saddlebag. I am going to the barn to fetch it."

Ethelred sat up. "You cannot go out in this storm! Send one of the thanes in the hall." He looked closely at Alfred and frowned, "Are you feeling ill?"

Alfred smiled crookedly. "No. But you know my stomach, Ethelred.

Strange halls and strange foods do not agree with it. I would have the medicine by me just in case of need." He began to walk to the door.

"Send one of the thanes," Ethelred said again as his brother picked up his cloak and went out into the hall.

But Alfred ignored the thanes sitting on the hall benches and crossed the room swiftly, looking neither to the left nor to the right. He pulled the door open, flung his cloak around his shoulders, and went out into the rain.

Lightning lit the courtyard. Alfred raised his face to the sky. The rain pounded on his skin, soaked into his hair. It felt cool and wonderful. He began to walk slowly toward the barn where the horses were stabled. Then the thunder crashed. The storm was still some distance up the valley, he thought.

The courtyard was deserted and the barn door was closed tight. Alfred opened it and stepped inside. A horse whinnied and kicked the wood of its stall. Another horse answered. "It's all right, my beauties," Alfred said soothingly. "Only a storm." He left the door open to allow some light into the dark barn and walked over to rub his chestnut's forehead. Lightning lit the world again, illuminating the barn. The stallion snorted and threw up its head. Alfred went back to the door to look out.

He loved storms. He had not forgotten his medicine at all, had only wanted an excuse to find someplace where he could watch the storm. Ethelred, he knew, would insist on hiding behind shuttered windows, no matter how hot. Ethelred did not like storms at all.

As he stood there at the door, a small figure came into view, wrapped in a hooded cloak and running across the courtyard. A serving girl, Alfred thought, then raised his brows in surprise as he realized that the figure was making for his barn. The girl did not see him standing in the doorway until she was almost on top of him; then she looked up and said, "Oh!" in a startled and oddly deep voice.

Lightning flashed again. The face under the brown hood was brilliantly illuminated: a child's face, black-browed, with black-lashed eyes of the darkest blue Alfred had ever seen. Thunder crashed. "You had better come in," Alfred said. "The lightning is getting closer."

The child came in the door after him and pushed back her hood. Two long glossy braids tumbled loose, falling straight to her waist. Alfred saw that the braids were as black as her eyebrows. "What are you doing here?" she demanded in an accent that could belong only to a Mercian noblewoman.

They looked at each other. Then, "Sheltering from the storm," Alfred replied, his clipped voice in sharp contrast to her deep drawl. "What are *you* doing here?"

She glanced inside the barn. "I came to be with the horses. They get restless during storms."

"I see." His face was perfectly grave. "Are you a groom?"

"Of course not!" The look she gave him was scornful. Then, as if the name should explain all, "I am Elswyth." He raised his eyebrows in elaborate mystification, and she deigned to add, "My brother is the Ealdorman of Gaini."

"I rather thought you might be Athulf's sister," he replied. "One doesn't often see black hair in Mercia." Then, with absolute courtesy, "I am Alfred, Prince of Wessex."

He watched as her blue eyes widened. Lightning flashed and the thunder roared almost immediately after. Inside the barn a horse whinnied frantically. Elswyth called something soothing but did not leave the door. Instead she pulled her cloak more closely around her shoulders and turned to look out into the courtyard. Alfred suddenly realized that she had been drawn to the barn for exactly the same reason as he. Lightning flashed again and he too turned to watch the storm.

For perhaps ten minutes neither of them spoke. They stood in the open doorway, letting the chill hard rain blow on them, watching the storm. Finally, as the lightning dimmed and began to move away, they turned to look at each other once more.

"Your presence certainly helped calm the horses," Alfred said.

She had her brother's arrogant nose, though hers was slim and elegant as well as haughty. Her eyes were a much darker blue. He had not thought eyes could be so dark and yet so blue. "And why were you not in the guest hall, Prince?" she retorted in her curiously husky unchildlike voice.

"I came to the barn to find something I had forgotten."

Silence fell as they regarded each other speculatively. Thunder rumbled in the distance. Then, at exactly the same moment, they began to laugh.

"I love storms," Elswyth confessed. "As soon as my mother began to close up the shutters, I slipped out."

"I did exactly the same." They were regarding each other now with distinct approval.

"You are the Lady Ethelswith's youngest brother?" she asked after a minute.

"Yes."

She nodded. "I have heard of you."

He smiled faintly and did not reply. She leaned her shoulders against the open door and looked him up and down. She could not be more than twelve, Alfred thought. Her self-possession amused him. "I met your brother earlier this afternoon," he said.

"Athulf. Yes." She shrugged. "He has been attending on the king since my father died. My other brother and I have just come to Tamworth to join Athulf and my mother. I can't see why I had to come. I usually bide in the country on our estates."

She did not sound pleased with her present situation. "Perhaps your brother wished to give you a treat," Alfred said.

"A treat?" She looked at him as if he were mad. "I can assure you, Prince, it is no treat to be cooped up here in Tamworth with my mother."

Alfred's lips quivered. He knew Eadburgh, Elswyth's mother, and he could see Elswyth's point perfectly.

"Speaking of my mother," she said glumly now. "She will be looking for me. I had better get back to our hall."

Without a backward look she walked out into the brightening yard. Alfred watched her small figure until it disappeared from view into one of the halls; then he too left the barn in order to return to Ethelred.

Chapter 6

*T*HERE was a great hunt on the day of Alfred's birthday. Burgred knew his young brother-by-marriage well enough to know that nothing would please Alfred so much as a hunt. Hunting seemed to be a passion that ran in the West Saxon royal family. Hunting and dogs.

Ethelred had his two new wolfhounds running beside his horse when Alfred trotted his own chestnut stallion up to stand beside his brother's bay in the bright morning sunshine. The weather had been considerably cooler since the storm, and the great courtyard of Tamworth was crowded and noisy, with nobles on horseback, and grooms and houndsmen and gamesmen on foot. The excited dogs milled around under the legs of the horses. Alfred noted with approval that none of the high-spirited Mercian horses had tried to kick a hound. Burgred's horses were well-trained, he thought, as his eye alighted on a small gray gelding with a particularly elegant carriage. A beautiful animal, he thought, and looked to see who was the rider. His eyes widened in surprise as he recognized young Elswyth, dressed in brown hunting tunic and cross-gartered trousers like all the men in the courtyard, and sitting astride the gray with perfect ease.

Alfred's finely drawn brows drew together. This was not a hunt for girls. What could her brother be thinking of? For Elswyth was obviously here with Athulf's permission; Alfred saw that he was sitting his own bay right beside his sister.

The tide in the courtyard seemed to shift suddenly and Alfred looked to see what was causing the disruption. A woman dressed in a cream-colored gown and blue tunic was threading her purposeful way on foot through the mounted men and the dogs. The shift in the tide had come from the efforts of the riders to draw back from her path. It took Alfred but a moment to recognize the woman as Eadburgh, wife of Ethelred Mucill, and Elswyth's mother.

Alfred looked back to Elswyth. She too was watching her mother draw ever closer, and she did not look happy. Before he consciously realized what he was going to do, Alfred was threading his stallion through the maze of horses and dogs, aiming in the direction of the Ealdorman of Gaini and his sister.

Eadburgh reached them before he did. "Are you mad, Athulf, to allow your sister to make such a display of herself?" Eadburgh was saying in an imperious voice as Alfred's chestnut came within hearing range of the small family grouping. Then, turning to her daughter, she said, "You are to take that horse back to the stable immediately, Elswyth."

Elswyth's face was stormy. In the bright sun of the courtyard Alfred could see that she still had the beautiful skin of childhood: pearly, close-textured, flawless. Her eyes glittered midnight blue as she looked down at her mother. "Athulf said I might ride with the hunt," she answered in a furious, husky voice. "I am a better rider than any man here! You know that, Mother. I am in no danger."

Alfred halted his horse and eavesdropped shamelessly.

Eadburgh spoke next, her well-bred voice cold as ice. "You will be in danger from me if you do not get off that horse immediately, Elswyth," she said.

"Now, Mother," Athulf put in placatingly, "I told Elswyth she might come with us. Why deprive the child of her pleasure? She will come to no hurt. I promise I will stay beside her the whole while."

Eadburgh's face was as cold as her voice. She started to reply to Athulf, but stopped as she saw another horse approaching. Then, "Ceolwulf!" she said to the new arrival. "Speak to your brother. He is allowing your sister to go on this hunt."

So this was the other brother, Alfred thought as he walked his horse forward once more. Ceolwulf's handsome face bore a distinctly troubled expression. He looked unhappily from his mother to his brother.

Elswyth said, "Do not seek to draw Ceolwulf into this, Mother. You know how he hates dissension."

Alfred's stallion came to a perfect halt beside her, and he smiled down into her startled face and said charmingly, "Lady Elswyth! I am so pleased to see you are joining my birthday hunt." He looked from her dark blue eyes to the lighter eyes of Athulf, and thence down to Eadburgh. He raised his brows in surprise, then frowned in concern. "My lady, what are you doing on foot in the midst of all these horses? Allow me to summon one of my men to see you to the safety of your hall."

There was nothing Eadburgh could do, as well he knew. He watched with a faint smile as she made him some sort of answer; then he gestured for a groomsman to come escort her from the courtyard. As soon as she was out of earshot he turned to her three children.

Elswyth was laughing. "Thank you, Prince. I owe you a favor."

"You can repay me by not hurting yourself," Alfred replied.

Her nose elevated in a gesture that was already becoming familiar to him. Athulf said with amusement, "Small chance of that. It is probably I who will get hurt, trying to keep up with her."

Ceolwulf said unhappily, "Mother will be furious. Why must you always defy her, Elswyth?"

"Mother wants me to be a replica of herself," Elswyth replied, "but I am not made that way." Then, with impatient exasperation, "You cannot always please everyone, Ceolwulf. There are times when you must make a choice."

The horns blew. Alfred saw Ethelred looking around for him, and with a nod in Elswyth's direction he squeezed his legs gently and moved forward to rejoin his brother.

Elswyth was gloriously happy. For one dreadful moment in the courtyard she had been afraid she was going to lose her chance to hunt; Athulf would go only so far for her against their mother. But the West Saxon prince had saved her. He had done it quite deliberately, too. She had seen that clear enough. He had had an unfair advantage of her mother, and he had taken it. Ruthlessly. Elswyth thoroughly approved of such tactics. Her only regret was that she herself held such an advantage all too seldom.

The summer day was warm; too warm in the sun, but under the canopy of trees in the forest it was cool and green and perfect for the hunt. Elswyth was never so happy as when she was out on horseback, wildly galloping after the hounds. Sometimes she thought that it was only with animals that she was ever really happy. People of late seemed to make so many demands, never seemed to be satisfied with her the way she was. Even her brothers, with whom she had lived all her life—even they had changed since her father died.

But she and Silken—and here Elswyth leaned forward to pat the shining dappled gray neck of her little gelding—she and Silken understood each other completely, were always in perfect accord.

The nets had been set by the huntsmen, and the hounds were doing their work of driving the game into them. Elswyth sat her horse at a little distance from the kill. It was the chase she loved, not its conclusion. It was not so much the blood that dismayed her as it was a sense of the unfairness of it all. The deer tangled in the nets did not have a chance against the men and the spears. Elswyth favored a fight that was more even.

Half an hour later, she saw one.

The huntsmen had found a boar in the thickness of the forest along the river. A huge boar, the largest Elswyth had ever seen. They had maneuvered him into a clearing around a forest pond, and he was standing there when they came up, his back to the pond, the sun shining on his hard gray bristles and wicked white tusks. The mounted nobles halted within the cover of the trees as he snorted and pawed the ground. He was a ferocious-looking beast, Elswyth thought in awe. She had not known boars could be so big. He snorted again savagely, planted his short legs wide, and lowered his snout to the ground. His small eyes glowed red as they surveyed the men and horses before him.

Suddenly, "He's mine!" called a crisp, commanding voice, and Elswyth saw Alfred leap from his horse and advance into the clearing, spear in hand.

Her heart jolted, then began to race. At her shoulder, Athulf voiced her own silent protest. "That boar is too big for the prince." Her brother looked around, but no one was moving. His black brows snapped together. "Alfred will never be able to hold him," Athulf muttered, jumped from his saddle, and took up his own spear.

The boar had seen Alfred coming and he pawed the ground again. Foam dripped from his jaws. The cruel, curving tusks glinted in the bright sun. The red eyes fixed themselves upon the prince.

Alfred must have heard Athulf's step, for he turned his head very quickly and snarled at the Mercian, "*Keep away.*" For a moment, with his glittering eyes and bared white teeth, he looked fully as dangerous as the boar.

Athulf stopped dead.

The boar charged straight for Alfred.

For a beat of time Elswyth felt as if her heart and breath had stopped. Athulf was right. The West Saxon prince was too slim, too light, to hold a boar of that size on his spear. Alfred knelt, spear advanced, and then the boar was on him. Elswyth shut her eyes.

A shout went up from the men around her. She opened her eyes in time to see Alfred rising to his feet. She stared, and realized with astonishment that he had got the boar right through the heart. As she watched, he turned in the direction of his brother, the king, and grinned. His entire right arm was covered with the boar's blood. Elswyth saw the white teeth flashing in the golden tan of his face. Then she looked at the boar, lying now on the bare earth of the clearing.

The prince was so slight. How had he managed to hold up that spear?

Beside her, Athulf was saying much the same thing.

A West Saxon thane passing Athulf said with a grin, "We all learned years ago never to come between Alfred and his boar. He'll have your head if you do."

"He is stronger than he looks," Athulf said.

"He's strong as a man twice his weight," the thane boasted. "He may not be big, but you'll find there's little our prince cannot do." Then he was by them, running up to Alfred's side and saying something they could not hear. Alfred laughed, put a hand on his arm, then turned away to reclaim his horse.

There was a feast after the hunt that day, also in honor of Alfred's birthday. Ethelswith loved to play hostess to her brothers and had done all she could to make the occasion as grand as possible. Though it was still daylight, torches were burning in the wall sconces of the great hall, illuminating with their glow the giant frescoes that were Tamworth's glory. The frescoes had been painted in the last century, in the glory days of Offa, and the most famous of all the paintings was the one of Offa's fellow monarch, Charlemagne, surrounded by his companions, among whom happened to be included Offa himself. There were other scenes from the life of Offa, and scenes as well from the lives of other heroes out of Mercian, Frankish, and Roman history. The frescoes were famous in England, and Ethelswith was very proud of them.

She had filled her hall this night with the high nobility of Mercia, summoned to this banquet in order to do honor to her younger brother. Burgred, of course, had the high seat, and Ethelred sat this night in her usual place beside him. Ethelswith had chosen to sit beside Alfred on the bench directly to Burgred's right, and on Alfred's other side she had placed Athulf, whom she thought Alfred would find congenial. Beyond Athulf sat his mother, his brother, and his sister.

The feast was to begin with the presentation of Burgred's gift to Alfred. Silence fell slowly upon the crowded room as the thanes and ladies along the wall benches saw the king rising to his feet.

Alfred sat beside his sister and listened with all outward attention to Burgred's extremely flattering speech. He did not dislike his brother-by-marriage, but too often he found Burgred somewhat wanting in quickness of wit. In truth, Alfred never spent above an hour in Burgred's company without finding himself pitying Ethelswith the dullness of her marriage. Then he would take himself to task for lack of Christian charity. Burgred was good and kind, he would chastise himself. The poor man could not help it if he was also dull.

But he *was* dull. It was nice, of course, that he thought so well of Alfred, but it would be even nicer if he would just stop talking and allow everyone to eat. Alfred affixed his alert, attentive expression even more firmly into place and began to replay in his mind the afternoon's hunt.

Suddenly his sister's elbow caught him in the ribs. He blinked, focused, and saw that Burgred was holding out a sword and looking at him.

"Go and take it from him," Ethelswith hissed into his ear.

Alfred rose from his place and went to bow gracefully before the King of Mercia. Burgred placed the sword into his hands. The king's fleshy face was beaming. Alfred felt the familiar twinge of guilt. Poor man. It was not his fault he was thick of body and dull of mind. "Thank you, my lord," he said with his quick charming smile. "I shall treasure this gift with all my heart."

He stepped back to return to his place, and a sigh of relief ran around the hall as the guests realized that he was not going to speak further. Alfred's eyes glinted with amusement, though his face was grave as he resumed his place beside his sister.

"Thank you," Ethelswith murmured in his ear. "Everyone is starving."

As the serving folk came into the hall from the kitchens, laden with heavy platters of meats and sauces and vegetables and breads, Alfred turned to look curiously at his sister.

Ethelswith was nine years older than he, the closest sibling in age to him, but he had never known her the way he knew Ethelred. Alfred had been but five when she was married to Burgred of Mercia and, except for infrequent visits, they had seen little of each other since.

She was still a pretty woman, he thought, looking at his sister's smoothly braided light brown hair and clear blue eyes. It had been several years now since Alfred had begun automatically to appraise every woman he met, with an eye to what pleased him and what did not. Yes, Ethelswith was definitely pretty. Much too pretty for Burgred.

She had been married for thirteen years and still she had no children. The pity that suddenly pierced Alfred's heart was of a different quality from the usual token flicker that his sister's marriage generally aroused in his breast. No children, he thought, and a husband she must find irksome. And she had been married to him since she was fourteen.

Not for the first time Alfred found himself reflecting on the bitterness of woman's lot when it came to matrimony.

"What do you hear of Judith?" said Ethelswith, and for one brief startled moment he wondered if she had been reading his thoughts.

Then, because she had surprised him, he blurted out what he would ordinarily have been more tactful in disclosing. "She has a son."

The flicker of pain on Ethelswith's face brought him to a swift realization of his callousness. He went on talking smoothly, to give her a chance to recover herself. "You know her father relented finally and agreed to recognize her marriage? Well, it appears now that Charles has done even more. He has made Judith's husband the Count of Flanders. A wise move on Charles's part. For one thing, once the pope recognized the marriage, there was nothing Charles could do about it. For the other thing, Baldwin Iron·Arm is just the warrior Flanders needs to keep it safe from the Danes."

Ethelswith's face was serene once more. She began to pile roast venison on her plate as she said to Alfred, a little caustically, "I must say, Judith has the most exciting life. I envy her."

"I hope she is happy," he said, and his own voice was very quiet. "She deserves to be."

His sister shot him a slantwise look. "That is right. I remember now she had you enslaved as well."

Alfred forced himself to remember that Ethelswith was married to Burgred. She had cause to be jealous of Judith. "I have always been very fond of Judith," he answered temperately.

"Are you speaking of Judith of France?" It was Athulf, from Alfred's other side.

"Yes," said Alfred. He too began to put some food on his plate. Athulf offered him the sauce and he shook his head. Bread, he thought, was probably safest.

"That girl must be quite a handful," Athulf said with amusement. "I am glad I'm not her father." He poured sauce over his own meat. "Imagine it. Your daughter, whom you have locked in your most secure castle because she refuses to marry the man of your choice, proceeds to elope with her jailer! Who also happens to be your most effective war leader!"

"She was aided and abetted by her brother," Alfred reminded him. "Baldwin is a fine man. I think she made a good choice." Alfred remembered how, after Ethelbald's death, Judith would sit in the garden at Wilton, staring at nothing.

"He may be a fine man, but he is certainly not fit to marry the Princess of France. I don't wonder that Charles was furious. Didn't he have all the Frankish bishops excommunicate him?" Athulf soaked up some of the excess sauce with his bread and put it in his mouth.

"He did," Alfred replied. "But then Baldwin appealed to Pope Nicholas. The pope was sympathetic and interceded for Baldwin and Judith with Charles. Once Nicholas took a hand, there was little that Charles could do."

Athulf frowned. "I am surprised the pope acted as he did. It is not the part of the church to encourage young girls to make their own marriages."

"Judith was twice a widow," Alfred said. "Hardly an inexperienced girl."

Athulf, whose mouth was full, shrugged.

Alfred contemplated the thin dark face of his neighbor. Then he raised a single delicately drawn eyebrow. "Judith wrote to me that Baldwin also told the pope that if his marriage was not recognized, he would join with the Vikings. As Baldwin has been one of Charles's main props against the Danes for the last few years, you can imagine Charles's reaction to that threat."

There was a moment of stunned silence; then Athulf began to laugh.

"My brother Ethelbald would have done the same," said Alfred. "I rather think that is why Judith married Baldwin. He sounds very like Ethelbald."

"One Ethelbald in the world was quite enough, I think," said Ethelswith, who had never forgiven her eldest brother for raising a rebellion against her father.

Alfred unconsciously touched his headband, which style he had adopted shortly after Ethelbald's death. Then, "There was much that was fine in Ethelbald," he said to his sister. His voice was contained but there was that in it that caused Athulf to feel he would be wise to change the subject.

"Well, I am glad that my own marriage is like to go more smoothly," Athulf said. "I am not one anxious to count the world well lost for love."

Ethelswith, who had also heard the warning note in Alfred's voice, followed Athulf's lead. "Athulf is to marry the daughter of the Ealdorman of Hwicce in the autumn," she said to her brother a little too vivaciously.

"I wish you every joy, my lord," Alfred said, and both his face and his voice were perfectly pleasant.

"Thank you. She is a good girl and we suit very well." Athulf nodded in the direction of a pretty girl seated further down the board. "That is Hild there, the blond girl in the yellow gown."

"She is very pretty," said Alfred.

Athulf nodded and picked up a leg of spiced chicken from the platter before him.

"Alfred, you have eaten nothing," his sister said. "You're too thin as it is. Eat."

"The food looks wonderful, Ethelswith," he said sincerely, then picked up a piece of bread and began to chew.

By the time Elswyth got to Alfred's birthday feast, she was starving. Like the rest of Burgred's guests, she thought that he would never stop talking; and her already good opinion of the West Saxon prince rose when he spared them a lengthy acceptance speech. As soon as the food was set on the trestle table before her, she filled her plate and then began to empty it.

"Elswyth," said Eadburgh beside her, "do not eat like a starving dog. You are a lady."

"I am hungry," Elswyth answered, but she slowed her chewing obediently. Eadburgh was already furious enough with her for going on the hunt. There was little to be gained by annoying her mother further.

"I like to see a healthy appetite," said the Ealdorman of the Tomsaetan, who was seated on Elswyth's other side. He reached over to pat her hand. "The Lady Elswyth is young," he said to her mother. "The young are always hungry."

Elswyth's narrow hand went rigid under his large puffy fingers. Then she pulled her hand away and cast a look of smoldering resentment at the man seated beside her.

Ealdorman Edred of the Tomsaetan was a tall, strongly made man of middle years; his hair was dark blond and his eyes were gray. The Tomsaetan were the chief of the Mercian tribes and their territory comprised the heartland of the country: the royal church at Repton, the bishopric at Lichfield, and the main residence at Tamworth. They had ever been administered by their own ealdorman, who, after the king, was the most powerful of all Mercian nobles. Edred had held his position for some ten years, and had been a friend of Elswyth's father's. Elswyth did not like him, but then, there were not many people Elswyth did like.

He smiled at her, not at all offended by her retreat. He had strong protruding yellow teeth. Horse's teeth, Elswyth thought unkindly. They looked well on a horse, not so well on a man. The West Saxon prince, on the other hand, had teeth as white and as straight as her own. Her thin, high-bridged nose, the feature that gave her face its look of haughtiness, seemed to grow even thinner as she regarded the smiling face of the Ealdorman of the Tomsaetan. "I have not eaten since the hunt," she said, her husky drawl more pronounced than usual.

"Ah, yes, I saw you in the hunt field today." Edred's gray eyes moved from her face to her throat. Elswyth felt angry color stain her cheeks. His eyes seemed almost to stroke her. Then he was looking at her mother. "Surely," he said gently, "Lady Elswyth is getting too old to be allowed to play the boy." He added, "How old is she now, my lady? Twelve?"

"Thirteen," said Eadburgh, and her mouth set into a long straight line. "And I agree with you, my lord, that she is too old to continue her hoydenish ways. It was her brother allowed her to join the hunt. Athulf is too lax with her."

"Ah, well," said the ealdorman genially. "Doubtless he is fond of his sister."

What did this interfering yellow-fanged old nuisance have to say about what Athulf allowed her to do? Elswyth's eyes were narrowed now, and so dark a blue they were almost black, always a dangerous sign. She opened her mouth to leap to her brother's defense, and felt her mother's hand close on her arm. Hard.

"That is so, my lord," Eadburgh was saying to Edred in a sweet voice. Her voice was so totally at odds with her iron fingers that Elswyth stared at her mother in astonishment. Eadburgh was continuing meaningfully, "But for all that she is young, she has been well-taught. Elswyth will know her proper place when the time comes."

Eldred nodded and smiled. Elswyth sat silent under her mother's grip. When finally it relaxed, she remained perfectly still, refusing to rub the hurt, which would leave bruises on her arm for several days.

She wished quite desperately that she was home at Croxden. She hated Tamworth, hated all the people at court, hated the way her mother was acting with Edred. Elswyth had never been one to adapt easily to change, and nearly all the people who surrounded her these days were strangers. She missed her horses and her dogs, missed the manor folk who were more her friends than her servants. She scarcely saw Athulf or Ceolwulf anymore, and was cooped up for whole afternoons with her mother and her mother's women.

There was nothing for Elswyth to do in Tamworth. The girls her age did needlework and talked about marriage. Elswyth hated needlework and planned to live the rest of her life with her brothers. She was bored. She was even beginning to become frightened. She bent her head and stared at her plate, her appetite quite vanished. She had asked Athulf today if they would be returning home soon, and he had avoided answering her.

Elswyth thought she would prefer even the Danes to another few months of Eadburgh and Tamworth.

Chapter 7

*E*THELRED and Alfred returned to Wessex in mid-July, to the usual round of travel from royal manor to royal manor. On the surface, nothing in Wessex seemed changed. But beneath the surface, Alfred felt an ominous sense of waiting, an impression that the collective breath of the country was being held. The Danes had conquered Northumbria. Where would they move next?

In October, word came that Ivar the Boneless had named a new king for Northumbria. He was an Englishman, not a Dane, and his name was Egbert.

"I never heard of him," Ethelred said to Alfred when they discussed this news together after the messenger from Burgred had been dismissed. "Egbert? He was not an ealdorman."

"Doubtless some spineless thane Ivar saw he could manipulate," Alfred replied. "He is of no account; a king who will move to Ivar's command the way a child moves a glove-doll." He frowned. "I do not think this appointing of a puppet king bodes well, Ethelred. If Ivar planned to remain in Northumbria, he would not have done thus."

Alfred's foreboding proved all too correct. In mid-November the Danish army, moving with a speed that astonished the shocked Mercians, came down the valley of the Trent to Nottingham, one of Burgred's towns that lay but thirty miles to the north of Tamworth. The Danish army then proceeded to systematically raid the countryside.

Burgred sent a frantic message south, to his brother-by-marriage the King of Wessex, reminding Ethelred of his alliance to Mercia and asking for assistance.

It was the end of December when Alfred and an escort of fifty thanes rode north to Tamworth in order to confer with the Mercian king and to gather information for Ethelred as to the actual situation in Nottingham.

The day was gray and silent, with a low sky that seemed full of snow, when Alfred reached Tamworth. It had snowed lightly the night before, and white sprinkled the roofs of the halls and covered the woodpiles stacked against the palisade walls. The great hall of Tamworth was decked with evergreens and the Yule log still smoldered on the hearth, but the faces that greeted Alfred as he came forward to salute his host were far from festive.

"It is good to see you, my boy," said Burgred heavily.

Ethelswith came to give Alfred the kiss of peace. Her lips felt chill as they touched his cheek.

Burgred had called together his witan to hear what Wessex would have to say, and the nobles and bishops of Mercia assembled quickly in the great hall as soon as they learned that Alfred was come. Alfred knew most of the Mercian ealdormen by sight. They were all older, save for Athulf, with whom Alfred exchanged a friendly smile.

The men sat along the benches in the great hall before the remnants of the Yule log. Edred, Ealdorman of the Tomsaetan and chief of the Mercian nobles, spoke first. "What does King Ethelred plan to do about these Danes?"

Alfred raised one perfect eyebrow and forbore to point out that the Danes in Nottingham were chiefly Mercia's problem.

Burgred said, almost querulously, "When Mercia swore allegiance to your grandfather, King Egbert, he promised to protect us. Wessex does owe us assistance, Alfred. Surely Ethelred recognizes that."

Now Alfred was really surprised. It almost sounded as if Burgred had nothing planned, was waiting for Ethelred to do it all. He looked around the circle of Mercian nobles and did not like what he saw. Athulf was the only man to meet his eyes, and Athulf was looking very grim.

Alfred looked back to his brother-by-marriage and said very evenly, "Ethelred is above all else a Christian king, my lord. In the face of such a threat as that posed by the Danes, it is essential for all Christian kings and Christian lands to stand together. Wessex will help Mercia in this time of need."

The heavy tension Alfred had felt in the hall shattered. For the first time since Alfred had arrived, Burgred smiled. "Thanks be to God," he said devoutly. Then, "What shall we do?"

Alfred looked at Athulf. The young Mercian refused to look back. The rest of the nobles were staring at the West Saxon prince, waiting for him to answer.

Alfred was astonished. Almost embarrassed. He laced his jeweled hands together on his knee and asked mildly, "What is the situation at present in Nottingham?"

At least the Mercian witan seemed to be well-informed as to what was happening in the Danish camp. The Danes apparently had made no attempt to move beyond Nottingham. They were behaving much as they had while they were in York—staying within their defenses save for quick raids into the surrounding countryside. "Most of the people within a ten-mile radius of Nottingham have fled," Athulf said. "The very name of Ivar the Boneless is enough to strike terror into the stoutest of hearts."

"No resistance has been offered to them?" Alfred asked.

"No," answered Athulf, and his blue eyes met Alfred's stoically. Athulf's eyes were paler by far than his sister's, Alfred found himself thinking inconsequently. Then Athulf added, "The king has not yet called up the fyrd."

So Alfred had begun to suspect. He looked around the circle of Mercian nobles, however, and said in surprise, "You have not called up the fyrd, my lords? But why not?"

"Not all the thanes of Mercia would be enough to defeat Ivar the Boneless and his godless, blood-soaked army," Edred answered him angrily. "In the name of God, Prince, these are the men who have spent the last ten years years despoiling the great cities of France! They are professionals! Compared to them, we know nothing of making war."

It was Athulf who replied to his fellow countryman: "We are going to have to learn, my lord." He looked around the faces of the nobles who comprised the Mercian witan, and added, "The Danes are not going to go away."

There was a brief unhappy silence. Then Alfred said crisply, "No, I fear they are not."

Burgred looked at him. "Alfred . . ." The Mercian king's voice was almost pitiable in its misery. "What should we do? What will Ethelred do to help us?"

"He will raise the fyrds of all the shires to come to your assistance," Alfred answered in the same crisp voice. "Ethelred suggests that we wait until the spring, when the roads are passable. Then will he march the combined fyrds of Wessex to join with the combined fyrds of Mercia before Nottingham. We think it is safe to wait until the spring. The Danes are unlikely to attempt a move in midwinter."

Athulf's thin dark face began to blaze. "Thanks be to God!" he said.

Even Edred was nodding judiciously. "Good. Perhaps one strike with our combined armies will be enough to rout this Danish threat forever."

Burgred said, "And perhaps the Danes will be satisfied with their plunder, will return to Northumbria before the spring."

There was a startled silence. Athulf looked disgusted. Even the Bishop of Repton looked at his king in wonder. Alfred said, "Perhaps they will, my lord. But I would not wager any money on it."

"Nor would I," Athulf said, and there was a general murmur of agreement among the rest of the Mercian witan.

"We will raise our fyrds, Prince," Edred said to Alfred. "And come the spring, let us see what we can do to drive the Danes from this land forever."

*   *   *

"Athulf!" Elswyth pounced on her brother as soon as he came out of the great hall after meeting with the witan and the West Saxon prince. "I must speak to you!"

Athulf tried to shake her hand off his arm. "I can't stop now, Elswyth. I have business to attend to." Then, when she showed no signs of letting go her hold on him. "When did you arrive in Tamworth? I thought you and Mother were at Croxden."

"Mother is still at Croxden," Elswyth replied. "I got to Tamworth but an hour since. I must speak to you, Athulf!"

He had been trying to walk forward, dragging her beside him, but now he stopped dead. "Mother is still at Croxden? Then how did you get to Tamworth?" He swung around to look at her, and for the first time noticed that she was wearing boy's clothes.

"I rode," she replied, the unmistakable ring of defiance in her deep voice. She dropped her hand from his arm.

"Who brought you?" His brow was beginning to cloud ominously.

She put up her chin. "I made two of the grooms come with me."

At that, his anger kindled. "God in heaven! *Elswyth!* The Danes are at Nottingham and you are careering around the countryside by yourself! Are you mad?"

She did not back away from his wrath. His anger had never intimidated her. "Not mad, Athulf," she replied. "Frightened. And not of the Danes." He noticed for the first time that there were shadows under her eyes. "Did you know that Mother is planning to marry me to the Ealdorman of the Tomsaetan?" she demanded.

Quite suddenly he could not meet her eyes. "She spoke to me of it, yes." Even to himself he sounded evasive.

"You cannot have agreed!" Her voice was passionate, her beautiful skin flushed with color. "Athulf, he is old! And . . . disgusting!"

Athulf cast a quick look around. "Hush. This is not the place to speak of such private matters."

"Then come with me to our hall."

He set his jaw. "I cannot. I have an errand for the king."

Her hand shot out to grab him once again. "Then you will have to speak to me here in the courtyard, for I am not letting go your sleeve until we discuss this." He recognized the stubborn expression on her face. When Elswyth looked like that, there was no moving her. "Oh, all right," he said, goaded, "I suppose I can spare you a few minutes. Come to the hall."

They entered their family hall and Athulf took her to his sleeping chamber for privacy. "Now," he said, turning to her as soon as the door had closed behind them. "I cannot approve your behavior, Elswyth. It was folly to ride through the countryside alone—" He ignored her defensive, "I had two grooms!" and continued inexorably, "Mother must be worried unto death about you. I shall have to send a messenger directly to assure her you are safe."

Elswyth, as ever, refused to be distracted from the main issue. "I will not marry Edred," she said. Her face was set and stubborn, her expressive mouth set into a thin line of determination.

She is but fourteen years of age, Athulf said to himself. *I will not let her rule me.* He clenched his teeth and said, "You will marry whomever Mother and I choose for you."

Her eyes darkened to midnight blue. The top of her head did not reach to his chin, but her will was stronger than his. He knew it. Her will was stronger than anyone's, save perhaps their mother's. He felt a flash of anger that Eadburgh had put him into this position and then failed to be here to support him. Elswyth said defiantly, "You cannot force me against my will. The church forbids it."

"The church enjoins you to obey those who are set in authority over you," he answered. Then, as her eyes flashed, "For the love of God, Elswyth, it is a splendid match! Edred is the most powerful noble in Mercia. He is rich. You will have all the comforts any girl could desire. He will be good to you. He cares for you. It was he who approached me, you know, not the other way around."

"I don't care about comforts," she said. This, unfortunately, was perfectly true. Athulf knew his sister cared for nothing that ordinary girls cared for, clothes and trinkets and such. She was as unlike other girls as a mountain lion is unlike a tame barn cat. "I never want to marry," she went on. "I want to go on as I always have, living with you and Ceolwulf."

He closed his eyes briefly, then opened them to find her looking pleadingly into his face. "Please, Athulf," she said. "I do not want to marry!"

Against his will, his heart was wrung with pity. He heard, and understood, the fear that was in her voice. Poor child, he thought. Then he told himself sternly that she was not a child any longer. She was fourteen, an age when many girls married. She must grow up sometime. She must marry. All girls must marry. Marry or take the veil, and Elswyth would go mad confined within the walls of a convent. Which meant it must be marriage, and they were not likely to get a better offer than Edred's.

It was for her own good, he told himself firmly. Once she grew accustomed to the idea, she would be all right. Elswyth had ever hated any sort of change.

"You cannot continue to live with me," he said, and now his voice was very patient. "I will be marrying shortly, and my wife is not like to want to share her home indefinitely with an unmarried sister. All girls must marry, Elswyth. Look around you. Even you must recognize that truth. Unless you wish to enter a convent?"

"No!" Her look of horror was instant.

"I cannot see you caged within the walls of a convent," he agreed. "So it must be marriage."

"But I do not like him, Athulf!"

"You do not know him," he answered, still in the same patient voice. "He is a good man. I would not wed you to someone I did not think well of. Come, Elswyth, your life with Edred will not be so unlike your life with me. He will give you all the horses and dogs you could possibly want."

Her face was stark, her eyes more black than blue. She said, "But I shall have to sleep in his bed."

His eyes fell away from hers and he felt color sting his cheeks. "Elswyth" —his voice was gruff—"you embarrass me."

For a minute she did not answer. Then, in the hard cold voice of an adult: "I tell you, I will not marry him. You cannot force me, Athulf. I am the one who must make the responses to the marriage vows, and I will not do it."

He said, "Then must it be the convent."

She stared at him in utter disbelief. "You would not do that to me."

"What else am I to do?" He forced himself to meet her appalled eyes and steeled his heart. It was for her own good, he told himself once more. "You cannot spend the rest of your life running wild in my household, Elswyth. I see now that I have spoiled you badly. Mother left you too much under the control of young men who knew nothing of how to rear a girl. But it cannot continue. Your childhood is over, Elswyth. It is time for you to take up the burdens of a woman. Now, I must send a messenger to Croxden." His voice was firm, adamant. "And, as I told you before, I have an errand to perform for the king."

It was with ill-concealed relief that he turned away from his sister and pushed open the door of his sleeping room to go out into the busy hall. He was sorry for the child, of course, but there was no other way. Girls must marry, and there was an end to it.

Elswyth stood where she had been left, statue-still, for a full three minutes.

What was she to do? In her heart, she had never thought that Athulf would force her to marry against her will. It was true that he had spoiled her, had given her her way ever since she could remember. She had never thought that he would betray her like this.

Perhaps Ceolwulf? But the thought was rejected as soon as it surfaced. Ceolwulf would feel badly for her, but he would never stand up to their mother or to Athulf. Ceolwulf had ever been one to seek the easiest way. Loyalty with him did not run as deeply as did his desire for peace.

At last she went out into the hall, and, without noticing the concerned glances that were cast her way by the thanes who were mending harness by the fire and who had heard somewhat of her discussion with Athulf, she opened the door and went out into the courtyard. She needed solitude and so she went to the one place where she had always gone when the urge to be alone was strong. She went to the barn.

The sun had not yet set, was a dull red ball hanging behind veils of thin gray cloud. It would snow later, she thought. The ground was hard under the leather soles of her shoes, hard and cold. She was cold. The whole world looked bleak and gray.

What was she going to do?

The barn felt warm as she came in the door. A groom was just finishing giving hay to the horses and Elswyth leaned against Silken's stall and watched the little gray eat his dinner. But the peaceful sound of animals crunching, which she usually loved, did nothing to loose the knot of fear in her stomach. The groom finished haying and left the barn. Once she was alone, Elswyth slipped inside Silken's stall and pressed her forehead against her horse's neck. She closed her eyes and slid her hands under the long silver mane, for warmth and for comfort. Silken continued placidly to eat his hay.

What was she going to do?

After a few minutes the barn door opened again, sending a gust of cold air down the stall aisle. Someone came in. Elswyth stayed perfectly still, hoping whoever it was would do what he had to do quickly and then leave. She was in no mood for talk.

Light footsteps came down the aisle, then stopped in front of the stall next to Silken's. "How are you, fellow?" came the clipped, distinctive voice of the West Saxon prince. There was the sound of crunching as his stallion took the apple he had been offered. Alfred stood for a moment, murmuring softly to the chestnut; then he too slipped into his horse's stall. "Let me see that leg," he said. Silken raised his head to eye the stranger in the next stall, and Elswyth turned to watch also as the prince bent down to feel the chestnut's off hind below the hock. As Alfred straightened up he saw her. Even in the pale light cast by the single lamp near the door, Elswyth could see how his eyes widened in surprise. He did not jump, however, made no move that would frighten his horse. "Elswyth!" he said. Then, frowning and peering at her in the dimness of the stalls: "Are you all right?"

To her own considerable surprise, she answered, "No. I am not."

They regarded each other gravely across the stall partition. Both horses lowered their heads to resume eating hay. Then Alfred said, "Might I help?"

She shook her head. "No one can help." She sounded utterly desolate.

He patted the chestnut's shoulder, opened the stall door, and went back into the aisle. Then, to Elswyth: "Come out. We can sit on the hay bales in the corner and you can tell me about it."

Rather sullenly, she did as he commanded. She dragged her feet as she followed him to the bales of hay, but she sat down beside him when he gestured to her, and looked at him almost sulkily. His return look was perfectly serene. "Now," he said. "Tell me."

"You cannot help me, Prince," she repeated. She heard herself, heard how like a spoiled child she sounded, and scowled ferociously.

"Call me Alfred," he said. "And we'll never know if I can help unless you tell me what is wrong."

She shrugged. He would be on Athulf's side, she thought. He was a man.

"Elswyth . . ." he said very softly. It was quiet in the barn, and the smell of horses and of hay was comforting. It could not hurt to tell him, she thought. And, pulling her cloak around her shoulders tightly, as if for protection, she recounted her interview with Athulf. "I thought they could not force me, you see," she ended bitterly. "But Athulf said he would put me in a convent if I refused." She still could not believe he had said that to her. But he had. And he had meant it, too. "I could not bear a convent," she said. "I should go mad shut up like that."

To her utter horror, her voice quivered and tears stung behind her eyes. She clenched her whole face in a frantic effort to regain her usual composure.

He seemed not to notice her humiliating lapse of control, but said only, "You have not the temperament for religious life."

His matter-of-factness helped where sympathy would only have deepened her shame. "It is not fair!" she said. "Just because I am a girl, I can be forced to a marriage I hate and fear. They would not do this to me if I were a boy."

She straightened her spine and stuck her nose in the air and waited for him to preach her a sermon on woman's lot in life. Instead, he said in a strangely quiet voice, "No, it is not fair. I have often thought that."

Surprise jolted through her. She stared at him, wide-eyed. "You do not think I am being unreasonable?"

"No." He was not looking at her now, was looking into the distance, as if he were seeing something, or someone, else. The lamp hanging near the door drew a faint glow from his hair. It was nice hair, she found herself thinking, smooth and shiny and the color of honey. Alfred was nice.

Her breath hissed in her throat as the idea struck with all the suddenness and brilliance of a bolt of lightning. "It does not seem unreasonable to me for a girl to wish to have a say in whom she shall marry," he was saying. "But, as you have discovered, all too often she does not."

She did not answer, but continued to stare at him, seeing him now in the illumination of this brilliant new idea. She saw that his features were very fine, very clearly cut. She liked his nose, which did not have the arrogant bridge that distinguished Athulf's, and to a lesser degree her own. His mouth was nice too, firm and cool-looking. Edred's always looked moist and . . . hungry. She said at last, very slowly, "It is all very well for Athulf to say Edred will give me horses and dogs, but I shall have to sleep in his bed."

At that, he turned to look at her. His eyes were a lovely color, she thought, and they met hers straight on, with no embarrassment. He said, "That, of course, is the crux of the problem."

She searched his face. "When I said that to Athulf, about sleeping in Edred's bed, Athulf was embarrassed."

"Athulf ought to be embarrassed," came the immediate forthright reply.

Elswyth smiled. Alfred, she thought, was very nice indeed!

"How old are you, Elswyth?" he was asking.

"I am just fourteen."

He said something under his breath that both startled and delighted her. Then, "When Judith of France married my father, she was but fourteen and the consummation of the marriage was delayed because of her age. Perhaps Edred . . ."

She thought of the way Edred looked at her. "I do not think so," she said. She tried to repress a shudder and was not entirely successful. She tried to explain. "He looks at me . . ."

Alfred's face wore an unmistakable expression of disgust. Elswyth's spirits soared. "Alfred . . ." she said. It was the first time she had used his name; she drawled it long and smooth off her tongue. She straightened the cloak on her knees and continued carefully, "Perhaps you can help me after all—"

He cut in before she could go on. "Little one, I am so sorry, but I do not see how I can. I cannot speak to your brother for you. I have no rights in this matter. Athulf would be furious if I attempted to interfere, and he would be entirely justified in his wrath." Alfred's fair brows were drawn together and he was watching her hands as they played restlessly with the brown wool of her cloak. "Perhaps I could speak to Ethelswith," he added. "She, of all women, must know what it is to be forced to a distasteful marriage . . ." He caught himself and looked up, directly into Elswyth's eyes. "I did not say that."

She smiled at him a little tremulously. "It will not help to speak to the Lady Ethelswith." She added with certainty, "No, Alfred, there is only one person who can help me, and that is you."

His eyes widened in surprise. "I?" He shook his head. "I wish I could, Elswyth, but—"

"*You* can marry me," she said.

He recoiled as if she had struck him. "*What?*"

She did not make the mistake of leaning toward him, of attempting to crowd him. Instinctively she held her own space and left him his. "Don't you see?" she said, the very model of sweet reasonableness. "You are even higher in rank than Edred. Athulf would be happy to take a West Saxon prince over a Mercian ealdorman. And your family is rich! That would weigh with my mother and Athulf too."

He smiled a little at her artlessness. "But don't *you* see, Elswyth, you would only be exchanging one husband for another. You said you did not wish to marry at all."

"I don't, but if I must marry, I would far rather marry you than Edred." Her dark blue eyes were clinging to his face. "It would be a good match for you also, Alfred." Her deep drawling voice was persuasive. "My father was one of the greatest of Mercia's nobles. And I have a rich dowry, or so my mother and Athulf say."

"You flatter me, Elswyth," he began, clearly intending to refuse her.

"I *like* you," she cried, and now her voice was anguished. "I *hate* Edred."

He was beginning to look harried. "Elswyth, you don't understand—"

But she would not listen. "How old are you?" she asked.

"Eighteen."

"Well," she said stoutly, "it is time you were married."

He began to laugh.

"You said you wanted to help me." She was being unfair. She knew it and didn't care. He was her only hope. "Well, help me, then. Marry me."

His laughter was quenched as abruptly as it had begun. His face grew grave. "I am sorry, Elswyth," he said. His voice was very gentle but very final. "I would like to help you, but I cannot marry you."

"Why not?" she shot back. Elswyth on the trail of something she wanted was relentless. "Are you betrothed to someone else?"

"No." A look of strain came over his face. It was not a look she had ever seen there before. It made him look older. "It is just . . . I have determined I shall never marry. That is all."

She saw that there was something more here than just a reluctance to wed her. Something deeper. She regarded him thoughtfully. He was looking off into the distance once more.

"Why not?" she asked again.

He laughed lightly and shrugged his shoulders. "Oh, like you, I am one who will do better alone."

"Perhaps you would," she answered slowly, "but that is not the reason, is it?"

He came back from wherever he had been and, reluctantly, he turned to her. Even in the dimness she could see that there was a white line around his mouth. She waited for him to rise and walk away from her, but he did not. At last he said, "No." He spoke unwillingly, but he went on. "That is not the reason. You see, I am . . . flawed . . . Elswyth. I am not fit to marry any woman. Though"—and even in his obvious distress he managed a quick, charming smile—"if I were to marry at all, I would be happy to marry you."

She looked him over, her eyes speculative. What could he mean, flawed? He was perfect to look upon. Beautiful, in fact. She had seen him kill his boar; he was strong enough, and brave enough. There was only one thing she could think of and, being Elswyth, she asked, "Are you gelded?"

She could see the shock that ran through him at her words. "Of course not!" The lamplight caught the burning gold of his eyes.

She said reasonably, "Well, what was I to think?"

After a minute he laughed unwillingly. "Exactly that, I suppose. No . . . there is something wrong with my head, Elswyth."

"Wrong with your head?"

"Yes." The white line had come back to his mouth. "I get terrible headaches. There is something wrong inside my brain, I think. I have prayed and prayed, but still the headaches come. I think now they will never go away." He spoke almost carelessly, as if it were of no great moment, but the line around his mouth was even more pronounced and she understood that this was a subject he almost never spoke about.

"How often do you get them?" she asked.

He shrugged. "It varies. Sometimes every few weeks, sometimes not for months."

She realized that these could not be normal headaches. He was not the sort who would exaggerate pain. Quite the opposite, she thought. Elswyth understood instantly, in her bones, how Alfred must feel about these headaches. And so she knew how to answer him.

"You are not perfect," she said, her face severe. "You cannot expect to be perfect. That was Satan's sin, was it not?"

He did not answer, but his eyes flared a sudden brilliant gold.

"Alfred," she said, and now she leaned a little toward him, the hunter closing in on her prey, "you are wrong if you think you can avoid marriage. You are a boy, and so they may not be able to force you, as they are forcing me, but neither will they let you alone."

He said nothing, just looked at her out of those brilliant golden eyes. She added cunningly, "Nor will you wish to have to explain why it is you do not wish to marry."

There was a long pause. Then, "You are diabolical," he said. He sounded as if he were out of breath.

She straightened her back and said with passionate intensity, "I would far rather marry you and your headaches than Edred."

Another pause fell, this one of a slightly different quality from the one before. This time it was Elswyth who held her breath. He was not looking at her. Finally, "Are you sure?" he asked. Then, with difficulty: "I wonder sometimes what will happen if the headaches become worse, start to happen every week, every day." His mouth was shadowed by that white line once more. "I could go mad with them, Elswyth. You do not know."

"Alfred," she said, "Edred's teeth are yellow."

The line disappeared and his face lit with amusement. "They are. Rather like a horse's."

They began to laugh at the same instant, as they had the last time they had met together in this barn. Then he said, a little breathlessly, "All right, little Elswyth. I shall see if Athulf will not accept me in place of Edred."

She heaved a great sigh of relief and he put his hand over hers where it lay, palm-up, on the hay between them. It was the first time he had ever touched her. His hand was thin and sinewy, adorned with golden rings, and she closed her fingers around it instantly. He stood up and pulled her to stand beside him.

"One more thing," he said, and now he was deadly sober.

"Yes?" She looked up at him, her eyes on a level with his nice, firmly modeled mouth.

"Do not worry about sleeping in my bed. Like my father, I think fourteen is too young for that sort of thing. I will wait."

Her smile was radiant. "Oh Alfred, thank you!"

"You are most welcome." His voice was rather ruefully amused. "Come along. I will try to see Athulf before dinner." He opened the barn door and they stood for a moment in the doorway, their arms touching. It had begun to snow.

"Put up your hood," Alfred said. And she, who hated being told what to do, promptly obeyed. She was so happy, she thought she could have hugged him.

"You go first," she said, suddenly circumspect. "It will not do for us to be seen leaving the barn together."

He laughed, showing nice white teeth, gave one of her long black braids a gentle tweak, and went out into the snow, his own head uncovered. He had a cat's assured, almost arrogant grace, Elswyth thought with satisfaction, watching him cross the courtyard in the lightly falling snow. He would get Athulf's approval, she was sure of it. There was that about Alfred that would always cause men to fall in with his demands. If she had to marry someone, and it seemed that she did, she could not have chosen better.

She settled her hood more snugly over her hair and went out herself into the snow.

Chapter 8

A THULF had come into his hall only minutes before Alfred arrived seeking him. Elswyth's brother seemed delighted to see the West Saxon prince, and seated his guest in one of the high-backed chairs that were set near to the fire. Athulf's hall thanes sat along the wall benches, talking and carving with wood or repairing leather, and the two young men were left to speak together in private.

"This business of the Danes is extremely serious," Athulf remarked to Alfred once they both had cups of ale in their hands. "Burgred deludes himself if he thinks they will come no further south than Nottingham." He added, with a swift sideways look at Alfred, "I thank God that Wessex will join with us in this campaign. The West Saxons have had far more experience fighting the Danes than have we Mercians."

"As I said in the witan, this is a time for all Christian men to stand together," Alfred answered. He ran his right index finger around the rim of his silver cup and added carefully, "I was . . . surprised . . . that Burgred had made no plans himself for defending Nottingham."

"We have grown soft in Mercia since the days of our capitulation to your grandfather, Prince," Athulf answered. His voice sounded bitter. "A conquered people lose their initiative."

Alfred was surprised at the bitterness and turned to look into Athulf's thin dark face. "Mercia has ever kept its own king," he said to Elswyth's brother slowly. "Egbert was Bretwalda, true, but he never tried to make Mercia a part of Wessex."

"We swore allegiance to Wessex. We were taught to look to Wessex for leadership. It is not fair to complain now, Prince, about what Wessex itself has wrought."

A small silence fell. Alfred looked from Athulf's taut profile back to his own ale cup and understood that the Mercian was deeply humiliated by his country's lack of initiative. "Perhaps you are right," Alfred said mildly, and took a sip of his ale.

Another silence fell. Then Athulf recollected his duty as host and cleared his throat. "But you did not come here to listen to my reproaches," he said to his guest, and managed a rueful smile. "How may I serve you, Prince?"

"I want to marry your sister," Alfred said.

Athulf's blue eyes opened so wide that it was comical. Alfred's eyes narrowed in concealed amusement. "I can offer a handsome marriage portion," he added.

"You wish to marry *Elswyth*?"

"Why not?" Alfred settled his shoulders more comfortably against the carved back of his chair. "She is a very desirable match."

"Of course she is," Athulf agreed hastily, aware that he had blundered. "Her birth is among the highest in Mercia. And she will have a rich dowry."

"That is nice," Alfred said.

Athulf was beginning to recover himself. Alfred watched him from under partially lowered lashes. "I am afraid, Prince," Athulf said hesitatingly, "that Elswyth is already promised."

"Has there been a formal betrothal?"

"No."

"Then there is no promise," Alfred said.

"Well, there is an informal . . . agreement."

Alfred shrugged the shoulders that were propped so easily against the dark chair back. "Break it."

"I . . . It will not be easy." Athulf rubbed his nose and stared into the fire.

Alfred said, "Tell Edred she does not like him, that he is too old, that she prefers to marry me."

Once more Athulf's eyes flew to the prince and stretched wide. "You have been talking to Elswyth?" he asked. Almost accused.

"Of course I have been talking to Elswyth." Abruptly all the amusement left Alfred's eyes. "God knows what she will do if you force her to marry Edred, Athulf. She fears him, is repulsed by him." His fully opened eyes glittered in the firelight. "Elswyth is not the sort to make the best of an unpleasant situation," he added. "She is one who will rebel."

"I know." Athulf's face was gloomy. "She has ever been thus. And she has been badly spoiled. My mother ever stayed with my father at court, and left her to me and to Ceolwulf."

"And so she was allowed to go her own way."

"All too often," Athulf agreed ruefully. "But she cannot continue thus, Prince. She is almost a woman."

The fire flared up suddenly as part of the huge log burning there cracked and fell. "Girl or woman, she is still Elswyth," Alfred said. "She will always be Elswyth. And she will do better with me than she will with Edred."

Athulf looked at Alfred's fire-gilded face. "Did she say she would marry you?"

"She *asked* me to marry her," Alfred answered, and humor quivered beneath the surface gravity of his voice.

"Oh, my God," Athulf groaned. "Only Elswyth would dare do such a thing."

"I like her," Alfred said. "I think we understand each other."

Athulf's dark, haughty face, also illuminated by the flaring fire, became very serious. "Prince," he said almost reluctantly, "I must ask you to think again before I give you an answer. You hold a great position in Wessex, you are secondarius, your brother's heir. You are deeply respected among your people; that is apparent immediately to all who do meet you. It is not impossible that someday you might be king." Athulf's arrogant aquiline nose looked pinched as he said, "I cannot see Elswyth filling the sort of position you would expect your wife to fill." Then he added with despair, "Every time you needed her, she would be out galloping her horse across the Downs."

At that, Alfred laughed. Then, sobering, he assured Athulf, "My brother, thank God, is young and healthy. And he has a son who will be able to succeed him in a few years' time. My position is not like to change, nor would I wish it to do so. My wife need be no finer than the lady of any ordinary thane, and that, Elswyth can be." He added with amusement, "She has pride enough to be queen, that is certain."

"All too certain," Athulf said. And breathed hard through his nose.

"Well, my lord, what is your answer?" Alfred did not sound as if he were in any doubt, and there was certainly no tension in his shoulders or in the relaxed hands that held his cup, but his expression was courteous.

"It is yes, of course. You must know you are a better match than Edred. And, more important, Elswyth apparently likes you." Athulf rubbed his nose, looked at Alfred, and said wryly, "I have not been liking myself much lately."

Alfred gave his future brother his quick, charming smile. "She is not an easy charge, that I can see."

"Well, she will shortly be *your* charge," Athulf retorted. "For which blessing I thank the good Lord."

Alfred set his barely touched cup of ale on the arm of his chair and leaned a little forward, as if to rise. "We will wait until after the battle with the Danes for the marriage," he said, still poised to rise from his chair.

"There is no need to wait for so long," Athulf assured him, but Alfred was shaking his head.

"If I died in battle it would not matter, that is true. But I have a deep objection to saddling a young girl with a man who is maimed. We will wait."

Athulf's face altered. "I had not thought of that."

"It is not something I dwell upon either," Alfred said lightly, "but in this case it has some bearing. Elswyth and I will marry after we have settled with the Danes."

"Very well," said Athulf. The two men stood up at the same time and regarded each other with approval. "I shall be honored to be your brother," the Mercian said.

"I too," Alfred replied. Athulf's dark face lit with a smile, altogether banishing the haughty look it wore in repose. Alfred put a hand upon the other's shoulder, then turned toward the door. "I must go and change before the banquet."

Athulf walked with him to the hall door, and when both men looked outside, they saw that it was snowing hard. "Good," remarked Athulf with satisfaction. "The more it snows, the less likely the Danes will be to raid the countryside."

"I pray they stay in Nottingham until the spring," Alfred said, and his voice was very clipped. "It is our great chance, Athulf, to catch them with both our armies at full strength."

"I know," Athulf said.

Alfred hesitated. Then: "I wish I could be sure that Burgred sees that."

"Burgred has a witan," Athulf answered grimly. "You may rely on us."

Alfred's hand closed for a minute on Athulf's arm; then the prince was gone into the swirl of snow.

Alfred returned to Wessex. Ethelred summoned another witan, and word was sent out across the country that the fyrds of all the shires were to muster in March, to move to Nottingham to meet the Danes.

There was no standing army in Wessex. The closest thing the country had to a permanent fighting force was the circle of companions who formed the king's bodyguard. These king's companions lived in the king's hall, were supported by the king's revenues, and to all intents and purposes were professional soldiers. Each ealdorman also had a hearthband of thanes who were sworn to serve him and who lived in his hall and at his expense. These two groups of thanes formed the fighting elite of the West Saxon army.

When an ealdorman called out the fyrd of his shire, however, he called upon other men besides his own hearthband. Chief, he called upon the shire thanes.

A shire thane lived upon his own manor, which had to be at least five hides of land in size and could be considerably larger. Though a shire thane did not live in the ealdorman's hall, still he was pledged to fight for the ealdorman of his shire when called upon. Each shire thane was further required to furnish to the fyrd an additional man for every five hides of land he possessed over and above the original five hides. Most often these extra men were ceorls, who owed loyalty to the shire thane whom they represented. It was the shire thane's responsibility to see that all his representatives were equipped with spear and byrnie and had been given basic training in the use of arms. The towns of Wessex were also assessed in hides and the townsmen were required to send for service in the fyrd a representative for each five hides of land the town was assessed.

These, then, were the kinds of men who had defended Wessex from the Danes for the past fifty years. The defense had in general been successful. Because the fyrds were local, they had the advantage of being able to gather quickly, and over the years, because the same men answered the call time and again, the thanes, ceorls, and townsmen who formed the shire militias had turned into decently equipped and experienced men-at-arms.

So in March, when the fyrds of Wessex mustered in response to their ealdormen's summonses, these were the men who gathered to march to Nottingham. There was not a man present, however, who did not realize that the army that awaited them in Nottingham was of a very different caliber from the raiding parties they had encountered in the past.

It was a hard time of year to take a farmer from his land, Alfred thought as the massed fyrds of Wessex moved slowly along the old Roman road known as the Fosse Way, north into Mercia. There were some four thousand men marching along this most westerly of all the great Roman roads this day, and most of them, shire thanes and ceorls, were landowners whose fields were in need of the plow if seed were to be sown this spring. It was going to be possible to keep together an army of this size only for a relatively brief period of time.

This was a thought that had been troubling Alfred for the last six weeks. The West Saxon men were mainly farmers who were used to scattering immediately after a fight to return to their homes and their fields and their animals. The Danes, on the other hand, were a professional army, joined together in the name of conquest, and living off the fruits of their plunder. The Danes would not scatter after a battle, of that Alfred was quite certain.

We must defeat them at Nottingham, he thought, and not for the first time. Alfred's stallion arched his gleaming chestnut neck in the chill damp air and snorted at the slow pace he was being forced to keep. The king's companions and the ealdormen were all mounted, but most of the men of the West Saxon fyrds were on foot, and the pace was suited to them and to the supply wagons drawn by slow-moving oxen.

It took a week to march from Chippenham, where they had mustered, to Tamworth. At Tamworth the fyrds of Wessex joined up with the Mercian army, and from thence they moved together to Nottingham, where they massed on the right bank of the Trent and looked across the river at high cliffs lined with the flashing arms of Danish warriors. Unlike the Northumbrians, Burgred and Ethelred had not been lucky enough to catch the Danes outside their fortifications.

The Danish fortifications at Nottingham were formidable indeed. The

Viking army had thrown up earthworks on all sides of Nottingham that were not protected by the river and the cliffs, and though they were outnumbered by the combined Mercian and West Saxon force, the Danes remained snug and safe within their barriers and showed no signs of issuing forth for battle.

The days went by. Alfred could see signs of restlessness growing among the fyrds. The weather was warming. At home the heifers and cows would be calving and work in the dairy would be under way. The pigs too would have littered, and as men clustered around their cook fires at Nottingham, eating their army rations, visions of roast suckling pig were dancing in more minds than one.

They could not afford to sit here on the riverbank and do nothing!

"What can we do?" Ethelred asked reasonably when Alfred expressed this thought to him for perhaps the dozenth time in one day. "It would be folly to attack the camp. You heard what happened to the Northumbrians once they got within the walls of York. If we are to fight the Danes, it must be out in the open."

"But they are not coming out in the open, Ethelred!" Alfred's voice was harsh with frustration.

"They will when they get hungry enough," came Ethelred's placid reply.

"By the time they are hungry enough, all our men will have gone home," said Alfred. And that evening he took a picked band of his own companions and rode south along the Trent to spy out the possibilities of crossing the river somewhere north of Repton.

"If we can get a party of men across to surprise the Danes from the south, then perhaps the rest of the army can successfully attack from the west," Alfred explained to Edgar, the young thane who was one of those companions closest to him.

"It is worth a try, my lord," Edgar replied promptly. Like Alfred, Edgar was young and frustrated by the inaction of the last two weeks.

Ten of them stole out of camp in the dark that night. Alfred had not told even Ethelred of his plans. To Alfred's disappointment, Ethelred had been deferring to Burgred's leadership ever since the armies of Wessex and Mercia had first merged. Alfred could understand Ethelred's reasoning, could even see some sense in it. As his one conversation with Athulf had shown him, the Mercians were extremely sensitive about Wessex' past overlordship. Still the fact remained that Burgred was too timid and indecisive to ever prove an effective leader. It was best, Alfred decided, to take action on his own authority.

The thanes who followed Alfred that night were all young, and could easily be distinguished as belonging to the prince by the headband all wore bound around their brows. It had become the fashion of late among Alfred's men, particularly the younger ones, to copy the prince's style. His men were all clean-shaven also, although Alfred's face was smooth because his beard had yet to grow and not because of any razor.

They moved carefully, keeping as much as possible within the trees to avoid being spied by the Danes on the other side of the river. The night was moonless, but the faint starlight gave them enough light to see their way. By daylight all but two of them had returned to the Saxon camp, with neither king realizing they had been gone. Edgar and his fellow companion, Brand, returned by noon, after verifying with the local folk that there was indeed a ford across the river at Willowburg. Then Alfred went to see Ethelred and Burgred.

Burgred would not hear of an attempt on the Danish camp. "The Northumbrians were slaughtered when they met with the Danes within the walls of York," he said stubbornly to Alfred. "We must fight in the open if we are to have a hope of victory."

"But they will not come out into the open, my lord," Alfred strove to keep his voice patient. The April sky was deeply blue, with high white clouds sailing across the Danish camp, so tantalizingly close on the far side of the river. "They know we outnumber them," Alfred went on. "They will keep within the safety of Nottingham unless we force battle upon them. And there is this ford—"

"No," said Burgred. Then, to Ethelred: "He should not have left camp without my permission."

Ethelred's brown eyes were clouded. He looked worriedly from Burgred to Alfred. "If we hold siege long enough," he said to his brother, "they will have to come out for food."

Alfred turned his impatient gaze to Ethelred. "The fyrds will never be able to hold siege for any length of time," he said. "Even now the shire thanes and ceorls are longing to be home. And we do not have enough men with just the hearthbands. We must have the farmers as well. You know that, Ethelred, as well as I."

Burgred drew his bulk up to its considerable height. "I am the leader of this army, Prince," he said to Alfred, looking down his broad fleshy nose. "You would do well to remember that."

"Alfred does not mean to be importunate," Ethelred said.

"He is more than importunate. He is impertinent," returned Burgred. "You have ever given too much heed to so young a boy, my brother. In consequence, he has too little regard for age and experience." And with these parting remarks, Burgred turned his back on the two West Saxons and lumbered away with dignity in the direction of his tent.

Ethelred looked at Alfred. His brother's young face was not wearing any of the expressions that Ethelred had expected to see. Alfred did not look angry or humiliated or contemptuous. Instead his eyes were cold, level, and implacably stern. He said to Ethelred, very quietly, "Burgred is making a terrible mistake."

"Perhaps," Ethelred returned. "But I cannot overrule him, Alfred. The Mercians will not follow me if their own king is against me. And the West Saxons are not strong enough to storm Nottingham alone. We have no choice but to hold siege for as long as we can, and hope for the best."

And so they waited. And while they waited the men of Wessex and of Mercia began to melt away. Few could see the point of sitting day after day on the banks of the Trent when there were more important things to be done at home. The shire thanes fretted that shepherds, cowherds, goat-herds, and swineherds would not be properly attending to their business in the absence of their lords. The ceorls felt their absences from home even more urgently than did the shire thanes. What work was done about the farm of a ceorl was usually done by the owner; if he was not home in the spring, it would be a hungry winter the following year.

By the end of April the combined armies of Wessex and Mercia had lost over three thousand men.

"I shall sue for peace," Burgred said. And Ethelred agreed. There was nothing else to do, he said to Alfred, considering the depleted state of the Saxon armies.

The peace was negotiated by Burgred's representative, Edred, Ealdor-man of the Tomsaetan. Ivar the Boneless drove a hard bargain. In order for him to leave Mercia, he demanded that Burgred pay him five thousand pounds in geld.

Alfred was livid when he realized that Burgred was going to agree to the terms.

"Where is the Mercian witan?" he stormed to Athulf. He had sought out the young ealdorman as soon as Alfred understood that his arguments would not persuade Burgred to reject the Viking demand.

Athulf's thin dark face was grim. "The witan agreed with the king," he answered tightly. "They want to buy the Danes off."

Alfred, who rarely swore, did so now. Athulf's mouth was thin as a sword blade. "I agree, Prince. I think we are making a grave mistake. But the king will not listen. He is . . . he is . . ."

"He is afraid," Alfred said.

There was a reverberating silence. Then Athulf let out his breath. "Aelle died hard," he said. "One cannot blame him, I suppose."

"Burgred is a king." Alfred's eyes were burning gold. "His thought should not be for his own safety but for his people and his God." The two young men were standing on the edge of the Trent, and now Alfred turned his face toward the rock of Nottingham, lying on the far side of the river. "*Now* is the time, Athulf!" His fists opened and closed at his sides. "God and all his saints, we *have* them! And instead, Burgred is paying them to go away."

"I said that to the witan, Prince." Athulf sounded more weary than angry.

"And the other ealdormen?"

"They agreed with Burgred." Athulf also stared toward Nottingham. "Mercia has never fought the Danes," he said then, his voice almost toneless. "We have no borders on the sea. The sight of Nottingham's fortifications frightened more men than Burgred, Prince. Nor is the fright unjustified. Our troops are raw and untrained. We are no match for the Danes."

"You have four thousand West Saxons to fight by your side," Alfred said.

"We are losing men daily. You know that."

"We are losing men because of our inaction!" Alfred was frustrated and furious.

A muscle in Athulf's jaw twitched, but he said nothing.

"Prince . . . my lord Athulf . . ." A voice from behind caused both young men to turn in haste, neither wishing their words to be overheard by other ears. A youngster of about fourteen stood there, hesitant but with a look about his mouth that said he would not easily be dislodged. "Is it true?" he asked, looking from Athulf to Alfred, then back again to Athulf. "Is the king going to pay the geld?"

Athulf did not dismiss the boy, but instead answered him. "Yes, Ethelred. I am afraid it is true."

The boy's hazel eyes flared very green. "But he cannot!"

Athulf glanced at Alfred, then said to the boy, his voice very flat, "He can."

"But . . ." The ardent green eyes turned again to Alfred. "What do the West Saxons say, my lord?"

Alfred looked at Athulf. "This is Ethelred of Hwicce," Athulf said. "The brother of my promised wife. His father is one of our ealdormen."

Alfred raised his brows in recognition. Then he looked back at the boy. Ethelred was a stocky youngster, with reddish hair and very fair, almost milky-white skin. "You are young to be bearing arms," Alfred said.

"I am fourteen, my lord." He raised his chin proudly: "I can wield my sword as well as any man."

"I see." Alfred's eyes were level as they watched the boy's face. He answered Ethelred's question: "The West Saxons must bow to the decision of Mercia."

A fiery flush stained the boy's milky skin. You are wrong!" he cried passionately. He bit his already-chapped lower lip: "I beg pardon, my lord, I do not mean to criticize, but do you not see that we must fight?"

Alfred's skin, tanned a deeper gold than usual by the sun, also flushed with emotion. "Yes, Lord Ethelred," he answered, "I do see. It is your countrymen who do not. Speak to your father. He is one of those in favor of peace."

Alfred's crisp voice was even more stinging than his words, and the boy's skin paled again. "I know that." Ethelred's voice was choked. "I hoped that the West Saxons would feel otherwise."

"The West Saxons cannot attack without the assistance of Mercia," came the chill reply. "And I do not think that the Mercian fyrds would follow the King of Wessex against the wishes of their own leaders." Alfred's face made it clear that this was a fact he deeply regretted.

Now Athulf's dark skin flushed with anger. "Mercia has its own king, my lord, and it is he who commands our allegiance."

"You have made that perfectly clear," Alfred snapped.

Ethelred looked from the fine-featured face of the West Saxon prince to the imperious and furious face of his future brother. He once more bit his maltreated lip. Then, uneasily: "I thank you, my lords. I did not mean to interrupt your speech." He looked from Alfred to Athulf once more, bowed, and began to walk away.

Alfred said to Athulf, "If the Mercian witan had half the mettle of that boy, we should be in Nottingham tomorrow."

The words were spoken to Athulf, but Alfred's crisp voice carried and Ethelred heard him quite clearly. The boy's milky skin flushed again, this time with a mixture of pride and pleasure.

Prince Alfred agreed with him, he thought as his steps took him farther away from the prince and Athulf. If the decision were Alfred's, they would fight. Ethelred could see that quite clearly.

He kicked a rock at his feet. He had not expected to find such a fighting spirit lodged within the slender, almost fragile-looking person of the West Saxon prince.

Alfred, however, was as powerless as he to change the course of events here at Nottingham.

Ethelred went off to spend the afternoon throwing rocks into the river, a pastime which served not at all to alleviate his humiliation and angry frustration at his king's unnecessary surrender.

Chapter 9

"**S**TAY still, Elswyth!" said Eadburgh, giving a none-too-gentle tug on the black braid she was plaiting.

Elswyth's eyes watered with the sudden sharp pain, but she made no protest. Eadburgh continued to weave threads of gold through the thick braids that were the chief adornment of any unmarried Mercian girl. "There," she said finally, stepping away to admire her handiwork. She added, almost grudgingly, "You have lovely hair, my daughter. If only you would take better care of it!"

"Thank you, Mother," Elswyth said tonelessly. Her chief conversation with Eadburgh this last month had consisted of Eadburgh scolding and Elswyth replying in monosyllables. Elswyth had long since discovered that any attempt at a genuine exchange of thought with her mother was a useless endeavor.

Eadburgh's mouth thinned. She had been at Croxden for the entire winter, seeing to Elswyth's bridal linens, and perforce mother and daughter had spent more time in each other's company than ever before in their lives. The interlude had agreed with neither's temper.

Eadburgh walked now to the clothes chest in the corner of the room and lifted out a cloak. It was a beautiful cloak, made of the softest wool and dyed a deep blue to match Elswyth's eyes.

"It is too warm for a cloak," Elswyth said.

"Every lady must wear a cloak," came the instant reply. "It is not seemly to go forth without one."

Elswyth curled her lip. Eadburgh's face hardened. She laid the cloak about her daughter's straight shoulders and fastened it with a large enameled pin. "Be sure you keep it on you," she said.

"Yes, Mother," Elswyth replied.

"You may send in Margit and wait for me in the hall." As Eadburgh watched her daughter walk to the door of the sleeping room, her lips folded in a thin straight line.

Elswyth found her mother's serving maid, then went herself to stand at the door of their hall to look out. From where she stood, the royal hall of

Tamworth was clearly visible. Though it was still light outside, torches were blazing beside the carved double doors. This night's great feast was being given by Burgred in honor of the saving of Mercia from the Danes.

Burgred had been in Tamworth since the previous week, bringing with him news of the peace and of its terms. Elswyth had been horrified when she learned that the Saxon armies had capitulated without a fight. When she had said this to Ceolwulf, however, he had assured her that Burgred had done the best thing. "We could not have fought the Danes within Nottingham," he said. "We would have been slaughtered trying to storm the town. You do not know how well they have fortified it, Elswyth!"

Elswyth, knowing her brother's peaceful tendencies, was not reassured. But Athulf had remained at Nottingham, as had all the West Saxons, and so there was no one else she could ask. Until now. King Ethelred and Alfred had ridden back to Tamworth today; it was their presence which had provided the occasion for Burgred's feast.

Elswyth leaned against the open door and looked out into the busy courtyard. Their own hall was unusually quiet; most of their thanes were still at Nottingham with Athulf. Only Ceolwulf and a few close companions had returned to Tamworth with Burgred. Athulf would be returning shortly, however, she thought. For her wedding.

Elswyth had not seen Alfred since their betrothal last Christmas. She would see him tonight, and in two weeks they would be married. Even though the evening was warm, Elswyth folded her arms as if she were chilled. Everything around her was changing, she thought desolately. The winter at Croxden with her mother had been dreadful. The Danes were still at Nottingham and unbeaten. In two weeks' time she would be a wife. She wished, with all her heart, that she could be a child again.

The royal hall was filled when Elswyth and her mother and Ceolwulf and his thanes entered, and the heat of the fire and the press of people immediately made her cloak feel too warm. She looked around but did not see Alfred. The high seat where the two kings would sit was still empty. "We are to sit to the right of the high seat," Ceolwulf was saying to Eadburgh. "Beside the West Saxon prince."

Their party began to cross the open floor. They were at the great hearthplace in the center of the room when Elswyth saw Alfred coming toward her, moving with his distinctive light grace. She stopped.

"Elswyth," Eadburgh began to say in annoyance, and then her mother too saw him.

"My lady. Elswyth." He was in front of them now, smiling and looking from the women to Ceolwulf, then back again to Elswyth. "Your hair is all a-sparkle with gold," he said.

Eadburgh, who had spent hours plaiting the golden thread into the thick black braids, smiled complacently.

"Mother did it," Elswyth said. "In your honor." She sounded as if she had been tortured.

Alfred looked from her to Eadburgh, then laughed. Elswyth, looking up into his amused golden eyes, felt as if a weight had been lifted from her chest. It was going to be all right, she thought. And smiled back, her thought as clear as crystal on her faintly flushed face.

Alfred took her hand, said, "You are to sit beside me tonight," and began to walk with her toward the benches.

Shortly after Elswyth was seated, Burgred and Ethelred made their ceremonial entrance. Then Burgred opened the feast by speaking about the peace he had made with the Danes. Elswyth watched Alfred's profile as they both listened to the king's speech.

"Wiser to buy peace with geld than to buy it with men's lives," Burgred said, and Alfred's perfectly straight nose seemed to her to grow thinner.

"The Danes will leave Nottingham as soon as the geld can be paid," Burgred said, and a muscle quivered under Alfred's smooth golden cheek. He was staring into space, Elswyth saw, and to one who was not as close to him as she, his expression would be inpenetrable.

When at last Burgred had concluded and the food was being put on the tables, Elswyth said to Alfred, "But where will the Danes go?"

He offered her a dish of spiced meat and, absently, she heaped her trencher. "Wherever there is more geld for them to collect," Alfred replied tonelessly.

She took a white roll and broke it open. "So we have bought our safety at someone else's expense."

He also took a roll. "You might say that."

She scooped up some meat, put it on her roll, and took a bite. On the other side of Alfred she could see that his brother and Burgred were talking. Ceolwulf, on her other side, was engaged in conversation with the man beside him. She asked, her voice low, "Why did we not fight, Alfred? You had so many men! Surely you should have met the Danes in battle, not left them free to prey upon some other kingdom. They will most like go to East Anglia next."

He too looked behind him and beyond her. Then he answered, his voice pitched low like hers, "Burgred did not wish to fight and your witan agreed with him."

"I see." She scanned his face. "And you?"

His long fingers, ringed with gold, were tearing apart the roll. He had eaten nothing as yet. "The West Saxons would have fought, but there were not enough of us without the Mercians." He glanced beyond her to Ceolwulf. Then: "Your brother Athulf would have fought also. But we were not the voices who carried the decision." The bitterness in his tone was faintly audible. He was not used, Elswyth thought shrewdly, to having his advice disregarded.

"Together we outnumbered them," he said. "We should have fought."

Elswyth watched the long, nervous fingers of her future husband shredding his roll. Then she said, slowly and thoughtfully, "When you train a horse, you must never let him see that you are afraid of him. Once he sees that, once he understands that he has only to lay back his ears and you will give in, then he is out of your control. Nor will he grow easier to deal with as time goes on." She raised her eyes to his face and found him staring at her. The white line was around his mouth again.

"Exactly," he said.

"Alfred . . ." said Ethelred on his other side, and he turned his head to answer his brother.

As the feast progressed, Elswyth noticed, without remarking upon it, that Alfred ate scarcely anything. She was her usual hungry self and consumed at least three times as much food as he, who was so much larger than she. And he was obviously preoccupied. While the scop was singing, he fell into a deep reverie and she thought he scarcely knew where he was or who was beside him.

" 'The gray gull wheeled about, greedy for slaughter; the candle of the sky grew dark,' " the scop sang, reciting the familiar Anglo-Saxon tale of the voyage of Saint Andrew to the land of Myrmidonia. " 'The terror of the tempest arose; the thanes grew afraid.' "

The terror of the tempest, thought Elswyth. That was what the Danes represented. And Burgred and the Mercian nobles had been afraid. Elswyth's dark blue gaze went to the figure of her king, sitting safe and well-fed this night on his high seat in his torchlit hall. Burgred was a fool, she thought. The Danes would despise him no less than she did. They would take his geld and go away for the winter, but they would be back. They would be fools if they did not come back; and Elswyth doubted that the Danes were fools.

For the first time the reality of the Danish threat was brought fully home to her. She had not felt it before, not even when her brothers and their men had marched away from Croxden to join the Mercian army at Tamworth. She had felt then, with serene assurance, that the armies of Mercia and Wessex would triumph in battle. Nor had she feared for her men. Elswyth herself was physically courageous. The thought of death did not frighten her, chiefly because she did not think of it.

But the thought of the Danes at Tamworth frightened her. They had taken Northumbria. If they took East Anglia, which was smaller by far than Northumbria, they would return to Mercia. And if they took Mercia, then they would turn to Wessex.

We should have fought them at Nottingham, Elswyth thought.

" 'God made the enemy weapons melt like wax in their hands,' " sang the scop. " 'The horrible foes could do no hurt by the strength of their swords.' "

But it would not happen that way, Elswyth thought, her eyes on Alfred's finally quiet hands. In the song of Saint Andrew, the heathen world was conquered by prayer and by miracle. Prayer might be efficacious in the real world also, but it would take the deeds of men to conquer the Danes. A strong leader was the miracle England needed now. And that leader was not Burgred.

Alfred's hand stirred and moved to grasp his cup. He turned his head, found her watching him, and smiled.

It was the month for sheep shearing and Ethelred sent his remaining shire thanes and ceorls home to Wessex, keeping in Mercia only his own king's companions and the ealdormen and their hearthbands. Half of the thanes remained camped near Nottingham, but the ealdormen and the chief thanes of the king's household came to Tamworth to see Alfred married.

Ethelred, who was determined to see his younger brother wed with all possible honor, had sent to Canterbury for Archbishop Ceolnoth, and the wedding party was forced to wait for the archbishop's arrival. Ethelswith prayed nightly that Ceolnoth's journey would prosper. It was costing her a fortune to feed the King of Wessex and all his retinue. Each night in the great hall they consumed ten jars of honey, three hundred loaves of bread, twelve casks of Welsh ale, thirty of clear ale, two oxen, ten geese, twenty hens, ten cheeses, a cask full of butter, five salmon, and a hundred eels. In order to supplement the food supply, she sent Burgred and his guests out hunting each day; but still the burden on her own stores was considerable.

Of all the principals concerned, Alfred was the one whose mind was least on his wedding. The thought of the Danes in Nottingham weighed like lead on his spirit. He could not rid himself of the thought that Wessex and Mercia together had thrown away a golden opportunity when they had backed down from a fight.

It bothered him also that for almost the first time in his life he was in disagreement with Ethelred. If Ethelred had asserted himself more forcefully, he could have won over the Mercians. Alfred was sure of it. And even if he could not . . . then should the West Saxons have taken the initiative. Enough Mercians would have followed to have made a difference.

Too late now, he thought. And even the excitement of the hunt failed to distract him from his preoccupation.

Ceolnoth arrived in Tamworth two days before Alfred's nineteenth birthday, and Ethelswith decided it would be lucky to wait the extra day and celebrate the marriage and the birthday together. Elswyth prayed fervently at the first Mass the bishop celebrated in Tamworth that she would last two more days without slaying her mother.

"It numbs the mind to think that any human person could show such concern over crockery and linen," she said to Alfred as they sat together at supper the evening of Ceolnoth's arrival. "The marriage settlements and dowry were agreed over the winter. We each know what the other is getting. Surely that is all that matters."

Alfred laughed at her grim expression. "Women are ever thus," he said. "And I suppose someone must be concerned with crockery and linen. You can be sure that I am not."

She looked at him. "I am not either." She felt it was only fair to be perfectly honest. "I have ever believed in leaving that sort of thing to the serving maids."

"You would concern yourself if you needed to," he answered carelessly.

"I suppose so." But she doubted it.

"In truth, Elswyth"—and he sighed a little wearily—"I wish crockery and linen were all we had to worry about."

"I know." She took a dish of chicken from the serving man and put it before Alfred. "There is your chicken," she said. For the last few days she had gone to the Tamworth kitchen herself to make sure there would be a plain roasted chicken for Alfred at dinnertime; she had begun to worry about his lack of appetite. He could not afford to lose weight.

He picked up a leg of the chicken, then turned to look at her. She had said nothing to him about food; the chicken had simply begun to appear at the table. "Thank you," he said. "Spiced food does not agree with my stomach."

She gave him a faint smile. "The Tamworth cooks are strong with the spices," she agreed. Then: "You don't plan to tarry long in Mercia once we are wedded, do you, Alfred?"

He began to eat the chicken. "No. The Danes are safe enough while the geld is still being collected. Why should they fight? They will profit handsomely enough without. We shall go to Wessex after we are married. There are things to be done at home."

"Good," she said with heartfelt approval.

He chuckled. "Poor little Elswyth. Two more days and you will be free from crockery and linen."

She was not hungry herself this evening, so she put down her knife and rested her cheek on her hand, turning her face to watch him eat. "I never thought I actually would be pleased to be getting married," she said in wonder.

His teeth were busy chewing but his eyes glinted with amusement. She went on, "I ever thought that leaving my home and my brothers would be the worst thing that could happen to me. But I scarcely saw my brothers all winter, and every time I took my horse out or flew my hawk or played with my dogs, there was my mother, scolding. It has been horrible!"

He put down the chicken leg, which he had stripped to the bone. "I am glad you prefer me to your mother."

"I would prefer Ivar the Boneless to my mother," she answered gloomily.

"I am flattered," he said.

"I did not mean that the way it sounded," she assured him. Then, when he cocked a quizzical eyebrow: "You know what I mean, Alfred. Don't tease."

There was a little silence as he picked up the next piece of chicken. She watched with satisfaction as he took a bite. He glanced at her and said, "You are not eating, Elswyth. Would you like some of this chicken?"

"No." She shook her head. "That is for you." She sighed. "Sitting within doors all day does not lead to a good appetite. *You* have been hunting."

He regarded her in silence for a minute. "Would you like to come hunting with me tomorrow?"

Her face lit like a candle. "Could I?"

"I don't see why not."

Her lower lip jutted out. "My mother is why not. She will be sure to have some stupid thing for me to do to keep me from coming with you."

He smiled faintly. "In two days' time you will be my wife," he said. "I think that gives me some rights in the matter."

She smiled back at him, her dark blue eyes glowing. "Oh, Alfred, I should love to hunt tomorrow!"

"Don't fall off your horse," he said. "I don't want a lame bride on Wednesday."

Her chin rose. "I never fall off my horse."

"Then you must be the best rider in the world."

She said, perfectly seriously, "I believe I am."

He shouted with laughter. When he had caught his breath, he said, "I think you are going to be good for me, Elswyth."

"I will try to be," she answered, utterly sober, as if she were making a solemn vow. "I like you, Alfred."

"I like you too." He finished his chicken wing and put the bone down. He said, his voice comically apprehensive, "Now, to talk to your mother."

She smothered a laugh at his expression, then assumed a very innocent face as Alfred rose and went along the table to where Eadburgh was sitting. Elswyth had no doubt that he would prevail. He knew how to make people do what he wanted, she thought. She watched out of the corner of her eye as he began to talk to her mother. He gave Eadburgh his sudden quick smile, the one that changed his face from gravity to charming intimacy and back again to gravity so quickly that you were left a little breathless. Eadburgh beamed.

I shall be hunting tomorrow, Elswyth thought with complacent satisfaction, and reached for a plate of spiced mutton. All of a sudden, she was hungry.

The night before his wedding, Alfred and Ethelred sat up late together talking. The summer night was pleasantly warm, and the brothers were both comfortable in short-sleeved shirts without tunics. Neither of them felt the least desire to go to bed, and so they once again went over their plans. They had decided weeks before that after his marriage Alfred would return to Wessex, to begin to see to its defenses, whilst Ethelred would remain at Nottingham until Burgred's Danegeld was collected and paid.

It was quiet in the hall outside Ethelred's room; the thanes who lay on the benches were all asleep. The soft murmur of voices from the king's sleeping chamber was not loud enough to disturb a child, let alone an adult used to sleeping amidst a crowd of other men.

"There is really very little we can do," Alfred said at last. His thin hands moved restlessly and he added, "Except wait to see what will happen next."

"That is so," Ethelred agreed, but not impatiently. Waiting agreed with his temperament far more than it agreed with Alfred's. The king continued, his face placid, "There will be business from the shire courts to see to. You will do that for me, Alfred?"

"Yes, of course." Alfred had often deputized for his brother in the hearing of law cases that required higher judgment than the shire courts. In fact, "ALFRED, FILIUS REGIS" appeared almost as often on official documents as did "ETHELRED, REX."

"Well, I suppose we had better get some sleep," Alfred said finally. "Tomorrow will be a long day." He yawned, stretched, then stripped his shirt over his head, folded it, and went to put it on the clothes chest in the corner.

Ethelred watched his brother finish undressing in silence. At last, when Alfred had sat down to take off his shoes, the king said softly, "For how long do you mean to delay the consummation of this marriage?"

Alfred looked up in surprise. He answered, as he began to untie the headband from around his forehead, "I don't know. Until Elswyth has grown up, I suppose."

"She is fourteen, Alfred. Full old enough to wed."

"She is a child," Alfred said. He raked his fingers through the long hair that, released from confinement, had fallen forward across his temples. "I can wait."

It was then that Ethelred asked the question that had been on his mind ever since Alfred had told him of the promise he had made to Elswyth. "Alfred . . . what of Roswitha?"

Alfred's hand dropped. The long green headband dangled from his fingers and touched the rush-strewn floor. He looked up at Ethelred, his fair eyebrows raised. "What do you mean, what of Roswitha?"

Ethelred chose his words with care. He knew his young brother's reluctance to share his most private feelings, but he felt this must be said. "Once you are wed, it would be adultery to keep up with her. I don't know if you have thought of that, Alfred. But it is so. And if you put aside Roswitha, and do not consummate your marriage to Elswyth . . . well . . . you are putting yourself into an awkward position, my brother. That is all I was thinking."

There was silence. It was dark in the corner where Alfred was sitting; Ethelred could not see his face clearly enough to read it. In the silence, and the shadows, it suddenly seemed to Ethelred as if the figure of Roswitha had come into the room.

She was the widow of a thane from near Southampton, a thane with a small holding of five hides, and Alfred had met her two years before when he had been at Southampton on some business for Ethelred. Their liaison had scandalized no one. Alfred had been seventeen and she twenty. Neither was wedded. These things happened all the time, even in families as genuinely religious as the West Saxon royal family. Athelstan, their eldest brother, had been born out of a liaison their father, Ethelwulf, had contracted before his marriage to Ethelred's and Alfred's own mother, Osburgh.

Ethelred had been neither surprised nor dismayed by Alfred's taking a woman such as Roswitha as his mistress. Such a liaison would be easy enough to break when it came time for him to marry, Ethelred had thought. But Alfred had shown evidence of an attachment for Roswitha that was deeper than Ethelred considered wise. Every time during the last two years that Ethelred had brought up the possibility of marriage, Alfred had made an excuse. Reluctantly the king had been coming to the unhappy conclusion that his brother's love for his mistress was what was standing in the way of his marrying. And Roswitha was not of high enough birth to be an appropriate wife for a prince.

When, like a lightning bolt from the sky, Alfred had offered for Elswyth of Mercia, Ethelred had been delighted. The match was excellent; the girl was of noble blood and connected to the Mercian royal house. Then, but a few weeks before, Alfred had told Ethelred of his proposed delay in taking the girl to his bed.

Ethelred did not like that at all. As he had just said to Alfred, he thought his brother was putting himself into an impossible position. He knew Alfred, knew how deeply religious was his spirit. Alfred would consider adultery a serious sin, and once he was married, the liaison with Roswitha would be adultery. There was no gainsaying that.

But Alfred was also a healthy young male; a healthy young male who had been living with a woman for the last two years. He was not going to find continence either easy or pleasant.

"I don't think you have thought this whole thing through, Alfred," Ethelred said again, gently. "You will be leaving yourself without either wife or mistress. And that you will not like."

There was continued silence from the corner. Ethelred was almost certain that Alfred had not thought of this before. His brother's mind had been too preoccupied with the Danes to consider the ramifications of such a marriage. Nor, evidently, had Roswitha said aught to him about the future. She was a clever girl. Ethelred had always thought so.

Finally Alfred stirred. "Well," he said, and his voice was deliberately light, "we shall see how things go. If Ivar the Boneless has aught to say, Ethelred, we shall both be too busy to worry about the women."

Ethelred deemed it best to let the subject drop. He had made his point. "True," he answered, and began to untie the strings of his own shirt. "It will be best for you and me to get some sleep."

Alfred came across the room. "Let us pray," he said, "that Burgred will not feel called upon to give a speech tomorrow."

Ethelred laughed, as he was meant to, finished undressing, and leaned over to blow out the candle.

Chapter 10

*T*HE day of Alfred's wedding dawned clear and warm. Alfred slept later than usual, then opened heavy eyes to find Ethelred standing over him. "Time to get up, my boy," his brother said boisterously. "We must be at the church in an hour."

Alfred lay perfectly still for a minute. Then, when Ethelred had turned away, he moved his head cautiously on its pillow. There was an ominous ache in his neck and behind his ears that he did not like. He closed his eyes briefly.

Please, God, he prayed, *not today.*

There was the noise of men talking and moving around in the hall outside the sleeping-chamber door. Alfred sat up carefully. There was no real pain, as yet. Only an ache, a feeling of tenderness.

Perhaps it would be all right, he thought. He had not had a headache in over four months. He rubbed his neck and prayed, once more, that he would not develop one today.

Sinulf, Ethelred's wardrobe thane, came into the room to assist the king to dress. The clothing both West Saxons were wearing for the wedding had been carefully chosen before ever they left Winchester, and as carefully packed for this moment. Alfred got out of bed, and while Ethelred dressed, he stuck his head into the bowl of water that had been laid out for washing. Then he splashed the water on his face and the back of his neck.

It felt better, he told himself firmly. It was going to be all right. Ethelred was dressed and Sinulf turned next to help Alfred. He submitted to being dressed in an immaculate new shirt and saffron-colored tunic, made for him by Ethelred's wife, Cyneburg. Cyneburg was near term with her fifth child and so had not attempted the journey into Mercia, but her kind efforts had provided Alfred with a new shirt and embroidered tunic in honor of his wedding day.

Once both king and prince were dressed, Ethelred's personal chaplain came in to offer morning prayers. Then it was time to leave for the church, where, at ten o'clock, Alfred and Elswyth were to be married by Ceolnoth, Archbishop of Canterbury.

The sun was very bright as Alfred crossed the courtyard toward the small wooden church where Elswyth awaited him. The ache had returned to the back of his neck and head. He held his head as still as possible and walked lightly, trying not to jar it. Ethelred said something to him, which he did not hear, but he smiled as if in agreement. Ethelred gave him a sharp look, and then they were at the door of the church.

Elswyth wore a deep blue overgown and a creamy white undergown, and the bridal crown was set on her flowing hair. He had never seen her hair unbound before, Alfred thought, and for a moment he almost forgot the pain in his head as he admired the shining blue-black mass that cascaded sheer to her waist. It looked too heavy a weight for her small head and slim, fragile neck to bear. Elswyth's eyes were a darker blue than her gown and she wore her haughtiest expression. He knew immediately that she was nervous. He smiled at her and said, "Courage!"

Her firm little chin rose, as he had known it would. "You're late," she said, and, as always, the huskiness of her voice surprised him.

"They were making me beautiful for you," he answered, and at that she grinned.

"They have succeeded," she said, appraising him from the tips of his soft leather shoes to the top of his neatly combed golden hair.

"You look nice too," he said.

She gave him a scornful look, but took the hand he was holding out. Her fingers were cold within his grasp and he closed his hand comfortingly to reassure her. Then they were walking up the aisle together, with the eyes of the whole church upon them.

They knelt side by side in front of Ceolnoth, who was dressed in splendid cloth-of-gold vestments, and the nuptial Mass began.

It will be all right as long as I don't get sick. That was the thought that Alfred kept in mind as the Mass went on and on and the pain in his head grew stronger and stronger. It had moved from his neck into his forehead and he knew he was doomed to eight hours of it. He could manage, though, as long as his stomach did not betray him. He would have to.

Thank God he did not have a wedding night to get through!

He made his vows in a steady voice, and Elswyth did too.

The archbishop gave a sermon that lasted nearly an hour.

Finally, after what seemed to Alfred an eternity, it was over. He and Elswyth were man and wife. They returned back down the aisle, hand in hand, as they had entered, and walked out of the dim church into the bright sunlit courtyard.

The light stabbed like daggers into his head and he stumbled. "Alfred . . ." It was Elswyth's voice, pitched low and close to his ear. "Are you all right?"

"Yes, of course." He could not see her very clearly, the sun was too bright. He narrowed his eyes like a cat. "The church was so much darker than the courtyard," he said.

"We have to go to the great hall for the wedding feast." She had taken his hand once more.

"Yes. I know."

There was a crowd of people around them. He looked for Ethelred and found his brother's familiar blond head close by. He thought, with relief, that if he needed help, he could count on Ethelred. Ethelred would know what was wrong.

Burgred insisted that Alfred and Elswyth sit together on the high seat. Alfred did not want to, but he could not refuse the honor. They sat down and the rest of the guests crowded into the hall.

It was very hot. The pain had begun to throb in tune with the beating of his pulse.

Burgred made a long speech; then the food was brought in.

The heat and the smell of the food began to turn his stomach.

"Alfred . . ." It was Elswyth's voice. "You are too pale. Is it one of your headaches?"

His stomach was churning now. There was no longer any hope of hiding it. "Yes. Elswyth . . . get me Ethelred. Please."

He sat with his eyes closed, concentrating on keeping his stomach under control. *I will not be sick in front of all these people.*

"Alfred." It was his brother's voice, thank God. "Is it your head?"

"Yes. Ethelred, get me out of here."

"All right." Ethelred's arm was coming around his shoulders and he allowed himself to be drawn to his feet. "There's a door behind us, we'll use that."

He made it to the courtyard before he began to retch uncontrollably. There was little in his stomach, however, as he had fasted for Communion and had eaten nothing since the previous night. Finally the spasms let up. Ethelred wiped his face with a soft cloth and said, "I'll carry you to the hall."

"*No!*" He drew a shallow, unsteady breath. "I'll walk."

He was aware of nothing but the storm of pain in his head and the reassuring presence of his brother at his side as they walked the distance from the great hall to the guest hall where they were lodged. He heard his sister's voice saying she would send for a doctor. He wanted to tell her that a doctor would do no good, but he could not make the effort. He was afraid to upset his stomach's equilibrium.

He had to get away from all those eyes.

At last they reached the safety of the hall and he could close the door of the sleeping chamber behind him. A number of people came into the room with him, but he leaned his hands on the posts of the bed and stared straight ahead. Ethelred handed him a washbasin and said, "I'll send for some cold cloths."

Alfred took the basin and was sick again.

"The feast," he said, when he could finally speak. "I shall be all right now, Ethelred. Go back to the feast."

"Certainly not," his brother said firmly. "You are too ill to be left alone."

All he wanted was to be left alone. He did not want to have the entire day ruined, all of Ethelswith's hospitality ruined, because of his headache. "Please," he said.

"The feast does not matter." It was Ethelswith herself, opening the door to a monk who must be her doctor.

"It does matter. . . ."

A drawling husky voice from by the clothes chest said, "I shall return to the great hall and see that the feast continues."

He sat down on the bed.

"You will return to the feast alone?" Ethelswith sounded scandalized.

"Alfred has a headache," Elswyth said. "That is no reason for hundreds of people to go hungry."

He managed to say clearly, "Thank you, Elswyth."

"You are most welcome," came her reply, and then the doctor was holding a cup of medicine to his lips.

"I can't," he said. "It will only make me sick again."

"Drink it," said his sister. So he did, and three minutes later he was retching over the basin once more.

The great hall of Tamworth was loud with speculation when Elswyth reentered some twenty minutes after Alfred's precipitate departure. She went quietly to where Burgred was still seated beside the archbishop. He looked worried and indignant both, and she bent over to say something into his ear. He nodded, turned to speak to Ceolnoth, then stood up and offered her his hand. Quiet began to fall as the king escorted Elswyth ceremoniously to the high seat, then assumed his own accustomed place. She sat down and he remained standing.

The hall was now perfectly quiet. Burgred spoke into the hush. "Prince Alfred has been taken ill, though not seriously," the king said. "He sends his apologies and bids you enjoy the feast in his absence." Then Burgred sat down, for once in his life understanding the value of brevity.

After a moment of continued silence, the murmur of voices began again. Servants came into the hall bearing platters of more food. Elswyth said to Burgred, "Thank you, my lord. Alfred would be most distressed should your splendid feast be spoiled due to his illness."

"But what is wrong with him?" Burgred asked. The indignation in his voice was clear. "He was perfectly well in church."

"I don't think he was," Elswyth replied. "He suffers from severe headaches, my lord, so severe that they overset his stomach."

Burgred's fleshy face did not register any sympathy. "Alfred is too highly strung," he told Elswyth. "I have always thought so. He should think less and eat more."

"Perhaps," Elswyth said shortly.

Burgred patted her hand. "Not a very pleasant wedding day for you, my dear."

She shrugged. "I am all right, my lord. It is Alfred who is suffering."

"Oh," the king said, "a headache. He will get over it, my dear." He heaped his plate full of food.

"Yes," said Elswyth. "I am sure he will." She put some food on her own plate, though she was sure she would choke if she tried to eat it.

The feast seemed to Elswyth to last forever. Ethelswith finally returned, then Ethelred, and the food kept coming in and the mead and ale kept passing around. The scop, who had composed a song in honor of the wedding, hastily substituted something else. Somehow it did not seem right to be singing a wedding song to a deserted bride.

Elswyth sat through it all, her head bearing its bridal crown held high, her haughtiest expression firmly in place. There had been no plans for a bedding ceremony, so all she would have to get through was this interminable feast, she thought as she pretended to eat and drink and listen to the scop.

She had sensed in the church that something was wrong. There had been a look of endurance about Alfred's mouth, a different ring to his voice. Then, when they had got to the great hall, she had known it. His lovely golden color had gone sallow, and the look of endurance had been etched into all the bones of his face. She had prayed he would be able to get through the feast, not because it mattered to her, but because she knew it would matter a great deal to him.

This illness humiliated him. "I am flawed," he had said to her when she proposed marriage to him in the barn. She understood; understood that, above all, he would hate to have his weakness exposed to the world. And there could be few things more humiliating to a man than to fall ill on his wedding day. The best thing she could do for him was to carry on as if nothing important had happened. He needed that far more than he needed someone to hold his hand. And so she gritted her teeth and determined that that was what she was going to do.

The afternoon waned and evening set in. Elswyth and Alfred had planned to spend the night at Tamworth before leaving on the morrow for Wessex, so for the moment no further plans would be disrupted. Elswyth had no way of knowing if, in fact, they would be leaving on the morrow, but for now she would carry on as if nothing unusual had occurred.

The women left the feast when the drinking started to become rowdy;

Elswyth withdrew in the dignified company of the queen. Ethelred had left sometime earlier, and Ethelswith said to Elswyth as the two walked down the steps that led from the great hall to the courtyard, "Ethelred tells me that these attacks customarily last about eight hours. Let us go and see whether or not Alfred is recovered."

The two women turned in the direction of the hall where Alfred was lodged. "I was never told about these headaches," Ethelswith said as they walked side by side across the hard-packed dirt. She did not look pleased. "Ethelred says that Alfred has suffered them for years."

"I do not imagine it is something he wishes known," Elswyth said.

"Did you know?" And the queen looked sharply at the girl walking beside her.

The weight of the bridal crown had been pressing into Elswyth's scalp all afternoon and she had taken it off as soon as the hall door closed behind her. She tightened her hand around it now, hard, and answered tersely, "Yes."

Silence fell as the two women approached the guest hall. "Well," Ethelswith said finally, when they were almost at the door, and there was the faintest trace of malice in her usually soft voice, "at least you will not be deprived of your wedding night. You were to have slept in your brother's hall anyway."

Elswyth shot the queen a quick inimical look from out the side of her eyes, but did not reply.

Then they were in the hall and Ethelred was coming to greet them. "How is he?" Ethelswith asked her brother.

"Better. I left him sleeping."

"Thank God." The queen's exclamation was heartfelt. She was genuinely fond of her younger brother.

Ethelred smiled at Elswyth. "You did the right thing by returning to the feast," he told her.

She nodded without speaking.

"Come and sit down." Ethelred gestured them to the hearth. The June night had turned cool enough for a fire and Elswyth followed brother and sister to the chairs Ethelred had indicated. The hall was quiet. Most of the West Saxon thanes were still at the feast, and the servants were upstairs in the loft room. Elswyth sat down and leaned her head against the carved high back of the chair. A bump on the carving jabbed into her and she sat up again, rubbing the spot on her head that had been poked.

"You should have told me about these headaches," Ethelswith was saying in an aggrieved tone of voice to her brother.

Ethelred shrugged. "He is sensitive about them, Ethelswith. And he has had them since he was eight years old. They are a family illness, I'm told. Eahlstan says that our grandmother suffered with them also."

Ethelswith was frowning. "And is there nothing that can be done for them?"

"Nothing. I have had the best doctors look at him, I assure you. He has taken every imaginable potion, gone to every imaginable shrine to pray for a cure. It is not a common illness, but it is not unknown." Ethelred sighed. "The Lord has laid this cross upon him, my sister, and he must bear it as best he can until the Lord sees fit to lift it."

Ethelswith bowed her head.

Elswyth spoke for the first time. "May I go in to him for a moment?"

"I think he is asleep, but if you wish to reassure yourself . . ." Ethelred smiled, not displeased with this evidence of concern on the part of his brother's new bride. "Go ahead," he said, and Elswyth rose, put her bridal crown on the seat of her chair, and went to open the door to Alfred's room.

The shutters had been opened at the single window and there was light enough still in the June night for her to see without a candle. She stood with her back against the closed door for a moment, looking at the bed. There was no sound. He must indeed be asleep, she thought.

She had no idea why she had come in here. She had just felt this sudden overwhelming need to see him, to make sure he was actually here. To make sure he was safe. She moved on light feet toward the great wooden bed that took up most of the center of the room, stopped at its side, and looked down.

He lay on his back, one arm flung over his hand, his lax fingers touching the wooden bed frame beyond the pillow. His hair fell in a tangle on the pillow and across his forehead. The ties of his shirt were open, bearing the upper part of his smooth chest to the cool evening air. Even the part of his skin that was not exposed to the sun had a faint golden hue. It was the first time she had ever seen him when he did not look immaculate, she thought. His face was peaceful. He looked very young; not at all like the clever, grown-up prince she knew. He seemed so . . . vulnerable, lying there. A sudden totally unexpected surge of emotion swept through her, stopping her breath with its fierce intensity.

The long gold-tipped lashes lifted and he was looking up into her face. For a moment he did not recognize her. Then: "Elswyth . . ." He blinked and moved as if he would sit up.

"Hush." She drew a steadying breath and put her hand on his shoulder to press him back. "The wretched banquet is over and I just came to see how you were faring."

He let her hold him against the pillow. The young, vulnerable look had quite vanished from his face. "Elswyth," he said again. "I am so sorry . . ."

She released his shoulder and answered scornfully, "Don't be a fool. You did not do it on purpose."

He raised himself a little on his elbow and, with his free hand, pushed the hair out of his eyes. "The banquet is over?"

"Well, the men are still there. Drinking. It was a great success, even without you."

"I am glad." He smiled at her crookedly. "Thank you for going alone."

"You already thanked me." Her face was grave. "The headache is gone?"

"Yes. It goes quite quickly, after about eight hours." Suddenly the skin under his eyes looked shadowed. "I suppose everyone knows what happened?"

"Burgred told them you were taken ill, that is all. The details are no one's business."

"They will be, quite shortly. Ethelswith must have called on every person she knows who owns an herb garden." The bitterness in his voice was faint but unmistakable.

That fierce instinct to protect him swept through her once again. It wasn't fair, she thought, to expose him when he was helpless with pain. "Do not worry, Alfred," she said, not realizing how coldly ferocious she sounded, "I will see to it that they keep quiet."

His lashes flicked upward, and startled eyes searched her face.

"I did not mean to wake you," she said, and her expression did not soften. "I just wanted to see if you were indeed all right."

"I shall be fine," he answered slowly. "We can leave for Wessex tomorrow as planned."

"If you are sure . . ."

"I am sure."

"All right." She smiled at him and at last looked like a young girl again. "Good night," she said softly. "Go back to sleep." And turned and went out the door.

Chapter 11

W HEN Ethelred took the throne of Wessex, he had given the royal manor of Wantage to his brother, to hold in Alfred's name and as his personal property until his death. It was to Wantage, therefore, Alfred's birthplace and favorite manor, that he and Elswyth went after their marriage. Half of the West Saxon ealdormen had returned to Wessex with them, and half had remained at Nottingham with Ethelred to support the Mercians in case the Danes should break their word.

It was summer and the days were warm, with the light lasting long into the evening. The ealdormen had sworn to see to the readiness of the shire fyrds, and the ealdormen would be the first to hear the law cases that had arisen in the local folk moots during their absence in Mercia. Alfred thought that he could fairly devote a month to putting his own affairs in order at Wantage. The manor reeve, Renfred, was efficient and honest, but there were decisions that only the manor lord could make.

The haymaking began shortly after Alfred's arrival at Wantage, and all the folk of the manor, both men and women, were busy working in the fields from dawn to dusk. Even hunting was curtailed, as the houndsmen and huntsmen were always pressed into service to help bring in the hay. For a small space of time Alfred found himself with little to do, and he decided to show Elswyth the Downs.

Elswyth was perfectly happy at Wantage. She loved the clutter of harness and animals that always filled the great hall of the manor. Her mother would never have tolerated it, but Elswyth did not at all mind the dogs that ran underfoot, or the saddles and bridles that had been brought in to be mended and somehow ended up reposing on the benches for days on end. The reeve and his wife saw that the important things that kept a house clean and comfortable were well-attended-to: the rushes on the floor were changed regularly, the linen on the bed was fresh, the food was well-cooked and well-served. Elswyth saw no necessity to meddle with perfection.

Alfred's companion thanes and other household retainers heartily appreciated the way their lord's new lady fit so easily into their comfortable household. All agreed that the prince could scarcely have found himself a wife better suited to the needs of his people.

Alfred and Elswyth rode out together one July morning during the haymaking, with three dogs following along at their horses' heels. They were alone this day, and Elswyth was dressed in the cross-gartered trousers that she found so comfortable for riding. Alfred had promised to show her the Blowing Stone, a fond memory, he said, from his childhood.

Elswyth immediately loved the Downs. As Alfred pointed out, she was seeing them at their most beautiful. The summer turf was lushly green, the hay fields like golden stretches of sand, the plowed chalk almost snowy in its misty whiteness, and the elms richly dark above the green corn. They had been to White Horse Vale the day before, and Elswyth had found the ancient figure of the strangely wrought horse, so high above the world, so brilliantly white against the lush green turf, an object of wonder and awe. They were taking a slightly different road today from the one they had ridden yesterday to White Horse Vale. The Blowing Stone was to the north of the horse, on the top of another very high hill, and Elswyth and Alfred tethered their horses and climbed the last part of the heights on foot, the dogs scampering ahead of them.

"This is it," Alfred said, placing his hand on a block of brown, ironlike sarsen stone. It stood on end, and it did indeed have what looked like a mouthpiece, a small roundish entrance to a funnel through the stone, which emerged as a larger hole down at the back. "Watch," he said and, bending, he blew.

A booming sound rang out over the hill and into the valley. The dogs howled and Elswyth jumped. Alfred straightened and laughed at her expression. "It is said to carry five miles, if blown long enough," he told her. "Would you like to try it?"

She did, but with less success than he. "I have not so much wind as you," she said regretfully.

"Just as well." He quirked an amused eyebrow. "Come over here and look."

She stood beside him and let him point out the various places of interest visible from the hill they stood upon. "That is Lambourn over that way," he said finally. "I have a manor there too. It is much smaller than Wantage, but I think you'll like it."

"I'm sure I shall." She had been shading her eyes with her hands and now she looked away from the view and up into the face of the man beside her.

The summer sun had burned his skin to a deep tan and bleached his hair a lighter color. Her own skin was too fair to tan; all she had to show for her hours outdoors was a faint peach-colored bloom in her cheeks. Alfred turned, looked down, and met her eyes. "I'm hungry," he said. "Let's eat."

They had brought bread and cheese in their saddlebags, and Elswyth unpacked the food while Alfred spread out the saddle rugs for them to sit on. "It is so peaceful here," she said almost dreamily when the bread and cheese had been consumed. "On a day like this it is hard to believe in the Danes."

He sighed. "I know." He had been putting the remnants of their meal back into the saddlebags and now he came to drop down beside her. He stretched his length comfortably on the saddle rug, leaning up on one elbow. He reached for a stalk of grass and began absently to chew it. The sun shone bright on his summer-light hair, held so neatly off his face by its blue headband. "But they *are* real, unfortunately."

Their horses peacefully cropped grass at a little distance. The dogs were stretched out in the sun, sleeping. The only sound besides the horses eating and the dogs snoring was the cry of birds in the blue sky. Elswyth clasped her arms around her knees and said, "If I were still at Croxden, my mother would be making me spin wool." She wrinkled her nose in disgust. "Or embroider a hanging."

He smiled faintly, but the preoccupied look on his face told her his thoughts were elsewhere.

I should not have mentioned the Danes, she thought, annoyed with her own stupidity. Now I have spoiled his peace.

"We should be doing something," he said suddenly. He sat up and threw away the stalk of grass he had been chewing. "It is folly for us just to wait, as we are doing, for the Danes to come down on us. We should be preparing."

"You are preparing," she said reasonably. "The ealdormen are seeing to the fyrds . . ."

But he was clenching and unclenching his fist. "Everything in Wessex is so spread out, Elswyth. I cannot put my hand on anything. And the Danish army is all together."

"But what can you do?" she asked. "You cannot call up an army just in case the Danes might attack. Who would work the land if you did that?"

"I don't know," he answered. "I wish to God I did. I just do not think that we are going about our defense in the right way."

"You summoned a great army to come to the aid of Mercia," she said. "Surely you will not do less if Wessex itself should be attacked."

"That is true. I suppose."

"Of course it is true." She spoke very firmly. "Your trouble is that you hate inaction. But would you really prefer to see the Danes sitting at the doors of Wantage?"

He laughed reluctantly. "No, of course not."

"SO." She reached out and with her forefinger smoothed the line that had etched itself between his brows. "You worry too much, Alfred," she said.

He caught her hand as she was withdrawing it, and her fingers turned immediately to curl around his. "Enjoy the summer," she said, her face very serious. "Who knows when we will get another."

Their eyes held for a minute; then he smiled ruefully. "You are right." He lay back down, still with her hand caught fast in his, and squinted up at the sky. "I said you would be good for me, Elswyth."

"You are good for me too." Her husky voice was very low.

"Mmm." His eyes had closed. She stayed very quiet, and within minutes he was asleep.

In August they moved their household to Lambourn. It was a much smaller manor than Wantage, as Alfred had said, and the main hall was crowded when the trestle tables were put up for supper, but the manor's setting on the Lambourn Downs was particularly beautiful. One of the main features of Lambourn manor was the separate living hall that Alfred's father had built for the manor's lord. This living hall had but a single bedchamber, however, so Alfred gave it to Elswyth and her women while he slept in the bedchamber of the great hall that had formerly belonged to the reeve.

This upheaval was not popular with the reeve, whose name was Godric, nor with Godric's wife, both of whom had to move into the loft. However, as Alfred had never remained at Lambourn long, the inconvenience was likely to prove temporary and so tolerable.

The law cases Alfred heard during the course of the summer were mostly simple ones. Godric had been reeve at Lambourn for many years, and he had always upheld the law in the neighborhood with great success. Rarely had the king been forced to listen to a dispute from the environs of Lambourn. The most disruptive event Alfred had to deal with all summer was a feud that developed between two of his own companion thanes over a local girl. The feud ended up in a fistfight of heroic proportions, which was finally broken up, at some cost to himself, by one of Alfred's closest companion thanes, Brand. Alfred handed out the prescribed fines of eight shillings for a front tooth and four shillings for a back tooth, then banished the thanes back to their own homes for a month, a punishment they felt much more deeply than they did the fines.

In September, while Ethelred was still in Mercia, a lawsuit of more serious proportions, one that required the attention of the king or the king's substitute, arose. The king's reeve who had charge of the royal manor of Southampton had sought to extend the pastures of his swine beyond the limits of the woodland the manor had, by ancient custom, used in the past. The Abbot of Netley, who owned the woods in question, protested to the king that the abbey had always used two-thirds of the woods and that the king had ever been entitled to mast, or forage, for three hundred swine only.

Alfred went to Southampton to hear the case. He left Elswyth behind at Lambourn.

During the last month in particular, the truth of his brother Ethelred's words on the eve of his wedding had been brought home most forcefully to Alfred. His body, deprived of the outlet it had become accustomed to, was in increasing rebellion at its enforced abstinence. Alfred had actually got to the point where he was not sleeping at night when the summons came from Southampton.

He thought of Roswitha constantly as he rode along the familiar old Roman road, lined for so much of the way by wild cherry trees. He stayed overnight in Winchester, leaving early in the morning to continue on toward Southampton. He would see her, he thought. He would have to see her. He could not, in courtesy, refuse to see her.

But he was married. Carnal relations with another woman would be adultery, a mortal sin.

He was married, but married to a child. Elswyth was a thoroughly delightful little comrade, no question, but . . .

What would Roswitha do when she saw him? Would she feel as he did, that his marriage had changed all between them? She had never said a word to him about the marriage all of last winter, had acted always as if nothing would be different. Had she spoken, perhaps he would have reconsidered . . .

By the time Alfred reached Southampton, he was in a torment of indecision.

He and his following of twenty companions rode into Ethelred's manor at three in the afternoon. At four he was in the saddle of a fresh horse and on his way to the small manor of Millbrook, some three miles north of the royal holding, where he would hear the law case on the morrow.

His intention was only to pay a call upon Roswitha. That was all. He would see her, assure himself that she was well, then return to Southampton. That was his intention.

She would know he was coming. He had sent messengers ahead to make sure the royal manor would be prepared to feed the men he was bringing, and one of the messengers had been instructed to ride over to Millbrook. She would be expecting him.

She was, in fact, standing on the front steps of her small hall when he rode in through the wattle fence that surrounded the domestic enclave of Millbrook. The late sun caught the bright gold of her hair, bundled carelessly into a net. He could not see her eyes but he knew well that they were gray. He dismounted and a man came running to take the reins of his horse.

"My lord," she said in her high clear voice as he came to a halt on the ground before her and looked up to where she stood above him on the steps. "You are most welcome. Will you be pleased to come in and partake of some refreshment?"

"Thank you." His mouth was very dry. "It is good to see you, Roswitha," he said, and let her lead him inside the familiar hall.

Roswitha tried very hard not to show her triumph as she took him into the small hall of her home and sent for ale and bread and cheese. She sat beside him on the bench as he was served and, choosing a safe topic, asked him about his dogs. She did not listen to his reply, however; instead she was remembering that time two years before when Alfred had come to Millbrook for the first time.

She had seen him first at Southampton manor, at a lawday he had held for his brother. She had presented a case having to do with her rights to firewood in the king's forest. He had heard the case, and ruled in her favor, and after, in the courtyard, he had sought her out. The next day he had come to Millbrook.

She sat now at her carved wooden table and watched his long ringed fingers wielding his knife, and remembered.

It had been she who had had to make the first move. He was younger than she, by nearly four years, and inexperienced. He had known, however, what he wanted; and when she had laid her hands upon his shoulders and tilted up her face, he had put his mouth on hers, hard, and drawn her close.

He had held to her alone for two long years, and she had even begun to hope that one day he might marry her. Then, last winter, he had come home from Tamworth promised to marry the daughter of a Mercian ealdorman.

Roswitha had been crushed, though she had striven not to show it. If only she had been able to give him a child! But she had miscarried twice, and though he had been all care and concern for her, she knew now that the miscarriages were what had sounded the death knell of her hopes. No great lord, let alone a prince, would marry a woman who could not bear.

His betrothal had been a bitter blow, but she had held her tongue. She had known then that she would have to settle for the part of his life that he could give her, and she had schooled herself to accept that. He had been engrossed all winter with the coming confrontation with the Danes, and in the time they had been together she had never once brought up the future. As long as he seemed to assume that she would always be there, she would assume so too. She could make herself accept his marriage. What she could not accept, would never accept, was that she had lost him.

She was an extraordinarily beautiful woman; she knew that. Her birth had not been as good as the simple thane's who had married her, yet he had been glad to do so. She could marry again if she wished; there were men enough of her own order who would take her, and her golden hair, and her ripe warm body, and her five hides of land, and count themselves lucky. But she did not want those men. She wanted Alfred.

He put down his knife, giving up any pretense of eating. "Alfred," she said softly, and leaned nearer. "I have missed you."

A muscle jumped in his cheek.

What was wrong? she thought. He was so tense. She could see the tendons standing stark in his wrist.

A horrible thought smote her. He was not going to tell her farewell?

No! she thought in panic. She stared at him, at the tawny gold long hair, at the chiseled, almost delicate lines of his profile. He looked so remote . . . then he turned to look at her and she saw his eyes. They were fire-gold with an emotion she recognized very well, and the panic in her heart subsided.

It was going to be all right.

"We should not see each other like this, Roswitha," he was saying, in direct contradiction to the message she read in his eyes. "Not now that I am wedded."

So that was it. She ran her tongue around her lips and saw how his eyes watched. She smiled and reached up to untie the headband from around his forehead. "What is between you and me is between you and me," she said softly. "It cannot hurt anyone else."

Still he sat, his eyes going from her mouth to her soft white throat, but his body still held aloof. She put the headband down on the table. "Alfred," she said, and pulling off the net that confined her own luxuriant hair, she laid it next to the headband. "My dearest."

He was staring now at the fine golden net that lay before him. Roswitha picked up one of the thin strong hands that lay so near the net and placed it on her breast.

It closed instantly, in a caress. She heard the sudden sharp intake of his breath.

"Roswitha." She saw his lips move, though no sound came forth. She leaned toward him, still holding his hand to her breast, and then, finally, his mouth was coming down on hers.

Thank God, she thought, felt the intense pleasure of his mouth, of his hand on her breast, and then all thinking stopped.

Alfred remained at Southampton for a month, leaving only when word came from Ethelred that the king was back in Wessex. Alfred went to meet him at Winchester.

"The geld is paid and the Danes are bound once more for York," Ethelred told his brother as the two men talked together in the privacy of the king's sleeping chamber shortly after Alfred's arrival in Winchester.

"With shiploads of Mercian geld." Alfred did not seek to hide the bitterness in his voice.

Ethelred agreed firmly, "With shiploads of Mercian geld."

Alfred's fingers played nervously with the cup of ale he was holding. "The Danes did no destruction?" he asked after a minute.

"No. They held to their word." Ethelred's hands were quiet and relaxed on the arms of his chair.

"For now," said Alfred.

Ethelred replied, still in the same firm tone of voice he had used earlier, "Perhaps they will be content with what they have won thus far. It is not inconsiderable, Alfred: all of Northumbria, as well as a goodly amount of Mercian geld."

"And all won so easily," Alfred pointed out. "If I were Ivar the Boneless, I should be inclined to see if the other Saxon kingdoms would pay as handsomely for peace as Mercia has done."

"Perhaps it was worth it to pay," Ethelred said. "Perhaps Northumbria wishes now that it had paid rather than fought. Certainly Mercia is in better condition than Northumbria. It is still an independent kingdom . . . no monasteries have been burned . . ." But the resolute firmness of the king's voice was beginning to waver. Alfred had not spoken, but Ethelred suddenly found it impossible to meet the look in his brother's eyes. He stared at Alfred's ale cup and said, "You do not agree, I see."

"No." The crisp voice offered no compromise. "I agree that the Danes will gladly take our geld to cry a peace. But what happens, Ethelred, when they come back the next time? What happens when there is no more geld in the kingdom with which to pay them?"

Ethelred said stubbornly, "Perhaps then they will go away."

There was an uncomfortable silence. "Perhaps," Alfred replied at last. The door opened and Ethelred's wife, Cyneburg, came into the room, her infant son in her arms. She smiled when she saw Alfred, and he went immediately to give her the kiss of peace.

"A handsome boy," he said, admiring his small nephew cradled in Cyneburg's embrace.

"He is a good baby," Cyneburg said placidly. On the instant, as if to prove her false, the infant began to cry. Cyneburg laughed, shifted him to her shoulder, and began to pat his back. "But where is Elswyth?" she asked Alfred. "I am longing to meet your wife, Alfred. It was a great disappointment to me that I was unable to attend your wedding."

"She is at Lambourn," Alfred answered readily.

"She will be missing you." The baby had stopped crying, but Cyneburg continued gently to rub the tiny back with one hand while she supported the insecure head with the other.

"I doubt it." Alfred's face was perfectly serene. "I am sure she is quite happy having Lambourn to herself."

Cyneburg's high-arched brows rose even higher and she looked to Ethelred. Her husband's brown eyes met hers and, very faintly, he shrugged.

The baby began to cry again.

"He's hungry," Cyneburg said.

Alfred moved toward the door. "I shall get out of here, then, so you can feed him."

His hand was on the door latch when Cyneburg said, smilingly, "Perhaps one day soon you will have a son of your own, my brother."

With his hand still on the latch, Alfred turned to look at her. "Not for a while, I fear. Elswyth is still but a child herself."

Cyneburg assumed an expression of great surprise. "I did not realize . . . I understood she was fifteen."

"No, she is but fourteen."

"Fourteen when you became betrothed," Cyneburg said gently. "When is her birthday?"

He was standing with perfect courtesy, waiting for her to release him. "I am not certain. Sometime in November, I think."

"Well, then," said Cyneburg with a teasing smile, "I am not so far wrong, Alfred. November is but one week away."

She saw his eyes widen in surprise. "So it is," he said then, slowly.

"You must bring her to meet me." And Cyneburg turned to carry the baby to a chair. Released from her attention, Alfred murmured a polite response, pushed open the door, and went out into the hall.

Cyneburg and Ethelred looked at each other. "I hear he has been one month at Southampton," she said.

Ethelred sighed. "You learn things more quickly than I, Cyneburg."

She sat in the chair and began to unfasten her gown. "What is the matter with this girl he has married?" she asked. "I was certain he must love her. He took her so quickly, and he had been so adamant in refusing all the girls you and I proposed for him."

"I don't know what his feelings are," Ethelred replied. Then: "Elswyth is certainly . . . unusual." He began to rub his right eyebrow with his finger. "She has little in the way of courtly manners, Cyneburg. In truth, she is a wild thing, wearing boy's clothes and riding out to hunt with the men. I cannot imagine what ever induced Alfred to offer for her. Were it any other man, I should say he was swayed by her family's name and connections; but not Alfred."

"No, not Alfred," Cyneburg agreed.

"I have always thought he would seek to marry a woman like Judith of France," Ethelred confided. "He admired Judith enormously. They still correspond with each other."

"This Elswyth is not like Judith?"

"Not at all." Ethelred was quite positive. "Judith was very beautiful, but it was more than just physical beauty. There was a serenity about Judith. A woman like that would be good for Alfred. I always thought he realized that himself."

The baby was now nursing vigorously. "Elswyth is not beautiful?" Cyneburg asked.

"She is beautiful, but in a haughty kind of way. Nothing like Judith. It was restful to look upon Judith. There is nothing restful about Elswyth."

Cyneburg was looking thoughtful. "Certainly she does not sound like the ideal wife for Alfred. But he must have seen something in her to his liking, Ethelred, else he would never have offered for her."

"I suppose that is true. But I mislike this news of his being at Southampton." He added with grim reluctance, "It is Roswitha who reminds me of Judith."

"Do you know for certain that he has taken up with Roswitha again?"

"Not for certain," Ethelred replied. "No one of his companion thanes will ever speak a word against him, not to me, not to anyone. You know how fanatically loyal they all are to Alfred. But, Cyneburg, why else would he have stayed for one month at Southampton?"

Cyneburg took the baby from her breast and put him on her shoulder again to pat his back. "There is no other reason." She put her lips to the fuzzy baby head. "Well," she said practically, "Alfred of all people has the brain to sort matters out for himself. We shall have to leave it to him, Ethelred."

Ethelred went over to drop a kiss on his wife's brown-blond head. "Not every man can be as fortunate as I," he said. She looked up into his kind face and smiled.

Chapter 12

*I*T was a day of half-mist, half-sunlight, the day Alfred returned to Lambourn after an absence of more than six weeks. The ripe scent of harvest hung heavy and sweet on the late-autumn air as his cavalcade of riders wound along the local road that followed beside the Lambourn River. The cornfields had been well-cleared of the wheat and barley crop, and Alfred saw with approval that the sheep had been turned into the stubble of the grain fields to glean what they could from the leavings.

It had been a fine autumn, and a fine harvest, Alfred thought with satisfaction as he sniffed the warm, mellow air. The storage barns would be full.

"A fine harvest, my lord," said the thane who was riding beside him.

Alfred turned to give him a friendly smile. "That was my very thought, Edgar. Godric knows his job well."

"He does." A shout from one of the fishermen along the river caught their attention and they turned to look. The sun glinted off the shining river water and the scales of the new-caught fish gleamed silver in the hands of the fisherman.

Alfred said, "It will be good to get home."

Half an hour later he and his party were riding into the small courtyard of Lambourn manor. Serving men came running to hold their horses, and Godric himself held Alfred's bridle while the prince dismounted. Once Alfred's feet were on the ground, the reeve turned his horse, Nugget, over to a groomsman and cried loudly, "Welcome, my lord, welcome!" The skin over the man's sharp cheekbones was creased with his wide smile. "We received your message and I am happy to report that all is in order to receive you."

"I am pleased to hear that," Alfred replied. Then, laying a gold-ringed hand upon the reeve's shoulder, he said, "The harvest looks to have been a good one."

"Indeed it was, my lord. I think you will be pleased to see how well we have done."

Next Alfred said, looking around, "Where is the Lady Elswyth?"

The reeve's face thinned to knifelike sharpness. "Out somewhere on the Downs, my lord. She is away from the manor for hours at a time, with only the company of Brand, my lord."

Godric sounded distinctly disapproving. Alfred felt a flicker of impatience with Elswyth. He had enough to worry about without having his reeves scandalized by their new mistress's careless behavior.

He patted Godric's shoulder once, then removed his hand. "I shall inspect the storage barns with you tomorrow," he said, and the man's smile returned.

"Thank you, my lord. I am sure *you* will be pleased." The reeve's expression turned sour. "I fear the Lady Elswyth knows little of the running of a manor."

Alfred groaned silently and was turning to enter the hall when there came the further noise of approaching hoofbeats. He looked around, and there, coming in through the gate, was a small gray gelding with a black-haired girl poised and erect in the saddle. Alfred thought, and not for the first time, that he had never seen anyone sit a horse as beautifully as Elswyth. He scarcely noticed the thane riding beside her.

She spied him immediately. "Alfred!" she cried, and trotted forward. The little gray came to a perfectly square halt just before him. Alfred did not see Godric's quiet withdrawal because Elswyth was giving him a radiant smile. "Finally," she said, "you are back."

He laughed and walked around to the gelding's near side to lift her to the ground. Usually Elswyth scorned assistance, but she gladly put her hands on her husband's shoulders and slid down along the length of his body, as unself-conscious as a child. When her feet were on the ground she stayed as she was, hands still on his shoulders, looking up into his face with those dark blue eyes that always seemed to be darker and bluer than he had remembered. "But what kept you for so long?" she demanded.

"Oh, there were more things to attend to than I had realized," he answered in an easy voice. "Then Ethelred returned from Mercia." He put his hands over hers for a brief moment, then took them from his shoulders, retaining one firmly in his own warm clasp. He turned toward the hall. "Have you heard that the Danes finally left Mercia?"

"Thank God," she answered promptly. "No, we had not heard." She fell naturally into step beside him and went with him into the hall, still talking of the Danes.

The remainder of the afternoon Alfred devoted to his dogs. He had left them at Lambourn with Elswyth and had missed them exceedingly. Godric asked to see him once, but Alfred put him off. He had a distinct feeling that his reeve was going to complain about Elswyth, and Alfred did not want to listen. He would have to eventually, he supposed, and he would have to speak to Elswyth if she was interfering with Godric's management of the manor. But not today.

Godric's wife, the Lady Ada, served a notable banquet that evening in honor of the return of Lambourn's lord. Elswyth was to share the high seat with Alfred, with Godric and his lady in the place of honor to Alfred's right. Before Elswyth came to join her husband, however, Alfred saw her deep in conversation with his thane Brand. The two had actually come into the hall together and were standing near the door, talking intently. Godric was staring at them, and the Lady Ada's face bore the exact same expression Alfred had often seen on Eadburgh's when she looked at her daughter.

Name of heaven, Alfred thought. He had left Brand behind with half of his companion thanes because he thought the young thane would be good company for Elswyth, but he had not expected quite the closeness that had evidently developed. If Elswyth had not the sense to realize that she was causing scandal, Brand should have.

The two Alfred was watching finished their conversation and parted, Elswyth to join Alfred in the high seat and Brand to take his place further down the board. The room settled down and Alfred's household priest for Lambourn manor rose to give the blessing.

Alfred tried to listen to the prayer, but his thoughts this night were not quiet. He had been restless the last week he was at Southampton, and all the while he was in Winchester he had been anxious to return here. But now that he was at Lambourn, the pleasure of homecoming seemed to have eluded him.

Alfred listened to Father Odo's monotonous voice and realized uncomfortably that he would have to confess his sin with Roswitha on the morrow. He had thought of going to confession to one of the priests at Winchester Minster; then he had procrastinated. But he could put it off no longer. He must confess. And make promise of amendment.

It did not make him feel better to realize that he had waited to confess to Odo because he knew the old priest would not have the nerve to upbraid him unduly.

The priest finished the blessing and sat down. The serving folk came around with the food. Alfred saw that Godric was engrossed in his dinner, turned to Elswyth, and said mildly, "You and Brand seem to be on good terms." He picked up his knife and began to butter a fluffy white roll. The wheat at Lambourn was very fine, and the baker talented.

She nodded vigorously, her mouth being full of fresh fish from the river. Then, when she could talk: "Brand is a good man. And he is good on a horse too. Some of the other of your thanes are horrified whenever I gallop."

He sank his teeth into the white bread. "They are not used to such a formidable horsewoman." The roll was delicious.

"Brand is a good man," she said again. She added somberly, "Which is more than I can say for everyone here at Lambourn, Alfred."

He hesitated, then decided he might as well hear her side first. "Oh?" He raised an innocent eyebrow. "Have you had trouble, Elswyth?"

"I would not call it trouble, precisely." Her black brows drew together over her thinly bridged nose. "But I think you should replace your reeve, Alfred."

He stared at her in astonishment. "Replace Godric? Why? I was just thinking, as I rode into Lambourn, how well-tended is the manor." He had turned so that his shoulder would effectively block Godric's view of their faces.

"Oh, the property is well-enough tended." The scorn in her voice was excoriating and she cast a narrow-eyed look past Alfred toward the reeve on his other side.

Alfred said crisply, "Elswyth, you had better explain to me what you mean."

She answered just as crisply, "Alfred, the folk of your manor of Lambourn have been going hungry."

"What?"

She nodded, her face very serious. "Yes. I went into the kitchen house one afternoon a few days after you left. For a little bite of something, you know. I was too hungry to wait all the way to dinner."

He kept his voice low. "Yes?"

"The men had just butchered a sheep and the cook was roasting it. It smelled wonderful. I sat down in the kitchen, just to smell the food and eat my bread and cheese. I often did that at home, you see. Then, suddenly, I saw how two of the serving girls were watching me. Not watching me, really, but watching my food. Then I looked at them. Closely. They were *thin*, Alfred. More than thin, they looked half-starved."

Now there was a deep line between his fair brows. "What did you do?"

"I asked them when they had last eaten. And what they had last eaten. Then I asked them to tell me what they had eaten for the last week." Her long black lashes rose and eyes of midnight blue looked into his face. "Alfred, those girls were not getting enough to eat. When I asked whose orders the cook was following, he said Godric's."

There was a brief hard silence. Then: "What did you do?" Alfred asked again.

"I told the cook to feed the sheep to the serving folk, and then I spoke to Godric. He did not like what I had to say, but the food has been sufficient since. But I do not trust him, Alfred. As soon as my back is turned, I fear he will cut the food again."

There was a white line of temper encircling Alfred's mouth. The noise in the hall was rising as the thanes paused to talk between courses. No one could hear Alfred and Elswyth's conversation. "His account books show a sufficient amount of food for the manor folk," Alfred said.

"I am sure they do." Elswyth was scornful. "But I think he is selling your foodstuff at market, Alfred. For his own profit."

The quality of the silence this time was dangerous. Alfred said, grimly, "If that is indeed so, more than his job is forfeit."

Elswyth said, "You have eaten nothing."

Still he paid no attention to the plate of food before him. "Why did you not say something to me this afternoon? I shall have to send someone I can trust to inquire of the local thanes and ceorls."

"I have already made some inquiries," she answered. "That is why I said nothing this afternoon. I was waiting for Brand. He has discovered some evidence that Lambourn food is indeed being sold in the neighborhood." She picked up her cup of ale and took a sip.

He watched the movement of her slim throat as she swallowed. "You have already made inquiries?" He heard himself how incredulous he sounded.

"Surely it was the reasonable thing to do." Her eyes were very blue against the black of her lashes and the white of her skin. "If the food was not going to the manor folk, and was not in the storage barns, obviously it was going somewhere else."

He said, his eyes watching her closely, "In the courtyard earlier, Godric told me you understood nothing of the running of a manor."

Her lips curled in derision. "I would not trust him with my dogs, Alfred. You should have heard the tale he spun to me about the necessity of conserving food for the spring. He must have thought me a fool."

He said, "Once you told me that you did not concern yourself with the running of a manor."

"I told you I did not concern myself with the linen and the crockery," she corrected him. "The people are somewhat different. It is not fair to take advantage of those who are unfree." She reached over and moved his plate closer to his hand. "The Lady Ada is every bit as bad as her husband," she added, her voice very low and close to his ear.

The white line about his mouth was back. "It is more than unfair," he said. "It is a very great sin. And Godric has been reeve at Lambourn since my father's time. I am much at fault for not finding his dishonesty sooner."

All of a sudden Elswyth grinned. "You don't spend enough time in the kitchen. I, on the other hand, pass many a pleasant hour there. You would be surprised what you can learn in the kitchen."

He did not smile back. "I shall speak to Brand after supper," he said. "I shall deal with Godric, Elswyth. You may rest secure that he will have no further chance to starve my folk here at Lambourn." There was an oddly still look on his face that Elswyth did not mistake for mercy.

"I knew you would be angry, Alfred," she said with approval. Then: "Will you please eat something!"

He nodded and picked up a slice of ham. Elswyth turned to speak to the priest who was on her other side, and Alfred dutifully chewed his meat. It tasted like ashes in his mouth. At his right hand, out of the corner of his eye, he could see Godric quaffing his cup of ale.

A rogue, Alfred thought. Why did I not see it before?

He answered himself: Because Godric's birth was noble, he ran a well-maintained manor, and his accounts were always in order. Alfred had never thought to look at the leanness of his servants.

He was bitterly angry and bitterly shamed. It had taken Elswyth but two weeks to see what was at hand. And she had dealt with it, without his authority and with surprising competence.

He looked once more at his child-wife as she sat talking to Father Odo. Within the month, he thought, she would be fifteen. And felt again the slender body that had slid so naturally along his when he had lifted her down from her horse. As if she could feel his eyes, she turned her head away from the priest to look at him. Her pure skin had the faintly glistening texture of fine pearls. Her braided hair was so black it shone blue in the light from the torch. He looked at her expressive mouth, at the cleft in her small firm chin. She leaned forward and said something to him about the scop.

"Yes," he said. "Of course."

She looked over his head, searching for the harper.

He remembered once again the feel of her slim pliant body against his; it was not a child's body anymore.

Brand had seen the close conversation between Alfred and Elswyth at supper and so was not surprised when he was summoned to speak to Alfred in the prince's sleeping chamber after supper was concluded. Godric, he saw, had also made an attempt to speak to Alfred but had been rudely ignored.

Alfred was rarely rude. Godric was looking extremely worried as Brand went to the door of the prince's room and knocked.

"Come!"

Brand entered to find Alfred squatting on his heels, looking carefully into a wolfhound's ears. "This should have some ointment put into it," the prince said; then he stood up. The dog immediately jumped onto the bed and stretched out, chin on paws.

"You have some information for me, I believe," Alfred said.

"Yes, my lord." Brand spoke steadily. What he had to tell his prince was not pleasant, and by the time he had finished he could see that Alfred was in a temper.

"And this has been going on for some time?" Alfred asked.

"For years, my lord."

"Did you manage to discover why no one thought to report this theft to me?" The words were bitten off with all the precision of icy rage.

"My lord, they were all afraid of Godric. He is of high birth, cousin to the Ealdorman of Wiltshire. Who were they to speak against him? He ever said that what he did, he did at your command."

"You are saying that my people of Lambourn thought that they were being starved on my orders?"

"No, my lord!" Brand had never seen Alfred look like this. His palms began to grow moist. "But you are rarely here. And Godric is here all the time . . ."

"What of Father Odo?"

"He is old, and . . ."

"And ineffectual."

"Well," said Brand unhappily. "Yes."

"If we have a trial, will oath-takers come forward to speak against Godric?"

Brand's hazel eyes widened. "A trial, my lord?"

"That is what I said."

Brand rubbed his palms against his wool trouser legs. "I am sure the local shire thanes would come forward, my lord. If they knew such action would not displease you."

"You may tell them that it would not displease me." The look on Alfred's face was so implacable that Brand felt a tremor of fear.

"Yes, my lord," he said.

"I will speak to Godric tomorrow," said Alfred. "Then you may speak to the shire thanes."

"Yes, my lord," Brand said again.

"You may go."

"Yes, my lord." And Brand turned thankfully to the door, leaving Alfred alone with his dog.

Godric went the following day to his interview with Alfred, a very determined look upon his face. When he left the prince's room his face was ashen. Alfred put him under guard and had the hysterical Lady Ada removed from the hall.

"Selling the prince's foodstuff for his own profit!" Edgar said to Brand, his blue eyes wide with horror. "It is hard to believe."

"It is not so unusual, Edgar," said Brand, who was a shire thane's son. "Particularly in a royal household which is bereft of its lord for most of the year. Godric's mistake was that he was too greedy. And the Lady Elswyth too astute."

"I saw the prince earlier," said Edgar. "Never have I known him to be this angry. Usually he is so good-natured."

Blue and hazel eyes met. "I know," said Brand. "Betrayal is an ugly thing."

The two young men had gone outside ostensibly to practice their sword-play, but neither of them had made a move to lift his sword. Edgar said now, "If the prince brings Godric to law, who will testify to the truth of his word?"

In Anglo-Saxon law, the defendant was not required to produce evidence about the facts of the dispute, but to bring before the court men who would swear that the oath taken by the defendant was pure. If the requisite number of oath-helpers was produced before the court, and the oath taken in full, the case was at an end.

Brand lifted eloquent eyebrows. "Who will stand up for a man who has betrayed his lord?"

"No one," Edgar answered.

"If the prince does indeed bring Godric to trial," said Brand, "Godric will die."

In Anglo-Saxon society, loyalty to one's lord was paramount. As Brand had said, once Alfred moved to bring Godric to trial, the conclusion was foregone. Godric had broken that loyalty and so Godric must die. If there were some who were surprised that Alfred had dealt so harshly with a man of such high rank as Godric, still no one dared to criticize.

"For all his good nature, the prince is not a man to cross," said Edgar. And that sentiment was generally agreed to.

It was Elswyth who knew that Godric's great sin had not been his own enrichment at Alfred's expense, but the starving of the manor folk.

"Most reeves cheat," she said to Alfred practically. "One must expect that. But this was something beyond."

"Yes," said Alfred grimly. "It was."

It was the day after the sentence had been carried out. Lady Ada had long since been sent away in hysterics to the manor of her brother. Elswyth and Alfred were riding together out toward White Horse Vale and now Elswyth said, "I think you should have hanged him." Hanging was the punishment for a commoner; a noble died by the sword. Alfred had given Godric the honor due to his rank.

"Dead is dead," Alfred answered. "Justice is one thing, vengeance another."

"I am for vengeance," she said, and for the first time in a week Alfred smiled.

"My little champion of the poor and the downtrodden," he said. Then: "What do you want for your birthday?"

Her reply was instant. "I want that chestnut filly."

At that he began to laugh. "Never say Elswyth does not know her own mind."

She was delighted to see this lighter mood and smiled back at him. "You know the one I mean, Alfred. The three-year-old you have in the far meadow."

"I certainly do know the one you mean. Nugget's filly out of Emma. The one with the beautiful gaits."

"That trot!" said Elswyth in ecstasy. "She floats." She said coaxingly, "I could make her into something extraordinary, Alfred. I know I could."

"She is very hot-tempered."

"I know. Put one of your heavy-handed thanes on her and she'd go wild."

Alfred said mildly, "I did not breed her for my thanes."

"You want her for yourself." Elswyth's eyes were blindingly blue as they scanned his face. "I did not know that, Alfred. Then of course you must keep her." She added with lavish generosity, "After all, you were the one who bred her."

A gust of wind whipped across the open turf. Elswyth's long black braids were too thick to be disturbed by the wind, though the hair at her temples stirred. Alfred smiled at his wife's small ardent face. "Birthday blessing to you, Elswyth. She is yours."

The blue eyes glowed impossibly bluer. "Do you mean it? She is really mine?"

He nodded, watching as the delicate color warmed the pearly curve of her cheeks.

"It's not that I don't love Silken," she said, as if to apologize to her little gray for a lack of loyalty. "I will always love Silken. But that filly . . . that filly is something special."

"Yes," said Alfred, his eyes still on that crystal-clear face. "I am beginning to think that she is."

Elswyth patted the dappled gray neck of her gelding, smoothed his mane, and gave Alfred a slanting look from under long thick lashes. "I'll race you to the trees," she said, and shot forward, going from walk to full gallop in just two strides.

His stallion overtook her just before the line of birches and they both pulled their mounts to a halt, laughing at each other in mutual satisfaction.

"I am so glad you have come home, Alfred," she said. "I missed you."

Actually, Elswyth had been surprised by how much she missed Alfred while he was away at Southampton. He had not suggested that she accompany him, and in truth she had been perfectly content to remain at Lambourn while he traveled south on his brother's business. However, as the weeks wore on and he did not return, his absence had weighed on her more and more heavily.

It was not that she was unused to being left alone, if a manor full of thanes and serving folk could be called alone. There had been numerous occasions during her growing-up years in Mercia when she had been the only family member to remain at a manor. She had rather enjoyed those times, with no one to gainsay her wishes, no one to tell her what she ought or ought not to do. She knew all the folk who dwelled on all her family's manors, and was perfectly content riding out with the huntsmen, helping the houndsmen in the kennels, visiting in the kitchen or the smithy, and in general doing as she chose to do when she chose to do it.

There was no reason, therefore, why life at Lambourn should be any different for her from life in Mercia before the intervention of her mother. True, Elswyth did not know the folk of Lambourn very well, and she was ever one who liked best what she knew. But she was mistress here, could do as she pleased, and for certain, after she had thwarted Godric, the folk of Lambourn liked Elswyth; indeed, they could scarcely do enough for her.

But as the weeks went by, and Alfred did not return, she felt a growing discontent. She missed him. She missed having him there to share things with, to laugh with. She missed being able to look at him. She loved to look at him, loved even to touch him. He was so beautifully golden and smooth. In general, Elswyth rarely touched another person, and hated to be touched herself. She had ever saved all her love for her animals. But Alfred was different. Right from the first time she had met him, in the barn at Tamworth in the middle of a storm, she had known that Alfred was different.

So she was delighted to have him return to Lambourn, although she was sorry to have to greet him with the news of his dishonest reeve. She would have dealt fully with Godric herself if she had been able, and spared Alfred the trouble, but she had not had the authority.

The next reeve, she thought with satisfaction, would be more careful.

It took most of November to find and to install a new reeve for Lambourn. The duties of the reeve of a royal estate were extensive and could not be trusted to just any man who had the proper noble birth. Besides running the estate of Lambourn, Alfred's new reeve would officiate at the Local Assembly or folk-moot, regulate traders in the area, exact fines and dues, witness property deals, trace stolen cattle, and fight along with the fyrd. It was an office of great responsibility and great trust, which was why the betrayal of such trust was so grave a matter.

Alfred finally settled upon a third son of the Ealdorman of Berkshire, in which shire Lambourn was set, and the arrangement seemed to please all concerned. Ulf settled into Lambourn with relative ease, and by the time Alfred and Elswyth left to pass Christmas at Dorchester, the new reeve had the manor well in hand to begin the winter months.

Chapter 13

SINCE his wedding Alfred had had but one headache, and that shortly before he left for Southampton. He had another the day before they were due to leave for Dorchester, but still they left on schedule. Alfred refused even to consider delaying their departure for an extra day.

The journey to Dorchester was very slow, mainly due to the oxen-drawn covered wagons that carried Alfred's contribution to Ethelred's Christmas feast: great barrels of ale, mead, and honey as well as salt meat and fish to supplement the gifts of the hunt and the pasture at Dorchester. Elswyth kept Silken beside Alfred's Nugget for most of the way. The big stallion and the small gelding had learned to get along together surprisingly well. Alfred was also taking his three favorite dogs to Dorchester, and they ran eagerly beside the horses, making forays into the woods whenever they became too bored with the road.

The party stayed overnight at several abbeys along the way, and for the first time Elswyth had a chance to behold what years of Danish raiding had done to many of the famous religious houses of Wessex. Mercia, being without a coast, had not seen its abbeys kindle to the torch of the pagans as had Wessex and Northumbria.

Alfred and Elswyth also stayed one night in the royal city of Winchester, then traveled west to Wilton, where they passed another night. The Roman road that went south from Wilton would take them directly to the royal city and manor of Dorchester, where the West Saxon kings tradition- ally celebrated Christmas.

Elswyth was particularly pleased to be going to Dorchester because it lay near to the sea. Alfred had been astonished when she told him she had never seen the sea. So much of Wessex was bordered by the sea that it was a part of life he took very much for granted. He had learned to swim almost before he could walk, and from youth had been able to handle the small craft the West Saxons used for fishing. But to Elswyth, child of Mercia, the sea was a foreign element, and she was wild to see it.

Ethelred and Cyneburg had been at Dorchester above a week when Alfred's party finally arrived. The sky was still light and the men were still at the hunt, so it was left to Cyneburg to greet her brother-by-marriage and his new wife.

Elswyth watched as Alfred exchanged the kiss of peace with his brother's wife. Cyneburg was soft and round and pretty; the exact sort of woman Elswyth would have expected Ethelred to marry. Then Alfred was turning to present his wife to his brother's wife, and Elswyth stepped forward politely.

"I am pleased to greet you at last, Elswyth," Cyneburg said. Her tone was gentle, but the light blue eyes that looked into Elswyth's face were sharply assessing. "I was sorry not to be able to attend your wedding."

"I was sorry also," Elswyth replied. Her husky drawling voice was carefully courteous. She looked back into Cyneburg's eyes and waited for her to say something else. When Cyneburg did not speak again, Elswyth added, "I am happy to be here."

"And we are happy to have you."

Another silence fell. Elswyth felt a flash of annoyance. Why did the woman look at her so strangely? Did she have dirt on her face? But she withheld the sharp remark that hovered on the tip of her tongue. Elswyth had determined to make friends with Cyneburg. She knew how fond Alfred was of Ethelred, and she knew he would be displeased if she did not get on with Ethelred's wife. So she strove to look pleasant, and racked her brain for something to say.

Into the silence there came the sound of a baby crying. Elswyth, who had never before shown any interest in children, spoke with sudden inspiration. "I should love to see your new baby, my lady."

Cyneburg's pretty face lighted to beauty. "Would you? Come along, then, and you shall see him right this minute. No, not you, Alfred." Cyneburg made a playful show of waving Alfred away. "Elswyth and I need some time to get acquainted. Isn't that so, Elswyth?"

Elswyth murmured a dutiful yes and trailed off after Ethelred's wife, so obviously determined to admire Cyneburg's child that Alfred hoped, half-humorously, that she wouldn't overdo it. He watched his wife's slim straight shoulders as she marched after Cyneburg, and it was not until the door had closed behind her that he turned to go into the courtyard to see to his thanes.

Alfred was always given the princes' hall at Dorchester, and even though it was the secondary hall, it was larger than the great hall at Lambourn. There were two separate sleeping chambers; Alfred took one and gave Elswyth the other. The thanes of Alfred's hearthband slept on the hall benches, as they always did. The clutter accumulated and the dogs roamed wherever they wished. Elswyth felt immediately at home.

Elswyth had admired Cyneburg's baby lavishly, which made her an instant favorite with Ethelred's wife. Elswyth then added to her good repute by spending the whole afternoon of Christmas Eve playing a board game with Ethelred's eldest son, Ethelhelm, who was confined to bed with a cough.

"It was fun," she said to Alfred when he commended her for her nobility. Her blue eyes glinted wickedly. "I taught him how to cheat when next he plays with his father. Ethelred will not know what happened to him."

"Wait until Cyneburg finds out what a bad influence you are upon her young," Alfred said. He laughed. Then, with mock severity: "What cheat did you show him? Do I know it?"

She smiled complacently. "Play me a game and we shall find out."

"You are an unprincipled brat," he said. "Did you show him how to fix the cards?"

She reached out and pulled his headband down over his eyebrows. "No." A dog whined at the door, wanting to be let out, and Elswyth jumped up. "Wait and see," she said over her shoulder, and went to open the door for the impatient hound.

Two days after Christmas, Alfred took her to the sea. The morning dawned very cold and very windy and he first suggested waiting for the morrow. But Elswyth's face grew so woebegone when he spoke that he changed his mind and said they would go if she wished. He would not take his dogs, however. His wife was one thing, he said, his dogs another.

The way to the coast led along yet another road left from the days of the Romans. As they rode south, Alfred told Elswyth about how, centuries ago, the legions had docked their ships in the bay near to Dorchester. Then the heights of Maiden Castle loomed before them.

"That is one of the old hill forts of the Britons," Alfred said in response to her question. Then, pointing, "See those earthworks? They were once the banks of a huge defense system that went round the whole hill." His tawny hair blew in the wind as he contemplated the ancient fort before them. "It did not stand against the Romans," he added.

A little silence fell as they sat their horses side by side, each imagining the bitter battle that must have occurred at this site all those long centuries ago. Then Alfred said, "If you climb around the hill you can even see the overlapping walls at the entrances."

"I want to do that," she said instantly.

At that he grinned. "Why did I know you were going to say that? Not today, though, Elswyth; not if we are going to ride to the coast."

"Will you take me some other day?"

"Certainly."

"When?"

"When I am able." He looked at her in mock exasperation. "Elswyth, sometimes you are worse than Ethelhelm."

"If someone makes me a promise, I like it to be clear." And she stuck her haughty, aristrocratic nose in the air.

"You like it written in blood and witnessed by three ealdormen," he answered.

Her lips curled. "I had not thought of that."

"We will go when I can find the time," he answered, and prudently she let the subject drop.

"I can smell the sea!" she said instead, sniffing energetically.

"The way this wind is blowing, you can probably smell the sea in Mercia," he replied with rueful humor. Even with his headband to hold it, his hair was whipping across his cheeks. Elswyth's nose and cheeks were scarlet.

"Let's canter," she suggested. "That will warm us up."

The two horses, tall chestnut and small gray, moved off together with alacrity. The horses seemed also to smell the sea.

Alfred took his wife to a pretty bay, sheltered from the southwest gale and safely rimmed with sand. Elwyth was wild with delight. In her boy's cross-gartered trousers, with her cloak and her braids flying out behind her, she raced up and down the sands like a wild young creature drunk on its first taste of freedom.

"Come," she cried, stopping for a moment by Alfred's side and catching his hand. "Let's play tag with the tide!"

The water shone brilliantly in the cold winter sun, the wind here was chill but not unbearable, and the sand was hard under their feet. Alfred laughed and let her pull him into her game.

They sat in the shelter of a rock to eat their bread and cheese. Wisps of hair had come loose from Elswyth's braids and hung down her back in an untidy tangle. Alfred reached out and took an ebony strand between his fingers. It felt like heavy silk to the touch.

"It will take Tordis hours to get a comb through it," Elswyth said through a mouthful of bread.

"Your hair is beautiful." He rubbed the shining blue-black strand between his fingers. "You shouldn't tie it up in braids all the time."

"I won't if you don't like it." She flashed her white teeth. "Perhaps I ought to wear a headband."

He laughed. "A headband would look a little odd on you, Elswyth."

"All the rest of your companions wear one."

"You are not one of my companions."

She sighed. "I know." Then: "Would you like some more cheese?" He accepted the piece she held out to him. "Was it here that the Danes first landed?" she asked.

"It was a little way further along the coast."

She drew up her knees and propped her chin on them. Her untidy braids framed a face that was suddenly sober. "The abbeys and monasteries we passed on the way south . . . I could see how they have suffered. So many new buildings hastily thrown up to replace those that were burned.

Such a destruction of libraries. We have been more fortunate in Mercia. I think that is why we don't realize as well as you here in Wessex just how dangerous is the Danish threat to our way of life."

"We have had a period of peace here in Wessex as well, while the Danes were busy in France," Alfred answered. "And in our last few encounters with them, the victory has gone to us. I think Wessex also is too complacent, Elswyth. I think my countrymen do not yet realize that this time we are not confronting a company of raiders. It is an army that sits there in York, an army that has no plan of returning home to Denmark."

She shivered, as she had not shivered in the cold. "We shall withstand them," she said.

His long firm mouth set into a line. "I pray we shall."

"We shall," she said. "We shall because we must. The alternative is unthinkable."

There was a little silence as he stared at her face. She put a hand up to brush a wisp of hair off her cheek, and he said, his voice sounding strange, "For a little girl, you often make a great deal of sense."

Her eyes, which were so much darker a blue than the deep winter sky, sparked with indignation. "Little girl! I am no little girl, Alfred!"

His mouth twisted in a wry smile. "Are you not?" He rose to his feet and held out a hand. "Come, we must be starting back to Dorchester."

When Elswyth appeared for dinner that evening, her hair was dressed differently. Instead of the usual braids, she wore it drawn back from her face, caught high with combs, and then coiled smoothly in a knot at the back of her small shapely head. It was a style similar to the one Cyneburg affected, and it was suitable to Cyneburg's soft prettiness. It was also suitable to Elswyth, though in a different way. Uncluttered by the childish braids, the hard, delicate bones of her face were clearly revealed, as was the slender, graceful length of her neck.

Alfred stared at his wife when she first appeared, and kept staring at her throughout supper. He had never before realized how much younger the braids made her look. Her whole face seemed changed, he thought in wonder. It was no longer round and childish-looking; the high cheekbones, narrow temples, and expressive, faintly disdainful mouth had suddenly turned into the features of a woman.

"Do you like my hair?" she had asked him as soon as they met. "You said not to wear the braids any longer."

"Yes." He could not stop staring at her. "It is very pretty this way, Elswyth."

She wrinkled her elegant nose. "It took forever to do. But if you like it . . ." She smiled and slipped her hand into his. "Too bad it is Friday. I am so tired of fish after eating it for all of Advent."

He made her some sort of an answer and they took their places at Ethelred's supper board.

Alfred was not the only one to notice the change the new hairstyle made in Elswyth. Both Cyneburg and Ethelred commented favorably on her looks, and she was forced to find a polite reply. Elswyth did not care for compliments, and after an hour of being stared at she was beginning to be sorry she had given up her braids. Even Brand stared at her out of strangely green eyes and told her hesitatingly that he thought she looked beautiful. Elswyth liked Brand, so she smiled and thanked him, but she was heartily glad when supper ended and she could go hide herself and her hair in her bedchamber.

She wore the hair up again the following day, however. Alfred had said he liked it and Elswyth reasoned that everyone's surprise would have worn off overnight and no one was likely to notice her hair one way or the other anymore. After breakfast it began to rain, a cold hard rain that looked to keep up for the entire day. Alfred and his thanes and Elswyth and her few ladies were forced to keep within doors in the princes' hall. The ladies spun wool. The men played at drafts and listened to Brand strum on the lyre. The dogs slept in front of the fire. Elswyth got out the checkered playboard and challenged Alfred to a game of boar and hound.

He accepted and they sat together before the fire, the dogs sleeping at their feet. Outside the rain soon changed to sleet, and the chill air creeping in from beneath the doors stirred the rushes on the floor. Elswyth tucked her feet under her for warmth, and frowned thoughtfully at the board. The flickering light from the fire cast a rosy glow on the pearly curve of the skin over her high cheekbones. Her long, lowered lashes were black as soot. She carefully moved a carved hound to another square, looked up with a brilliant flash of blue, and grinned wickedly.

"I've won!" she crowed.

Alfred made himself look at the board. "Yes, so you have." Even to himself, his voice sounded odd.

"And I did not even cheat." She tilted her head in the way she had that managed to be both arrogant and charming at the same time. "You were distracted. I'll play you again." She was generous in her victory.

"No." He stood up. "I must go to see Ethelred."

The amazing blue eyes widened in surprise. "It's sleeting outside," she said.

He shrugged. "No matter." He began to back away, signaling for his cloak.

She watched him, and trouble began to crease her brow. "Are you all right, Alfred?"

"I am fine," he replied hastily. "I just thought of something I must discuss with Ethelred." He took his cloak from Brand, who had seen him gesture for it, and headed for the door of the hall.

Outside the wind tore his cloak and the sleet beat against his face. He made it to the safety of his brother's hall, and spent the remainder of the afternoon playing drafts with Ethelred.

That night he lay awake in his solitary bed and thought of his wife. The storm had gathered strength and tore and howled and shook at the shuttered window and caused the tapestried hangings on the wall to billow inward.

He lay there starkly awake, shaken by an emotion that was as intense and as turbulent as the storm without.

Elswyth. For how long, he wondered, had he loved her? For that was the emotion that was rendering him sleepless this night, he had no doubt of that. Love. And desire.

He had loved her, he thought, for a long time. Whatever it was in the mixture of her personality that attracted him so strongly, it had worked its spell right from the start. He would never have agreed to marry any other girl he found weeping her heart out in a barn.

Elswyth would be quick to point out to him that she had not been weeping.

He smiled a little painfully and stared above his head into the dark. It was Elswyth, he thought, who had drawn him back to Lambourn; Elswyth who had made his last encounter with Roswitha so strangely unsatisfying. And it was his joy in his wife's companionship, mixed with the frustration of his incomplete marriage, that had rendered his return to Lambourn so difficult.

She was so close to him this night. Only on the other side of a thin wooden wall. He could see her in his mind's eye perfectly clearly: the line of her beautiful cheekbones; the cleft in her small determined chin; the curling, ironic, tantalizing mouth. She would be sound asleep on this wild and stormy night, wrapped in her beautiful hair, completely unaware that aught could be wrong between them.

For she loved him too. He did not doubt that. There was an understanding they had together that he did not think many people were fortunate enough to find. They were different in many ways; yet in the great and important things of life, somehow they were alike. They understood each other's feelings.

She understood him in all but this one great thing.

She was fifteen and no longer a child. He remembered, far too vividly, the feel of her body against his when he had lifted her down from her saddle at Lambourn. But because he too understood her, he understood that in this one thing she was not yet a woman. "Thank you, Alfred!" she had said when he promised her an unconsummated marriage. He remembered her radiant smile, remembered her words about Edred: "But I shall have to sleep in his bed."

He could not betray her trust. He could not ask something of her she was not yet ready to give. He would simply have to go on waiting.

Alfred did not fall asleep until the dawn was breaking. When he entered the hall the following morning, heavy-eyed and short-tempered, he saw Elswyth and knew his only hope of peace was to keep away from her. The weather was vile, but he took his thanes and went out hunting. Nor would he let Elswyth accompany him.

When the Christmas celebration was over, he thought, he would send Elswyth back to Wantage and he would begin to travel the country, checking on the readiness of the shire defenses. He had only to get through Christmas. Surely he could manage that.

Elswyth sensed the change in Alfred instantly, but was at a loss to account for it. All she knew was that he no longer seemed to want her near him. He spent his days hunting with the men, and never once did he find the time to take her back to Maiden Castle.

Then he started to get headaches: one the day before the New Year and another one two days after.

He would not let her come near him. It was Cyneburg who brought the cold cloths for his head, and Ethelred who kept the door barred against intruders.

At first Elswyth was hurt. Bitterly so. And then she began to grow afraid. Perhaps there was something wrong with Alfred that he was trying to keep from her. This quick succession of headaches was not usual; Ethelred unbent enough to tell her that. And Elswyth could see how tightly strung Alfred was, even when he was not in pain.

Something was wrong with him. What if he was seriously ill? What if he was going to die?

Never in her life had Elswyth been afraid as she was afraid those days at Dorchester. Never had she felt so alone. What would she do should something happen to Alfred?

It never once occurred to her that she was the problem, that he wanted her, and felt bound by the promise he had given her, and was thus driving himself into a state of extreme nervous tension that would inevitably result in headaches.

Alfred had rightly understood that Elswyth's thoughts were far from sex. But it was not immaturity that kept her ignorant; it was innocence. She knew she loved Alfred. She knew she would die of loneliness if ever she lost him. She, who had ever sought only solitude, now found that another person was as necessary to her as the air she breathed or the water she drank.

She knew nothing of the necessities of sex, knew nothing of its pleasures. Elswyth had never in her life sat with other women and gossiped about such matters. It never once occurred to her that Alfred's problem could be so simple. She had always assumed that when he wanted to consummate their marriage, he would. It never crossed her mind that she was the one who must make the first move.

"Consummate this marriage!" Ethelred said to Alfred two days after the second headache. "You are making yourself ill. The girl is old enough, Alfred. And she worships you. All can see that. What are you waiting for?"

"I do not want to discuss this, Ethelred." Alfred's voice was cold and final. "Do I ask you about your relationship with Cyneburg?"

"There is nothing wrong with my relationship with Cyneburg," Ethelred was beginning to answer, when Alfred turned his back and precipitately left the room.

"Send him to Southampton, my lord," recommended Ethelred's seneschal, Odo, an old thane who had served Ethelwulf years before. "Anything is better than another headache."

"I really do not think the girl has any idea of what it is that is distressing Alfred," Cyneburg said to her husband when he reported Odo's recommendation to her.

"If that is true, then perhaps Alfred is right," Ethelred said heavily. "Perhaps she is still too much a child."

"No." Cyneburg shook her head. "She loves him. That is clear enough. She is just . . . unawakened. Elswyth had a very strange upbringing, Ethelred. From what Alfred says, she was put under her brother's care and simply allowed to run wild. Her mother utterly neglected her. Poor child, no wonder she is so backward. She had no woman to guide or teach her."

"I don't think Elswyth and her mother liked each other very much," Ethelred said.

Cyneburg made a soft sound of distress.

Ethelred smiled. "Not all mothers are as tender as you, my dear. Nor all children as malleable as ours."

"Nevertheless," said Cyneburg, "Alfred could teach her to love him well enough, if only he had the sense to try."

"I fear Alfred is not thinking very sensibly just now," Ethelred said dryly. "And it is impossible to discuss the subject with him."

"Then it had better be discussed with Elswyth," said Cyneburg.

Ethelred looked troubled. "I do not know . . ."

"What is the alternative?" His wife stared at him with gentle exasperation. "Will you send him to Southampton?"

"No." Ethelred's mouth set. "I cannot play so carelessly with the health of his soul."

"Just so." Cyneburg's pretty face looked amazingly resolute. "It is time someone talked to Elswyth. And it seems the someone," she concluded, "must be me."

Before Cyneburg could put her resolution into practice, however, Alfred had another headache. It was exactly the twelfth day of Christmas, and after Cyneburg saw that Alfred had a good supply of cold cloths, she went into the adjoining room to speak to Alfred's wife.

She found Elswyth pacing up and down like a caged panther, her skin nearly transparent with strain, her blue eyes glittering. "What is it?" she demanded of Cyneburg the moment she came in the door of Elswyth's room. "Why is he having so many headaches? You are all hiding something from me. I know it. Is he terribly ill? Is he going to die?"

Elswyth came to a halt in front of Cyneburg, and now she grasped Cyneburg's arm and shook it. Elswyth's voice shook also as she cried furiously. "Tell me!"

Cyneburg replied in a quiet voice, "It is not so bad as that, Elswyth. It is simply that Alfred is a man, and this unconsummated marriage is taking its toll."

Elswyth chin rose, and her narrowed, glittering eyes seemed to widen. She took a step back from Cyneburg. "What do you mean?" she asked in genuine bewilderment.

"He had a lady before he married you," Cyneburg said. "He is nineteen years old, Elswyth, and not a monk. I think, if you are unwilling to be a true wife to him, you ought to send him back to Roswitha."

There was a stunned silence. Then: "Roswitha?" Elswyth was no longer looking at Cyneburg, was looking into the empty air beside Cyneburg's ear. Abruptly the dark blue eyes swung back to meet the paler ones of her sister-by-marriage. "This Roswitha, does she live at Southampton?" Elswyth asked.

Cyneburg did not allow her satisfaction to show. "Why, yes," she said. Very gently. "She does."

"Does Alfred love her?" Now midnight-blue eyes were glittering through dangerously narrowed, long-lashed slits. There was a white line running down the entire length of Elswyth's narrow aristocratic nose. Cyneburg stared at her in considerable awe and answered hastily, "I am sure he does not. He would not have married you if he loved Roswitha."

"But if what you say is so, why has he said nothing to me?" Elswyth turned her beautiful, fierce, disquieting face away from Cyneburg and began once more to pace the room. Cyneburg waited. Finally Elswyth turned to her again and said, "Surely he could not be foolish enough to make himself ill over such a little thing!"

"Men," said Cyneburg wisely, "can be remarkably foolish."

"Not Alfred," came the immediate reply.

Cyneburg smiled. "Not usually," she agreed.

Elswyth came a step closer. "You are saying he is having these head-aches because he wishes to bed with me?"

"That is what I am saying."

Elswyth stretched upward on her toes, as if a great weight had just been lifted from her back. She stretched her shoulders. "Well, that is soon enough mended," she said.

Cyneburg nodded and folded her arms. "So I thought."

Elswyth regarded Cyneburg suspiciously. "What does this Roswitha look like?"

"I understand that she is pretty," Cyneburg answered.

Elswyth drew her lips away from her teeth. "I will never give him up to her."

Cyneburg stared at that fiercely beautiful face. "So I thought." She walked to the door and put her hand on the latch. "Well, my dear," she remarked, "I believe the rest is up to you."

Elswyth went next door to Alfred's room. He was lying on the bed, a cloth laid over his forehead. She stalked to the bedside and stared down at him. His eyes, clouded with pain, looked back.

"Elswyth." He sat up and she did not try to stop him. "What are you doing here?" His voice had the note it always held at such times, as if he were speaking with great difficulty.

"I have come here to tell you that if ever you go near Roswitha again, I will murder her," Elswyth said.

The heavy eyes, darker than usual with pain, stared at her in astonishment.

"From now on, it is my bed you will be sleeping in." She glared at him. She sounded as if she were talking between her teeth. "Do I make myself clear?"

"I . . . Yes."

"Good," she said. "You married me. You are stuck with me. I'll come back when you are feeling better." And she turned and stalked once more out of the room.

In the end, it was he who came to her. The pain lifted sooner than he had expected, and Elswyth was still in her own room, brushing one of the dogs to pass the time, when Alfred came in the door. Her head shot around as soon as she heard the latch lift. "Alfred! Are you all right?" She put the dog away from her and jumped to her feet.

"I am perfectly fine," he answered.

She crossed the room to stand before him, her eyes lifted to his face. The room was lit by a single lamp and by the brazier that burned in the corner for warmth. In the soft glow she could see that he looked pale still, and heavy-eyed. Then he smiled.

It was all right, she thought. It was going to be all right. And she slipped her hands into his and smiled back.

"Did you mean what you said?" he asked.

"Yes." The heaviness in his eyes was different, she thought, had nothing to do with the headache. He raised one of her hands, curled so confidingly within his, and looked at it. His smile faded, leaving his face very grave. He spread out her fingers carefully and linked them between his own. Then he raised her hand to his mouth.

She felt his kiss on each separate finger, and her lips parted. "Do you realize . . . ?" he said, and his voice too was heavy and different. Husky-sounding, not his usual tone at all. "Can you possibly realize how much I have longed for you?" And he looked down into her face once more.

She shook her head, her eyes held by his. Deep within the gold of them, a flame had begun to burn. "You should have told me," she whispered. "I did not understand."

"I promised you." He raised her other hand and began to kiss those fingers as well. "I promised you I would wait."

"You have waited," she said. "Now your waiting is over."

At that, he drew her close against him. She slid her arms around his waist and pressed her cheek into his shoulder. It was so safe here in his arms, she thought. So wonderfully, wonderfully safe. She felt his lips brush over her hair, her ear, across her cheek. The soft linen of his shirt was warm against her cheek and she could feel the muscles of his back under her hands. She sighed.

"Elswyth." The word was a whisper, a caress. "Elswyth." It came again and, a little reluctantly, she raised her head from his shoulder and looked up.

He was so beautiful. She loved him so much. She heard him murmur something under his breath, and then his mouth was bending to hers. Its touch was gentle at first, and she leaned against him, her head bent back over his arm, her hair beginning to loosen and fall from its coils. His mouth grew harder, more demanding. Never had she dreamed a man's mouth could feel thus against her own.

"My little love." He was steering her across the room, to the chair that was set beside the brazier. He sat down and drew her to him once again, holding her between his knees as he kissed her. She pressed against him, her warm young flesh seeking his, her arms going out to encircle his neck. The charcoal glowed warm against the cold January air. The dog she had been brushing lay stretched out on the rushes, basking in the warmth of the brazier. Alfred's fingers moved over her back, her shoulder, while his mouth taught her how to kiss him back. His hand moved lower to caress her narrow waist, then moved upward again to cup one little breast. It answered to his touch instantly, rising to meet him.

She sank against him, heedless of all but the sensations his touch was arousing. His fingers slipped within her gown; then she felt their warmth on her bare skin. She whimpered with pleasure.

"Elswyth." Now his voice was urgent with desire. "Elswyth, come to bed."

Her lips moved along the edge of his jaw, where a beard had yet to grow. "Yes," she said. "Alfred, this is wonderful."

His laugh was not steady. "Elswyth . . . the first time, it may hurt."

"I don't care," she said. And spoke the truth.

It was so wonderful to be able to touch him. She had always loved to touch him, and now to be able to run her hands all along that smooth golden body, to feel the sleek muscles of it, the strength. It mattered not at all that it hurt when he came into her. It was a matter of awe just to see how much pleasure she was able to give to him.

"I love you," he said into her ear. She pressed her lips against the tawny gold head that was resting on her breast. "I have been going mad for love of you."

"I love you too," she answered, her lips still buried in his hair. "Surely you knew that. Why did you wait so long?"

"I had promised you . . ." She felt the sweep of his lashes against the bare skin of her breast.

"You frightened me so," she said. "I was afraid there was something terribly wrong with you . . . all those headaches . . . you should have told me."

"Mmm." He was sounding sleepy. "It seems I certainly should have."

She cradled him in her arms. "You are weary," she said softly. "Go to sleep."

He raised his head and looked down at her. His headband was lying on the floor and his hair hung forward, framing his face with gold. The curve of his mouth was very tender. "Don't go away," he said.

Looking at him, she felt such a pain around her heart. Why should such happiness give her such pain? "I won't," she answered softly. And drew him down to rest in her arms once again.

Chapter 14

ATHULF was to be married immediately after Easter, and the end of March found Elswyth and Alfred traveling to Mercia for both the holy day and the wedding. It was the time of year to prepare the fields for the corn crop, and all along the road Alfred's party could see oxen toiling slowly up and down the fields of manor and village, the farmers behind steering the plows, furrowing the earth for the seeds of barley, wheat, and rye, that would be sown as soon as the plowing was done.

"March is not the best of times for a wedding feast," Alfred remarked to Elswyth. They were fording a small forest stream on the second day of their journey to Croxden manor in Mercia and he raised his feet a little to keep them from getting wet. It was true that weddings were rarely held in the spring. Spring was a time when both food and fodder were scarce after the winter. And there was the added factor that the church forbade marriages during Lent. In Anglo-Saxon England, weddings were far more likely to be held in autumn than in spring.

"Athulf and Hild were to have married last October," Elswyth replied as Silken splashed tentatively through the cold running water. The little gray did not like to get his feet wet. "But then her father became ill. It did not seem right to hold a wedding while the bride's father lay dying, so they waited. He died but last month."

The horses were through the water now and scrambling up the small bank on the far side. Once they were back on the path: "Hild's father was Ealdorman of Hwicce, was he not?" Alfred asked, looking thoughtful.

"Yes." Elswyth leaned forward to straighten Silken's mane. He arched his dappled neck as if in acknowledgment.

"Who do you think will be named the next ealdorman, Elswyth?"

Elswyth, smiling with amusement, was patting the little gray's neck. Then she turned to her husband. "Hild has a brother," she said. "He is young, but perhaps he will be appointed. The honor has been in that family for several generations, and Mercia has more a tradition of family inheritance in these matters than you have in Wessex."

"Her brother?" Alfred frowned in an effort of memory. "Does her brother have red hair?"

"Yes. His name is Ethelred. A good man on a horse."

Alfred laughed. "Elswyth, you judge everyone by how well he sits a horse."

"It is not so bad a system," she retorted. "The way a man treats his animals can tell you much about his character."

"I suppose that is true." They were walking the horses slowly along the path and now Nugget stopped to rub his knee with his nose. Silken stopped also and watched the chestnut stallion with polite interest. Alfred said, "About this Ethelred. I met him at Nottingham and he was hot to fight the Danes. If he is indeed appointed in his father's stead, that will be good news for Wessex."

Elswyth's delicate lips curled in a distinctly sardonic smile. "If he is hot to fight the Danes, it would be well if he kept his eagerness to himself. Burgred is not likely to be seeking an ealdorman with a lion's heart."

The thoughtful look returned to Alfred's face. Nugget stopped scratching and began to walk forward once again. "That is so," Alfred answered. He added, "Is Ethelred likely to be at this wedding?"

"He is Hild's eldest brother. I would be surprised were he not present."

"Good. Then can I speak to him."

At that Elswyth grinned. "You can advise him to hold his tongue, you mean," she said.

He laughed a little in acknowledgment. "I am always on the lookout for an ally."

They were riding through deeper woods now, and the path had narrowed so that they were forced to go single file. Elswyth went ahead of Alfred, as Silken fretted when he was behind. Suddenly there came the sound of something rustling in the trees to their right; then an animal screamed. Silken jumped, bucked, and bolted. Nugget tried to follow, but Alfred pulled the stallion down with a ruthless hand. The sound of a horse galloping on his heels would only spur Silken onward. Elswyth disappeared into the trees. Alfred shouted over his shoulder to Brand to keep the others to a walk and trotted forward, fighting a horse that wanted to run. It was not long before he saw the figure of his wife, walking her little gray sedately back along the path in his direction. His grim face lightened and he brought his own excited horse to a halt.

"Did you enjoy the run?" he asked her as they met face-to-face on the forest path. The rest of their party were further behind, and for the moment they were alone.

She laughed. Her cheeks were flying flags of color and her brilliant eyes were blue as sapphires. "He wasn't really frightened," she said. "It was just a good excuse."

He nodded. "So I thought. We had better wait a minute for the rest to catch up."

She turned Silken and, as the path was wider here, Alfred came up beside her. The horses stood quietly, Silken very pleased with himself and Nugget resigned to the fact that he had better obey the hands holding his reins. Quite suddenly Elswyth leaned over and picked up one of those thin, surprisingly strong hands. Bending her head, she kissed the long fingers, then returned it to its original position. Alfred raised an inquiring eyebrow. "What was that for?"

"There is not another man I know who would have trusted me to control my own horse," she said. "Even Athulf would have come galloping after me."

"A horse on his heels would have really frightened Silken," Alfred returned serenely.

"I know that." She smiled at him, a faint but very intimate smile.

"You ride better than I do," he added.

"Alfred," she said, "I adore you."

He grinned. "Tell me that again tonight."

"I think we are staying in the abbey near Bordesley tonight," she answered regretfully. "I doubt that I shall even see you."

All the good humor abruptly left his face. "Don't they have a guesthouse?"

"They have a house for women. The men must lodge with the monks."

He said something under his breath. Then he looked ashamed. "The good monks have promised a lifetime of chastity to God. I suppose I should not grudge him one night."

"We will be at Croxden on the morrow," she said. "Then will we be lodged together."

The sound of horses' hooves and the jingle of bridles came floating on the air, and then their escort of thanes was coming out of the narrow path between the trees to fall in behind them. Alfred and Elswyth moved forward again, their pace decorous, their conversation impersonal.

There was not a large party gathered at Croxden for the wedding of Athulf, Ealdorman of Gaini, to Hild, daughter of the Ealdorman of Hwicce. As Alfred had noted, early spring was a difficult time to feed an increased number of people and horses. And the bride's father's recent demise gave good excuse for keeping the celebration small.

Eadburgh was there, of course. And Ceolwulf. And Hild's mother. And her brothers, Ethelred and Aelfric.

Ethelred remembered Alfred well, and was eagerly looking forward to meeting the West Saxon prince again. All that had happened since the Danes' departure from Nottingham had only confirmed Ethelred's belief that Burgred had been wrong to let the enemy slip away. Ethelred wanted to know what Alfred's plans were regarding the future. The Mercian nobility, even including Athulf, appeared resigned to a posture of passive waiting.

It was Ethelred, who had been on the watch for them, who first caught sight of the party from Wessex as it came through the gates of Croxden manor. He stood on the steps of the guest hall where he was lodged and watched Alfred swing down from his saddle. Ethelred had developed a case of hero worship for Alfred last year in Nottingham, and he recognized now the easy grace that had so impressed him and that he had since tried so fruitlessly to imitate. Ethelred was not slim and lean and catlike and his stocky, short-legged body had been a source of frustration to him all the winter.

The sun caught the green of Alfred's headband and drew gleams of light from the tawny gold of his hair. He handed his horse to a groomsman and turned to his wife. Ethelred's eyes also swung to the girl on the small gray gelding and then they opened wide.

Surely, he thought in startled confusion, surely this could not be Elswyth? True, the hair was the right color, and the horse was hers also, but . . .

The West Saxon thanes of Alfred's escort were dismounting, and now Ethelred saw that Croxden's reeve was coming down the steps of the great hall to greet the newcomers. "My lady!" he cried, and the pleasure in his voice rang loud enough for Ethelred to hear it clearly. "Welcome home."

Alfred was laughing as he lifted the slim black-haired girl down from her saddle. Then she was saying to the reeve, who was now standing before her, "Many thanks, Offa. It is good to see you also."

It was her voice that Ethelred recognized. There could be no mistaking that dark, almost husky drawl.

The reeve had begun to escort the prince and his wife across the courtyard, and hastily Ethelred stepped forward from within the shadow of the guest-hall door.

"Welcome to Croxden, my lord," he said as he reached Alfred's elbow a few paces before the steps of the great hall. The prince stopped to look at him. Ethelred held his grave expression and hope desperately that Alfred would remember him. "I have been looking forward to meeting you again," he added.

The prince's golden eyes, the color of which Ethelred had never seen on any other human, lighted with pleasure. "Ethelred," he said. "I have been looking forward to meeting you also."

Ethelred could feel the ready color rise to his cheeks. He hated the way his pale skin showed every change in his emotions. He wished his skin would tan, like . . .

"Greetings, Ethelred," said Alfred's wife. "For how long have you been here?"

Ethelred forgot his own embarrassment and stared at this beautiful girl who was, astonishingly enough, really Elswyth. He had known Elswyth for years, ever since his sister had become betrothed to her brother over four years before. They were of an age, and they had been comfortable companions on the occasions in the past when his family had visited Croxden. They had hunted together, and he had thought her braver than most boys he knew, but it had never occurred to him to find her pretty. He had been deeply surprised to learn she was to marry Alfred. He could not imagine the hoydenish Elswyth married to anyone, let alone his secret hero.

So he looked now in some confusion at the finely boned blue-eyed face of this beautiful girl who was Elswyth. It was her hair, he thought. She looked completely different without the ubiquitous braids. He was still too young to disguise his thoughts, so he blurted out before he could stop himself, "You look so different, Elswyth!"

She grinned and for a moment the gamine he had known returned. "It's my hair," she said. "You look the same, though, Ethelred. I'm glad you are here. Is Burgred going to name you ealdorman in your father's stead?"

"Nothing like going straight to the point," Alfred murmured as they all began to walk slowly toward the steps.

"I hope so," Ethelred replied. "I have an uncle, but he is not well. My mother has spoken to the queen and she thinks it will be me. Athulf will speak for me also." He looked at Alfred. "I am to go see the king after the wedding."

"Ah," said Elswyth, and she looked also at Alfred.

His lips twitched. "You and I must have a talk sometime, Ethelred," he said. "I would very much like to see you named ealdorman. We two have much in common, I think."

Ethelred's hazel eyes glowed very green. "Yes, my lord."

Suddenly Elswyth's face changed. Ethelred's eyes turned in the same direction as hers and he saw that Eadburgh had come out the door of the hall and was awaiting them at the top of the steps. They stopped on the step below her and their hostess said to Elswyth with regal composure, "Welcome to Croxden, my daughter." Next Eadburgh looked at Alfred, and now she smiled graciously. "Welcome to you also, Prince."

"Thank you, my lady," Alfred replied in his clipped West Saxon voice. Ethelred saw how his hand lifted casually to rest on his wife's shoulder. "We are pleased to be here to help celebrate Athulf's marriage."

Eadburgh was looking once more at her daughter. "You look very well, Elswyth. I am glad to see you are wearing proper clothing for a change."

Ethelred was the only one to see how Alfred's fingers tightened on his wife's shoulder. There was a moment's pause; then Elswyth said in a sweetly husky voice that brought a look of wonder to the reeve's eyes, "Thank you, Mother. It is wonderful to see you also."

Eadburgh looked taken aback. There was a brief silence. Then she said, "Why are we standing here on the stairs? Bring your husband into the great hall, Elswyth."

Alfred gave his mother-by-marriage a charming smile. "Elswyth is tired, my lady. Might we be shown to our lodging instead?"

"Certainly." Eadburgh turned to Elswyth. "I have given you your old room in the bower, Elswyth."

"Oh, good." her daughter lifted a glowing face to her husband. "My old room," she said.

"The older and more familiar it is, the better Elswyth likes it," Alfred remarked to Ethelred when he saw the boy's face. "I comfort myself that by the time I am an aged old grandfather, she will like me very well indeed."

Elswyth chuckled, a deep, dark, delicious sound. "Come along," she said. "I'll show you the way. Offa will take care of our thanes."

Ethelred stood in silence on the top step and watched the figures of Alfred and his black-haired wife as they recrossed the courtyard toward the small hall that was the girl's bower. Elswyth was talking, looking up into Alfred's face, and then she slid an arm around his waist and leaned against him. Linked thus together, they walked in through the door of the bower.

"Well," said Eadburgh, and Ethelred turned to see that he was not the only one watching. Eadburgh and Offa stood beside him. Eadburgh looked outraged; Offa looked delighted. "That girl has no sense of decorum," Elswyth's mother said, and pinched her lips together.

"The lord Athulf did the best he could, my lady," Offa replied piously. "But he lacked a woman's touch."

Eadburgh shot her reeve a distinctly nasty look, then turned and walked away. Ethelred pretended he did not hear the unflattering comment the reeve made under his breath, and went himself to get ready for dinner.

After a week of stringent prayer and even more stringent meals, Easter came to set the household free from the penance of Lent. Then, three days after Easter, Athulf's household priest married him to Hild. The wedding banquet was presided over by Eadburgh and Hild's mother, the recent widow, and was not jolly. Athulf took his new bride early to bed, and the rest of the party broke up with obvious relief.

"Lucky man," Ceolwulf remarked gloomily to Alfred as the two returned from a very perfunctory bedding rite for the newly wed pair. Then, "You also, Prince. I am the one who needs must retire to a lonely bed."

Alfred smiled at him. This brother of Elswyth's was just his own age, and very personable. Alfred liked him. It was hard not to like Ceolwulf. "You should get married, Ceolwulf."

"It's not marriage I need," Ceolwulf returned. "It's escape from my mother." He gave Alfred a deliberately comical look. "Do you know how grim life has become at Croxden since Elswyth left? Life was uncomfortable enough last year, with Elswyth and my mother constantly in battle, but now things are even worse."

"Why so?" Alfred asked absently. His mind was on Elswyth and his bed, not on Ceolwulf's complaints.

"I don't believe any of us realized how much this manor depended upon Elswyth," Ceolwulf replied. There was an odd note of wonder in his voice. He looked at Alfred, his gray eyes wide. "She never seemed to do anything!" Alfred grinned and Ceolwulf went on, "My mother is certainly a more conscientious mistress. She supervises the work in the bakehouse, the weaving house, the dye house, the kitchens. Yet under Elswyth, all seemed to run better." There was a pause; then Ceolwulf's brows drew together. He corrected himself. "No, not better, perhaps. All was happier. The serving folk were happier and the service was more willing. These days, all we seem to have are brangles."

"It is that to Elswyth the manor folk are all individuals," Alfred replied. His smile was gone; he was utterly serious. "The rest of us, we see the groom and the beekeeper and the goose girl. Elswyth sees Oswald and Wulfstan and Ebbe. Free or unfree, it makes no difference to her. All are individuals. And they know that. It is why they love her, would do anything for her. Even in the few short months she had been at my own manors of Wantage and Lambourn, I can see this. It is her great gift, this ability to see the person and not just the rank."

Ceolwulf was looking at his brother-by-marriage, his gray eyes a little puzzled. Then he shrugged, finding his own solution. "She has ever been a strong-minded brat. From the time she was five years old, she had her way of Athulf and of me." He smiled wryly. "It was not so difficult to get her way of me, perhaps, but Athulf is another story. Yet rarely could he stand against her. I think the manor folk felt the same."

Alfred grinned again. "Very likely."

They had reached the door of the small hall where Ceolwulf was lodged. He sighed once more. "Well, Prince, I wish you a good night."

Alfred responded pleasantly and went toward the bower, his stride quickening noticeably as he approached the door. The benches in the small bower hall were empty, as the maids slept in the attic room above. There was a light showing under the door of Elswyth's sleeping room, and it was but a few long strides until Alfred could push it open and go in to his wife.

She was sitting cross-legged on the bed, a blanket draped over her thin linen undershift, her long hair tied at the nape of her neck with a strip of embroidered tapestry. There was an oil lamp lit on the table beside the bed, and she was throwing dice on the bedcover. She looked up when he came in, smiled, and remarked, "What a gloomy wedding. Poor Athulf. I will wager you that his path and my mother's rarely cross again."

"Your mother is not exactly what I would call a jolly person," Alfred agreed. He unbuckled his belt and began to pull his tunic over his head. Elswyth scooped the dice up, put them on the table, and leaned back against her pillow, watching him. "I think I ought to go to Tamworth with

Ethelred," he said, his voice a little muffled as it came from beneath the blue wool of his tunic. His head emerged and he began to fold the tunic to put it on top of the clothes chest. Next he began to take off his shirt.

"Do you?" she responded almost lazily.

"Yes." He came back to the bed and sat down to take off his soft leather shoes. She reached out and laid a hand on the warm, smooth skin of his back. The muscles flexed under her hand as he reached to push his shoes under the bed. "It is important that Wessex and Mercia continue to hold together." He straightened, turned, and looked down at her. "I had another thought too. What if we found a West Saxon girl for Ceolwulf to wed? If Ethelred is appointed ealdorman, and if Ceolwulf is bound to Wessex by marriage, that will be two more Mercians inclined to assist us."

"Hmm." She clasped her hands around her updrawn knees and regarded him thoughtfully. "We could do that, I suppose. But, Alfred, I would caution you not to expect too much from Ceolwulf. He is my brother, and I am fond of him, but Ceolwulf will ever take the easiest way." She shrugged. There was pity in her eyes, and the faintest trace of contempt. "He cannot help it. It is his nature."

"Still," Alfred said, "if we make ours the easiest way . . ."

She shrugged again. "It is worth a try, certainly."

"We must find him a nice docile girl who will not threaten his peace," Alfred said. Now there was laughter in his eyes. "Someone like you."

"True." She smiled at him sweetly. "Ceolwulf and I have ever got along well."

"That is because you have him thoroughly intimidated," her husband retorted. He reached out to pull the ribbon from her hair and watched as the shining blue-black mass slid over her shoulders like a silken cloak. "Poor man, after you and your mother, a sweet-natured West Saxon girl will seem like an angel from heaven to him."

Elswyth's blue eyes flashed. She sat up straight as a spear. "Do not compare me to my mother! We are not at all alike."

"You both have wills of iron." He was pushing her back against the pillow, stretching out beside her.

She tried to draw away. "Alfred, take that back. I am not like my mother."

He took a fistful of her hair and held her still. "You are not like your mother," he repeated, imitating her Mercian drawl.

She laughed unwillingly and reached out to pretend to push him away. "If I am such a shrew, you can scarcely wish to sleep with me."

"But such a beautiful shrew," he murmured, sliding his leg over hers to hold her down. She was under him now, her hair spilled like an ebony halo on the pillow around her face.

He could see her wondering if she would be strong enough to push him off. He let her try. Then, when she fell back again against the pillow, her breath coming a little short: "And I would find a sweet-natured West Saxon girl so tedious."

"You are a devil," she said. But the struggle had heated her blood; he could see that from the glitter in her eyes.

"Elswyth," he said. The teasing note had quite gone from his voice. "God Almighty. Elswyth." And he set his mouth against hers.

Her arms came up instantly to draw him close. "I love you," she said after a while, her husky voice close to his ear. He pushed up her shift to get it out of his way, and she ran her hands up and down his smooth naked torso. He touched her and she shuddered.

Athulf and his new bride were asleep long before Alfred and Elswyth that night.

Chapter 15

ALFRED and Elswyth returned to Wessex at the end of April, Alfred well-pleased with the naming of Ethelred as new Ealdorman of Hwicce. The Danes remained in York. Alfred collected his food rents, the seed was sown, the lambs and piglets and calves were born. June came and the sheep were sheared and the fleeces gathered into the barns to be combed and spun into wool by the women. Fences were built and repaired and new fishing weirs were constructed. Then the summer was upon them.

Elswyth stood without the door of the hall at Wantage one light summer night late in July and breathed in the cool evening air. It had been hot during the day and the heat still lingered within the hall. The courtyard was empty, but she could hear the sound of music and laughter coming from the far side of the stockade fence. The manor folk were having a dance this night, to celebrate the conclusion of the haymaking.

Alfred was not at Wantage this week, having ridden to Mercia on business for his brother. Elswyth was near four months gone with child, and though she was feeling better now, she had been ill in the mornings for the first few months. She had decided to forgo the long ride to Tamworth and back in favor of remaining at Wantage and working with her filly while still she could ride.

Ethelred had sent Alfred into Mercia in response to Burgred's most recent message that the Danes were making ready to leave York. For all this past year the Mercians had kept watch on York, and now the dreaded signs at last were visible. Actually the Danish army had remained in the north for longer than anyone had dared hope; they must have eaten the land bare these last six months.

Elswyth crossed her arms on her breast and shivered a little in the cool night air. She had been so happy these last six months with Alfred. She had clung fast to the joy of the moment and refused to let her happiness be marred by the uncertainties of the future. It was one faculty of childhood she still retained, that ability to live in the present.

But their peace was over. She felt it this night, as she stood in the solitude of her safe courtyard and listened to the mirth of the manor folk floating on the soft summer air. The Danes were once more on the move. Whither would they march next?

The music was still playing when Elswyth turned back to the hall to seek her lonely bed. She did not sleep, however, until long after the last merrymaker had fallen into his cot and lay deep in the sodden slumber of the weary and the drunk.

In August the Danish army came pouring down the old Roman road that led from York directly into the monastery-rich fen country of East Anglia. Monasteries that had been centers of civilization since the time of Saint Guthlac gleamed as rich prizes before a Viking army which had fallen on lean times at York this last year.

It was Elswyth's brother Ceolwulf who brought Alfred the news of the Danish move into East Anglia. Ceolwulf had been sent as messenger by Burgred and had ridden straight through from Tamworth to Lambourn, where Alfred and Elswyth were housed this time of year. He stopped to see Alfred first, since Ethelred, Wessex's king, was further to the south and the east, in Sussex.

"All the fen country is afire," Ceolwulf said as he sat with his sister and her husband in the hall at Lambourn. Ceolwulf was eating as he talked, having barely halted for food on his ride south. "Farms, manors, monasteries—all within the path of the pagan march is going up in smoke."

"What monasteries?" Alfred asked bleakly.

"Crowland, for one." Ceolwulf swallowed the ham in his mouth. "One of their novices, a boy who is half Mercian, escaped the blaze and made it to Tamworth. The story of Crowland is just one example of what is happening all over East Anglia."

"What happened at Crowland?" Elswyth asked.

Ceolwulf put down his knife. His gray eyes were very somber. He said, "It is an ugly story, my sister." Then, when no one spoke: "From what the boy told us, they had sufficient warning that the Danes were coming. They could see the fires in the towns around them, you see." Alfred and Elswyth nodded their understanding. Ceolwulf began to play with his knife. "Well, the abbot and the monks first buried most of their treasure—the sacred vessels and the gold." Ceolwulf turned the knife over and over in his fingers. "Then the abbot said Mass for all the folk of the monastery. They were still in the church when the Danes burst through the monastery gates. Most of the monks tried to hide, but the pagans hunted them through all the maze of the monastery buildings. Hunted them down and killed them."

There was a pause as Ceolwulf put down his knife and then looked up. His handsome face was very pale. "This boy had remained in the church with the abbot. They were both within the vestry, the abbot still clothed in his sacred vestments, when the hounds out of hell broke into the church and cut the priest down." He looked at his brother-by-marriage. "In his own church, Alfred! Almost before his own altar!"

The flesh around Alfred's mouth and nostrils was lividly pale; the line of his jaw stood out whitely. The only color about his face was the burning gold of his eyes. "Go on," he said to Ceolwulf.

"They killed them all, save this one boy. Then, when they could not find the gold, they were so angered that they piled all the dead bodies up in one heap and set fire to them, together with the church and all the buildings."

"May God damn their souls to hell," Alfred said, through his teeth.

"Why did they spare this one boy?" Elswyth demanded.

Ceolwulf's smiled was crooked. "Because of his beauty. And he *is* a beautiful creature, my dear. All big eyes and delicate bones. Luckily for him."

"Where in the name of God is Edmund?" Alfred still sounded as if he were talking through his teeth. "England cannot afford to lose centers of learning like Crowland!"

"It is not just Crowland," Ceolwulf returned. "From what this boy said, the Danes were going on to Medeshamsted."

"And thence to Bardeney and thence to Ely." Alfred's eyes were slitted and glittering, hawk eyes. "Ceolwulf, *where* is East Anglia's king?"

Ceolwulf could not meet those eyes. He looked at his ale cup. "I do not know." He took a sip. "But he made peace with the Danes when first they landed in East Anglia. Perhaps he can do so again."

"Make peace with them?"

Ceolwulf flinched

"You must be mad," Elswyth said incredulously. "How can one make peace with such as these?"

"Burgred did," Ceolwulf said. "You were there, Alfred—"

"I was there and I thought he was wrong. But the Danes did not burn down half of Mercia before Burgred consented to make peace!"

"Sometimes," said Ceolwulf stubbornly, "it is better to make peace and take what one can get, rather than fight and risk losing all."

"I do not agree," Alfred said. His voice was like ice.

Ceolwulf ran his hand through his light brown hair. "Edmund is still young—" he began.

"Then should he have some fire in his belly." There was fire enough in Alfred's belly, to judge by the fire that blazed in his eyes. "I shall ride with you to Sussex," he told his wife's brother. Then, to Elswyth: "Ceolwulf and I will leave at dawn tomorrow. I'll go now and give orders for the thanes and the horses."

"All right," she said in reply, and managed to keep from begging to be allowed to accompany them. Alfred would be riding hard, and in her present condition she would only hold him up. She watched her husband leave the hall and knew by his leopard's stalk that he was furious. She turned slowly back to her brother. His gray eyes, turning from the door that had closed so firmly behind Alfred, were hurt.

Poor Ceolwulf, Elswyth thought with the familiar mixture of pity and scorn. Ever the peacemaker. Unfortunately, the time for the peacemaker was long since passed.

Ceolwulf looked back at her. "This is not a raiding party, Elswyth," he said. Very quietly. "This is an army of seven thousand men. An army on horseback. An army that does not have to till the fields or keep the swine or cut the timber. An army of pagans, with no Christian scruples or concerns. We cannot stand against them. It is as simple, and as fearful, as that."

Ceolwulf the peacemaker, she thought again. But Ceolwulf was not stupid. Alfred had often said many of the same things. The difference between the two men was that Alfred would seek for a way to negate the Danish advantages, while Ceolwulf would simply give up. But she had a fondness for Ceolwulf, who had always been kind to her. "What does Athulf say?" she asked instead.

He shrugged. "Athulf has the heart of a fighter. But he sees the reality too."

"We should have fought them at Nottingham! We had them there."

"Have you seen their swords?" Ceolwulf asked. "I came by one this winter. They are more efficient weapons than ours, Elswyth. Stronger and easier to wield."

"You must show it to Alfred," Elswyth said immediately. "Perhaps he can have it copied."

"If Alfred thinks he can fight the Danes," Ceolwulf said, "he is wrong."

But Elswyth would never tolerate criticism of Alfred. "You are beaten before ever you have fought," she told her brother contemptuously. "You make me ashamed of my blood. Do all in Mercia feel like you?"

He shrugged, not dismayed by her disdain. "Young Ethelred of Hwicce is like Alfred, all afire for Edmund to fight."

"I hope to God he does," said Elswyth.

"If he does," returned her brother, "I hope you will pray for his soul."

All through the early fall, the Danes ravaged and burned the monasteries of East Anglia. Then the Danish leader, Ivar the Boneless, sent a messenger to the young East Anglian king demanding that Edmund yield to the Danes a considerable part of East Anglia's wealth, and reign henceforth under Ivar's own overlordship.

The demand made clear to all, Edmund included, that this time the Danes would not be bought off. They wanted what they had won in Northumbria, a subject kingdom. From his manor of Hoxne in Suffolk,

Edmund replied to Ivar that as a Christian king he had no such love of this life on earth that he would submit to a pagan lord.

Ivar roared with pleasure when he heard the reply, and set off immediately with his army to meet Edmund at Hoxne. The East Anglian fyrd rallied to its king, and the two forces met and clashed on the fields near the king's royal manor. The East Anglians were crushed and their king, Edmund, was taken prisoner alive.

In November 869 Ivar the Boneless, leader of the Danish Great Army, performed the blood eagle on Edmund, King of the East Angles, the last successor of the Wuffingas of Sutton Hoo. With the martyrdom of their king, all resistance in East Anglia collapsed. For the rest of the autumn and for all of the following year, the Danes remained at Thetford in East Anglia, living on the harvests and farms of the country.

Northumbria was gone. East Anglia was gone. Now there were but two independent Anglo-Saxon states left in England: Mercia and Wessex.

"Which of us will be next?" Ethelred asked Alfred as they gathered for a grim Christmas at Dorchester.

"It will be Wessex," Alfred answered somberly. "Mercia lies too far from the sea to be easy of access, and those parts of Mercia most easily reached, in the north and east near to Nottingham, have been recently plundered. Wessex, on the other hand, has been untouched for years; and we are easily reached from East Anglia by the Icknield Way. We must prepare ourselves, Ethelred. The Danes will come to Wessex next."

"I think you are right," Ethelred said. His kind brown eyes regarded his brother for a long quiet minute. "You were right in Nottingham, as well. We should have fought then, while the advantage was ours."

Alfred's mouth set. "No point in regrets. We had best keep scouts posted on the Icknield Way. We do not want the Danes in our courtyard before we have had a chance to call up the fyrd."

"I shall send to Burgred to see what assistance he can render us."

"Do you want me to go?"

"No." Ethelred gave him a strained smile. "Your child is due to be born shortly. You must stay with Elswyth. I shall send someone else."

Elswyth's child was born in the deep cold of a January afternoon, when the snow lay thinly over the halls and barns and fences of Dorchester, where she and Alfred had remained ever since Christmas. It was a long labor, and a silent one. Alfred alternately prayed and paced the floor of the princes' hall, refusing all the distractions that a kindhearted Ethelred tried to offer. Cyneburg herself was attending Elswyth, and would periodically come out into the hall to reassure the nervous husband that all was going well.

"It is taking so long!" Alfred said to Ethelred for perhaps the hundredth time. "She started with pains during the night. Why is it taking so long?"

"The first child is often long in coming," Ethelred answered, with all the wisdom of a man who was a father five times over. "Cyneburg says Elswyth is in no danger. There is no need to fret yourself so. You will end up with a headache if you continue thus."

"She is so young. Too young. This is all my fault." Alfred continued his prowl, reminding Ethelred of nothing so much as a great golden cat stalking within the confines of a cage.

"Every man feels thus at such a time," Ethelred assured his brother. His brown eyes were very faintly amused. "You will feel differently when you hold your son in your arms."

Alfred did not reply, but continued pacing. A serving man came to add a log to the fire, and Alfred suddenly said, "I am going back to the church."

Ethelred sighed but made no move to stop him.

Outside, the sky was steel gray. It would snow again before nightfall, Alfred thought. He crossed the frozen courtyard and made his way to the church, a walk of some five minutes. It was bitterly cold within the wooden church, but he knelt and prayed until he was so stiff with the cold that he could scarcely rise again to his feet.

Surely all would be well, he thought as he walked down the narrow aisle toward the wooden door. Elswyth was young and healthy. She had made the journey from Wantage to Dorchester with no ill effect. Alfred had wanted to remain at home, but she had insisted on traveling to Dorchester for Christmas and the birth.

"Dorchester has special memories for me," she had said with a faint intimate smile. "I would like to spend Christmas there once again."

Alfred had agreed, principally because he thought Elswyth wanted to have Cyneburg near when her time came due. Elswyth was not on close terms with many women of her own order, but she and Cyneburg had ever seemed to get on well. Alfred, too, had been relieved at the thought of having his brother's wife in attendance when Elswyth gave birth. And he knew he would be glad to have Ethelred. So they had made the arduous winter journey to Dorchester, and now the time had come.

The wind caught the church door as Alfred was trying to close it, and slammed it against the building. He had to push hard to close it against the wind, and as he turned away toward the path that would take him back to the hall, he was struck with a sudden memory: the morning of his father's death. He had been in the church when it happened, he remembered. He had gone back into the hall and . . . Abruptly he began to run.

He was out of breath and his chest hurt from the cold air when he pushed open the hall door violently and almost crashed inside. The atmosphere in the hall was different. He felt it immediately. His heart began to pound so loudly he could hear it in his head. He could not speak.

Then Ethelred was coming toward him. It took a moment before Alfred saw that his brother was smiling. "Felicitations," Ethelred said. "You have a daughter."

At first all Elswyth could feel was gratitude that it was over. She had known childbirth would be painful, but still she had not been prepared for the reality. All she could do was set her teeth and endure in hard silence. When Cyneburg recommended that she scream to ease the strain, she only gritted her teeth even harder and shook her head. There was no privacy, the women were handling her body at will, her pride was in the dust, but she could at least keep silence.

When they told her the child was a girl, all she felt was surprise. She had never once thought it would be a girl. She lay passive with fatigue all the while the women washed her and brushed her hair.

Then Cyneburg put the baby into her arms.

Elswyth had anticipated being fond of this child. Of course she would be fond of Alfred's son. He would have his nurses to take care of him, and when he grew a little older she would play with him for some part of each day. Alfred would like to have a son.

Elswyth looked now for the first time into her daughter's face. It was tiny, amazingly tiny, and the fair skin was mottled red and white. The small head was fuzzy with dark gold hair. The eyes were a very pale blue. The baby moved her lips and began to cry.

"I think she is hungry," Elswyth said to Cyneburg anxiously.

"You will have to nurse her," Cyneburg said. "I'll show you how."

Alfred came in just as Elswyth was finishing nursing the baby. Cyneburg shooed the other women out of the room and then left the new mother and father alone.

"Isn't she wonderful?" Elswyth breathed, her eyes on the small fuzzy head at her breast.

Alfred stared in awe. "She is so small."

"I know." She cradled the baby in the crook of her arm so that Alfred could see his daughter's face. "She has your hair, Alfred. But look at the color of her eyes!"

"They will probably change," said Alfred, the knowledgeable uncle. "Babies' eyes often do."

Silence fell as they both stared with fascination at the small, perfect face of their daughter. She yawned. Her parents exchanged a look of mutual wonder and delight.

Then Elswyth said very softly, "She is tired."

Alfred looked from his daughter to the rapt face of his wife. The women had combed her long hair and it hung now in a sheet of shining ebony over the clean white linen of her fresh undergown. There were dark shadows under her eyes and her cheeks looked hollow. "You should sleep also," he said, and his usually clipped voice was soft with tenderness. "It was a long labor."

"It was horrible," she answered honestly. "But I thought of you, and how you endure." She looked up, her eyes meeting and holding his. "And you don't have the joy of this at the end."

But he was looking angry. "There can be no comparison between my stupid headaches and what you underwent this day!"

"It is so humiliating," she said.

His frown smoothed out. His mouth curved downward wryly. "Yes," he said with resignation. "It is."

The baby smacked her lips in her sleep and they stared at her in speechless admiration. Then Cyneburg was coming back into the room.

"It is time that Elswyth slept," she said to Alfred practically, and bent to take the baby from Elswyth's arms.

"Alfred too," said his wife, looking at his face with knowing eyes.

He did not answer, but bent his head and kissed her on the mouth. Then, under the stern eye of Cyneburg, he reluctantly quitted the room.

II

THE STORM BREAKS
A.D. 871, The Year of Battles

Chapter 16

WHEN Erlend Olafson rode into the Danish camp at Thetford the middle of one cold damp November afternoon in 870, it was plain by the bustle of purposeful activity that something of importance was at hand. Grooms and horses were everywhere, and a train of store wagons was being loaded with extra arrows and food supplies. The boy and his small following of three men had little trouble finding someone to direct them to his uncle Guthrum's quarters. It was slightly more difficult gaining access to his uncle, who was in council with the kings and jarls who comprised the Danish army command in England. Finally Erlend convinced Guthrum's followers to let him wait in his uncle's hut.

The day was chill and there was no fire within the temporary wooden hut that was Guthrum's. Erlend looked around the bleak bare room and struggled to keep his courage high. Suddenly this journey of his from Denmark to England seemed a mad undertaking. Suddenly he wished he were safe at home in Jutland. What troll had prompted him to cross the sea on such a wild venture as this?

Erlend answered his own question immediately. The troll's name was Asmund, his mother's second husband, and it was because of Asmund that Jutland was no longer safe for Erlend. To the contrary, it had become chillingly clear these last months that Asmund had decided that the neatest way to take for himself Erlend's father's estate of Nasgaard would be to ensure that Erlend himself was no longer alive to claim it.

The cramp of horror in Erlend's stomach had never quite left him since the day he first understood what was afoot at Nasgaard, the day he had first realized what all those strange accidents befalling him must mean.

He had gone immediately to his mother. Even now he could not bear to remember the look that had crossed her face when he had told her. He would not believe that she had aught to do with Asmund's schemes, but she would not intervene. He had seen that clear enough in the quick flash of her green eyes before they had lowered to her lap. Asmund was her husband now, the father of the child she carried, and she would not step between him and the son of a former marriage.

143

Nor was there anyplace in Denmark outside of Nasgaard where he could turn for justice. There was no high king in Denmark these days, not since Horik had been killed in the invasion led nearly twenty years since by Erlend's own grandfather. Since Horik's demise, the petty kings had done as they would; there was no longer any strong central power to redress the wrongs done by the overgreedy. It was a wolves' den in truth in Denmark these days, with every man reaching for what he could get. Those who could not prosper in Denmark must seek their fortunes elsewhere.

Erlend's father's brother Guthrum had sought his fortune with the sons of Ragnar Lothbrok in England. When Erlend had begun to seek in his mind for someone who would help him in his feud with Asmund, his thoughts had turned to Guthrum. Erlend had no recollection of ever meeting this uncle, who had been ten years younger than Erlend's father; but surely, he thought, surely Guthrum would not wish to see one of the greatest estates in Jutland stolen away from his kindred.

Bjorn had agreed with him. Bjorn had been husband to Ragnfrid, the foster mother who had nursed Erlend and whom he had ever loved more than his own mother, Eline. Bjorn had no power, but Erlend trusted him, and when Bjorn advised him to get away, Erlend had not hesitated.

So here he sat in this strange room in this strange land waiting for this strange kinsman to decide his fate. If Guthrum should turn him away . . . But he did not think Guthrum would do that. Erlend represented Nasgaard, and Nasgaard was too rich a prize for any man, particularly a Viking like his uncle, to turn his back upon.

After nearly an hour he heard the sound of a new voice outside the planked wooden walls of his uncle's booth, and then the door was pushed open and a man was coming into the small cold room. Erlend stood, his hands hanging empty by his sides, his whole thin, adolescent's body tensed and quivering, like a hound that has sighted a wolf. The man stopped by the oil lamp that burned beside the straw-filled platform bed that was the room's only furniture. His shoulders were so wide they blocked half the room from Erlend's view. Dimly Erlend remembered that his father had had shoulders like that. "So," Guthrum said in a deep bell-like voice, "you are Olaf's son."

"Yes, my lord." Erlend's own voice, so clear and true when he sang to his harp, betrayed him now with a quiver. He flushed with embarrassment and pretended to clear his throat.

"And what are you doing in England, Nephew?" Guthrum asked. "The heir to Nasgaard has no need to go a-viking to increase his wealth."

"My mother has remarried," Erlend replied, willing his flexible voice to remain expressionless. "There is little love betwixt my stepfather and me, and I deemed it wisest for my health to put some distance betwixt us as well." Then, chin up, eyes level on the huge blond giant standing before him: "Asmund has an eye to my father's lands, my lord. He has an eye to my life as well. That is why I am here."

Silence fell as the two in the booth regarded each other with measuring eyes. Erlend thought that his uncle was one of the most splendid-looking men he had ever beheld. Guthrum's hair was the pale yellow color so often seen in Denmark, but he wore it cut shorter than Erlend was accustomed to seeing. It was a style that he had noticed among other men in the Thetford camp as he rode in, cut short to hang level with the earlobes, with a long straight fringe of bangs cut off just above the eyebrows.

It was something else, though, that caught the attention when one looked at Guthrum, something besides the obvious good looks. There was an air of suppressed violence about the man, Erlend thought. It was there in the glittering blue of the eyes, in the thin yet sensual line of the mouth under the short mustache.

Guthrum must be wondering where Olaf had got him from, Erlend thought with a distinct twinge of bitterness. For Erlend was small for his age, and thin, and his hair was brown and his eyes green. Looking at his uncle, Erlend thought that Guthrum would have been able to handle Asmund easily should their situations have been reversed. A man like Guthrum would not have had to come crying for help to an unknown kinsman.

Guthrum spoke at last. "How old are you?" he asked Erlend.

"Sixteen, my lord."

"You look younger."

"I know." Bitterly.

There was another short silence. Then: "There was no one else to whom you could turn for help? Nasgaard is yours from your father; it cannot be given through your mother."

"There is no one in Denmark these days who cares for aught that is not his," Erlend replied, his voice even more bitter than before.

"By the Raven, but things have come to a pretty pass!" Guthrum moved again, gestured Erlend to a skin on the floor by the wall, and dropped to sit cross-legged himself on another skin. For such a big man he was very supple. "Well, brother's son," Guthrum said, "perhaps you have done the right thing in coming to me. England looks to offer more these days to men of enterprise than aught in Denmark can." He raised a thick blond eyebrow. "You are small, but if you are your father's son, you can use your weapons."

"Of course," Erlend said. He frowned. "But what of Nasgaard?"

"I have no intention of resigning Nasgaard to the tender care of this new husband of Eline's," Guthrum replied. He bared his teeth at Erlend. "You are your father's only son; I am his only brother. If aught should happen to you it is not this Asmund who should inherit Nasgaard, but me. And I promise you, Nephew, I do not let anyone take what is mine."

The relief Erlend felt was mixed with a trace of wariness. That was a wolf smile his uncle had given him for sure. "I am glad to hear that, Uncle," he said cautiously.

"But Nasgaard can wait for now," Guthrum said. "It will still be there when I want to put my hand on it. For now, England looks to be better game."

Erlend wrapped his arms around his knees. "How is that?" he asked.

"Already we have taken the kingdoms of Northumbria and East Anglia," Guthrum told him. "Mercia has paid us a great fine in geld to leave it alone. You see the preparations; we march within the week for Wessex. It should not be long until the whole of this island, its lands and its riches, lies securely under our rule."

Erlend could feel his eyes stretching wide. "Is it so?" He had had no idea that the Danes in England were so successful.

Guthrum nodded and regarded him out of speculative eyes.

"Ivar the Boneless has led you well," Erlend said.

Guthrum shrugged. "Ivar the Boneless is no longer with us. He went this winter to take over the rule in Dublin. Halfdan is our sole leader now." Guthrum's eyes flickered. "Halfdan and I have ever seen eye to eye," he said.

Erlend considered this news. Ivar the Boneless was a legend in his own time even among his own people. It surprised Erlend that such a man would leave so seemingly successful an army, and he said so now to Guthrum.

"Dublin holds sway over the whole of Danish Ireland as well as over all the shipping on the Irish Sea, Nephew," came the somewhat scornful answer. "The ruler of Dublin holds a position of great power."

"Ivar the Boneless," Erlend said, pronouncing the name with genuine awe. "I have never seen him, Uncle. Is it true he was born with only gristle in his body?"

"I do not know what is inside him," Guthrum answered, "but truly I have never seen a man so flexible." His sensual upper lip lifted a little in disgust. "It is not pleasing to look upon." The blue eyes studied Erlend's face. "You came alone?" he asked.

"I came with Thorkel, the son of Bjorn, my foster father, and with his two cousins, my lord." Erlend's green eyes burned. "I had no power at Nasgaard," he said. "All the rest of my father's men cleaved to Asmund."

The fair eyebrows disappeared for a minute under the thick yellow bangs. Then: "I cannot let go this enterprise in England to jump to your command, Nephew. But once I have finished here, and have won my own land, then I will see what we can do with this usurper in Jutland. I recommend that you bide with me until then. Who knows? You too may increase your holdings by the worth of your sword."

There was the faintest suggestion of amusement in the deep bell-like voice. Erlend's hand suddenly itched to smash across his uncle's handsome, violent face. Instead he said softly, "I thank you, my lord, for the invitation. I will stay." Then, as Guthrum rose to his feet: "Will there be a battle soon, Uncle?"

Guthrum shrugged. "Who is to say? These Saxons are marvelous quick to spend their geld before ever they spend their lives. And the West Saxon king was at Nottingham when the Mercians chose to decline a fight. But if they do not fight, they will pay. Either way, brother's son, we are the winners." He looked Erlend up and down once more. "Fetch your belongings, Nephew, and set them down in here. On the morrow you can show me just how well you handle sword and ax."

"Yes, my lord," Erlend said, and went to do as he was bid.

The royal household was holding Christmas at Dorchester when word arrived that the Viking army had come down the Ridgeway from East Anglia into Wessex and encamped at Reading. First, Ethelred sent a rider to order the Ealdorman of Berkshire to call up the Berkshire fyrd immediately; second, he sent a messenger to Burgred of Mercia. Next Ethelred set about gathering the remainder of the West Saxon fyrds into one great army. The machinery for such a swift summoning had been put into place by Alfred during the previous year, so all concerned knew what must be done. It took but four days for the combined fyrds of all Wessex to arm and gather at Winchester.

Elswyth accompanied Alfred to Winchester even though she was but six weeks away from giving birth. She rode in a litter and he did not try to dissuade her from coming, knowing she was perfectly capable of following him on horseback the minute his back was turned.

One of the greatest tests her courage had ever faced was to send him off to Reading alone.

"I wish I could go too!" she said to him fiercely when finally they were alone together the night before the army was to march. "It is wretched being a woman and having to stay at home!"

"I wouldn't like it at all if you were a man," he replied teasingly. He flicked a finger against her thin cheek. "For I would love you still, no matter what your sex, and think how strange that would make me."

They were in their sleeping room in the secondary hall at Winchester. Their daughter, Ethelflaed, whom they called Flavia, was asleep with her nurse in the room next door. The hall outside was packed with thanes sleeping two to a bench. All the halls and houses of Winchester were filled to overflowing tonight, and men were camped all along the city wall and on the outlying fields as well. On the morrow, five thousand West Saxons would march forth from Winchester to confront the Danes at Reading.

She did not want Alfred to go. Everything in her was crying out to him to stay behind, to stay with her. There would be a battle. He could be hurt or maimed . . . he could be killed . . . She could not bear it, she thought. She could not bear it.

"Elswyth?" Alfred said. He had put his shirt on the clothes chest and was coming toward her. She drew a long breath and forced herself to look at him. His eyes had darkened; they looked almost brown in the light from the oil lamp. He came to sit beside her on the bed and drew her into the circle of his arm. She sat perfectly still, listening to the steady beat of his heart beneath the smooth bare skin pressed against her cheek. "You will be all right?" she heard him ask softly.

She heard the fear he was trying to conceal. Oh, God, she thought, I cannot let him go forth like this! Somehow, somewhere, she must find the courage to free him from the fetters of his love for her. Of his fear for her.

Blessed Mary, she prayed. You stood by and watched while they cruci-fied your son. Help me now. Give me the courage that I need.

Alfred was not afraid to die. His faith in God was too strong for him to fear death for himself. It was for her that he feared, for her, who would be left behind without him.

"I shall be all right," she answered. Miraculously her voice was strong, steady. "I have our children to see to. Do not fear for me, Alfred. You do what you must do, and I shall do the same."

He loosened his arm so he could look down into her face. She made herself look back at him steadily, fearlessly. He cupped her chin in his hand. "I love you more than anything in the world," he said. His eyes were growing golden again.

It took all the willpower she possessed to keep her face calm, to keep from clinging to him, from pleading with him to come safely back to her. "I will wager you anything you like that Cyneburg is weeping all over Ethelred," she said. She even managed to curl her lip. "I am made of stronger stuff."

The agony was worth it, for he smiled. A genuine smile, delighted and tender and relieved all at once. "So you are," he said. Then: "Elswyth . . ."

No one ever said her name as he said it, short and clipped, with more an emphasis on the closing consonants than on the opening vowel. She had never liked her name until she heard Alfred say it.

She cursed the heavy, clumsy body that stood between them. He bent his head and kissed her, then held her against him so that his body was a shelter for hers. She pressed her face against his bare shoulder. His skin was so warm under her cheek. So warm. So smooth. So alive. His hands were hard and callused on the tips, but so gentle as they held her, so strong with life. She ran her own hand, flat-palmed, up and down his back, feeling the muscles under the smooth warm flesh. He was so perfect. She could not bear to think of him injured or hurt. It was anguish to have him here like this and know that in a few days he could be dead.

I cannot bear it, she thought. She felt his lips on her hair, turned her face into his shoulder once more, and knew that she would have to.

*   *   *

The Danes made their camp east of the royal manor of Reading, in a place where the junction of the rivers Kennet and Thames gave them good protection on three sides. It was a matter of hours to throw up an embankment on the fourth, exposed side of their position. Once the bank was up, it was time to look around the country for food and for plunder.

"Sidroc is leading a raiding party down the river tomorrow," Guthrum said to his nephew on the evening of December 29. "Would you like to be of its number?"

Erlend regarded his uncle from beneath half-lowered lashes. Guthrum's face was perfectly bland. "Yes, of course," Erlend answered. There was no other answer he could make, and both knew it. "And you, Uncle?"

Guthrum shook his head. "This is Sidroc's party. But you are anxious to blood your sword, I know, so I asked him if he would include you among his men."

"That was thoughtful of you," Erlend answered, and if there was irony in his reply it did not color his voice. He was well aware that Guthrum would shed no tears if aught should befall him on the field of battle. Then would Guthrum have the unquestioned claim to Nasgaard. But he did not suspect his uncle of actively plotting his death. In that, Guthrum would be more honorable than Asmund. Or so Erlend hoped. And in truth, Erlend was not an ill hand with weaponry. Despite his size, he could hold his own against much larger men. He would go with Sidroc without complaint.

The night before they were to set out from Reading, a sleeting rain fell, and the early-morning frost froze it on the ground. Consequently the footing was slippery when the Danes set out to follow the Kennet west in search of food, fodder, and whatever else they might carry off from the rich Berkshire countryside. Erlend's horse was full of energy and Erlend fought to keep him to a steady walk; too fast a pace, and both horse and rider would be down on the ice.

The raiding party's breaths were white in the chill air. Like the others, Erlend wore his leather tunic but not his mail byrnie. They did not expect to meet with armed resistance. It would take weeks for the West Saxons to organize, if indeed they meant to offer resistance at all. Guthrum seemed to think they would be more likely to offer geld.

At the first farmstead they came upon they took five sacks of barley, a wagonload of baled hay, three cows, and a horse. The house was deserted and some of the men wanted to search the woods for the inhabitants, but Sidroc called them off. "Women come last," he said. "First come supplies."

They went along the river for a few miles, then cut north and west, where the richer farms seemed to lie. Erlend was given the job of herding the cattle, and by the time they reached the small market village called Englefield, he was heartily sick of the raid and wishing they were back in Reading again. He had never liked cattle.

Suddenly, out of the trees surrounding the market common where the Danes had halted to rest, there began to rain a deadly shower of arrows. Chaos reigned in the Danish camp as men sought for weapons and cover. Erlend could hear Sidroc's deep bellow as he grabbed for his shield, sword, and ax. The arrows came again; then men were pouring out of the woods. Before the Danes could do more than clutch their weapons, the West Saxons were upon them.

The ground was still icy and Erlend fought to keep his balance as he hacked with his ax at bareheaded men amidst the plunder wagons, horses, and bellowing cattle. The confusion was terrible. Then the cry came, "More men are coming!" All around Erlend men began to break away and run. It took Erlend a minute to realize that it was the Danes who were running. A tall oxlike West Saxon was coming at him with sword upraised. Erlend ducked under a wagon loaded with barrels of honey and took to his heels. He was lucky enough to catch a horse at the edge of the field; most of Sidroc's raiding party had to run all the way back to Reading.

Word came of Ealdorman Ethelwulf's victory at Englefield while Ethelred and Alfred were at Mass the morning the West Saxon army was set to leave Winchester. The news flamed through the ranks of armed men. The Danes were not invincible!

"This could not have fallen out better," Alfred said to Ethelred as they stood side by side on the steps of the minster. "Such news will put heart into our men."

"Yes," Ethelred agreed. He added cautiously, "But remember, Alfred, it was only a raiding party Ethelwulf attacked."

"And Ethelwulf had only the Berkshire fyrd," Alfred retorted immediately. He grinned. "Don't be so cautious, Ethelred. This is wonderful news!"

Ethelred's returning smile was not nearly so carefree. "I know, I know." Then, with a sigh: "Well, I suppose it is time to be off. The men seem ready."

"The men are ready and so are we." The king's and Alfred's horses were being brought up by Ethelred's horse thane. Alfred swung into the saddle with his distinctive lithe grace, took up his reins, and waited while Ethelred mounted more slowly. Then the brothers moved forward to join the mounted ealdormen at the head of the vast army of foot soldiers. By ten in the morning the West Saxons were on the road that led to Reading.

It took the slow-moving supply wagons two days to reach the old Roman town of Silchester. The army encamped behind the crumbling walls, and Alfred said to Ethelred, "I think we should try a surprise attack."

Ethelred did not answer.

"They cannot know that we are here," Alfred continued persuasively.

"Considering how long it took Burgred and Edmund to gather their forces, the Danes must think they have weeks before we will come up on them. Surprise is to our advantage, Ethelred."

"I am not sure," Ethelred said slowly. "By all accounts, they have fortified Reading very well."

"They fortified Nottingham very well also. The Danes will always choose a site that is easily fortified. We are fooling ourselves if we think they will give us the advantage in that respect."

Ethelred began to pluck at his eyebrow. "That is true, I suppose. Still, Alfred . . . I am not sure that we should be the ones to make the first move. Perhaps we ought to wait, see what they are going to do . . ."

Alfred strove to contain his impatience. He said calmly and reasonably, "Ealdorman Ethelwulf made the first move, and see what happened."

"Ealdorman Ethelwulf was not attacking the whole of the Danish army!"

Alfred's face wore an uncharacteristically hard expression. Quite suddenly he looked ten years older. He said, "Ethelred, we must act whilst we have the fyrd out in force. Otherwise the same thing will happen that happened in Mercia. The men will begin to go back to their farms. If we wait until that happens, if we wait for the Danes to move first, then we are lost."

Ethelred looked for a long moment into the face of his brother. Then he said, "Perhaps you are right, Alfred. For certain, we should have listened to you at Nottingham." He dropped his hand from his eyebrow. "All right," he said with decision. "We will try a surprise attack upon Reading."

"Tomorrow?"

"Tomorrow." Ethelred quirked his much-abused eyebrow. "Why wait?"

Alfred laughed and once more looked his age. He got to his feet and asked, "Shall I pass the word to the ealdormen?"

"Yes," said Ethelred quietly. "Do so."

Reading was surrounded by rivers, the Kennet to its southwest, the Thames to its north, and the Loddon to its east. On its southeastern exposure the Danes had built earthworks to protect their camp. The West Saxons came from the south, up the Roman road, along the Kennet as it wound into Reading, right to the base of the earthworks. The surprise was absolute. They fell on all the Danes who were outside the walls and slaughtered them.

Erlend was within the camp when the cries went up from without the walls. He had been playing his harp for his uncle, who had evinced surprising interest both in Erlend's skill and in the large number of Saxon poems that Erlend knew.

"Name of the Raven!" swore Guthrum, his blue eyes glittering in the cold January sun. The noise from without the walls was bloodcurdling. "The bastards are attacking!"

Within the camp all the men were running for armor and for weapons. Erlend kept beside his uncle as Guthrum mustered his men. "Fall on them like wolves!" Guthrum shouted. And, with his glittering eyes and his white teeth bared in the sunlight, he did indeed look like the wolf he invoked. Guthrum slammed his helmet down over his short hair, lifted his sword and his battleax, and made for the ramparts. His men followed, each taking his accustomed place in the fighting wedge favored by Viking warriors.

The Viking army was extremely well-trained. That was something Erlend had noted and admired in the weeks since he had joined his uncle. Guthrum's men had been with him for years, as had the men of most of the other kings and jarls. Most had been ships crews originally, with muscles hardened by rowing and comradeship strengthened by facing together the storms of the North Sea. There was no social distinction made in the crews of the long ships. All were warriors. And here on land, the strength, the discipline, the comradeship they had learned on the sea made them superior soldiers, brave and skilled and loyal to their leader. There was not a man among the Danes who went over the wall on this cold clear January day who did not think they would drive this upstart West Saxon army to its knees.

And indeed the Danes were a fearful sight as they swarmed out of Reading to fall upon the West Saxons. The sun shone upon the metal of their helmets and on the gold or silver bracelets that encircled their arms and their wrists. It shone on their swords and their battleaxes and their polished byrnies. It brought out the brilliant colors in their shields, in their pennants, and in the grim banner of the Raven that floated over Halfdan, their battle leader. Their battle cries were bloodcurdling and for a moment the West Saxons swayed and began to fall back.

Then there came a shout, a cry of "*Wessex! Wessex!*" and the fyrds were pressing forward again. For nearly an hour the battle raged at the gates of Reading. But the West Saxons, busily engaged in front, did not realize that Halfdan had sent a party of men under the jarl Harald to slip around to their rear and cut off their retreat to the south. It was not until the cry went up from the rear, rolling like thunder over the ranks of hard-fighting men, "*We are trapped! We are trapped!*" that Ethelred and Alfred realized what had happened.

Guthrum turned to Erlend with a wolfish grin. "Harald has cut off their escape. They are hemmed in by the rivers now. We have them."

"God Almighty, Alfred," Ethelred cried to his brother. "What shall we do? They have us trapped!"

"Fight on!" Alfred answered. But even as he spoke, he could see that panic was beginning to spread among the fyrds. In a very short time the men would break and run. And once they did that, they would be cut down without mercy.

God. Alfred forced his brain to function. He knew Reading, knew these rivers. He stood for a moment, safe within the midst of a circle Ethelred's companion thanes, and said to his brother, "There is a ford over the Loddon at Twyford. We must fall back on Wiscelet."

"All right," Ethelred turned to his thanes with the command and soon word began to pass to all the ealdormen.

Fall back on Wiscelet. Hold together and fall back on Wiscelet. We shall cross the Loddon at Twyford.

The army rallied to the call of its leaders. Holding together under their ealdormen, the thanes and ceorls and townsfolk who comprised the West Saxon fyrds began an orderly fighting retreat to the west. An hour later they thoroughly surprised their pursuers by fording the Loddon where the Danes did not think it could be forded. The Danes hesitated, chose not to follow, and the West Saxons were free in the world.

Chapter 17

*T*HE West Saxons went north and west, toward the Ridgeway and the Downs; in winter it was essential to keep to a traversible roadway, and the Ridgeway was an all-weather track. As soon as they were safe away from Reading, Ethelred sent a rider galloping to Mercia to request that Burgred bring the Mercian fyrd to the immediate aid of Wessex. Ethelred fixed the meeting point at Lowbury Hill, the highest point on the eastern part of Ashdown, the name given by the West Saxons to this eastern line of the Berkshire Downs. Lowbury was a well-known spot, marked by its height and by an ancient earthwork from the days of the Old Ones. The Mercians should be able to find it with little trouble.

The weather held cold but clear as the West Saxon army made its way through the deserted countryside. They had sustained hard losses and been driven from the field, but even so, their spirits were high. They had fought well and their leaders had extricated them deftly from what could have been a fatal situation. They had hurt the Danes, that was sure. The very fact that the enemy had not pursued them once they crossed the river was an indication of how badly the northmen had been hurt.

Alfred's thoughts reflected those of his army. They had come so close! If it had not been for their inexperience in letting the Danes get behind them . . .

Among the list of the West Saxon fallen was Ethelwulf, the Ealdorman of Berkshire who had won the field for them so bravely at Englefield. "A courageous leader," Ethelred said when learning the news from one of the ealdorman's hearthband thanes. "A bitter loss."

Most of the Saxon dead had been left behind before the walls of Reading, but Ethelwulf's thanes had brought the ealdorman's body across the river with them. One of the first things the army did when it reached Lowbury Hill on January 5 was bury Ethelwulf decently, with prayers said by the king's own household priest.

The West Saxons made camp right on the Ridgeway half a mile to the southwest of Lowbury Hill and prepared to wait for Burgred and his Mercians. Alfred also sent to his nearby manors of Wantage and Lambourn for reinforcements. Free or unfree, went the order, all able-bodied men who could carry a spear were to report to the army camp on Ashdown. By nightfall of January 7 there were several hundred more West Saxons in Ethelred's camp.

The guard stationed on Lowbury Hill by day and night kept the watch toward the north, the direction from which the Mercians would come. The short winter day waned toward dusk. The West Saxons repaired their weapons and fed their bellies and waited. Finally, as the light was dimming fast, there came the sound they had all been listening for: galloping hooves from Lowbury Hill. The king and Alfred were on their feet when the scout came thundering into camp.

"My lord! My lord!" The thane was one of Ethelred's, young and chosen for his unusually sharp eyes. He was out of breath. It was not gladness that rang in his voice, however, but fear. "Coming up the Ridgeway, my lord! From Reading! It is not the Mercians I see. It is the Danes!"

The West Saxon attack upon Reading had completely surprised the Danes. "They actually attacked," said Guthrum to Erlend in astonishment as they prepared for sleep in Guthrum's booth on the night of January 4. Guthrum's teeth gleamed whitely in the light of the oil lamp. "Wonderful. It seems there is one English kingdom after all with stomach enough to fight us."

"Did not East Anglia fight?" Erlend asked. Since coming to England he had done his best to acquaint himself with the course of the Danish army's campaign.

"Not until we left them no choice." His uncle's voice was full of contempt. "Nor could they keep the field against us for above fifteen minutes."

"These West Saxons seem strong enough," Erlend ventured. Having been both at Englefield and at Reading, he felt he had the experience to make a judgment.

"They let themselves be outflanked today. If it had not been for that ford . . ."

Prudently Erlend kept silent. The Danish leaders were not pleased with the escape of the West Saxons across the Loddon. Halfdan's curses had been heard round the camp when he learned what had happened.

"They are a pack of farmers only," said Guthrum. He leaned to blow out the lamp. "In the open, in fair battle, they could no more stand against us than did the East Anglians."

Silence fell. Erlend heard Guthrum turn over in the straw of his bed, preparing to sleep. "Uncle?" he asked very softly. "Will we seek a battle, then?"

"Perhaps." Guthrum sounded sleepy. "The war council will meet tomorrow." Then: "Go to sleep, Nephew."

Erlend lay down on his own straw. He was wide-awake. He had killed a man this day. The first man he had ever killed. He had felt surprise when he saw the man go down. It had been a strange feeling, not at all the wild triumph he had thought he would feel. Then another sword had hacked at his mail-protected shoulder, and he had forgotten the man on the ground at his feet.

From the other camp bed came the sound of Guthrum snoring. Erlend closed his eyes and the battle raged before him once again. He opened his eyes and stared into the dark. Slowly, carefully, he stretched and flexed his legs, his arms, his shoulders, his back. He was alive. Guthrum snored louder. Suddenly Erlend felt weary. He closed his eyes and this time saw only the dark. He pulled his cloak over his shoulders and then he too fell asleep.

The Danish leaders—Halfdan, his fellow-king, Bagsac, and the jarls—met in council the following day and decided to march forth from Reading to seek battle with the West Saxons.

"One battle won us Northumbria and one battle won us East Anglia," Halfdan said to his war council. "My aim is to add Wessex to our holdings. I see no reason why we should not triumph again. And if we are to move, it would be well to move quickly, before the Mercians have a chance to come to the aid of the West Saxons."

There was not a single dissenting voice. Scouts were sent out to determine the West Saxon position, and on the morning of January 7, another bright clear cold winter day, the Danish army issued out of Reading in full battle array and marched up the Ridgeway toward Lowbury Hill, where the West Saxon army was camped.

The West Saxon surprise was as great at the Danes' had been when the fyrds attacked Reading. Neither the king nor his councillors had expected the Danes to leave their base camp, and the whole end of the Ridgeway toward Reading had been left open and unprotected. Most devastating of all, the West Saxons had left the ridge just to the southeast of their camp unmanned. Halfdan camped in a slight hollow behind it and immediately posted scouts on the unprotected ridge, but one thousand feet from the West Saxon camp on the Ridgeway below.

Alfred swore bitterly when he realized what had happened. The Danes had always been so reluctant to leave their base camps! He had never dreamed they would come out into the open like this.

"We should have occupied that ridge," he said to Ethelred. "It is inexcusable of me to have neglected it."

"Too late to bemoan our mistake now," Ethelred said. His face was drawn and grim. "We must decide immediately whether to fight on our own or try to escape in the night. If we stay, we will be facing battle tomorrow."

The two brothers were alone for a moment, awaiting the arrival of the ealdormen who had been called for a war council. Ethelred's eyes were steady on his brother's face. Ethelred wanted the two of them to decide now, Alfred realized, before the ealdormen arrived. He forced himself to push aside his fury at his own stupidity and concentrate on the problem at hand. A battle, he thought. Tomorrow. Without the Mercians.

"The men are in high heart, Ethelred," he said slowly. "Even if the Mercians do not come in time, I think we will be all right. Worse to run. That would surely knock the heart from the fyrds. Twice now they have fought the Danes and held their own. They have confidence. They will fight well if we fight tomorrow."

"I think you are right. And God knows when we shall have such an army collected again." Ethelred's brown eyes were clear as he looked at his younger brother. "Alfred," he said, and stopped. Then, very carefully, still with those clear steady eyes: "Should anything befall me on the morrow, it is you who must take the kingship."

Alfred's head jerked up. His face went very pale and his eyes widened and darkened. He did not answer. "I love my sons," Ethelred went on, still in that same careful voice. "But they are still boys. Wessex needs a king who is a man." He paused. Then, again: "It must be you."

Alfred's throat moved as if he were trying to talk but could not. He wanted to protest, to tell Ethelred not to speak so, but his voice stuck in his throat. His heart was rejecting utterly what his brain knew to be true: Ethelred was mortal. Finally, after a struggle that Ethelred could clearly see, Alfred gave up trying to answer and nodded.

Ethelred put a hand on his brother's shoulder. Alfred covered it with his own. Then, as if the touch had released his voice, he said urgently, "Whatever happens, Ethelred, do not let yourself be taken alive!"

His brother smiled. Wryly. "I will remember that." He looked over Alfred's shoulder. "Here come the ealdormen."

It was full dark when a single horseman, coming from the north, rode into the West Saxon camp and asked for the king. Alfred knew as soon as he saw the face of Ethelred of Hwicce that the news was not good.

"The Welsh have risen," the young Mercian ealdorman said to the king and his brother. "Burgred and the rest of our ealdormen are fighting on our western border. They cannot come to the aid of Wessex."

Ethelred and Alfred exchanged a grim look. They had resigned themselves to the fact that Burgred would not arrive before the morrow's battle, but they had yet been counting on future assistance from the Mercians. Alfred thought of the thousands of West Saxons who had marched to Nottingham, and shut his mouth hard.

Ethelred said to his Mercian namesake, "Thank you for bringing us this word, my lord ealdorman. "You look to have had a hard ride. Come and take some food."

Alfred looked at his brother's quiet, dignified face and felt a fierce surge of love and pride.

"I have brought you my sword as well," the redheaded Mercian answered. From the expression on his face it was clear Ethelred of Hwicce felt bitterly humiliated by the news he had been forced to carry. "If you will accept it, of course," he added stiffly.

"We will gladly accept your sword, my lord," Ethelred the king replied with his gentle courtesy. "And your valorous heart as well. The fight will be on the morrow. Those are Danes you see on yonder hill."

"Tomorrow?" said Ethelred, startled. Then, with heartfelt fervor: "Thank God!"

At that Alfred grinned. "It has been a long wait since Nottingham, my friend."

"That it has." Young Ethelred blazed a returning grin and ran a dirty hand through his hair. "If you will just show me where I can get some food, my lord . . ."

Alfred walked around the camp till quite late, talking with thanes he knew, exchanging a jest with a man here, an encouraging word with one there. The temper of the army was confident. Far from being discouraged by being driven from the field at Reading, the men seemed to be looking forward to this next encounter. This time, they told their prince, there would be no rivers with which to trap them!

When Alfred finally returned to his own tent, he was content. The ground was frozen with the cold and the sky was a great bowl of stars overhead. The weather looked to play no part in the morrow's encounter. The numbers of the armies were close to even. The victory would fall to whichever army fought the harder.

Please God that army would be the West Saxons'!

The Danes were stirring as soon as the first light began to streak the sky. The West Saxons ate their bread and cheese and watched the enemy slowly marshaling their troops into battle lines on the ridge above them. The leaders of Wessex—the king, the king's brother, Alfred, the ealdormen, the king's companion thanes, and the lone Mercian nobleman who had come to their assistance—met before the king's leather tent in council of war.

"They are forming into two columns," said Osric, Ealdorman of Hampshire. All the men in the group turned to look once more to the ridge. The hill was divided by the Ridgeway, and on one side of the ancient track was a column flying the Raven banner of the leaders, the kings Halfdan and

Bagsac. The other column was mustering under a variety of individual pennants.

"Those pennants on the left belong to the different jarls," Ethelnoth of Somerset said.

"So," said Ethelred, "king's men on the right, jarls' men on the left."

The men of his council grunted in agreement.

"We shall form up in two columns also," Ethelred said. "I shall lead the column opposing Halfdan, Alfred shall lead the column opposing the jarls."

A startled silence fell and the ealdormen looked at each other. Ethelnoth of Somerset, who had fought at Aclea with Ethelbald and been his friend, said, "My lord, the prince is brave as a lion, no doubt about that. But he is twenty-one years of age. Full young for such a responsibility. Give the left to me, or to another of us older men who has more battle experience."

Alfred said nothing, but his face was taut and his eyes were narrowed and blazing.

"No," said Ethelred. "Alfred will take the left. And, my lords, should aught happen to me on the field of battle today, Alfred has my name for the succession."

This command of the king drew no opposition. There was not a man present who wished to see a child at the helm of Wessex today. "Very well," said Ethelred quietly. "Let us arm ourselves for battle and pray to our Lord and all his saints for victory."

Alfred was very silent as he donned his battle dress. Brand, who was assisting the prince, looked at the familiar face and did not after all say the words that had been on the tip of his tongue. Alfred's mind was not on Brand. The thane lifted the prince's mail byrnie to slip on over the leather tunic that Alfred already wore. As the mail coat settled into place, Brand lifted the prince's swordbelt. Alfred looked from the belt to the man who held it, and for the first time his intense preoccupation lifted. The golden eyes registered his thane's face. "God be with you this day, my lord," Brand said fervently.

"And with you." The familiar clipped voice was just the same as always. Brand smiled and after a minute Alfred clapped his thane on the shoulder. "We shall beat them, my friend." He grinned. "I know it."

Suddenly Brand knew it too. His greenish eyes glowed. "Yes, my lord!"

Alfred rammed his sword into his belt and put his sax dagger through the swordbelt on the other side. His hair was bound by his distinctive green headband. The West Saxons still fought unhelmeted. "Arm yourself, Brand," he said crisply, "and follow me."

Brand moved hastily so as not to be far behind.

By the time the full light of morning was blazing in the sky, the two armies had taken up their positions. The Danes had the higher ground, on the ridge to the east of the Ridgeway. Ethelred had moved his own men to a slight rise that rose behind his camp to the southwest of the Ridgeway. The pure cold January sun shone brilliantly, the two armies faced each other with but a thousand yards separating them, and the ritual shouting of abuse that presaged every battle began. Swords banged on shields. The noise from the Danish ranks was tremendous, and as they stood waiting in the bright sun, tension began to rise in the West Saxon lines. In the war council, the leaders had determined to take the offensive. Only so could they hope to negate the Dane's advantage of holding the hill, to break the force of their charge. Yet here they stood in the cold sunlight, waiting.

Alfred stood under his own personal banner of the White Horse and looked to the other wing, for his brother. The Golden Dragon of Wessex flew, but the king was not in place beneath it.

"Where is the king?" he asked Osric, the Hampshire ealdorman, who was fighting under his command.

The ealdorman's face was grim. "Hearing Mass in his tent," he replied.

Alfred looked toward the king's tent, pitched now to the rear of the lines. His response was involuntary. "Surely not now?"

"Yes, my lord," came the stoic response. "Now."

On the opposite hill the masses of men were beginning to move. Then horns blew and an even louder shout went up from the Danish ranks. They raised their brightly colored shields and began to advance slowly down the hill. They blanketed the hillside and the noise they made was absolutely petrifying.

"Brand!"

"Yes, my lord?" The thane was at Alfred's side instantly.

"Run to the king and tell him the Danes are advancing. We must attack now!"

Brand was gone almost before Alfred had finished speaking.

The Danes still held their charge, but their battle horns were blowing. The West Saxon fyrds were becoming restive. Alfred could see the men looking at him, then looking toward the king's banner.

God in heaven, he thought. *Ethelred must attack now!*

Brand was beside him again, his breath heaving he had run so hard. "My lord, the king says that he will not leave the altar until the priest has ended the holy rite. That would bring the worst ill luck of all, he says."

Osric, hearing Brand's reply, looked at Alfred. "What shall we do, Prince?" he said. "If we wait longer, we shall have to retire from the battle."

"The king's prayers may well be in our favor," Alfred replied grimly. "But it is needful also for us to help ourselves." He drew his sword. "We will attack."

Osric looked unsure. "Without the king?"

Alfred could feel the restlessness in the army. Another minute and all would be lost. He turned to Osric, and his face was bright and falcon-fierce. "Without the king," he said. "Follow me." And raising his sword, he gave the cry of his house, *"Wessex! Wessex!"* and charged down the hill. The men of his command poured after him. After a brief moment's hesitation, the king's leaderless column followed.

The Danes, seeing the West Saxons beginning to charge, ran forward themselves. The two armies met with a clash at the bottom of the valley and the shock of the West Saxon charge was so fierce that it forced the Danes to fall back slightly up the hill whence they had come.

Brand struggled to keep his place at Alfred's back. The prince was in the forefront of the battle, with Edgar on his right holding his banner high to show to all on the field Alfred's position. The West Saxons pressed forward eagerly, inspired by their prince's ferocity. Up and up and up the hill they went, pressing the Danes back. Halfway up the ridge was a road junction, a place where five ancient trackways met. This junction was marked by a single stunted thorn tree, and there the Danes steadied. The slow backward retreat halted and the men under the banner of one of their jarls, the banner of a great golden eagle, rallied.

Erlend fought to keep close to Guthrum's eagle banner. Hammer of Thor, he had not known fighting could be so fierce! The West Saxon who fought under the banner of the White Horse was like a wild boar in full charge. Erlend had begun to think that nothing could stop him. But Guthrum was holding on now, shouting and blazing and urging his men to press forward, to push the West Saxons back down the hill. The fight between the leaders concentrated around the thorn tree. Concentrated and stuck and held. It was man against man, a clashing of sword and battleax and spear, a bloody give-and-take, with the dead falling under the feet of the living, and the wounded lying unheeded in agony while the battle raged back and forth on top of them. Erlend saw his uncle, surrounded by a wall of dead men, climbing over those he had felled to get at the ones coming next.

Pride and the fire of battle burned in his own veins. He fought to get to his uncle's side. His arm was bloody up to the shoulder and he hacked and swore and killed with the rest of Guthrum's followers. Under the banner of the White Horse the men of Wessex raged full as fierce.

Hammer of Thor, Erlend thought as he took a blow on his mailed shoulder and turned to give back as good as he had taken. The day would end with not one of them left alive to claim the victory!

Then, from the bottom of the hill, came a shout of triumph. Erlend saw Guthrum look toward the noise, and he locked his shield with the man's beside him and looked also.

Fresh troops were entering the field on the side of the West Saxons.

"Forward, sons of Odin!" Guthrum shouted. But the men around him had begun to waver.

"Reinforcements. They have got reinforcements." The word was running all through the ranks of the Viking army now. They had scarcely managed to hold their own against the troops on the field at present. Fresh men would turn the tide quickly. Slowly the Danes once more began to give ground.

"Is it the Mercians after all?" Alfred shouted to Edgar, miraculously still unwounded and still clutching the White Horse banner.

"I don't think—"

"It is not the Mercians, my lord," yelled Brand behind him. "It is the king. The king and all his hearthband, come from Mass to join the battle!"

Alfred's face was streaked with blood from where he had wiped his hand across it. His hair, too, was matted with the blood of his enemies. But the sunlight showed his eyes clear and golden, and his teeth flashed in a brilliant grin. "Ethelred!" he said. "Perfect!" And turning back to the battle, he hurled himself once more into the fray.

Ethelred's thanes, all trained warriors frantic to join the action, thrust themselves forward with wild enthusiasm. The fresh assault took the heart from the Danes. Slowly at first, then with growing speed, the Vikings began to turn and flee from the field. Guthrum held out longer than most, but when he saw that he alone of all the jarls was left on the field, he too called his men to a retreat. The area around the thorn tree was knee-deep in the dead when Alfred turned at last to go and confer with his brother, the king.

"A victory!" Ethelred said when he saw Alfred approaching. Then: "Holy God, Alfred! Are you hurt? You are covered with blood."

"It is none of mine," Alfred replied, wiping his hand on his trousers. "Ethelred, I think we should go after them. They are in no condition to harm us now, and the more of them we kill, the fewer there will be to meet us tomorrow."

"I agree, my lord." It was Ethelnoth of Somerset coming up now. "They are in full flight. Let us follow them until we lose the light."

"Very well," said Ethelred. "Give the order for the fyrds to pursue."

Ethelnoth nodded but did not immediately turn away. Instead his eyes went to the blood-covered figure of the king's brother. "Never again will I question your leadership, Alfred of Wessex," the older man said deliberately. "You are a true son of your house, a battle leader I shall ever be proud to serve under."

"I thank you, my lord of Somerset," Alfred answered, full as gravely. "But it was the king's coming up when he did that won us the day." He looked at his brother and grinned. "You came so hard, Ethelred, I thought you were the Mercians!"

Ethelred, whose battle dress was scarcely stained, put an arm around his brother's shoulders. "You held them for me, Alfred. Ethelnoth and all the army knows that well." He laughed a little unsteadily. "I can scarce believe it is true. We won!"

The brothers stood close together and surveyed the scene before them. All over the hill and the valley the ground was thick with the fallen. Most of the West Saxons were now in full pursuit of the fleeing Danes, save for the parties of men searching among the bodies to separate the wounded from the slain. The winter sun shone on this scene out of hell, and Alfred said to Ethelred, very grimly, "Yes, Ethelred. We won."

Chapter 18

ERLEND and Guthrum did not reach the safety of the walls of Reading until after dark. The following day, when the war council gathered once more to plot the future, the full extent of their defeat became evident. Bagsac was dead, as were five of their jarls, among them the venerable Sidroc, who had been with Halfdan for more years than any could count. And nearly two thousand had fallen.

Guthrum sat silent in Halfdan's booth and listened to the talk flow around him, his face unreadable. He had brought out a large number of his own men, but the thought did not console him. Guthrum had never yet lost in battle. He did not like the feeling.

"Who was the leader who fought under the White Horse?" he asked at last, when there came a lull in the discussion and all were beginning to look at him in puzzlement at his silence.

"The king's brother," Halfdan said. His seamed and weathered face looked the same as ever. Halfdan had been fighting for too many years to be dismayed by one lost battle. "Alfred, he is called. He is full young, I hear. Not yet in his mid-twenties."

Guthrum grunted. Alfred, he thought, and saw again in his mind's eye the slender figure under the waving scarlet banner of the White Horse. That was the one who had led the attack, had kept the West Saxons pressing forward. Guthrum was an inspired battle leader himself; he recognized his like.

"Their king was not on the field, my lord," said one of the other jarls. The Viking war council exchanged looks of contempt. It was inconceivable to them that a leader would let his men go out to fight while he himself stayed safe behind.

"He fears the blood eagle," said Halfdan. He showed his stained and broken teeth in a pleased smile. Then he looked once more around the diminished circle of his war council and issued his decision. "We cannot let them rest on this victory," he said. "They will expect us to lie quiet, to lick our wounds for the winter. That we will not do. We will strike. We will carry the Raven banner into the very heartland of their country. We will aim for their chief city of Winchester. And sack it."

The West Saxons posted guards to watch the Viking camp at Reading and quartered their own forces at Silchester, at the junction of the two Roman roads the Danes would be most likely to take should they try to break out of Reading. Alfred volunteered to take the news of their victory to Winchester.

"I want a bath," he said to Ethelred the morning after Ashdown. "Let me bring the news to Elswyth and Cyneburg, and I will be back to you in two days' time."

Ethelred looked at his brother with wry amusement. "Elswyth will scarce recognize her spotless husband," he said. "You are filthy."

Alfred had done his best to wash in the icy conditions of the camp, but he was far from being his usual immaculate self. His hair was so stiff and matted that he had simply used his headband to tie it out of his way at the nape of his neck. He answered Ethelred now a little irritably, "I have dried blood in my nails and in my hair and I cannot get it out without hot water and soap."

Ethelred peered more closely. He had teased Alfred for years about his fastidiousness. "In your ears too," he said. "However did you get blood in your ears?"

"I don't know. All I know is, I want it out!" There was a note of muted panic in Alfred's voice, and Ethelred's amusement died on the instant.

"Go to Winchester," he said. "Nothing is like to happen here, though we shall keep our watch on Reading."

"I shall be back in two days," Alfred said.

"No need to rush," Ethelred said comfortably. "The Danes will wait for you."

Alfred took Brand and Edgar and set out for Winchester down the Roman road. The weather had turned even colder, and the sky looked to be building up for snow. The three men kept mainly to a steady canter, for warmth as well as for pace. The dark was coming on when finally they saw the walls and gates of Winchester before them. They rode in with the first snowflakes.

All Alfred wanted was a bath. But Cyneburg had come running out onto the steps of the great hall and he had to go to her. There was no sign of Elswyth, so he turned to Brand and asked, "Will you tell my wife I am here?"

"Yes, my lord," the thane answered immediately, and giving the reins of the horses into other hands, he set out for the princes' hall. Alfred went to meet his brother's wife.

"Ethelred is well," he said as soon as he came within hearing range. "There was a battle and we won."

Cyneburg's strained face lightened. She smiled up at Alfred as he reached the top step. "Our prayers have been answered," she said fervently. "Come inside and get warm."

Alfred followed her into the hall but refused to sit. "I am not fit to sit before any woman's fire, Cyneburg," he said firmly. "I need a bath. But the news I bear is heartening. We drove the Danes back to Reading and slew upwards of two thousand of their men." He gave her a small smile. "Ethelred led the charge that broke them."

"But he is all right?"

"He is in perfect health."

Cyneburg smiled radiantly. "Thanks be to God."

The door to the hall opened again and the voice he had been waiting for said, "Alfred! You won?"

He looked at his wife. "We won." Then he said stupidly, as if it was all that mattered, "Elswyth, I need a bath."

"Well, come with me and I'll get you one," she answered. She was at his side now and he looked down into the dark blue eyes he loved. He made no move to kiss her or touch her in any way, and after the briefest of moments she turned to Cyneburg. "Alfred brought two of his thanes with him. Will you feed them, my lady?"

"Certainly," Cyneburg answered. "And they can tell me all about the battle. No need for you to return to the great hall this night, Alfred."

He scarcely had time to thank her, Elswyth was moving so briskly toward the door. He caught up to her and they went out together into the early-winter dark. There was snow on the steps of the hall now. Alfred made a move to take his wife's arm, stopped himself, and instead said sharply, "Be careful. It's slippery."

She nodded and went down the steps beside him, sure of foot even though she was great with child. They walked side by side to the princes' hall, scarcely speaking. As soon as they were in the door, Elswyth called for the wooden tub they used for baths.

"Papa!" His daughter had seen him and was coming across the rush-strewn floor on steady feet. Flavia was an extremely agile and precocious child, had both walked and spoken at ten months of age. Her four little teeth were flashing in a wondrous smile and she held out her arms to be picked up.

Alfred recoiled. It happened before he knew it was going to happen, so he could not disguise it. Flavia stopped and looked from him to Elswyth. "Mama?" she said, uncertain where she had never been uncertain before.

Elswyth stepped forward and picked the child up. "Papa is all dirty, Flavia," she said calmly. "He doesn't want to touch you until he's had a bath."

"Dirty?" said Flavia and looked at Alfred from the safety of Elswyth's arms. Her blue-green eyes were wide with wonder. "Papa?"

"Very dirty," Alfred said.

Flavia peered closer. "Dirty!" She sounded extremely pleased.

Elswyth was looking around for Flavia's nurse, and as the woman came forward she handed her daughter into another pair of arms. Flavia screamed in protest. Elswyth ignored her and said to Alfred. "Come into the sleeping room. They'll have a bath for you very shortly."

It seemed to take forever for the tub to be filled. Serving girls kept coming in and out with buckets of water. Alfred stood, his hands clasped out of sight behind his back, and listened to Elswyth telling him about a new litter of pups in the kennel. Finally the tub was filled and he could shed his clothes and submerge his filthy, bloodstained body in the hot water. Elswyth handed him a cake of soap and went out to the main hall. He ducked his head under the water and washed his hair. Three times. His nails washed clean as he was doing his hair. He scrubbed at his ears, at his face, at his chest, at his knuckles. The tub had been set before the brazier, but even so it was cold in the sleeping room. The water was turning chill when finally he felt that he was clean enough. The serving girl had left a towel on a stool near to the tub, and he wrapped himself in it as soon as he stepped out. He dried his body hastily and reached for the clean clothes Elswyth had left out for him on the bed. He was fully dressed and sitting on the room's one chair crossing the garters that bound his trouser legs when Elswyth came back into the room.

He looked at her, a full long look, the first he had permitted himself since he came home. She smiled. "All right now?"

His returning smile was wry. "All right."

She came to stand beside him, and picking up the towel, rubbed his hair to dry it. He sat perfectly docile under her touch. He did not move even when she fetched a comb and dragged it ruthlessly through the still-damp tangles. It wasn't until she had finished that he spoke.

"I couldn't bear to touch you," he said. "I felt so . . . unclean. I killed so many men, Elswyth." He was still in his chair and she was standing now before him. He looked up at her, his eyes dark. "I couldn't touch you or Flavia with all that blood still on me."

"I know," she said. Her beautiful face was very grave. "I saw."

He shuddered. "Ethelred said it was even in my ears!"

At that she stepped nearer and drew his face against the bulk of her stomach. "You are clean now," she said quietly. "The blood is all gone."

He pressed against her and she held him tighter. Finally, in a muffled voice that yet held a distinct edge of bitterness: "At least I did not get sick in front of all my men."

She smoothed the hair that would not show gold again until it was dried. "Hawks kill without thought or without mercy," she said. "So do wild boars. It is well that men are different from beasts. Is that not why God gave us souls?"

There was a long silence. Then he said, "You do not think I am craven to take killing so ill?"

"No." The baby within her kicked so that they both felt it. She said softly, "I have carried life and know how precious it is, with how much care and toil it is brought into the world. It is well to mourn its passing, even by necessity."

Slowly he moved away from her, and slowly rose to his feet. They stood there in silence for a moment, the chair between them. He looked into her eyes. "On the battlefield," he said honestly, "I killed without thought and without mercy. It was not until after that . . ."

Her answer was prosaic. "Once committed to the battlefield, Alfred, there is no choice but to kill. That or be killed. And to me you are worth more than the whole Danish army. So bear that in mind when you take up your sword."

He did not answer, but his eyes were his own again, clear and golden; the dark look was gone. She reached for his hand. "Come and make your peace with Flavia," she said. "Or she will give us none of our own."

Alfred's sleep was restless and he woke the following morning to a headache. Nor was he surprised to feel the familiar, unwelcome pain in his forehead. All his life, it seemed, after great emotional turmoil would come a headache.

Elswyth did not seem to be surprised either. "It's snowing," she said to him. "You could not have left in any case." Which made him feel somewhat better, and he settled in to endure.

The headache lifted toward evening and he fell asleep. When he woke again it was full dark and the lamp had been lit. Elswyth was sitting in the chair next to it, and in its clear yellow glow her unguarded face was laid bare.

His first thought was that she looked tired. There were faint shadows he had not noticed before beneath the blue eyes, and hollows beneath the magnificent cheekbones. She looked older, he thought, immeasurably older than the girl he had married but two years before. She did not know that he was watching her, and she shifted on her chair as if she were uncomfortable. Her hand went to her side and she shifted again.

Two babes in two years, he thought bleakly. True it was that a child was a gift from God, but even so, Alfred had not felt joy when Elswyth told him he was to have another child. He knew how fettered she had felt while carrying Flavia; and then, so soon, to face again the long weary months of bearing.

What had she said to him yesterday? "I know with how much care and how much toil life is brought into this world." He felt a sudden flash of anger and frustration. He had not married her to burden her like this!

It had happened so quickly because Elswyth had stopped nursing Flavia, or so Cyneburg had said. Elswyth had come down with a fever that was short but fierce enough to dry up her milk. Flavia had had to be put with a wet nurse, and within a month Elswyth was once again with child.

She would nurse this child until it could ride a horse, Alfred thought now savagely. And, as if she sensed his unrest, her head turned.

"Alfred. You are awake." She rose and came to stand beside the bed. She smiled. "Better?"

She was still in her blue day gown and her hair was pulled away from her face and set in a crown of braids on top of her head. How few women could bear that severity of hairstyle, he thought. But the hollows in Elswyth's face only emphasized the beauty of her bones. "Yes," he said at last. "Much better." He sat up and fixed the pillows to make a backrest beside him. "Come and join me," he said. "You look tired." When she hesitated, he got up, came around the bed, picked her up, and deposited her gently into the nest he had made. She laughed and settled back, trying to get comfortable. He tucked a pillow into the small of her back. "Better?"

"Yes."

He went round the bed again and rejoined her, picking up her thin hand and holding it in his. "It will be soon," he said softly.

She sighed. "I hope so." Then: "The snow stopped earlier, but now it has begun again."

"I have to start back tomorrow. I promised Ethelred I would not delay."

She was looking at their clasped hands lying so quietly on his thigh. He too was wearing his clothes, but without the thonged garters and without shoes. "I want to go to Wantage," she said.

"Wantage is too close to Reading, love," he answered, still softly. "Nor are you in any fit condition to travel."

Still she stared at their hands. "I hate it here in Winchester. There is nothing for me to do."

"I know. When once the babe has come, I shall move you to one of our manors. If not Wantage, then to Chippenham, or perhaps into Sussex."

"I like Wantage best. Wantage or Lambourn." She sounded fretful, not at all like herself.

"As soon as the Danes leave Reading, you can return. I promise, Elswyth."

At that she raised her eyes to his face. "Winchester doesn't feel like home."

"Doesn't it?" He put an arm around her and drew her close against him. She laid her head on his shoulder and he heard the sound of a weary sigh. The fist of his hand that was not holding her clenched. But his voice was quiet as he said, "I knew I would get a headache. It was inevitable. And all

I could think was that I must get home before it happened, that I could not have one in the camp."

She stirred a little. "So Winchester is home to you?" She sounded surprised.

"No," he answered simply. "You are."

There was a long pause. The charcoal brazier glowed in the corner, a dimmer light than that cast by the oil lamp. "Yes," she said finally. "That is it. No place is home if you're not there. But Wantage would be better than here."

He laughed a little unsteadily. "I shall do my best to chase the Danes out of Reading, love, so you may go to Wantage."

"No!" She pulled away from him at that, and twisted to look into his face. "You are safest with them at Reading. Don't mind me, Alfred. I am just feeling sorry for myself. Pay no heed to what I have said."

"I always pay heed to what you say," he replied. "You usually make a great deal of sense."

"Not now, I don't." She picked up his hand and held it to her cheek. "Once the babe is born, it will be better."

"I know it will. And let us hope that there will be no more babes for a few more years."

"I will say amen to that," said Elswyth, and for the first time he could hear an undercurrent of bitterness in her voice.

He laid his cheek against her hair and thought that perhaps it was no bad thing that he would be away at war. It would give her a respite.

It snowed through the night but stopped once again with the dawn. Alfred and his companions rode out of Winchester as soon as the sun was fairly up. The road was not so easily traversed in this weather, and it was a long ride to Silchester. By nightfall it had begun to snow again.

The camp at Silchester was still when Alfred finally rode in, the snow muffling all sound. In the morning the crystal beauty of the world was breathtaking, but the snow had severe consequences for the West Saxon army. More and more men began to slip out of camp to return to their homes.

"Is there nothing we can do to stop this leakage of our troops?" Alfred asked Ethelred furiously. It was but ten days since their great victory, and the West Saxon army was at less than half the strength it had been at Ashdown.

"It is the snow," Ethelred replied. His face and voice both were weary. "The women at home will not be able to do all that is needful with this amount of snow. The men are returning to their farms out of necessity, Alfred. If their cattle are not fed, they will die."

"The Danes are more important than the cattle," Alfred said. His face was set and stern; there was a white line around his mouth.

"To you they are," Ethelred answered. "To me. Not to most of the men who comprise the fyrd." Then, to his brother's implacable face: "Be fair. Our wives are not struggling to maintain a precarious existence in our absence. Our children are not like to go hungry. The same is not true for most of our men."

There was a moment'a pause; then Alfred let out his breath. "You are right." He gave his brother a crooked smile. "I wonder if the West Saxons realize how fortunate they are in their king?"

Ethelred sighed. "I doubt it." His brown eyes were somber as he surveyed the diminished numbers in his camp. He was fully as aware as Alfred of the problems such leakage raised. "We thrashed the Danes soundly at Ashdown," he said now to his brother. "Let us pray that they keep to their camp at Reading for the winter. Come spring, we can raise the full fyrd again."

"Spring will be the time for the sowing," said Alfred. "Something else the Danes do not have to concern themselves with."

Ethelred shrugged. "We will do the best we can with what we have. And trust to God for the rest."

"Amen," said Alfred, and went off to speak to the guards who were next on watch at Reading.

On the night of January 20, the night that Elswyth's son was born, the Danes crept out of Reading under cover of darkness and slipped past the West Saxons at Silchester, moving south. It was not until near morning that Ethelred's scouts at Reading realized what had happened and galloped to the king's camp to sound the alarm.

"God in heaven," said Ethelred. "They are past us and heading for Winchester!"

"We must go after them," Alfred said. His face was no less grim than Ethelred's.

"We are at less than half-strength."

"We have no choice," said Alfred, and after a moment Ethelred agreed. "You are right. We must go after with all speed. But first I shall send a messenger to Winchester to warn the city. Cyneburg and Elswyth must be prepared to flee if necessary."

"Elswyth is near her time, Ethelred," Alfred said, his voice as clipped as ever it got. "She cannot flee." One fist clenched. "At all costs, we must turn the Danes back from Winchester!"

The diminished West Saxon army was on the march by morning's end. The Danes, their advance scouts told them, had not pushed straight through to Winchester but had taken up a position near the market town of Old Basing, some fourteen miles to the south of Reading.

"As ever, they have chosen a good defensive position," Alfred muttered when told the news. "The water meadows of the Loddon will protect them well."

It was dark when the king's forces stopped, some three miles from the Danish camp. Ethelred set guards to watch the Danes, with instructions this time to watch through the night as well as the day. Then he and Alfred and the ealdormen met.

"They have a larger force than we," said Ethelnoth of Somerset. "We cannot look for a repeat of Ashdown."

"We do not need to beat them," Alfred answered. "We need to stop them."

A murmur of agreement went up from the other men in the council at these words. Then Ethelred said, "Granted that this is true, how is it best we go about our task? Shall we straddle the road south and offer battle?"

"That would be folly," said Ethelnoth instantly. "They outnumber us. I doubt our men would hold."

"Storm the camp, as we did at Reading," advised Osric of Hampshire. "Even if they drive us off, as they did at Reading, still we will inflict hurt on them. And they will know we are yet in the field and prepared to fight."

There was a pause as all considered this possibility. Then Ethelred said, "I would say, my lord, that you have named our best course of action."

Murmurs of agreement came from the rest of the council. "Alfred?" asked Ethelred. "What say you?"

"I agree, my lord. I think we should storm the camp."

"Very well." Ethelred looked around the circle of men who sat on their heels around his campfire. "Tomorrow," he said. "No sense in delay."

Ethelnoth grunted. "No sense at all. I shall tell my men to prepare for battle."

"And I. And I. And I," said Osric of Hampshire and Ethelm of Wiltshire, and Ceolmund of Kent. Before they lay down to rest that night, the West Saxons had once more prepared their weapons and their souls to go out to fight the Danes.

The women at Winchester posted their own scouts on the road that the Danes would come by, and prepared if necessary to flee. "You cannot, Elswyth," Cyneburg said when she realized that Elswyth had dragged herself out of bed to practice walking around her room. "If the worst comes to the worst, you must hide somewhere within the city. You cannot possibly ride in your condition. And what of the baby!"

"I can if I must," Elswyth replied stubbornly. "I will not stay here to be taken as a hostage to hold at Alfred's throat."

"You cannot take an infant out on the roads in this weather."

"Edward will have to stay," Elswyth conceded. "He will be safe enough. Who is to notice one more babe in the town? But my face is known; for enough geld, someone might well betray me. I cannot chance it. If I must, Cyneburg, I can ride. And so can Flavia."

Cyneburg looked at her with a mixture of exasperation and admiration, threw up her hands, and bustled out of the room.

The news of the battle came to Winchester on the morning of January 23, brought by a thane who had ridden through the night. The West Saxons had attacked the Danish camp at Basing and been driven back. "But it was a fierce battle, my lady," the man told Cyneburg, who relayed the news to Elswyth. "Though outnumbered, our men held firm for many hours. We drew off to the south, so the Danes know they will have to fight again if they wish to try for Winchester. We hurt them. We took hurts ourselves, but the king and the prince and the ealdormen are safe. Now we must just wait to see what the Danes do next."

On the morning of January 25 the Danes moved out of their camp at Basing and returned the way they had come, to the north. Unlike the West Saxons, the Viking army traveled by horseback, and by evening they were once more safe within the rivers of Reading.

"We won," Alfred said to Ethelred when they learned this news. "We lost the battle at Basing, but we won the most important battle of all. Winchester is safe."

"For now," said Ethelred.

"For now."

"And you have a son," said the king with a smile. That news had been sent to the camp immediately after the baby's birth. "Tomorrow we shall ride to Winchester and see him."

Chapter 19

*T*HE Danes lay quiet at Reading, guarded alternatively by Ealdorman Ethelm of Wiltshire and Ealdorman Ailnoth of Berkshire and their men. All those who were not of the hearthbands of the king or the great nobles went home to their farms, prepared if necessary to answer another call to arms. After Basing, Ethelred had been forced to send the fyrds home. It was not just a problem keeping the men away from their land, it was a problem feeding them as well.

"The Danes can live by raiding the countryside," Alfred said bitterly to Elswyth one rainy March night as they sat together before the fire in the princes' hall at Wilton. "Ethelred cannot so prey upon his own people. It gives the pagans a distinct advantage."

"That it does." She stretched her feet to the warmth of the fire and wiggled her toes. She could hear the sound of the rain as it beat against the wooden walls of the hall. Elswyth loved the sound of rain at night.

Alfred was silent, his somber gaze fixed on the fire. He had been like a caged wildcat all this last month, Elswyth thought. There was nothing to do but wait for the Danes to make their next move, and he hated inaction. It was also Lent, and the general darkness of the season and the liturgy was not contributing any lightness to his spirit.

"The world lies sunk in gloom, waiting for Our Lord to be risen," he said now, eerily echoing his wife's thoughts. "Appropriate, Elswyth. Only, where is the savior for Wessex?"

He really was in a black mood. Elswyth herself was feeling much more cheerful. Today she had had her first good long gallop since the baby, and her muscles felt pleasurably sore. It had felt so good to be outdoors on a horse. To feel her body light and free once again. The gloomy weather and the gloomy season were as nothing compared to this exhilarating sense of freedom. She felt a flicker of annoyance with Alfred. Things were not as bad as all that.

"You have done very well, I think," she said now, consciously reasonable. "You have held your own against the Danes each time you met them, and at Ashdown you actually took the victory. I see no reason for things to change."

"They can wear us down," he said. "For how long can we go on calling up the fyrds, letting them go home, then calling them up again? Our men will weary of it, Elswyth. And the Danes . . . they will just go on."

"Then why don't you surrender now and get it over with?"

He had been slumping in his chair, and at her words his spine straightened and his head snapped up. "What?"

"Since all is so hopeless and gloomy, why don't you just surrender? What is the point in fighting if you are bound to lose in the end?"

Glittering hawk eyes stared at her. "I did not say we were bound to lose!"

"Well, that is what I thought I was hearing."

"I never said we would lose. I said it would be . . . difficult."

"Oh." She looked at him out of wide-stretched eyes that were as dark a blue as the night sky. Her cheeks were faintly flushed with rose from the warmth of the fire. "I must have misheard you."

He gave her a reluctant grin. "You did not mishear me. But I was only talking."

"I know." She leaned over, grasped his hand in her own, and squeezed it. "But you are so depressing! You are spoiling all my pleasure in the sound of the rain."

He became instantly somber. "I doubt the men on guard at Reading take quite the same pleasure in it."

She wiggled her toes again. "I am sure they don't. The most pleasurable part is the knowledge that it is cold and wet and miserable out and you are safe and warm and dry within." She stared dreamily into the fire. "When I was a little girl I used to wrap myself in a blanket and stand on the porch to watch the night rain. When my mother wasn't around, that is."

He looked at her, and this time the smile reached his eyes. He asked, "Do you want to do it now?"

She gave him a delighted look. "Go out on the porch and watch the rain?"

"The thanes will think we are mad, but why not?"

She grinned. "The thanes already think *I* am mad, but I would hate to ruin your standing."

"Get the blankets," he said.

Two minutes later, giggling like children, the Prince of Wessex and his lady, wrapped in blankets, crept out onto the porch of the princes' hall and stood there huddled together to watch the rain.

The Danes had spent the winter making brief forays into the countryside around Reading, raiding food for their men and fodder for their animals. They also gathered as much information as they could about these unexpectedly warlike West Saxons. One of the chief of their scouts that winter had unexpectedly turned out to be young Erlend.

Despite his small size, Erlend had proved himself a worthy son of his father in the Wessex campaign. But Erlend possessed two other skills that the rest of the Danes did not: he was a skilled harper and he spoke the Saxon language fluently.

"A Saxon harper stayed one whole winter at Nasgaard the year that I was twelve," Erlend had explained to his curious uncle when Guthrum questioned him about his abilities. "He taught me many of his songs and I learned somewhat of his language as well."

Guthrum, like most of the Danes, had only some basic Saxon words, and Erlend's ability to speak in full sentences impressed him greatly. "Could you pass as a Saxon?" he asked his nephew, and Erlend could tell from the gleam in his uncle's eyes that he had some scheme in mind.

"No," Erlend replied promptly. Then, thoughtfully, his eyes intent upon Guthrum's face, "But I could pass as a Frank. My Frankish is better than my Saxon, and these men of Wessex would scarcely realize that I was speaking with a Danish accent."

And so Erlend was not surprised when he was called before Halfdan one day and asked to go out among the West Saxons in the guise of a wandering harper.

"No one would suspect you," the Danish leader had said, his eyes raking the small thin figure of the heir to Nasgaard. "You do not look Danish at all."

"What would you want me to discover, my lord?" Erlend asked, his voice neutral, his face expressionless.

"I have need to know all you can learn about this West Saxon king, Ethelred," Halfdan said to the boy. "I have need to know about his army. My other scouts say to me that they have disbanded, but I find that difficult to believe." Halfdan frowned so that his bushy graying eyebrows met together over the bridge of his broad nose. "In short, son of Olaf, I want to know all the information you can glean. Nothing is too unimportant to be of interest to me. Leave us for a month, go and play your harp among these West Saxon villages and manors, then come and report to me all you have learned."

Erlend had looked from the craggy face of Halfdan to the bright blue eyes of his uncle, then back again to Halfdan. It would not be a poor idea to win the respect of Halfdan, Erlend thought before he answered. One day he very well might find himself in need of an ally against his own present ally, Guthrum.

And so Erlend had agreed to Halfdan's proposal and taken to the roads and byways of Wessex in the guise of a wandering harper. Such musicians were not an uncommon sight in the countryside, and no one seemed to find the Dane at all suspicious. Erlend played in villages and farmsteads, and one night even found him within the walls of the royal manor of Lambourn. Alfred was not in residence, but the folk of the manor gave Erlend a fine welcome and he played his harp for them for half the night.

The talk among the manor folk in Lambourn was little of the king and all of the prince. Many of the Lambourn men had been at Ashdown, and it was from them that Erlend learned the story of Ethelred's refusing to take up arms until Mass was finished.

Two brothers of such differing temperaments, Erlend thought as he listened to the tale. There could scarcely be much love between them. "Has Ethelred sons?" he asked casually, strumming a few careless notes on his harp.

"Ethelred's sons are too young to take up the kingship as yet," came the ready answer. "Should aught happen to the king, Alfred would be his heir."

Erlend raised his eyebrows in astonishment. "How young are the sons?" he asked.

"One is a mere babe. The eldest, Ethelhelm, is ten or eleven. Too young to lead the country in such a time as this."

Not so young, Erlend thought, as he smiled agreement with the man who had answered him. For certain an eleven-year-old would not relish his kingship being usurped by an uncle. And where there was discontent among royalty, there were always nobles ready to take advantage.

Should the West Saxons become embroiled in a war over the succession, the way would lie open for the Danes. It was an intriguing thought that Erlend stored away to repeat to Halfdan upon his eventual return to Reading.

Meanwhile, back in Reading, Halfdan was not idle. Over the winter he had sent to one of his brothers in Denmark for reinforcements to replace the men he had lost at Englefield and Reading and Ashdown. In early March came reply that a new army would reach Reading in mid-April, at the start of the season the Danes called Cuckoo Month. This was good news for the Danish war council, which met in discussion one day toward the middle of March, shortly after Erlend's return from his wanderings.

"The conquest of Wessex can begin in earnest once we have increased our numbers," Halfdan said to his men as they met within the confines of one of the wooden booths the Danes had erected for shelter at Reading. "Cuckoo Month and Lamb's Fold Month are ill times for a farmer to be away from his land. From what Erlend Olafson has reported, Ethelred may have difficulty summoning an army at that time of the year."

"And even if he does, he cannot keep it long." Guthrum's white teeth flashed briefly. "He cannot feed so many men without despoiling his own land. As Erlend has also reported." It had been Guthrum's idea to send his nephew out as a spy, and he was not at all loath to take credit for Erlend's accomplishments.

"Erlend has done very well," Halfdan grunted. Then, rubbing the side of his face with his hand: "The number of Saxons on guard here at Reading is small. We can break through easily enough anytime. And I think it will be well to venture further afield before the summer army arrives, to test the waters to the west of Reading. There are roads that will take horses with little trouble."

There were grunts of assent from the jarls of the war council. Over the winter, Reading had become too confining for most of the Danes.

Guthrum spoke up. "I have been thinking, my lord, that in both Northumbria and East Anglia the defense of the country collapsed with the death of the king. And from what my nephew has reported, these West Saxons might well find themselves embroiled in a dispute over the succession, should Ethelred die. There is Alfred, but there is also a near-grown royal prince."

Halfdan smiled, his broken and stained teeth almost hidden in the bushiness of his mustache. "I have thought on that also, Guthrum. It would be well for us, should the West Saxons begin to fight among themselves. Then could we come at their throats with ease, and set up our own king, as we have done in Northumbria." The Danish king's smile grew. "I give this charge into your hands, Guthrum. If the West Saxons rise to meet us, see that you either take or kill their king."

Guthrum's eyes were vividly blue as he answered with real zest, "My lord, I will."

On March 17 the Danes marched out of Reading, this time in full numbers. "Not a raid," a thane from Ealdorman Ailnoth reported to Ethelred at Wilton. "There were too many of them, my lord, for us to attack. Ailnoth says to call up the fyrds. We will keep track of them and bring news of their destination."

Within an hour horses were galloping out of Wilton, flying to the west and to the east, bearing word to Somersetshire and Wiltshire and Hampshire and Essex and Sussex and Kent and Surrey that the shire ealdormen must call up their fyrds and march immediately to join the king at Wilton.

On March 20 the Somersetshire and Wiltshire and Hampshire fyrds marched into Wilton. Late in the afternoon of the twentieth, one of the men from the Berkshire fyrd, which was keeping watch on the Danish army, rode in to tell Ethelred that the Danes had marched to the west, up the Ridgeway toward Chippenham. Early the following morning, without waiting for the other shire fyrds to arrive, the West Saxons marched out of Wilton and headed toward the old Roman road that led from Winchester to Marlborough.

The road was in poor repair and mired deep in mud. The marching was not pleasant, but the men of the fyrds tramped along doggedly. There was not a man of them following under the banner of his lord who did not understand the danger of this Danish thrust to the west.

They camped beside the road and continued onward with the early-morning light. While they were yet ten miles to the south of Marlborough, the Berkshire scouts found them.

"The Danes are at Meretun, my lord, but two miles to the north of you," the leader of the scouting party told Ethelred and his council. "They know you are coming and are ready to fight."

"Well," said Ethelred grimly, "so are we."

When the West Saxons came upon the Danes an hour later, they found the scene at Meretun not unlike that at Ashdown two months since. The village lay at the place where the Ridgeway intersected the Roman road, and once again the Viking army had divided into two wings and straddled the Ridgeway. Also as before, the West Saxons divided their forces to oppose them. The Danes looked to be larger in number, but not overwhelmingly so. It was high noon when the initial charge was made, and the two armies locked in bitter combat.

Guthrum was not fighting with the other jarls this day, but under the command of Halfdan in the king's column. As expected, the West Saxon king had taken the opposing command, and as the battle raged on, Guthrum kept the Golden Dragon banner of Wessex ever in his eye. He had picked a few of his own following to stay by him throughout the day until their mission was accomplished, and he was pleased to see the faces he needed still around him when, after nearly two hours of almost evenhanded fighting, Halfdan gave the order to begin a retreat. The battle was still holding steady, so all the Danes understood what was meant by the order. Halfdan would feign a retreat, lure the West Saxons into a pursuit, and when once the enemy had broken their lines, the Danes would reform and attack the now-disorganized and vulnerable West Saxons, and slaughter them.

Before he retreated, however, Guthrum was going to kill Ethelred. He looked around at his men and saw they understood. Then, as the Danes began to melt back and the West Saxons to press forward, Guthrum began to move toward his prey.

The king's hearthband were unprepared for the savage attack that seemed to come from nowhere out of a retreating army. The enemy were falling back, seemingly beaten, and then there came this sudden mad-dog spring of some twenty Danes led by a great snarling beast of a man who felled three thanes with one swing of his bloody battleax.

Ethelred too was unprepared. But he had his sword up by the time Guthrum was on him, and though he was not the warrior the Dane was, neither was he unskilled. He staved off the killing blow by leaping to his right side, and the ax, instead of taking him in the throat, took him in the shoulder. Ethelred thrust with his own sword, and for a brief intense moment his eyes were locked with the fierce blue eyes of his attacker.

Then the men of his hearthband were closing in and the Danes were forced back. In less than three minutes the assassins had melted into the general retreat of their army and disappeared.

"My lord, you are hurt!" Blood was pouring from Ethelred's upper arm, and now for the first time he felt the pain. "You must retire from the field," said Bertred, and his treasure thane slipped an arm around him to bear him up. "If that wound is not attended to, you will bleed to death."

Ethelred had begun to feel light-headed. He wet his lips. "Tell Alfred . . . he is in command now," he said. Then: "Ethelm is to take command of my wing."

"It shall be done," said a voice. Someone else was applying a cloth to his shoulder. "Get a horse," he heard from a very far distance. "The king cannot walk." And then he fainted.

To Alfred and his men it seemed a miracle when the Danes began to retreat, and with wild enthusiasm they plunged after in pursuit. The West Saxons remembered well the slaughter they had done in the pursuit of the Danes after Reading, and saw no reason they could not duplicate that feat this day.

The pursuit lasted for over an hour. Alfred, when finally apprised of the news of Ethelred's injury, had pulled his own hearthband back to the Ridgeway, and so he was not among the pursuers when the Danes finally turned.

This time the slaughter fell the other way. The West Saxons, spread out and totally unprepared, were as lambs before the slaughter of the massed Danish army. It was only when the first West Saxons came racing back into Meretun that Alfred realized what had happened.

"We must get the king away from here," he said grimly to Ethelred's companion thanes. They had been so confident of victory that Ethelred was still at Meretun, being tended to in a tent they had rigged. "Get on the road to the south," Alfred said now, "and I will try to hold the Danes here at Meretun for some further time."

And so it happened that as the frantically fleeing West Saxons came racing into Meretun, they were greeted by lines of their own men, who urged them to join. When the Danes finally made their own appearance, expecting to find the battleground empty, they were astonished to be met by a rain of arrows, and then the advancing shield wall of the West Saxon fyrds.

The final battle was not so fierce as the first one had been; both Danes and West Saxons were wearied from the chase. As dark began to fall, Alfred called his men off, and at his word the men of the fyrds turned and fled unashamedly into the growing dusk, leaving their wounded on the field. It was too dark for the Danes to follow.

They had lost, but Alfred's final stand had given Ethelred the time he needed. As dark fell, the wounded West Saxon king was safely away and on the road that would take him back to Wilton.

The journey to Wilton exhausted Ethelred, but once he had been in his own bed for a few days it seemed he would make a good recovery. Half of the Danish army, under Halfdan, returned to Reading, while the other half remained at Meretun. Alfred took the men of the Sussex fyrd, who were still at Wilton when he returned, and went north once more to harry the Danes at Meretun as best he could. The men of Surrey he sent to relieve the guard at Reading. Both the Wiltshire and the Berkshire fyrds had done more than their fair share of the fighting this spring.

Alfred had ridden back to Wilton once more to check for himself on Ethelred's progress, when word came from the Ealdorman of Surrey, who was in charge of his shire's fyrd at Reading, that shiploads of reinforcements had come up the Thames to join Halfdan at Reading. Several thousand new men, the ealdorman's thane reported grimly. And supplies as well.

Alfred swore when he learned this news. The West Saxon army was not likely to be at full strength again this spring. The ealdormen of Wiltshire and Berkshire had been blunt about their chances of being able to call up their men yet again. "There is little point in saving the country, if you are like to starve because there is no food at home," Ethelm of Wiltshire had said bluntly. "Myself and my hearthband you will have, but the shire thanes and the ceorls . . . I think not."

Alfred rode north again, determined to slay as many of the Danes at Meretun as he possibly could. It was not possible to engage in a full-scale battle; the West Saxons instead lay in cover and fell upon the Danes whenever they emerged from their base in order to raid the countryside for food and fodder.

It was Good Friday when one of Ethelred's thanes came to find Alfred to tell him that his brother was dying.

Chapter 20

ALFRED galloped straight through from Meretun to Wilton, changing horses several times at manors along the way. Only Brand and Edgar rode with him, and the pace was too hard for conversation. But Alfred's mind was ablaze with a wild mixture of disbelief and fear.

Dying. How could that be? Ethelred had been on the road to recovery. He was strong and young, not yet thirty-five years in age. True, the wound had been serious. But not fatal! How could he be dying?

And then the frightening thought, pushed down deep whenever it surfaced, only to resurface yet again: *If Ethelred dies then I shall be the king.*

It could not be, would not be. Not Ethelred. Anguish caught at the back of his throat. Make it not true, he prayed. Dear God, dear God, dear God. Not Ethelred.

Elswyth must have been watching for him, for she came running into the courtyard as soon as his horse was in through the gate. "What has happened here?" he asked her as he vaulted to the ground. "The messenger said that Ethelred was . . . was . . ."

"He is dying, Alfred," she answered when his voice trailed away. Her face was very pale, her blue eyes looked almost black. She put her hand on his arm and began to walk with him toward the great hall. "The wound has turned sour," she said. "It is going all through him."

He stopped and closed his eyes. He could feel her body close beside him. She said nothing. He opened his eyes and forced himself to walk forward. "Can nothing be done?" But he knew the answer before ever she replied. Once the poison started to spread, there was nothing that could be done.

"They have tried everything. I wanted to send for you on Wednesday, but Ethelred would not have it. Then, on Thursday, he wanted you." Her husky voice sounded even huskier than usual.

They were in the hall now. Elswyth said, "Go in to him," and took her hand from his arm.

Alfred nodded without speaking and crossed the floor with long strides. He paused for a moment before the door to Ethelred's room, and the thought crossed his mind, like a shiver of doom, that this was the room in which Ethelbald had died. Then he pushed open the door and went in.

Cyneburg was sitting by the bed in the very chair that Judith had once sat in. Ethelred's household priest was on the king's other side, chanting prayers in a low voice. Both bedside watchers turned to the door as it opened, and when they saw who it was, both Cyneburg and the priest stood up.

Cyneburg looked from Alfred back to the man in the bed. "Here is your brother," she said to Ethelred, her voice very gentle; then she motioned to the priest, and both walked to meet Alfred at the door. Cyneburg's face seemed very composed. "I'll leave you alone together," she said to Alfred. He nodded, unable to reply, and she went out, taking the priest with her. Alfred crossed the floor and stood beside his brother's bed.

Ethelred's face was flushed with fever, his lips blistered and cracked. But the brown eyes knew him. "Ethelred," Alfred said.

The feverish lips moved in a small smile. "I was beginning to fear I had waited too long to send for you."

Alfred tried to answer, and found that his throat had completely closed down.

"I did not want to die without seeing you again," Ethelred said.

Alfred sat in Cyneburg's chair and bowed his head onto the edge of the bed. "Ethelred." It seemed to be the only word he could get out. Then he felt his brother's hand on his hair.

"You know it must be you," Ethelred said. "I have written it in my will, Alfred. Over there." Then, as Alfred still did not raise his head he said, "Go and get it for me."

Alfred raised his head. His eyes were wet. "Where?" he asked huskily.

"In the small chest. Near to the treasury chest." And Ethelred gestured painfully.

Alfred went to the chest that contained Ethelred's important documents and found the will on top of several charters. He brought it back to the bed. Ethelred said, "I had it written into the will some months before by one of the monks in Winchester. You are to succeed me. Do you see?"

Alfred looked through the closely written script. "Yes, I see it."

"Show that to the witan. They would choose you anyway, but it will be well to have my word and my seal."

"I . . . I will try to be as good a king as you, Ethelred." Alfred set his teeth into his lower lip. "You have ever set me the example of what a Christian king ought to be."

The cracked and swollen lips moved once more in a smile. "You will be a better king than I, Alfred. It eases my mind to know that I leave Wessex in such capable hands." He moved his fingers a little and Alfred's hand shot out to grasp his brother's. Ethelred's skin felt hot and dry to the touch. Then Ethelred said, "You will look after my children for me."

It was not a question, but Alfred answered it anyway. "As if they were my own."

"I know." Ethelred sighed and closed his eyes. "I am tired," he said.

"Rest, my brother." Alfred stood, then leaned over to touch his lips to the hot flushed forehead. "I have ever loved you better than any other man in the world," he said, and his eyes once more were wet.

His brother's eyes flickered open. "And I you," said Ethelred. Alfred nodded, forcibly controlled his face, turned, and walked out the door.

Ethelred died as the sun was rising on Easter Sunday. He had asked to be buried at Wimborne Abbey, and arrangements were made for his body to be carried there forthwith. Most of the ealdormen would be in attendance at the funeral, as the election and coronation of the new king would take place immediately after.

It took but a day to bring Ethelred from Wilton to Wimborne. They used horses in front of the cart carrying the coffin instead of oxen. Everyone knew that Wessex could not afford to be too long without a king.

Alfred rode behind his brother's coffin and remembered the funeral journey of his father. Ethelred had been with him then; Ethelred had always been with him. He remembered his brother's words to him on the day his father had died. "I will take care of you, little brother," Ethelred had said. "I will take care of you."

Ethelred had held to his word, had been father to him as well as brother and friend. Never again would any man be as close to him as Ethelred had been; never again would he know that deep friendship of the mind and the heart and the spirit that he had known with his brother.

Always there would be this great aching void, the place that Ethelred had filled in his heart that could be filled by no one else.

Ethelred had known him, known his weaknesses as well as his strengths, known the true Alfred in a way that none of his companion thanes ever would. It was not safe to let any of the rest of them too close.

No one must ever know how bad the headaches really were.

No one must know. Not now, not when they were depending on him to be strong, when a whole nation was looking to him for its very survival.

He would be the king. It was a fearful prospect, one he had never ever expected to face. How could he have thought thus, he, the youngest of five brothers? How could he have expected that such a thing would ever befall him? And to have it happen now . . . when the Danes were at their throats . . . when they were fighting for their very lives.

Dear God, dear God, dear God. Where was he to find the wisdom to see them through this?

"Ethelred will help you." It was Elswyth's husky drawl echoing his thoughts in the uncanny way she often had. He turned to look at his wife, who was riding close beside him. Her eyes were fixed on his face. "He was a truly good and holy man, Alfred," she said. "I think he must be very close to God. Ethelred will intercede for you." Her eyes were a darker blue than the spring sky. "How can God not listen to such a voice as his?" she said.

He looked back into his wife's gaze, and some of the weight on his heart lifted. She was right, he thought. If ever mortal man deserved to be saint, that man was Ethelred. Ethelred would help him. He nodded, unaware of the shadowy look below his eyes that was so worrying her. "Yes," he said. "That is true."

She smiled. Her eyes were so beautiful, he thought. Then: I am not alone, after all. I have Elswyth.

"His love will give you strength," she said.

"Yes."

She was right, he thought, facing front and letting his eyes rest on the tapestry-covered coffin on the cart before him. Ethelred had always given him strength.

Then, with a gut twist of anguish that no faith, however sincere, could completely relieve: *Oh Ethelred, I shall miss you so.*

Cyneburg broke down during the funeral Mass. Her audible, broken-hearted sobbing made it much harder for Alfred to bear. He would have to settle some manors on Cyneburg, he thought, trying to distract himself, horribly afraid that he would break down also. Ethelred had left all the royal property in his hands. Alfred did not look forward to talking privately with Ethelred's wife. He feared she might be bitter that the kingship had been taken from her son. Surely she had expected that the boy would succeed his father.

So had Alfred.

He met with Cyneburg late in the afternoon, after Ethelred had been interred within the abbey grounds. The sky was still light when he requested an interview with his sister-by-marriage and they went together into the abbey garden to talk.

"You must tell me which of the manors you would like most to live at," Alfred said, "and I will see them made over to you by charter."

"Thank you," she replied, her voice expressionless.

"Cyneburg . . ." He looked at her helplessly. They had ever been friendly, but never close, and he felt the distance between them now most sorely. "Ethelred's children are as dear to me as my own," he said at last. "You must never hesitate to ask me for aught that they might need."

They were standing facing each other before a small clump of flowering apple trees. The scent of the blossoms was sweet on the air. "I understand that the kingship must go to you, Alfred," Cyneburg said now tonelessly. "Ethelred explained it to me and I understand. Ethelhelm is too young to take command of the country at such a perilous time. I see that. But . . ."

She looked at him directly for the first time since they had left the guest hall. "I want you to promise me you will name Ethelhelm as your heir," she said.

He looked at her, his face very grave. "He is still too young, Cyneburg. If I should die in battle, it will fall to the witan to name a king who is of full age to lead the country. I cannot name a child to succeed me. Even if I did, it would not be heeded by the witan."

"I mean . . ." She bit her lip. "I mean for later, for when the children are grown up." She set her jaw and said it. "I want you to promise me you will name Ethelhelm over your Edward."

He was surprised by the anger he felt at her request. How could she think to bind him so at such a time as this? "When the time comes to name my heir, be sure I will name the one I think is best fit to serve the country, Cyneburg," he said. His face had a look about it that caused her to take a step back, away from him. "That is something I learned from Ethelred. And from my father. A king must ever put the good of the country above his own personal ambition."

She looked away from him. It had seemed such a good idea when she had thought of it . . . to protect Ethelhelm's future as best she could.

"Ethelred would be ashamed to hear his wife speaking so," the stern, clipped voice of her brother-by-marriage said now, and tears sprang to her eyes again. She began to cry bitterly.

"I am sorry." His arm came around her. "I did not mean to make you cry, Cyneburg. I know you are not yourself. I know how much you miss him. I . . . I miss him too."

She knew he did. She knew that Alfred had truly loved Ethelred. She was ashamed, and that made her weep all the harder. She leaned against the slender body that felt so surprisingly strong. His arm tightened and she let her head fall onto his shoulder.

"Come," he said gently. "Let me take you to your women."

The witan met the following morning in the monks' refectory at Wimborne. Athelred, the new Archbishop of Canterbury, was there, as were the bishops of Sherborne and Winchester, and Ealhard, the Bishop of Dorchester, too. The religious head of Wimborne was not present. Wimborne was a double monastery, housing both men and women religious, and its head was an abbess. Women were not permitted to join the councils of the witan.

The only ealdorman not present was Godfred, Ealdorman of Dorset. There were, as well, a number of the higher-ranking king's thanes, those who had sat on the witan often before. In total, the council numbered near thirty men.

The Archbishop of Canterbury, premier cleric in the land, headed the meeting. "We are met, my lords," he intoned solemnly after the opening prayer, "to choose a successor to our dearly loved Ethelred." The men of the witan, all seated at the simple wooden tables whereon the monks ate their meals, looked back impassively. Alfred sat within the circle of nobles. Ethelred's will lay on the table before him, and his eyes remained fixed on the parchment as the ponderous opening of the witan continued. Then finally the archbishop was saying, "The king has left us a will, which we by rights must hear before we proceed further." All eyes swung to Alfred, and he picked up the parchment and rose from his bench.

He was so young, Ethelnoth of Somerset thought as he listened to the precise, perfectly pitched voice reading Ethelred's wishes in regard to the succession. But twenty-one years old. And the task before him was staggering in its enormity. The only English kingdom with a hope of standing against the Danes was Wessex. And should Wessex fall . . . should it fall, then would England be no more. The Danes would control the entire island. Everything the Anglo-Saxons had done since first they landed here so many hundreds of years ago would be gone, obliterated under the heel of the pagans from the north.

It did not bear thinking of.

Not for the first time did Ethelnoth curse the loss of Ethelbald. There was a king who would have been able to face the Danes!

And yet . . . Alfred was a valiant youngster. Ethelnoth had seen that well at Ashdown. Nor did he shrink from making a decision. There was talk of some illness that hampered him, but Ethelnoth had never seen sign of it. And he was a prince of Wessex' royal line. He traced his ancestry back to Cerdic and Ceawlin. If Wessex would follow any man, it would follow Alfred.

The prince had finished reading and now the archbishop was speaking again. Suddenly a man to Ethelnoth's left was getting to his feet. "My lord bishop." Heads swung to see who was speaking. It was Cenwulf, Ethelnoth saw, king's thane of Dorset. "My lord," the thane was going on, "there is another with a better claim to the kingship than Prince Alfred, and I put his name before you now."

A hum of surprise rose from the benches. Cenwulf raised his voice above the sound. "Athelwold, son of Ethelwulf's eldest son, Athelstan. He it is whose name I place before you, my lords. This prince is full old enough to take up the kingship, as he was not when his father so untimely died."

So, Ethelnoth thought. That was why Godfred of Dorset was not here. He had not wanted to find himself caught between two loyalties.

"How old is Athelwold?" barked the Bishop of Sherborne.

"Twenty, my lord," Cenwulf replied strongly. "But one year behind Prince Alfred."

Ethelnoth's eyes went to Alfred. The prince had seated himself and was looking now at Cenwulf, his face perfectly calm, perfectly sealed.

"Athelwold has the right over Alfred," Cenwulf was continuing. "He is the son of the eldest son of Ethelwulf. It is Athelwold whom we should name to be our next king."

"How many battles has he fought?" It was Ethelm of Wiltshire's harsh voice ringing out. "We have fought with Alfred all this spring. We know his mettle. He is a battle leader we can trust. Now is not the time to name an untried boy to lead Wessex."

"Aye!"

"That is so!"

"Truly spoken!"

"My lords, my lords." The Archbishop of Canterbury struggled to regain control of his meeting.

"Athelwold has the right!" Cenwulf shouted over the archbishop's protesting voice.

"There is no right to the throne of Wessex." Now Ethelnoth himself was on his feet. He looked around at the faces of his peers and saw they agreed with him. "In Wessex the right to name the king falls to the witan," he continued, his hard gray stare now alighting on Cenwulf, who was standing just down the table from him. "It is our right and duty to name the prince of the royal line who seems to us best fit to serve the country. And I say that man is Alfred."

A roar of approval went up from the benches.

"My lord." Now it was Alfred rising to his feet. His crisp voice easily cut through the noise in the room, and quiet began to fall. Alfred looked at Cenwulf, the only thane still remaining on his feet. "If you please, my lord," the prince said, "I should like to speak."

Ethelnoth watched with interest as the king's thane from Dorset, good friend of Ethelwulf's son Athelstan, hesitated, then sat down. That boded well, Ethelnoth thought. There was something about the boy that commanded obedience.

"My lords." Now Alfred was addressing the entire group. "God knows, I never sought this honor. You all do know how much I loved and revered my brother Ethelred." The quiet voice was perfectly steady, yet somehow Ethelnoth could sense the intense emotion behind Alfred's words. And it was true. Scarcely were two brothers ever closer than Ethelred and Alfred had been. Alfred was going on, "But Ethelred, that best and most Christian of kings, has left us and we are forced to choose another. He has asked that the responsibility fall upon me. Almost the last words he spoke to me . . ." For the first time there was a quiver in the perfectly controlled voice. Alfred paused, then continued, steady once again. "Almost the last words he spoke to me were: 'It eases my mind to know that I leave Wessex in such capable hands.' "

Alfred had been looking at the parchment containing Ethelred's will, which lay on the table before him, but now he raised his head. His eyes, darkly golden like his hair, went from face to face around the room. "I do not know if I can lead you to victory over the Danes," he said. "But I will promise you this. I will never give up. I will never surrender. I will keep the fyrds of Wessex in the field, summer and winter, until the Danes are beaten or I am dead." His voice was not emotional; it was cold. Cold and level and implacable. As was his face.

For the first time all morning, the room was deathly silent. In the stillness, Ethelnoth got once more to his feet. He looked at Alfred, then at the circle of men seated on the refectory benches around him. "My lords," he said into the quiet, "I propose the witan name Prince Alfred to be our king."

The silence was shattered as the entire room, with the exception of Cenwulf, rose to its feet with a roar.

Later, when the clamor had somewhat subsided and the men were standing in groups of twos and threes talking, Osric of Hampshire came up to Ethelnoth. The two stood for a moment in silence, looking at the figure of Alfred standing in the midst of a circle of taller, heavier men.

"Do you realize," Osric said softly, close to his ear, "that the fate of England hangs today on the heart and brain and arm of that young man?"

"Yes," said Ethelnoth in a voice almost as clipped as Alfred's. "I do." Then, more deeply: "We must all pray that he proves himself equal to so high a task."

"Amen," said Osric, as if in answer to a prayer.

The witenagemot was held in the morning, and in the afternoon Alfred was crowned. It was a hasty ceremony, held in the abbey church, with little of the splendor that had attended the crowning of Alfred's brothers. But the coronation was perhaps the most portentous that Wessex had ever held. If the Danish army was not turned back, this might be the last king of their own that the West Saxons would ever raise. This was the thought in everyone's mind as they went through the all-too-familiar ceremony that would give Wessex a new king.

Alfred's headache started midway through the Mass. There was no warning for this one; it came on swiftly, like a herd of thundering horses. Within fifteen minutes it was in full force, hammering its agony through his temples and across his brow.

He held steady for the whole of the ceremony. To Ethelnoth's discerning eye, the young king looked curiously rigid, with his jaw set and his mouth shut in a hard straight line. As he left the church, Alfred was very white and carried his head in its new gold circlet stiffly, as if he went on holding it erect only by the sheer force of his will.

Overcome, Ethelnoth thought grimly, by the sheer immensity of what he had undertaken. No wonder.

A headache, thought Elswyth, following behind in the procession as they left the church. Then, in despair: Why were all the momentous occasions in Alfred's life doomed to be spoiled by headaches?

As soon as they were in the great court of the abbey, she pushed forward to her husband's side. Relief briefly flickered on his face when he heard her voice.

"My lords," she said firmly, putting an arm through Alfred's. "If you wish your new king to be strong enough to lead you, then I suggest you allow him to get some rest. He has grieved sorely for his brother."

A ring of startled eyes stared at her. The thanes of Wessex were not accustomed to hearing a woman issue orders.

"Of course, my lady." It was Ethelnoth of Somerset, she saw.

"My wife is right. I am . . . tired." Alfred's voice had the hollow sound Elswyth knew, but clearly no one else suspected aught was amiss with him. "I shall speak to you later," he finished.

Then they were free and she was steering him firmly toward the guesthouse in which they were lodged. To the men behind, he must look perfectly upright. Only Elswyth knew how he was leaning on her for guidance. "Can you see?" she asked him in a low undertone.

"The light . . ." he said. "It is hard in the outdoors."

"There are two steps before the guest hall," she said. Then, raising her arm a little: "Now."

She got him to their room and closed the door.

Three hours later, a rider came galloping in from Reading. Knowing that most of the West Saxons were in Wimborne, the Danes had attacked the men of Surrey who were keeping watch on them, and cut them to pieces.

"It was a slaughter, my lord," the messenger reported bitterly to his ealdorman. "We had no chance against them. Those of us who could run got away. I rode as fast as I could to Wimborne to bring you the news."

"We must tell the king," said Ulfric of Surrey. And a grim detachment of ealdormen and king's thanes marched out into the great court and moved in a body toward the guesthouse where Alfred was lodged.

Elswyth stepped before them when they were halfway across the hall. "Alfred cannot be disturbed," she said. "He is sleeping."

"He will be disturbed for this, my lady," Ulfric said, and continued to walk forward.

"*I said to stop.*" It was the tone of her voice more than her words that halted them in their tracks. Six pairs of male eyes stared in amazement at Alfred's wife. She said, her Mercian drawl very evident, "What is so important that you must see my lord? If it is indeed that serious, then I will wake him for you."

To his own astonishment, Ulfric told her.

"I see." The girl's blue eyes, for she *was* no more than a slip of a girl, Ethelnoth thought, flicked from face to face. They waited. "I will bring him," she said. "Wait here." And she turned and went into the room.

There was an uncomfortable silence among the ealdormen. Then Ethelnoth laughed. "Never did I think to find myself faced down by a woman," he said humorously. His words broke the tension and the rest of the men laughed as well. Then they looked at the door of the king's room and waited.

It did not take long. Suddenly the door opened again and Alfred was among them, fully dressed and in perfect command of himself. At least, thought Ethelnoth, he did not take long to wake.

It was Elswyth's face more than Alfred's that gave away to Ethelnoth that something was wrong. She watched her husband with such fierce intensity. Just so, he thought, would a wild creature watch her ailing young. He looked again at the king.

There were shadows like bruises under the too-dark eyes. He stood too still, and he never moved his head. Suddenly Ethelnoth realized what was wrong. Alfred was in pain.

He remembered the rumors about an illness. So, he thought. They were true.

Whatever the problem, however, Alfred's brain was still functioning. Their orders were very clear. They were to call up as many men as they could and ride for the standing cross that marked the crossing of the Roman roads that led south from Meretun and Reading to Winchester and to Wilton. "If they are coming for the heart of Wessex, they will take one or both of those roads," Alfred said. "Time is imperative. Do not linger to collect the unwilling. Take what men you can find and meet me at the standing cross. I will be there tomorrow."

"My lord," they said. "We will."

Within an hour the ealdormen had ridden out of Wimborne to collect an army for the king.

Chapter 21

*T*WO thousand men met at the standing cross the following day. Alfred had sent thanes from his own hearthband north to scout the situation in both Meretun and Reading, and the West Saxon army waited to learn what news they could of the Danes. They waited also for their supply wagons to come up.

"They can yet get by us if they take the road direct from Reading to Winchester and bypass meeting up with their forces from Meretun," Alfred said at the end of the first day's wait. And he sent Ethelnoth with the men of Somerset to hold the main Winchester road while the rest of them kept guard at the crossroads of the two other roads that led into the heart of Wessex.

After three days the scouts returned with the news that both parts of the Danish army had joined at Reading and were moving south along the main road toward Silchester. At Silchester they would have the choice of either of two roads, the one Alfred was guarding, which led toward Wilton, or the one guarded by Ethelnoth, leading to Winchester. Alfred gritted his teeth and waited. The following day further news came that the Danes were pitching camp in Silchester.

Alfred was bitterly disappointed. He did not have the men to attack a Danish camp, and had hoped to be able to meet them out in the open, where the West Saxons had had some success in the past. The longer he had to wait, the harder it would be for him to keep his men in the field.

He decided to march north to see if he could harry the Danes badly enough to force them to leave Silchester.

"Every time we send out a raiding party, we lose men." Guthrum was disgusted. The men lost in the last raid had belonged to him. "They won't come out and fight. It's just arrows falling from nowhere, and then nothing."

"They remember what happened when the men they left to guard Reading made themselves too visible," Erlend replied. He and his uncle were lodged within one of the crumbling old Roman buildings in the ancient town, and now he plucked a few strings on his harp. Then he said, "Clearly they do not have the numbers to attack us directly."

"Their king is dead." Guthrum's blue eyes gleamed with the thought. He had been bitterly disappointed not to have slain Ethelred on the battlefield. The king's subsequent demise from his wounds had been eminently satisfactory to the jarl.

"Ethelred is dead," Guthrum repeated now, "but still we know little of the succession. Heretofore the West Saxons' strength has lain in their unity. I wonder if that unity will survive the death of Ethelred."

A little silence fell, and Guthrum ran his fingers through the heavy yellow bangs on his forehead. "I would give much to learn the answer to those questions," he murmured half to himself.

Erlend ran his fingers over his harp strings, calling up a dazzle of notes. "Would you like me to try to find out?" he asked.

Guthrum's head turned sharply. "You?"

Erlend shrugged. "I can take my harp around the countryside once more."

Guthrum frowned with impatience. "Your little disguise will not serve us this time, Nephew. Simple country folk will not yet know what has taken place in the councils of the great."

Erlend's face stiffened. The hint of scorn in his uncle's deep voice rankled. Guthrum had not belittled his "little disguise" when he had proposed it to Halfdan last winter. Nor had he hesitated to take the credit for Erlend's accomplishments.

"Perhaps," Erlend said, producing yet another elaborate shower of sound, "perhaps I can find my way into the household of one of their nobles."

There was a long pause. Then Guthrum said, "Your confidence has grown, youngster. It is one thing to fool the simple, another to hoodwink the great."

"Not so much difference," Erlend replied. His greenish eyes flicked over Guthrum's face. He had no illusions about the way his uncle's mind was working. Should Erlend fail and be discovered, then Erlend would be out of Guthrum's way. On the other hand, should Erlend succeed, then would the Danes have some useful information. And Guthrum would manage to take the credit for having such a clever kinsman.

Guthrum smiled. His wolf smile, Erlend thought. "It is not an ill idea," his uncle said. "Find out who has been named king, and who is opposing him."

"My lord . . ." Erlend bared his own teeth in a return grin. "I will."

After two weeks the only troops remaining to Alfred were his own household thanes and the thanes of the ealdormen's hearthbands. It was May, and at home the farmers were facing their yearly problem of keeping their animals fed until the spring grass was thick enough for grazing. The fodder problem was always serious in the spring, and spring had been late in coming this year.

Alfred himself fell back on Wilton, sending Ealdorman Osric and his men to occupy Winchester. It would be easier to feed the thanes of the hearthbands from the royal manors than it was in the field.

It took Alfred three days to move his men to Wilton, encumbered as they were with the supply wagons, and it was at their first overnight camp near to Wodnesford that they were joined by an itinerant harper. It was Edgar who first spotted the boy lurking by the side of the road and called him into the light of the fires.

"I'll play you a song for some supper, my lords," Erlend said, looking around the firelit faces with his most winning smile. He ran his fingers over the strings enticingly. He was an excellent harper.

The West Saxons waved him closer and he took a place among them, fitted his harp into the crook of his arm, and asked simply, "What will you have?"

"Eat first, lad," said the thane beside him good-naturedly. "No cause to play on an empty stomach."

"That is so," said someone else, and brought to Erlend a bowl of stew from the pot on the cookfire.

"Where are you from, lad?" another man asked as Erlend began to eat. The stew was surprisingly good.

"I am Frankish, my lord," the boy returned.

"What brings you to Wessex?" asked yet another. There was no suspicion in the questions, and Erlend had grown comfortable with his story over the course of the winter.

"I had a fancy to see the world," he answered readily. "There were ten of us at home, and no tears shed to see me go."

The men around the fire nodded and shrugged. So went the world. Erlend finished his stew and took up his harp. "I know some of the song of *Beowulf*," he said.

"That will do," said the man beside him, and Erlend ran his fingers over his harp, bending his ear close to listen to each individual string. Then he raised his head and shook back his hair from his brow. He did not wear it short like the rest of the men in the Danish camp, but shoulder-length, in the style of the West Saxons.

" 'Hark!' " he began, and ran through the notes again, " 'to the story of the bygone glory of the Danish kings and the doings of their princes. Of how Scyld Scefing, the dread of armies, brought hostile nations into thrall and struck grim terror into the hearts of their lords.' "

His voice was clearly chanted, his harp the perfect background for the stirring words. A sigh of satisfaction ran around the circle of men and they settled down more comfortably to listen.

Erlend played for fully an hour, and all during that time men kept moving closer and closer to the fire around which he sat. When finally he put aside the harp, they paid him the tribute of silence.

Then, "Very well sung," said a crisp voice from the far side of the fire. It was one of the men whom they had made room for early in the song. "What is your name?"

"Erlend, my lord," the boy replied. He had decided last winter he would be less likely to make a mistake if he used his own name.

"Erlend," said another voice. "This is not a Frankish name."

He had his reply ready. "My mother's mother was from Norway, my lord."

"Give the boy a drink," the man with the distinctive voice said. "He must be thirsty after such an effort."

"Yes, my lord!" Three men made to get up, one said, "I'll get it," and the others sat back down.

A drink of ale was brought to Erlend, and as he sipped it gratefully, he looked across the fire. The flames showed him the figure he sought. That color hair looked familiar, he thought. Then, as the man rose to his feet, Erlend recognized him. He had seen that way of moving once before, on the battlefield at Ashdown. Even in full battle dress, Alfred had moved like a cat.

Erlend finished his ale as Alfred, followed by three of his men, left the fire. The boy wiped his mouth with his sleeve, turned to the thane next to him, and asked guilelessly, "Who was that man with the golden hair?"

The man's firelit face broke into a smile. "Why, that was the king, my boy. That was Alfred himself."

"Oh." Erlend let his eyes widen into awe. "I did not know I was playing my harp for a king!"

Good-natured laughter rose from those who were listening. Erlend drew up his knees and propped his chin on them. He looked about fourteen sitting there, and he knew it. "I did not even know who the new king was," he said.

The man beside him looked surprised. "There should have been little doubt in the country about who would be chosen. Alfred is the only one to lead us in such a time of peril. Surely all of Wessex knows that."

"But did not King Ethelred have sons?" Erlend's eyes were round with assumed innocence.

"The boy is a Frank," a voice to his left said, as if Erlend's nationality would explain his ignorance.

The man beside him retied his garter as he told Erlend kindly, "Ethelred's sons are too young. Ethelred himself knew that. In his will he named Alfred, his brother, as his heir."

"He did?" Erlend did not have to feign surprise. This emotion was genuine. "That was . . . selfless of him," he said. "Few kings would choose to bypass their own direct descendants."

"The royal house of Wessex is not like other kingly houses," came the proud reply from somewhere down the circle. "Your Frankish princes would cut each other's throats before they would assist each other. The house of Cerdic is not like that. They are for the country first. All of Wessex does know that."

Erlend's neighbor added, "And all of Wessex does know the love and the trust King Ethelred had for his brother. Alfred was the only choice in such a time as this."

Erlend listened hard but there was not the hint of a dissenting voice in the group. The young Dane lay down to sleep in the midst of the West Saxon thanes and mulled over what he had learned.

If what the thanes had said was true, then truly the house of Cerdic was singular among the race of men. But these were Alfred's own men, Erlend thought. As were the folk at Lambourn, who had given him a previous report of the relationship between Ethelred and his brother. Erlend strongly doubted that things in Wessex were as unified as these thanes would have him think. It was not in the nature of man to be, as one of the thanes had said, "for the country first." Erlend had no doubt that he lived in an age of wolves. Now that Wessex' crowned king was dead, the wolves would be out and snarling over the kingdom he had left.

Erlend decided he would stay with the army for a little longer, to see just who the wolves turned out to be.

The Saxon army was up early the following morning, but to Erlend, who was accustomed to the speed with which the Danes could move, Alfred's men seemed ponderously slow. It was the lack of horses, he supposed as he marched along in the midst of the fyrd, his harp over his shoulder, listening to the talk about him. An army that traveled by foot was considerably slower than an army that traveled on horseback, he thought. The only men on horseback among the Saxons were the king, his immediate companion thanes, and the ealdormen. In contrast, every Danish soldier was mounted. The East Anglian horses they had acquired upon landing in England had proved invaluable.

A distinct advantage for the Danes, Erlend thought, they could outrun the Saxons anytime they chose. A useful piece of information for him to pass on to Halfdan and Guthrum when he returned to camp.

The rows of thanes moved slowly down the thinly graveled Roman road, and Erlend's green eyes flicked from line to line of the marching men, counting numbers. Not nearly the number that had fought at Ashdown, he thought. But all the men seemed well-accoutred, and carried swords as well as spears, the sure sign of the upper class. The farmers, apparently, had gone home.

Erlend found his eyes going back again and again to the figure of Alfred, riding his chestnut stallion so confidently at the head of his marching men. Erlend could almost find it in his heart to pity the boyishly slender West Saxon king. Alfred could not possibly stand against the army the Danes had collected at Reading this April. He was outnumbered nearly four-to-one.

The West Saxon thanes seemed to expect that Erlend would make camp with them and he was tuning his harp, waiting for the cookfires to be lit, when a clean-shaven young man with brown hair and greenish eyes rather like his own came up to him and said, "Harper, the king invites you to sup with him this night."

Erlend got slowly to his feet. The thane's resemblance to him did not extend to size. He had to look up to meet the other man's eyes even when he was finally standing. "I am honored," he said softly, and slinging his harp over his back, he fell into step beside Alfred's man.

"We do not have any harpers with the fyrd," the thane told him as they walked together toward the king's camp place. "In truth, the royal harpers have all grown too old to march any great distance. So it is a boon to have you fall in with us like this." The man, who looked to be but in his early twenties, smiled down at him. "My name is Brand," he said. "I am one of Alfred's companions."

"Is that why you wear a headband?" Erlend asked ingenuously.

Brand laughed. "Yes. It has been our badge ever since Nottingham."

Erlend deliberately slowed his steps. "Nottingham?" he asked, widening his eyes with simulated wonder. "Was there a battle at Nottingham? I thought the Mercian and West Saxon kings chose not to fight."

"It was the Mercian king who did not want to fight." This was evidently a sore point. "They should have listened to Alfred," Brand said. "We had the fyrds of two countries at Nottingham and we let the Danes go free."

"Alfred wanted to fight?" Erlend asked.

"Yes. Do not think, Harper, that it was the men of Wessex who backed away from Nottingham. It was the Mercians." Brand sounded as if the word "Mercian" left a bad taste in his mouth.

Before Erlend could ask another question, however, they had reached their destination. "Come," said Brand, and the thane walked directly up to where the king was standing, with Erlend trailing behind him. "I have brought the harper, my lord," Brand said. And turned aside to gesture Erlend closer.

It was the first time Erlend had ever seen Alfred up close, and he bowed his head, then looked with candid curiosity at the man standing before him. Alfred was taller than Erlend, but still no one would ever call the West Saxon king a big man. His shoulder-length hair was a unique shade of dark gold, and he was almost boyishly slim in build. He was clean-shaven, and in the glow from the cookfire his skin gleamed with a faintly golden glow. If he were a girl, Erlend thought, you would have called him beautiful.

Erlend thought of the strong bones and massive muscles of his uncle. Next to Guthrum, Alfred of Wessex would look like a child. If Erlend had not seen Alfred fight at Ashdown, he would have wondered how the West Saxons ever chose him to be their king.

But Erlend remembered Ashdown all too well, and he remembered also the defense this man had organized to cover the retreat of his wounded brother from Meretun. For all his apparent delicacy, Alfred was a man to be reckoned with.

Alfred said to him, "I am pleased to welcome so accomplished a harper into our camp." Erlend's musician's ears noted that the king's voice was of the middle register, but his way of speaking was short and clipped.

Erlend suddenly remembered that no poor lowborn harper would stare quite so boldly at a crowned king, and he dropped his eyes. "Thank you, my lord," he replied, and shuffled his feet a little to denote his awe. "It is my good fortune to have fallen in with so generous a group," he added.

"We will make you sing for your supper," Alfred said. "I heard you last night. You are very good."

The words were certainly not extravagant. There was no reason for such a thrill of pride to run through him. Erlend frowned, annoyed with himself. "Thank you, my lord," he said shortly, aware that he sounded ungracious, and was even more annoyed.

Alfred appeared not to notice, but gestured the boy to a place near the cookfire. Seating himself, Erlend was startled to find the king was taking the place beside him. Brand served Alfred his dinner, which tonight was dried fish, and next he served Erlend.

Harpers, Erlend knew, were honored by the West Saxons, but he had not quite expected this.

"You are Frankish?" the king asked pleasantly as Erlend took up his fish.

"Yes, my lord," Erlend replied cautiously. Guthrum had said truly that it was one thing to fool the simple but another to hoodwink the great.

"My father's second wife was Frankish," Alfred said. "She was a very great lady. Judith of France. She is married now to Baldwin of Flanders."

Erlend knew the story of Judith of France. All of Europe knew the story of Judith of France. Another beautiful woman who had trampled all decency in the dust in order to get the man she wanted into her bed. What had Alfred called her? A very great lady? Erlend's mother was a very great lady also. He did not think much of the breed.

"I am the son of simple folk, my lord," he said now, woodenly. "I know little of princes."

"Yet you know the courtly songs," came the easy answer. "And the harp you carry is a fine one."

Erlend made himself chew his fish slowly. So there was a brain under that gleaming golden hair, he thought. He felt a pleasant sense of exhilaration stir within him. He was going to have to think. He swallowed his fish. "I learned to play from a wandering harper, my lord." He took a bite from his barley bread. Better not to volunteer too much information, he thought. Only answer direct questions. "He had played all over England and Europe at one time," Erlend mumbled rudely around the bread in his mouth. "He was old when I met him, and when he died he left me his harp."

"I see," Alfred said. He had not eaten the fish, Erlend noticed. Now, for the first time, he took a bite of his bread.

"We should reach Wilton by midday tomorrow, my lord," Brand said on Alfred's other side. "The weather looks to hold fair."

"That will be good," Alfred replied tranquilly. "It is always good to come home."

Erlend was still with the Saxon army when it arrived at the royal manor of Wilton the following afternoon. He stayed partly because he still did not have the information he wanted, and partly because it was a challenge he could not resist, to come within the very halls of the enemy's stronghold and still maintain his disguise. The West Saxon thanes welcomed his company good-naturedly and told him there was always room on a hall bench for a harper of his talent.

It was danger of a very different sort from the kind offered on the field of battle, and Erlend was discovering a distinct taste for it.

They rode into Wilton under a cobalt-blue sky. Erlend, who had never seen the palaces of France, was impressed with this dwelling of the kings of Wessex. There were five substantial-size dwelling halls within the wooden palisade fence of Wilton, as well as the church and the outbuildings and the barns. Each of the halls had a second floor, where the serving folk slept. The chief thanes slept in the halls beneath, with the remainder of the army camping out within the perimeter of the manor walls. Erlend was surprised to be given a bench in the smallest of the dwelling houses; another sign, he thought, of the respect for harpers evinced by the West Saxons. The sleeping room in this particular hall was being occupied by the Ealdorman of Kent, Ceolmund by name, and it was Ceolmund's thanes among whom Erlend was quartered.

The small hall was soon filled with thanes, arranging their gear and checking their weapons. Erlend put his harp carefully under his allotted bench and decided to go outdoors into the courtyard, away from the noise and the clutter that was accumulating so quickly indoors.

The courtyard was busy as well, with serving girls scurrying with buckets of water and serving men running back and forth with messages and food. A number of Alfred's thanes lounged comfortably in the sun, leaning against a hitching post before the great hall. Suddenly, through the open gate there came a single horse and rider. Erlend, like everyone else in the courtyard, turned to look.

It was a black-haired girl, Erlend saw in surprise, riding the most beautiful filly he had ever seen. The filly snorted in surprise at the number of people before her and reared. The girl leaned forward a little and patted the gleaming chestnut shoulder. The filly came down, halted, and stood watching the scene before her out of wide white-rimmed eyes. The girl made no attempt to press the horse forward, but from the movement of her lips, Erlend could see she was talking.

The door of the main hall opened and Erlend saw Alfred come out. There was a very small girl riding on his shoulders, and from the color of the child's hair Erlend guessed she must be his daughter. Alfred came lightly down the stairs, his hands raised to hold the child's small hands in order to balance her, and walked across the courtyard toward the girl on the chestnut filly.

A voice floated to Erlend's ear. "Mama!" He realized in some surprise that this black-haired girl must be Alfred's queen.

The filly's ears pricked forward as Alfred approached, but she stood quietly enough. The girl—the queen—remained in the saddle until her husband was by her side. They remained thus for a few minutes, talking. Then Alfred went to the filly's head and held the bridle while the girl dismounted.

She swung down with effortless ease and Erlend was shocked to see that she was wearing trousers, just like a man. Alfred beckoned, and a serving man, one of the twenty or so people who had been watching this scene with silent fascination, came running forward to take the filly's reins and lead her to the stable. The king and the queen came across the courtyard toward the main hall, deep in conversation. The child was still perched on her father's shoulders, but now her hands were wound into his hair for balance.

The three went up the steps and into the hall, out of the view of those in the courtyard. The thanes and serving folk, who for the last five minutes had been frozen into stillness, began to talk and move about again.

Erlend realized that someone was standing beside him, and he turned to the thane and asked, "Was that the queen?"

"We do not have queens in Wessex," came the unexpected answer. "But that was Alfred's wife, the Lady Elswyth."

"No queens?" Erlend was surprised.

"It is not our custom." The thane, who was of Ethelnoth's hearthband, looked at Erlend with tolerance. "It is never wise to give a woman too much power," he said.

There was a brief pause as Erlend pushed away from his mind's eye the image of Eline's small heart-shaped, green-eyed face. "I suppose that is true," he answered then, his clear harper's voice a little harsh.

"That was the king's daughter," the thane continued.

"I thought so. They have the same color hair."

"There is a son also." The thane seemed eager to establish that fact. "He is but a few months old, but very promising, they say."

"I am certain that he is," Erlend replied politely. His own half-brother back at Nasgaard would be older than that, he thought. Would be as old as the little girl who had ridden so securely upon her father's shoulders. Was Asmund carrying his son about in such a loving and paternal way?

Somehow, Erlend doubted it.

Chapter 22

*T*HE following morning Alfred's personal household priest said Mass in the church for the king, the ealdormen, and the thanes of the witan. One of the first things Alfred had done after his coronation was to find a congenial personal priest to travel with him. While he was but second in command, the manor priests had been sufficient, but the king must always travel with a priest for himself and his men. Alfred had bypassed Ethelred's chaplain, a man pious enough but unlearned and simple, and named a man from Canterbury, one of the few priests left in Wessex who could somewhat read and write in Latin.

Consequently, while Father Erwald said Mass in the church, the household priest of Wilton said Mass in the great hall for the rest of the thanes and the household folk. Erlend went with the others, afraid to differentiate himself in any way.

It was the first time the Dane had ever attended a Christian religious service, and he was extremely disappointed. He did not understand the Latin. There was no sacrifice, no banquet. He had always understood that Christians feasted on the flesh of their god, but there was nothing like that. The priest gave out small pieces of bread, which were received reverently by about half of those present, and that was all. Erlend did not go forward to take the bread. He had been careful to imitate the actions of those around him, but he was not at all certain of the ritual and did not want to make a mistake.

It did not seem like much, he thought, watching as the thane next to him bowed his head and moved his lips in what Erlend supposed was prayer. Depressingly tame, in fact. Erlend had expected more.

In a mere hour it all was finished and the trestle tables were being set up for breakfast.

A tedious religion, Erlend thought. Guthrum would laugh at it. Assuredly, it held no interest for a warrior.

After a breakfast of bread and honey and porridge had been served, Erlend slipped away from the hall and went out through the manor gate.

He thought he would spy out the countryside as best he could. He had not been this far south and west during his travels last winter.

It was another magnificent spring day. The grass had greened and thickened these past weeks, and the fenced pastures lying without the manor walls looked temptingly rich and lush. Certainly the horses turned out in the nearest pasture seemed to think so. They were all grazing industriously and did not even raise a head when Erlend began to walk toward the wattle fence that held them in. All, that is, except the beautiful chestnut filly Erlend had seen Alfred's wife riding the day before. The filly was standing nearest the fence, head already lifted, gazing in the direction of the manor. Erlend walked slowly in her direction, wishing he had a treat he could offer her.

The chestnut filly remained where she was and watched him come. When he reached the five-foot wattle fence he halted and looked her over with reverent awe. Like most Danes, Erlend was a good horseman, and his father had kept some highly bred stock in the pastures of Nasgaard. He knew a good animal when he saw one.

This one was almost perfect, he thought. Her legs were long, slender but strong, the knees flat and the canon bones sufficiently short. Her shoulder had admirable length and slope and her withers were well-defined for so young a mare. Her hindquarters showed great depth, with strong muscling through the stifle and the gaskin. Her head was particularly beautiful, he thought, lost in admiration of the big eyes, small neat ears, and chiseled shape of her nostrils. Her coat gleamed reddish gold in the bright sunlight. She was beautifully cared-for, Erlend thought with approval, and obviously well-treated. She watched him with mild interest and absolutely no fear. Then, all of a sudden, her ears pricked.

"What a complete beauty you are," he was saying in reverence when a deep drawling voice spoke from behind him.

"And well she knows it." Startled, Erlend turned and saw Alfred's wife standing there on the grass. Elswyth smiled at him. "Her name is Copper Queen. Copper for short. I think she likes your compliments. She is very vain."

"I . . . She is beautiful . . ." Erlend stammered.

The darkest blue eyes he had ever beheld looked forthrightly into his. "You should see her gaits," Elswyth answered, and came forward to stand beside him.

Erlend found himself at a loss for words. He had been at some distance from Alfred's wife in the courtyard yesterday and had not had a really good view of her face. Up close and under the brilliant glare of the merciless sun, he realized that she was extraordinarily beautiful. She was not wearing trousers today, but a blue gown that was obviously old. Erlend had to look down to meet her eyes, which pleased him tremendously and gave him a little courage.

"Her hooves are a trifle small," he said. "That is the only flaw I can see in her."

The blue eyes flashed, then narrowed thoughtfully. "Perhaps they are a trifle small," the girl admitted after a moment. "But they have given no trouble thus far. She is so very well put together otherwise that there is little shock to her feet when she moves."

"Yes, I can see that she must be a comfortable ride," he said. "The slope of the shoulder . . ."

He broke off because suddenly she was smiling at him. He realized, as he gazed in wonder at that lovely face, that she was very young. As young as he, he would wager. "You do know horses," she was saying in warm approval. "How nice."

Erlend dragged his eyes away from hers in a little confusion. "What is that you are carrying?" he asked hurriedly, gesturing to the equipment she was holding in her hands. As far as he could see, she was carrying a long rope, a bridle, some separate reins, a girth, and a whip.

"I am going to work Copper today on the long rope," Elswyth answered.

"What is the long rope?" She was so matter-of-fact that he found himself losing his awe and becoming more comfortable. And he really was interested. He had always been very fond of horses; his pony, in fact, had been the best companion of a lonely childhood.

Copper nickered, not pleased by Elswyth's neglect. Elswyth laughed and went to hang her equipment on the fence, answering briskly as she moved, "It is a system I invented when I was with child and unable to ride. I found that in some ways the long rope is more effective than riding, particularly with a young horse. The horse isn't trying to find her balance under an additional weight, you see."

"But what is the point of it?" asked Erlend. "What are you trying to do?"

"I am teaching Copper to carry herself properly," came the surprising answer. Elswyth had been rubbing the filly's forehead and now she proceeded to give her an apple.

"Carry herself?" Erlend said in bewilderment as the filly crunched enthusiastically. "All horses know how to carry themselves."

"All horses go on their front legs," Elswyth said, proffering the other half of the apple. It was accepted with alacrity. "I like my horses to use their hind legs. If a horse has his hind legs active and under him, the rider has more control. And the horse is lighter and in better balance, able to do what you ask with dexterity and ease."

"I never heard aught of this," Erlend said with wonder.

"Alfred says there is a book by some Greek that tells about the training of the horse. He wrote to France to try to procure it for me." The single braid she wore was as thick as his wrist and fell sheer to her waist, gleaming blue-black in the bright sunlight. "The Greeks used horses in battle," she added, "so control and dexterity were of prime importance to them." She rubbed Copper's forehead again, then turned to walk along the fence to the gate. The filly, on the other side of the fence, walked right along with her.

"Can you read?" Erlend asked in astonishment.

She flashed him a grin over her shoulder. "No. But Alfred can. He can even read Latin, and he says he will translate this book and read it to me when once he gets it."

"Oh," said Erlend, amazed by a king who, in the midst of fighting for his country's very life, would take the time to send for a book. For his wife.

"Would you like to watch while I work with Copper?" Elswyth asked.

"Yes. I would like that very much."

An approving nod was tossed his way before she began to bridle her horse. "It is nice to find someone who is knowledgeable about horses," she said. "Most of the thanes, though they take good care of their animals, have not the patience to properly train and ride a horse." She was putting the girth on now, which was not properly a girth but a long band that went around the horse's whole middle. Then she attached the long reins she had brought from the girth to the bit rings.

"How did you learn, my lady?" he asked, coming to hold the gate for her as she led the filly out.

"What I know I figured out for myself," the king's wife answered. "But how I would love to get my hands on that book!"

Erlend spent the morning watching Elswyth, completely forgetting his initial plan of spying out the country surrounding Wilton. He found her work with the long rope utterly fascinating. It seemed that all she did was hold the rope and whip and make Copper Queen trot in a large circle around her, but Erlend was perceptive enough to see how the filly's way of going changed after about five minutes. By the end of the session Copper's hind legs were stepping into the marks made by her front hooves, and she was carrying her head stretched out low and almost on the vertical. It was beautiful.

"I must feed my son," Elswyth said as they walked together back toward the manor gates. "But why do you not come and play your harp for me this afternoon? I should like to hear you."

After a fractional hesitation, Erlend agreed.

At midday a party of men Erlend had not seen before rode into Wilton. From the quality of the leader's horse and clothing, Erlend thought he must be important. The leader disappeared into the great hall, and perhaps half an hour later Erlend followed, carrying his harp.

The great hall of Wilton was the only one of the manor halls that did not have a second floor. The ceiling here rose very high, with beams supporting the roof. There were tapestries adorning the wooden walls, and a display of arms hung over the high seat. The hearthplace in the center of the hall was unusual in that it was made from brick and not stone.

There were a few thanes sitting on the benches; the spring day had called most of the men outdoors. But Alfred was there, sitting on a bench beside the high seat, three dogs sprawled at his feet and the man who had just ridden in sitting beside him. They were deep in talk. Erlend hesitated just inside the door. There was no sign of Elswyth.

The door of the sleeping room at the far end opened and a small girl came tumbling out, spied Alfred, and made for him with arrow-straight determination.

"Papa," she called. "I am awake!"

"So I see," replied the king, and continued his conversation. When his daughter reached him, however, he leaned down and lifted her to sit on his lap.

"Is this your daughter?" the man to whom the king was speaking asked in obvious astonishment. They were not talking loudly, but Erlend had excellent ears and could hear them quite well.

"Yes." Alfred smiled. "This is Flavia."

"I thought she was but a babe."

"Not a baby!" Flavia said with indignation. "Edward a baby. I a big girl."

"So I see," said the young man. "And very beautiful too."

Flavia was not impressed by compliments. She leaned against Alfred's chest and said, "Who you?"

The redheaded young man grinned. "I am Ethelred," he said. "A friend of your father's."

The young man's voice had the same drawl that had sounded in the Lady Elswyth's, Erlend thought. A few of the thanes on the bench had begun to look at Erlend now, and he walked toward them slowly, still listening to the conversation at the high seat.

"The Lord Ethelred comes from the same country as your mother, Flavia," Alfred was saying. He spoke to the child as if she were much older.

"Where that?" came the instant demand.

"Mercia, love."

Oh, oh, Erlend thought. Mercia. Were the two Saxon countries about to band together? If so, that was not good news for the Danes.

"What do you want here, Harper?" one of the thanes asked. The question was not belligerent, but it was quite deliberate.

"The Lady Elswyth asked me to bring my harp this afternoon to play for her," Erlend answered. "But I do not see her. . . ."

"Oh." The faint wariness in the group relaxed. "She is most likely with the young prince. You may wait here with us if you like."

Erlend nodded and took the bench that had been indicated. The men ignored him and went back to their conversation.

"Curse Burgred for a mewling coward," one of them said. "We went to his aid last year."

Another grunted in agreement. "And if Alfred had had aught to say, we would have fought at Nottingham. It was Burgred who lacked the nerve."

Burgred, Erlend knew, was the King of Mercia. So. It seemed the Mercians would not be coming to the aid of Wessex after all. That was good news.

"Young Ethelred is the only Mercian with fighting blood in his veins," the thane called Edgar said now.

The one named Brand replied, "Ethelred and the Lady Elswyth."

They all laughed. "Aye," a dark-haired man said. "Elswyth would rouse all of Mercia to arms if she were the one to lead." A distinct note of pride sounded in his voice.

"And God help the poor thanes who did not follow her!" They all laughed again.

At that very moment the sleeping-chamber door opened once more and Elswyth herself came out into the hall. Erlend saw that she had changed her gown to one more seemly for such a great lady. And her hair was no longer in its long braid.

"Ethelred," she said, her deep husky voice audible even to those who had not Erlend's sensitive hearing. One of the dogs jumped up and went to greet her, his tail wagging.

"Ethelred has red hair, Mama," Flavia announced, and Elswyth nodded.

"Yes, Flavia, I know." She had reached the high seat now and she and Ethelred exchanged the kiss of peace. She sat down and the dog curled himself at her feet. "What news from Burgred?" Elswyth asked.

"What you would expect," came the terse reply.

"He is still fighting the Welsh?" The scorn in her voice was bitter. The Mercian shrugged and did not answer.

"What the Welsh?" Flavia asked.

Alfred said to his wife, "Will you get her nurse, Elswyth? It is impossible to have a discussion with an echo seated on one's lap."

Flavia shrieked. Elswyth signaled to one of the serving maids who had just come into the hall. "Hilda, take Flavia to Tordis, will you please?"

"Yes, my lady." The girl took his daughter from Alfred after he had unwound her small arms from about his neck, and bore her relentlessly from the room.

"She is beautiful," Ethelred said sincerely.

"She has a will like iron," Flavia's loving father replied.

"I cannot imagine whom she inherited it from," her mother said blandly.

"*I* know," both Alfred and Ethelred replied in unison. Then they both began to laugh.

"She is just like Alfred," Elswyth said to her fellow countryman. "Do not let him fool you with that mild manner, Ethelred. I have never yet seen the man not get what he wanted."

"He didn't get a battle at Nottingham last year," Ethelred replied.

"True." The humor of their conversation died utterly. Elswyth sighed. "That mistake has certainly come back to haunt us."

At this point all the thanes on the bench were openly listening to the conversation of their betters. Erlend rubbed his finger over the wooden frame of his harp and listened as well.

"What of Athulf?" Elswyth asked.

"Athulf is doing the best he can to fortify the towns and the monasteries of Mercia. But he has no authority to call up the fyrd, and Burgred has made no move to do so."

There was a speaking silence. Then, "I wish he would catch a fever and die," said Elswyth.

"Elswyth!" Both Alfred and Ethelred sounded horrified.

"It is true." She was unrepentant. "He is like a deadweight at the top. Nothing can be done while he lives. Not only does he endanger Mercia, but he is useless to Alfred as well. Useless and dangerous. The Lord would do us a favor by taking him."

There was silence. It was evident that both men agreed with her, although they neither felt quite comfortable in saying so. Then Alfred said to Ethelred, "When you returned to Mercia after Ashdown, I did not think to see you again so soon."

"I can do more good for my country fighting with you in Wessex than I can sitting on the Welsh border with Burgred," Ethelred replied grimly. "That is, if you will have me."

"Of course we will have you," Alfred said.

"Oh, Erlend is here." Elswyth had just seen him. "The Frankish harper," she explained to Alfred. "I asked him to come play for me this afternoon."

"A little harping would not come amiss just now," her husband replied. "Have him over."

And so Erlend found himself approaching the King of Wessex, his wife, and one of the chief ealdormen of Mercia. Elswyth said to her husband, "I was talking to Erlend this morning, Alfred. He is a very good man."

"He must know horses," Alfred said instantly.

"You are so amusing," and she gave him a haughty look.

"Know horses?" Ethelred was puzzled.

"Elswyth's measure of a man is how well he sits a horse," Alfred informed his guest.

Elswyth's nose was still in the air. "I did not see Erlend ride," she told her husband. Then, with a faint grin: "But he did watch me work Copper on the long rope and he was able to understand what I was doing. It takes a good eye for a horse to do that."

The king's golden eyes rested on Erlend's face. They were less friendly than his wife's. "If my wife says you are knowledgeable, Harper, then you are." A beat of silence. "I wonder where you learned to judge fine horseflesh?"

Once again Erlend was aware of how quick Alfred was to pick up an incongruity. He answered before ever he knew what he was going to say, "I have not always been fortunate enough to earn my meat by my music, my lord. I have been stableboy too in my time."

"I have ever found that people either have a natural eye for a horse or they do not," Elswyth said. "Look at that dreadful nag Wilfred bought. He thinks it beautiful, and it would be, I suppose, if you cut off its legs." She looked at Erlend. "Its canon bones are thin and long, it's over at the knee, and it's sickle-hocked as well."

One of the thanes on the bench Erlend had left rustled with indignation. Elswyth called over to him, "It is true, Wilfred, as I told you when you bought him."

Erlend smothered a smile; Elswyth's husband did not even try to hide his grin. Ethelred said, "You haven't changed at all, Elswyth."

"I never change," she said complacently.

"Well," said Alfred, and looked at Erlend, "let us have some music."

Two days later a scout came flying into Wilton manor with the news that the Danes were on the march. The word went out to Alfred's thanes: "Coming toward Wilton." And the fighting men began to prepare.

Alfred sent his wife, his children, and an escort of thanes south to Dorchester. Erlend watched them leave, Elswyth riding a small gray gelding and holding her infant son in her arms. Flavia rode with Ethelred of Mercia, whom Alfred had asked to lead the escort guiding his family to safety. Ethelred also was charged with seeing to the defenses of Dorchester, whence the men of Wessex would retreat in case of necessity.

Erlend then judged it was time for him also to depart from Wilton. It was almost a certainty by now that Alfred was not going to be able to collect any meaningful number of reinforcements, so Erlend would be able to give an accurate report of the enemy's numbers to Halfdan. None of the West Saxons were either very interested or very surprised at his going. Clearly they had not expected a small Frankish harper to feel called upon to fight alongside them.

Erlend came upon the Danish army a little to the southwest of Andover. First he sought out Guthrum, who listened to his tale in silence and with somewhat grudging admiration.

"You have done well, Nephew," he said finally when Erlend had finished. "They still do not know who you really are?"

"No."

Guthrum's face took on the look it always wore when he was plotting something. He said nothing further, however, just told Erlend to come with him to see Halfdan.

"You outnumber them by better than four-to-one," Erlend was telling his leader some five minutes later. "Most of their men have gone back to their farms. Alfred has with him only the thanes who live in his hall and the thanes of his ealdormen."

"What is the disposition of the land?" Halfdan wanted to know.

Erlend told him as best he could.

"This Alfred will not want to meet us in the open, then," Halfdan said decidedly. "Not with so little forest to shelter in and with the numbers as uneven as you say. He will either shelter within a fortified position or try to run."

"This Wilton manor is surrounded by stout timber walls," Guthrum said. "Erlend says the West Saxons were preparing for battle, not for flight. They will most likely try to defend the manor."

Erlend agreed with his uncle. "I do not think Alfred will run. He was most certainly preparing to make a stand, and with the shortage of men under him, a defense from behind stout walls is the best that he can do."

"Good," said Halfdan. The Danes were experts in siege warfare. "Then that is where we shall go."

"One other thing, my lord," Guthrum said softly. "I think it would be well for Erlend to keep out of the sight of the West Saxons."

Halfdan looked at the jarl, his bushy gray eyebrows eloquent with surprise. "Why?"

Guthrum smiled, the smile Erlend always classified in his mind as his wolf smile. "They have admitted Erlend to their hearth. He has played for their king, and spoken to him as well. If necessary, he can play the harper again and gain access to their councils."

Halfdan grunted. "A good thought." He showed his own stained teeth. "Better, though, to finish our work at Wilton."

"Yes, my lord," uncle and nephew chorused in reply, then left the king to rejoin their own command.

Chapter 23

*T*HE May weather continued unusually fine and hot as the Danish host poured down the Roman road leading toward Wilton. It was late in the afternoon of May 28 when they turned west onto a local track that Erlend told them would take them directly to the royal manor of Wilton, behind whose palisade they expected to find the men of Wessex awaiting them.

A mile along the track brought them to a meadow situated right beside a stream that fed into the River Wilye. A sloping hill rose to their east, and the track to Wilton stretched before them. The river afforded drink for their horses and the meadow was rich with grass for grazing. Halfdan, whose army outnumbered Alfred's by over four-to-one, confidently ordered his men to make camp for the night. The West Saxons would know he was coming, he thought. There was no hurry. Best to let them sweat a bit and think on the fate of Northumbria and East Anglia.

The light faded late. It was not until after midnight that Alfred was able to move his men from near Old Sarum, where the West Saxons had lain concealed all through the day. Old Sarum was four miles to the east of Wilton, two miles to the east of the meadow whereon the Danes were encamped.

The West Saxons had spent the early part of the night in prayer and in the hearing of confessions. It was a bold gamble they were taking, this meeting of the Danes in open battle, and all knew it. Their chances of success, however, greatly increased when the Danes decided to halt in the meadow instead of pushing on for Wilton. A fight in front of the walls of Wilton would not suit Alfred so well as the grounds he was now likely to get.

Alfred was gambling on several things in this particular venture. He was gambling on the overconfidence of the Danes, that they would not bother to post scouts to their east. If guards were indeed posted and sounded the alarm to Halfdan, it would be impossible for Alfred to gain position on the heights, and the surprise maneuver would end in disaster for the West Saxons.

A desperate gamble indeed, but no other course had been open to him that held out any hopes of survival. Alfred had never had any intention of trying to last out a siege within the walls of Wilton manor. His plan had been to fall on the Danes from the rear, inflict as much damage as possible, then withdraw into the forest of Selwood. But now . . . if the men of Wessex could gain position on the hill and stage a surprise attack at dawn, then perhaps they would even have a chance for victory.

All was quiet when Alfred and his men reached the far side of the hill that lay to the east of the Danish camp. The night was moonless, lit only by distant points of unusually bright stars. The leaders left their horses at the foot of the hill, and the West Saxon thanes, some fifteen hundred strong, began to climb the grassy slope. No cry of alarm disturbed their progress. The Danes, never dreaming that Alfred would have the audacity to offer battle in the open, had not bothered to post scouts.

The West Saxons took up their positions just below the top of the rise and settled down to wait out the night. All was silence. Finally, in the sky to their rear, the waiting thanes could see the sky turning to the light gray of dawn. Then shafts of red began to streak the heavens, and finally it was light enough to see.

All the eyes of the West Saxons were fixed on the slim, bareheaded figure of their king, who was leading the shield column on the right. It was the first time Alfred would be fighting under the royal banner of Wessex, not his own personal banner of the White Horse.

As the eyes of ealdormen and thane watched, the banner of the Golden Dragon was raised on high. The cry came through the early morning air, clear and thrilling. *"Wessex! Wessex!"* And the king was running forward.

His thanes answered him with a roar. *"Wessex! Wessex!"* Then the entire West Saxon army was over the top and thundering down the hill into the unprepared Danish camp below them.

Guthrum could not believe what was happening. They had attacked! He was scarcely out of his bed, had not time to don his armor, time only to grab sword and shield and race forward, his hird of followers at his back, to meet the onrush of West Saxons who had fallen upon them with the unexpected power of an avalanche.

Had the Danes been a less experienced army, Alfred's charge would have carried the day. As it was, many of the Danish warriors, weaponless and unprepared as they were, fell in the first few minutes of the fight. Then they rallied, strong in their discipline to their leaders, strong in their sense of comradeship with each other.

The battle roared on amidst the tents and the cookfires of the Danish camp. The horses, which the Danes had hobbled and set out to graze the night before, went wild with the smell of blood, and the screaming of injured men was punctuated by the screaming of frantic horses fighting to get free of their hobbles.

The Danes struggled to form up into two rough wedge formations, Halfdan commanding one and Guthrum the other. Red streaks of dawn had long since brightened into the full light of day when the first sign of a break came in the deadlock between the two armies. Little by little, the Danes began to retreat.

Guthrum, who knew the mind of Halfdan very well, rallied his men to him and held them together as they slowly let themselves be pushed back by the West Saxons. Erlend, who had been as astonished as anyone by Alfred's attack, and who had been fighting alongside his uncle's hird, was surprised to find that their men were retreating. He said so to the man beside him.

"We'll lure them out of formation," the man grunted to him, his eyes on Guthrum, not on Erlend. "As soon as the jarl gives the signal, see . . ."

And all of a sudden Guthrum's column broke. All around him Erlend saw men beginning to turn and flee. "Come along, you little fool!" someone shouted at him, and then Erlend too turned and followed the Danes as they raced from the field, evidently in fear of their lives.

Ethelnoth was commanding the men opposing Guthrum, though the fighting had been so haphazard and spread out over the littered field that it was truer to say that each man was commanding himself. Consequently, when Guthrum's men turned to flee, there was little Ethelnoth could do to stop his own men from racing in hasty pursuit. After a moment's hesitation, the ealdorman followed as well. Then Halfdan's men began to run from the meadow, and the rest of the West Saxons, flaming with the fire of unexpected victory, tore after.

Alfred swore with frustration. But there was nothing he could do to halt his overeager thanes. In too short a time the meadow was emptied of all but the dead and the dying. All Alfred could hope for was that the Danes were indeed in flight, that this was not another ruse such as they had played on the West Saxons at Meretun.

Surely it could not be, he thought desperately as he stood on the battlefield surrounded only by his personal hearthband. The Danes had been thoroughly surprised. They had not had time to prepare any trick maneuvers. Surely this time they had really been put to flight.

"We beat them!" Edgar, the bearer of the dragon banner, was in no doubt about the outcome of the day.

"Do you not wish to join in the pursuit, my lord?" asked Wilfred, obviously fretting to join the hunt himself.

"No. The ealdormen will command their followers." Alfred looked around. There were perhaps fifty of his own men left on the field. Many faces were looking openly disappointed at his decision. Alfred spoke very crisply. "We will load as many of our wounded as possible onto the Danish horses. Then I want you to ride for Dorchester."

"Now, my lord?" Wilfred was clearly bewildered. "Would it not be best to care for the wounded first, without moving them?"

"Now," Alfred repeated. His face did not look triumphant; it looked worried. "I want the wounded away from here. And I want as many of the Danish horses as we can manage to take." He looked from one dirt-and-blood-smeared face to the next. His own expression was at once both fierce and bleak. "Quickly," he said.

The thanes moved, half going to find bridles from among the litter in the Danish tents, the other half beginning the gruesome job of sorting out those who were wounded but able to ride from those who would have to be left behind.

Within an hour they had mounted fifty men. Alfred sent the party off, escorted by twenty of his own thanes, each of whom was leading two more horses. Then Alfred said to the thanes remaining with him, "Catch and bridle as many horses as you can," and they set to work.

Two hours after the Danish retreat had begun, the tattered remnant of the West Saxon army began trickling into the meadow. The Danes had indeed waited until their enemies were hopelessly spread out, then gathered and turned and cut them down. Fewer than four hundred men made it back to the meadow, and they found their king awaiting them with a supply of bridled horses. "Ride for Dorchester," each was told, and the West Saxon thanes asked no questions, but mounted and fled down the Roman road to the south.

Alfred waited until he could hear the war cries of the pursuing Danes before he mounted Nugget and galloped off after his men.

The Danes returned to the meadow, trimphant in the knowledge of a nearly total victory. Alfred's army had been decimated in the pretend retreat. It was not until half an hour after they had begun the grim work of counting the dead and wounded that word came to Halfdan that they were missing hundreds of their horses.

"Alfred cut the hobbles and let them go," Guthrum said to Erlend with faint scorn. "I did not see him among those pursuing us. He must have been busying himself with the horses. It is a nuisance, of course, but we will catch them. The sound of grain in a bucket will bring them running quickly enough."

It was not until the bridles were missed that the Danes realized what had really happened.

"He stole our horses! Over five hundred of them!" Guthrum was scornful no longer. "We beat him into the ground, but he has five hundred of our horses! Name of the Raven, but he is a resourceful bastard."

"He is clever," Erlend said with narrow-eyed intensity. He was standing beside his uncle in the midst of their scattered belongings.

Guthrum pushed his bloody hand through the evenly cut bangs on his forehead. "We lost two jarls in the initial surprise attack. Two jarls and near a thousand men. We should have posted a guard to the east." His brilliant blue stare was directed at Erlend. "You were the one to say he would try to defend Wilton, Nephew."

Erlend was only too well aware of his own advice. "You outnumbered him over four-to-one," he said. His eyes were very green. "None of you expected him to attack."

After a minute: "That is so," came the somewhat grudging reply. "It seems this Alfred is an opponent worthy of the name."

"It might have been wiser," said Erlend grimly, "to have left them Ethelred."

"We must have a mounted fyrd," Alfred said to Elswyth. "The Danes can move so much faster than we; it is one of their greatest advantages."

It was a warm and hazy July day. Alfred had been away from Dorchester for weeks, and upon his return he and Elswyth had taken their horses and ridden out alone to Maiden Castle for the afternoon. "Do you mean a cavalry, like the Romans?" she asked. They had left their own horses to graze and were stretched out side by side on the grassy hillside where once those very Romans had defeated the native Britons, centuries before the Saxons had ever set a foot on English soil.

"No. The Danes do not fight from horseback, nor has it ever been a tradition of the Anglo-Saxons to do thus. But the Danes travel by horseback. And they move their supplies by river. We cannot hope to keep up with them, Elswyth, unless we learn to imitate them." He punched the grass beside him. "They moved from Wilton back to Reading in a day and a half! It would have taken us three times that long, with our supplies traveling by ox wain."

"They are also reinforced by ship," Elswyth said. "How many more troops sailed into Reading this spring from Denmark? You need to be able to stop them on the sea as well as on the land, Alfred."

"We have no ships!" he cried in frustration.

She shrugged. "You will have to build them."

"We do not have the time to build ships," he said. His voice was quiet now. Quiet and bitter.

She turned her head and looked at him. He was thinner, she thought, thinner and harder. He himself had been in the field almost constantly this spring and summer, leading his own hearthband and small groups from the shire fyrds on flying raids against the Danes, who had settled in at Wilton for a month before finally returning this last week to their base at Reading.

"They pillaged the country around Wilton pretty thoroughly," she said now, "but they did not try to come further south."

"Yet."

She continued to regard him for a minute in silence. He was very tan, and his hair had streaks of blond amongst its usually darker gold. She said at last, her voice carefully neutral, "You know that you should buy them off."

"*No!* I will not stoop to Burgred's level!" His usually controlled voice rasped raw with unsuppressed emotion.

She propped her chin on her updrawn knees. The day was very warm and they both were wearing short sleeves. His muscular forearms were as brown as his face. There was a pulse beating against the skin of his throat. She could see it clearly in the open collar of his shirt. "Wessex is exhausted," she said. "You yourself have just said that you need to reorganize, to change the way you have been fighting. You need time to do that. Buy the Danes off for now, Alfred."

"When I accepted the crown, I told the witan that I would never give up." He reached for a small rock and threw it down the hill. After it had bounced to the bottom and lay still, he said, "How can I sue for peace, Elswyth? It is impossible." He picked up another rock and threw it after the first.

"The Danes have not beaten you," she said. "You are still king, you still have an army in the field. Buy them off and Wessex will still be an independent kingdom. The Danes could not do to you what they did to Northumbria and East Anglia. The folk of Wessex know that well. Their spirit is not broken. They will understand, if you buy a peace, that it is only for a while, that you are buying time to prepare for the future."

"I sneered at Burgred when he bought a peace at Nottingham," he said. She had scarcely ever heard him sound so bitter. "And now you suggest I do the same thing myself?"

She said, "It sounds to me like your pride is getting in the way of your good sense."

There was a reverberating silence. Then, with a fierce lithe movement, Alfred jumped to his feet. He turned his back on her and threw another rock. It arced out into the air, soaring with the force with which it had been thrown, and Elswyth laughed. "Alfred, stop being so dramatic. Cry a peace. Collect more horses for your fyrds. Build some ships. Then, when they come back, we will be ready for them."

He turned to stare at her. His eyes were blazing. "It is not funny!" He was furious.

"The situation is not funny," she said. "You are." Then, impatiently: "For heaven's sake, Alfred, no one is like to confuse you with that fat slug Burgred. They are far more like to praise your good sense. Stop taking the situation so personally."

An odd, arrested look came over his face. He said slowly, "I remember what my father said to me once. It was when he resigned his kingdom to my brother Ethelbald without a fight. He said, 'A true king is one who ever sets the good of his kingdom above his own personal ambition.'"

"Very good advice," Elswyth said.

"I thought then that he was wrong, that he should have fought."

"The Bible says that there is a season for everything," Elswyth said. "A season for fighting and a season for peace. I think Wessex needs a season of peace, Alfred. Even if it hurts your pride to sue for it."

Another silence fell, this one of a considering sort. He turned away from her again and stared off toward the north. "There are other things that need to be done," he said. "We need to start to build fortifications for our people to shelter within. They are too vulnerable, left alone on their farms."

She did not say anything, but her dark blue eyes never left the back of his head. "We need a better system of communication, also," he said.

Silence fell again. The birds circled overhead, the insects buzzed. A white cloud very briefly blocked the sun. Alfred turned at last and looked at his wife. "You are right," he said. His voice was quiet, but the bitterness had gone. "I must sue for peace."

"You knew it all along," she said. "You just needed a push."

He held out his arms and she jumped to her feet and went to him. "I hate it as much as you do," she said, her arms locked about his waist, her cheek against his shoulder. "I want them dead, every last one of them. But you cannot keep an army in the field long enough to finish the task."

"Not this year," he agreed with a sigh. "But I will never give up, Elswyth. They will have to kill me first."

"We will none of us give up," she answered, tightening her arms. "I am not so good a Christian as you, Alfred, but I can see that if we allow the Danes to triumph, we will have plunged England back into the pagan dark. We cannot allow that to happen."

His mouth was pressed against the top of her head. "No." His voice sounded muffled.

"You will have to teach many of the ceorls to ride," she said. "I will be glad to help with that."

He looked down into her face, and his own suddenly blazed with laughter. "The poor ceorls! The minute one jabs a horse's mouth with the bit, you will murder him."

"I certainly will." Her blue eyes were filled with zeal. "You will have to break horses to pull supply wagons too. As you said, the oxen are too slow."

"And will you help with that?"

"Certainly." She grinned at him. "It is going to be fun."

He bent his head and kissed her. Hard. "Elswyth," he said, "I love you."

"Not as much as I love you."

"I do too." They began to walk toward their grazing horses.

"How much do you love me?" she asked, beginning a familiar game which kept them occupied most of the way back to Dorchester.

*   *   *

There was no opposition to Alfred's decision to sue for peace. As Elswyth had said, Wessex was exhausted. Exhausted, but not defeated. If the West Saxons had not triumphed, then neither had the Danes. In the eight engagements fought during 871, the Danes had lost one king, nine jarls, and thousands of soldiers. When Alfred proposed a peace, Halfdan accepted.

The Danish terms were hard for Alfred to swallow. The Vikings were to keep all the plunder they had amassed and be given free passage out of the country. Alfred also had to collect and pay a sum of gold, not near the amount Burgred had pledged, but still enough to hurt Alfred's pride. He did it, however, and the thanes and ceorls of Wessex paid ungrudgingly.

In September the Danish Great Army left Reading and moved down the River Thames to London, the chief port of Mercia. Alfred sent a small band of thanes under Ethelred of Mercia to keep watch on London, and settled down himself to ready Wessex for when the Danes returned. No one in Wessex had any doubt that they would.

III

THE PEACE
A.D. 872–876

Chapter 24

*I*T was a gray-blue February day and the melting snow had turned the road into a quagmire of slush and mud. Erlend pulled his cloak more closely about his shoulders and toiled onward, his head bent a little against the gusting wind. Another day, he thought, and he would be at Wantage.

This new venture into Alfred's territory had been Erlend's own idea. The Danes had settled down in London most comfortably this past autumn and winter. There had been scarcely any need to fight. A few simple raids, and the King of Mercia had agreed to exact a general levy from his kingdom in order to keep the peace.

"A mewling coward," was Guthrum's opinion of Burgred. "We will milk all the geld from his kingdom, then take the rest by the sword." He shrugged his big shoulders. "Burgred is a fool."

"Alfred bought peace also," Erlend had said.

"Alfred knew what he was about." The name of the West Saxon king had wiped all the contempt from Guthrum's face. "That one is no fool. Nor will he be wasting his time while we are busy elsewhere."

That was when Erlend had offered to take his harp and once again go in disguise into the kingdom of the West Saxons.

"Let the boy go if he wishes to." Halfdan had shrugged when Guthrum brought the matter before him. "It can do no harm and he may even discover something useful to us. He is of no value to us while we lie here in London. Let him make himself useful elsewhere."

Guthrum sent out scouts, who discovered that Alfred was at Wantage. Then Guthrum had Erlend sail up the Thames almost to Reading before being put ashore to walk the roads in his guise of wandering harper. Erlend had been walking west along the Thames for almost a full day now, and a short way ahead he would intersect with the old Roman road that went north toward Oxford. He knew, from his previous travels, that he could take the road north for some miles before cutting west again to the royal manor of Wantage.

Erlend had not proposed this new venture to Guthrum on a whim. It was something he had been thinking of all the while the Danes were so comfortably established in London. He knew he could insinuate himself back into Alfred's camp, and it was a prospect that pleased him. For one thing, he had enjoyed himself thoroughly all the time he was at Wilton; he had felt clever and resourceful, making fools of the enemy while gathering information for his own people. It had been much more satisfying than merely wandering the roads playing his harp for the poor folk of the land.

In fact, Erlend had felt personally affronted by Alfred's attack on the unprepared Danish camp near Wilton. After all, it was Erlend who had told Halfdan the numbers of Alfred's army; it was Erlend's valuable information that had caused the Danes to let down their guard.

Name of the Raven, who would have expected Alfred to attack? He had been outnumbered more than four-to-one!

It was some small comfort to Erlend that the West Saxons had suffered heavy losses in the feigned Danish retreat, but the Danes had also lost many men in that first charge. And then Alfred had taken their precious horses. Nearly five hundred of them!

All the long autumn and winter, while the Danes made merry in London, Erlend had brooded. He felt he had a score to settle with Alfred of Wessex.

And, too, there was one other thing that Erlend held against the King of the West Saxons. It was the way Alfred had taken his kingship at the expense of his younger nephew. It rang all too clearly of the way Asmund had taken Nasgaard from Erlend himself.

For Erlend had not forgotten what he had left behind him in Jutland, nor had he resigned himself to its loss. He had vowed, as he sailed out of sight of Danish land, that one day he would win back his patrimony, that one day Nasgaard would once again be his. It was a vow he intended to keep.

He had gone to Guthrum seeking aid for the achievement of that vow, but he did not entirely trust his uncle. Guthrum would help him, true enough, but Erlend was not sure who would end up as lord of Nasgaard once Asmund was driven out: himself or Guthrum.

Consequently, Erlend had determined that he needed a champion other than Guthrum if he were to see his rights restored in Denmark. Halfdan, he thought, could be such a champion. A son of Ragnar Lothbrok was still a power in Denmark. If Halfdan would stand up for him, then Erlend thought he could oust Asmund from his wrongfully held lands and still manage to keep them clear of his uncle's big-fisted grasp.

If only Erlend could somehow put Halfdan into his debt . . . if he could find a weapon to put into Halfdan's hand that would assist the Danes in their conquest of Wessex.

For Wessex was not going to be easily taken. The Danes had beaten Alfred again and again, yet still he had come back. He had ambushed so many of the raiding parties the Danes had sent out from Wilton to plunder the countryside that Halfdan had eventually decided to move his army back to Reading. In fact, Alfred had made such an effective nuisance of himself that when eventually he sued for peace, Halfdan had accepted with alacrity.

Treachery from within. That was what Erlend was seeking in this new venture into Alfred's court. West Saxon or Dane, it did not matter, all men were out for their own aggrandizement. Erlend had taken as his mission the task of finding the weakest link in Alfred's defenses. This was a king who had taken the throne over the better right of others. There would be someone who hated him, someone who would be willing to betray him. Erlend would find that someone.

This might be the way to Alfred's downfall.

Only the king's companion thanes were attending him at Wantage, and it was Brand who recognized and went to welcome Erlend as he came in through the gates of the royal manor. The young thane had ridden in himself but a moment before and was handing his horse over to a groomsman when he spied Erlend.

"Welcome, Harper," he said as he came to meet Erlend in the center of the courtyard. "You come in good time. Alfred's harper is ill and we have been reduced to listening to my own poor strumming these past two nights."

Erlend smiled. "That is a fine welcome indeed, my lord. I shall be most happy to play for the king."

"Come along," said Brand, placing a friendly hand on Erlend's arm, "and I shall find you a bench to sleep upon."

Erlend walked beside Brand toward the great wooden hall of Wantage. This manor, he saw, was not as large as the one at Wilton. Here there were but three living halls, all smaller than the ones Erlend had seen last spring at Wilton. There were few men in the courtyard this time of day, but the hall benches were full when Erlend followed Brand in through the great door. The fire in the central hearth was burning brightly, but the smoke was drifting high and going out the smoke hole in the roof. Erlend slowed his steps and looked around, admiring the great tapestry depicting a white horse that hung over the high seat. The hall was filled with the deep, comfortable rumble of male conversation. "The king did not go hunting today," Brand said to explain the profusion of men in the hall. Then: "There is an empty place over here, I think."

A few of the men called a greeting to Erlend as he crossed to the benches that lined the hall along its long right side. "Here," Brand said, indicating a section of bench that did not have a shield and sword hanging over it. "You may sleep here."

"Thank you, my lord," Erlend replied, dropping his small bundle of belongings on the wooden bench. His harp he placed carefully under the bench, where it would be safe.

"Where have you been, Harper, since you left us at Wilton?" Brand asked, sitting down beside Erlend's bundle and stretching his long legs out before him.

"In Sussex and Kent, mostly," Erlend answered evasively. He smiled deprecatingly at Alfred's thane. "I was not overeager to see a battle, my lord. Fighting is not good for a harper's health. Particularly a harper as small as I am."

Brand laughed good-naturedly. "You have grown, I think, since last we saw you." He stood up again. Erlend's head reached only to the level of Brand's eyes. "Height and weight are not everything, boy. Look at Alfred. Speed and agility can compensate for height and heft. He is living proof of that."

"Where is the king now?" Erlend asked, looking involuntarily toward the closed doors of the sleeping rooms.

"Out checking the horses," came the easy reply. "We go from checking the ships to checking the horses."

Erlend made himself widen his eyes. "I heard you stole a great many horses from the Danes at Wilton."

Brand grinned. "Near five hundred. The whole time the two armies were chasing and killing each other around the countryside, Alfred had us bridling horses. We have three hundred of them here at Wantage, eating their heads off."

Erlend pretended to fuss with his bundle. "You were talking of checking ships? What ships?" he asked over his shoulder.

Brand answered readily, "Alfred is building ships. The Danes, damn them to hell, rely on the sea for reinforcements. We must stop that if we ever hope to win this war."

A small silence fell as Erlend digested this information. "The king has been busy," he said.

"The king is always busy," replied Brand. "Now, if your things are arranged to your satisfaction, come to the kitchens with me and I will see you get something to eat."

"You are very kind," Erlend said. And was surprised to find that he meant it.

The king and his wife rode into Wantage an hour after Erlend had arrived. They came into the great hall together, and this time Erlend was not shocked by Elswyth's trousers. Three dogs had followed them in, and the thanes who had been lounging comfortably on the benches all straightened and looked toward their king. Alfred and Elswyth went immediately to the hearth and held out their hands to the fire. Elswyth looked up at her husband and said something in too low a voice for Erlend to hear. Alfred bent his head and listened intently.

A thane with striking red-gold hair, whom Erlend had not seen before, detached himself from a bench and approached the king. "Did you find all to your satisfaction, Uncle?" His voice was a clear tenor, perfectly audible to Erlend, indeed to all in the room.

Uncle? Erlend thought. He had understood that Ethelred's sons were much younger. This man looked to be about Alfred's age.

"The horses look to be thriving," Alfred replied. His clipped voice was perfectly civil.

"You can be certain that any horse left in my care will prosper, Athelwold." It was Elswyth. Erlend would have recognized that husky drawl anywhere. She sounded distinctly annoyed.

The redhead hastened to make amends. "I did not mean, my lady, that you would be remiss. I only meant—"

The black-haired girl who was Alfred's wife gave Athelwold a brief dismissing wave of her hand, turned to her husband, and said, "I had better go and see to the children."

Erlend watched her walk to one of the sleeping-room doors, and wondered how so small a female figure, and one clad in men's trousers at that, could yet look so formidably imperious.

The red-haired thane began to talk to Alfred, but now his voice was lowered and thus inaudible to the rest of the room.

Erlend turned to Edgar, who was sitting on the bench closest to him, whittling a figure out of wood. "Who is this Athelwold?" he asked, his own voice carefully modulated. "He was not with the king when I was at Wilton. That is not a color hair I would have missed."

"Athelwold is Alfred's nephew," Edgar replied. "The son of his eldest brother, Athelstan."

Erlend assimilated this information for a minute in silence. He said then: "Athelwold is the eldest son of the eldest son?"

"Yes."

"Then he should be king, not Alfred." The words were out as soon as they were thought. A mistake, Erlend thought, watching Edgar's face change.

"Not so," Alfred's thane growled. "In Wessex we do not choose our kings solely by line of descent. Alfred was duly chosen by the witan because he was the one most fit to lead us—and he was chosen over Athelwold, too." Edgar put down his whittling for a minute and stared at Erlend out of challenging blue eyes.

"I see," Erlend replied hastily. After a minute Edgar picked up his wood again. "What is that you are making?" the harper asked, deeming it wise to change the subject.

"A figure of a deer. For Flavia." Edgar's skillful fingers were carving with careful authority.

"Flavia?" Erlend asked.

"The Princess Flavia. Alfred's daughter."

"Oh, yes," said Erlend, remembering the small figure riding on her father's shoulders in the courtyard at Wilton. "A pretty child," he added.

"She is a terror," Edgar said with palpable pride. "And she is beautiful."

"There is a son too, if I remember."

"Edward. Yes. Two fair children does Alfred have."

Erlend watched in silence as Edgar began to carve an antler. But after a minute his eyes went from the delicate work of the wood to the figure of the tall young man with the red-gold hair standing beside the smaller figure of the king.

Athelwold. Son of Alfred's eldest brother. The weapon he was searching for might lie right there, Erlend thought, in that flaming red head. "How old is Athelwold?" he asked Edgar.

The thane's fingers never faltered. "Twenty-one," he answered.

Twenty-one, Erlend thought. Full old enough to be king. "Why was Alfred chosen over Athelwold?" he asked Edgar, careful to sound merely curious.

"Athelwold has never yet seen battle. It was deemed wisest to choose the man everyone knew could lead in battle as well as in council." Edgar shrugged. "There was really never any question as to whom the witan would choose. Ethelred named Alfred in his will. No one even thought of Athelwold. It was a shock to all when Cenwulf did place his name before the witenagemot."

Erlend raised his brows. "Who is Cenwulf?"

"A shire thane of Dorset. A friend of Athelwold's father, Athelstan." It was Edgar's turn to ask a question. "Why are you so interested in Athelwold, Harper?"

Erlend shrugged, then grinned. "A harper ever has a nose for a good tale, my lord. And a Frank is more aware than others of the enmity that may lurk within a royal house."

"You are looking in the wrong place for your story," Edgar answered bluntly. "The West Saxons are not like the Franks."

Erlend smiled agreement, but in his heart he knew that what Edgar had said was false. All men were alike, ruled by greed and guided by treachery.

He must try to make friends with this Athelwold, he thought. After all, they were two who had much in common.

Erlend played in the great hall after supper that night, and Alfred spoke him fair and gave him a gift of a fine golden ring. The young harper lay down on his bench with the rest of the king's companion thanes, well content with the place he had won for himself. Considering the enthusiastic response to his playing this night, he should be able to stretch his stay at Wantage into a month easily. He went to sleep dreaming of Nasgaard.

He awoke some hours later to the sound of a sleeping-room door opening. Then Alfred's voice came from within the room, sounding sharply
alert. A child's quavering voice answered, "I had a bad dream, Papa. Can I
come sleep with you?"

Alfred's voice came again, then Elswyth's. Erlend heard the sound of a
child's running feet. Then Elswyth said, "Close the door, Flavia." Footsteps once more, the sleeping-room door closed, and silence descended on
the hall again. Erlend lay and stared at the smoldering fire in the middle of
the hall.

He also had had bad dreams, he remembered, when he was a child. For
days at a stretch sometimes he had feared to go to bed, feared to close his
eyes because of the monsters that chased him through his sleep. When he
had told his nurse, she had scolded him for being a baby. He had never
told his father or his mother. It had never once crossed his mind that he
might find comfort in their bed.

At last Erlend drifted back to sleep. He woke to find the household
preparing itself for Mass.

Erlend did not immediately find an opportunity to speak to Athelwold.
Alfred and his thanes rode out to hunt immediately after breakfast, and
Erlend, who did not have a horse, was forced to remain behind.

Elswyth stayed at the manor as well, and Erlend filled the day by
keeping watch on Alfred's wife. She intrigued him, this black-haired girl
who was not like any other woman he had ever met. Erlend knew two
kinds of women: the kind who followed the Danish army and the kind who
were ladies, like his mother. Erlend was old enough to have made use of
the first kind and to have learned to be wary of the second. Alfred's wife
did not seem to fit into either category.

Elswyth spent the day with her children. Flavia, the child who had
awakened in the night, was two years old and full of boundless energy; in
all the day, Erlend never once saw her walk. She ran. Constantly. The
baby, Edward, was just learning to walk, and so was necessarily slower.
But he too was in constant motion. Erlend discovered this fascinating
information from Elswyth when she invited him to join her after seeing
him playing his harp a little lonesomely in the corner of the hall.

Two fair children does Alfred have, Edgar had said the day before. And
they were fair indeed, Erlend thought as he followed along beside Elswyth
on their way to the kitchen house. Flavia's hair was the same color as
Alfred's, a rich dark gold, while Edward's was so blond it was almost silver.
Both children had extraordinarily striking blue-green eyes.

"Such beautiful eyes your children have," he said to their mother. "I
have never seen their like before."

"They are a color that runs in the West Saxon royal house," Elswyth
replied. "Alfred says that his brother Ethelbald had eyes of a like color, as
did his grandfather." She was carrying Edward in her arms and now she

boosted him a little higher on her shoulder. He was a big boy, weighing nearly as much as his elder sister.

"Would you like me to carry him for you?" Erlend surprised himself by asking.

"If he will go to you," Elswyth answered doubtfully. But she stopped and Erlend did the same, holding out his arms for the child. No fear of Edward being delicate, he thought as the considerable weight of Alfred's son was put into his arms.

Edward looked from his mother to the strange man who was now holding him. It was astonishing, Erlend thought, how so small a face could yet be so distinctively male. Erlend smiled at the baby and walked forward again, saying to Elswyth, "He is no lightweight!"

She laughed. "Alfred says in fifteen years' time he is sure to be looking up at Edward. I think he is right."

Edward had apparently decided that Erlend was an acceptable substitute for Elswyth, for he put an arm around Erlend's neck and said something utterly indistinguishable.

"He likes you," Elswyth said, and Erlend felt an absurd thrill of pride.

The Lady of Wessex was greeted in the kitchen like an old friend. The huge kitchen fire was roaring, and Elswyth, Erlend, and the children settled down in the fragrant warmth and were given some porridge and bread left over from breakfast.

Edward fed himself and made an utter mess of it. His mother smiled at him and absently wiped his face with the edge of his cloak. One of the serving girls mopped up the scarred wooden table in front of the baby, and the women went on talking.

Flavia looked into every nook and cranny of the kitchen. Erlend was afraid she was going too near to the fire, but Elswyth replied tranquilly, "Oh, no. Flavia knows the fire is dangerous. She won't touch it," and went back to gossiping with the serving maids. Edward began to bang his spoon against the table and sing to himself.

Erlend was amazed by the informality that prevailed between the lady of the manor and her underlings. One of the cooks, a buxom matron of some forty years, was instructing her young mistress in the remedies for teething. Elswyth listened with rapt attention. Edward finished banging his spoon against the table and one of the maids took his hand and walked him around the room, showing him things. The room was wonderfully warm and redolent with the smell of cooking. Erlend could not remember ever being so comfortable.

After almost an hour, Elswyth rose to go. As she was fastening the children's cloaks around their shoulders once more, Flavia asked, "Where we go now, Mama?"

"To visit the lambs."

Two small faces lit like candles. "Oh, good! We go to see the lambs, Edward!" Flavia said to her brother, and the baby echoed, "Ambs, ambs!"

Elswyth laughed and Erlend bent to shoulder the burden of Edward once more.

The month-old baby lambs held the children's attention for nigh on half an hour. Elswyth leaned on the fence of the pen within which the lambs and her children were contained, and watched her young splashing in the mud.

"Where have you been these last months, Erlend?" she asked the harper, who was leaning beside her.

He gave her the answer he had given Brand. She nodded. A wisp of hair had come loose from her single thick braid and was blowing across her cheek. She pushed it back behind her ear and said, "We have need of a harper. Alfred's harper has grown old; his fingers are bent and it is difficult for him to pluck the strings these days. He will stay with us, of course, for as long as he likes, but he cannot play more than a song or two." She turned to look at him. "You are a fine harper, Erlend. I would like you to stay."

He stared back into the blue eyes of Alfred's wife. He had never before seen such eyes, he thought, and he came from a land of blue-eyed people. They were so dark. So dark and yet so blue. He said, "I am no highborn thane, my lady. My birth was simple, my folk poor."

She shrugged. "What matter, Erlend? You are a fine harper." She flashed him a smile. "I like you. If you would care to stay with us, we will be happy to have you. You will find that Alfred is a generous lord."

She never referred to her husband as "the king." It was always "Alfred."

It was far more than ever he could have hoped for. A permanent place in the household of his enemy. How Guthrum would roar with laughter when he heard.

Why, then, did he feel so uncomfortable? Why did he find it so difficult to meet those forthright blue eyes?

He said, "It is all right with the king if I stay?"

"Of course." She sounded surprised. "You are a good harper and I have told him that I like you."

"That is right," Erlend said, remembering. His small pale face was turned toward the children in the pen. "He said I must know horses."

Within the pen Edward sat down suddenly in the mud. His mother laughed. Erlend said in a strange voice, "I would have gotten a beating if I came home looking like that."

They both contemplated the wet, muddy, thoroughly happy children cavorting among the lambs. "Children should be dirty," Elswyth said. Then, shooting him the sidelong look of a conspirator: "The best part of having children, Erlend, is that one gets to do all the things one wanted to do as a child, and couldn't."

He laughed. "I'll wager little stopped you from doing what you wanted to do, my lady," he found himself saying. It simply was not possible to be formal with Elswyth.

The King of Wessex' wife said, "After I put the children down for their naps, I will show you Copper. Then we shall have to find you a horse of your own, Erlend. You ride, do you not?" She sounded perfectly confident.

"Yes, my lady," Erlend said. "I do."

Chapter 25

"**I** have found us a new harper," Elswyth said to Alfred as he changed his clothes from the hunt in preparation for supper that evening.

"I knew you must have something on your mind when you did not come hunting today," her husband said. "Erlend?"

"Yes. And I found him a horse from among the ones you stole from the Danes. He is a good rider, Alfred. He has nice light hands."

There was a little silence as Alfred untied the laces on his shirt. Then he said, "Where, I wonder, did such a boy learn to ride with nice light hands?"

Elswyth had been changing her own gown, and she turned now to look at him, clad only in her linen undershift, her long hair streaming down her back. "You asked him a similar question once before and he said he had worked as a stableboy."

"Stableboys groom horses; they don't ride them. You know that."

She sat down on the bed and stared at him. "You are not usually so suspicious."

"I know." He had removed his headband and now he ran his fingers through the loose hair on his brow. "But there is something about the boy that does not ring quite true, Elswyth. I feel it." He pulled the shirt over his head.

"The dogs like him," she said. "Edward likes him. *I* like him."

"Oh, well," he said, and dropped the shirt on the clothes chest. "Perhaps I am just jealous." And he crossed the room to where she sat on the bed and put his hands on her shoulders.

She looked up at him. He was bare from the waist up save for the medal he always wore on a gold chain about his neck. Even in winter his smooth skin was faintly golden. He looked sleek and strong, and a familiar hunger began to stir within her. His fingers on her shoulders moved caressingly. Their eyes met and held. "You are not jealous," she said.

"Am I not?" His hands moved from her shoulders to her neck and then her face. Long fingers traced the line of her lips, then came to rest in a gentle curve about her chin and cheeks. "I never have you to myself," he murmured. "Even at night we seem always to have one child or another in the bed with us."

Her breathing was slightly hurried. "Not to mention the dogs," she said. She ran her tongue around winter-dry lips. "We are alone now."

His eyes were very serious, very intent. "So we are," he said, and straightened away from her. He did not bother with his shirt, but went straight to the door. Elswyth heard him telling one of the thanes that he was not to be disturbed and then he reclosed the door behind him and fastened the bolt. The men in the hall would all know what their king and his wife were doing, but Elswyth did not care. She lay back on the bed and watched him come to her.

The royal household remained in Wantage for the remainder of February, then removed to Lambourn, a few miles to the south. Erlend had been in Lambourn the previous year, and the folk of the manor remembered the itinerant harper with pleasure. In fact, Erlend would have thought himself living well were it not that it was the Christian season called Lent.

He did not understand half of what Lent was about, and since he was supposed to be Christian himself, he could not ask. He did know that he was always much hungrier than he expected to be in a rich household such as Alfred's. Nor did the king try to escape from any of the burdens the lesser folk had to bear: endless Masses in the cold morning air, and endless meals of fish. Alfred, who was not fond of fish, visibly lost weight. Erlend could not understand it at all.

One thing Erlend was able to do during the long cold hungry days of Lent was cultivate the acquaintance of Athelwold. He found what he learned of the red-haired thane to be extremely interesting.

Athelwold had been reared in a part of Wessex called Dorset, the shire from which his mother's family came. He had been but four when his father died, and had no memory of him, but he knew very well that his father was Ethelwulf's eldest son. His mother had kept ties with this Cenwulf, her husband's dearest friend and Athelwold's godfather, and it was Cenwulf who had put it into Athelwold's head that he and not Alfred should be the King of Wessex after Ethelred. When that attempt failed, it had been Cenwulf who brought Athelwold to join Alfred's household.

So much Erlend learned directly from Athelwold. In fact, an odd and twisted kind of rapport had sprung up between the two young men during that dark and hungry Lent of 872. It could not be called friendship, for neither man particularly liked the other. But there was a deep and subterranean understanding that, in some ways, they were very much alike.

They most resembled each other in their dislike of the king. It was a dislike they both kept well-hidden from the rest of Alfred's court, but each recognized in the other the reflection of his own resentment.

Athelwold was a good dissembler. Erlend did not think anyone else suspected how bitterly Athelwold resented Alfred's popularity, Alfred's secure hold on the kingship that Athelwold thought should be his. Nor did Alfred's refusal to name Athelwold as his heir help to mollify his nephew's animosity.

It was not unreasonable for Athelwold to ask to be named his uncle's heir. Athelwold was the oldest male member of the house of Wessex after Alfred. Under similar circumstances, and considering the youthful ages of his own sons, Ethelred had named Alfred to succeed him. But Alfred had brushed aside Athelwold's request. Alfred had no secondarius. To all intents and purposes, his formal heir was still his one-year-old son, Edward.

The king had given no reason for refusing to name Athelwold secondarius. Nor had anyone, Athelwold included, dared to press him too hard. Alfred was the most amiable and approachable of kings, but when he did not wish to discuss a matter, one simply did not discuss it.

Erlend sometimes wondered if there was perhaps one other person—the king himself—who was aware of Athelwold's bitterness. Erlend was never quite sure what was going on behind the pleasant smile and masked golden eyes that Alfred most often turned upon the world.

The royal household was moving to Wilton in order to celebrate Easter. Before they left Lambourn, however, Erlend managed to slip away for a few days to ride to London. There was a girl, he told Elswyth, shuffling his feet in pretended discomfort. He wanted to see how things went with her, perhaps leave her some of the gold he had won for his harping.

Elswyth had laughed and sent him on his way. Erlend was always comfortable dealing with Elswyth. The king, however, was a different story. More and more Erlend was beginning to wonder just how much the king saw. Alfred was always courteous to him, always generous. But there was a look in his eyes sometimes that told Erlend that Alfred did not trust him the way Alfred's wife did. Of that Erlend was becoming uncomfortably certain.

"The king's harper!" Guthrum's blue eyes blazed with a mixture of triumph and amusement. "Name of the Raven, youngster, but you have pulled off a feat!"

"Things have fallen well for us," Erlend replied. He looked around the comfortable house wherein Guthrum was established in London. "How goes the tribute collection?" he asked.

"Well enough." Guthrum shouted to the back of the house for some ale. "Burgred delivered the first installment two days since. He has had to milk the whole of his kingdom to pay what Halfdan asked."

A girl came into the room carrying the ale cups. She was not a girl Erlend had seen before. She gave a cup to Guthrum and bore the other one to Erlend. Erlend took it, looked into her face, and saw that she was young and very fair. The girl did not meet his eyes, but ducked her head and left the room quickly.

"That was a new face," Erlend said to Guthrum.

The Dane grunted. "London has provided more than geld," he said. "A nice change from the usual camp followers."

"She is Mercian, then."

Guthrum drank some ale. "If you want her tonight, you can have her." He wiped his mouth and grinned. "The king's harper deserves some sort of reward. Now, tell me, what have you learned? . . ."

Half an hour later, Erlend was saying, "I must leave tomorrow. They will be suspicious if I stay away longer."

Guthrum said, "There may be trouble in Northumbria."

Erlend's triangular eyebrows rose in a question.

"Apparently there is a rebellion being raised against our client king, Egbert. We shall have to see how successful it proves."

"What if it is successful? What will Halfdan do?"

"We will have to go north again. But it will not be for long. More and more I am coming to the conclusion that the key to England is Wessex." Guthrum frowned. "I do not like the news that Alfred is building ships. I do not like that news at all."

"He is clever," Erlend said, as he had said before. Then, almost reluctantly: "His people like him well, Guthrum. They will follow him again if he asks it."

"Men will ever follow a leader who is strong," Guthrum said.

Erlend thought of Asmund. "Yes," he agreed a little bitterly. "That is so."

"We will go together to see Halfdan," Guthrum said, draining his cup and getting to his feet. "He will be pleased with you, Erlend."

That, of course, was Erlend's hope, and he rose with alacrity to follow his uncle.

That night Guthrum sent him the Mercian girl. Erlend found her waiting in his room when he returned there after a great banquet in Halfdan's new-acquired London hall. She was sitting on his bed when he came into the room, her hands folded in her lap, her head bent.

He halted at the door in surprise, then slowly closed it behind him. She did not look toward him, but he could see by the lamp how tightly her hands were clasped together.

"What is your name?" he asked her in Danish.

At that she looked toward him. She shook her head and answered in Saxon, "I do not understand you, my lord." Her voice did not have the exaggerated drawl of Elswyth's, but still it held a cadence that was somehow disconcertingly familiar.

"What is your name?" Erlend asked again in his excellent Saxon.

Blue eyes widened. Then she answered reluctantly, "Edith."

"Edith." He began to walk slowly toward the bed. She watched him come, her eyes wide and frightened, her hands clasped so tightly the knuckles were white. "Are you a serving girl, Edith?" he asked.

Her chin rose a little. "This is my father's house," she said.

"Where is your father?"

"You killed him," came the flat reply.

He too sat on the bed, careful to keep some distance between them. "I never saw your father," he said. "How can you say I killed him?"

"You . . . your people . . . Guthrum," she answered. She said his uncle's name as if it were a curse. "My father tried to protect me from him, and he killed him. Killed him and then ravished me." She was staring at her hands. "He sent me to your room. He said you wanted me."

She was a very pretty girl. Her hair was pale brown and fine as silk. Her eyes were a mix of blue and gray. Erlend remembered suddenly an incident that had occurred at Lambourn some weeks ago. One of the minor shire thanes who had a manor near the royal estate had raped the daughter of a ceorl. The ceorl had appealed to the king for justice, and Alfred had made the thane marry the girl.

Erlend had been shocked by the judgment. The girl was of no consequence, far below the social level even of a shire thane. He could not believe that the thane had accepted the king's decision.

"It was better than being gelded," Brand had said bluntly when Erlend questioned him. "Nothing makes Alfred more furious than seeing the powerful take advantage of the powerless. The man can count himself lucky all he had to do was marry the girl." Alfred's trusted thane had shrugged. "Perhaps it will teach a few others to be more careful. There are whores enough in all the towns. No need to hurt a simple maid."

Erlend looked now at the slim figure beside him and remembered Brand's words. No need to hurt a simple maid. He said, "I will not hurt you, Edith."

She did not move, did not look at him, only sat there, still as a wild creature at bay. "I will not touch you," he added, clarifying matters as best he could.

At that her head turned. He smiled a little, trying to reassure her. Then, awkwardly he said, "I am sorry about your father."

Tears brimmed suddenly in her eyes. She nodded, unable to reply.

"Stay the night," Erlend said. "That way, he will not . . ." His voice trailed away. She was looking at him warily. "You can have the bed and I will take the floor," he said, and her eyes widened in amazement.

And so Erlend Olafson, whose grandfather had deposed a king, who was rightful heir to one of the greatest estates in Jutland, spent the night on the floor so a merchant's daughter could sleep unmolested in his bed.

* * *

The royal household remained at Wilton for all of March. The weather was fine and the fields of Wessex went early under the plow. Alfred had brought a hundred of the Danish horses with him to Wilton, and after Easter the ceorls who were members of the Wiltshire fyrd came to Wilton to learn how to ride.

"They need to be able to steer their horses and not fall off," Alfred warned his wife, who, to the astonishment of no one who knew her, was undertaking to lead this training. For form's sake, Alfred had assigned a number of his thanes to the task, but everyone knew who was really in charge. "They do not have to ride like centaurs, Elswyth," he said now warningly. "Do not be too fussy."

"What are centaurs?" Elswyth asked.

"Creatures out of Greek myth," Alfred replied. "I saw some paintings of them once when I was in Rome. They are supposedly half-man, half-horse."

"Do not worry, Alfred," Elswyth assured him with a sunny smile. "I will not be too harsh on your poor ceorls. I promise."

Alfred's heart was not with the horses these days, but with his ships. They were being built at Southampton, and every chance he could get, Alfred rode south to see how the work was coming along.

Erlend had been shocked when first he saw the size of Alfred's ships. He had not paid much attention to talk of the ships before going to Southampton. The Anglo-Saxons had been too long away from the sea, he had thought, for them to pose any threat to the Danes on that element. Fishing ships were most likely what Alfred was building in the fond hope of challenging the Vikings on the sea.

Then he saw the long ships already in the water at Southampton. Two of them had sixty oars. The sides were higher than the long ships used by the Danes, and they rode extremely steady in the water.

Name of the Raven, Erlend swore under his breath. Where had the West Saxons learned to build such ships?

Then he met the Frisians.

Apparently Alfred had realized his countrymen's lack of expertise in this area also, and he had induced a whole company of Frisian shipbuilders to come to Wessex to build ships and teach the West Saxons to sail them. Alfred was one of their most enthusiastic pupils.

Erlend had learned to sail a longboat before he was ten, but he deemed it wisest to conceal his knowledge. Alfred already thought him more accomplished than was easily explainable by his fictive background. Add a mastery of sailing to mastery of harp and horse, and his diguise would be in shreds.

The sailing weather was particularly good that spring, and Alfred remained at Southampton for longer than he had originally planned. Erlend and Athelwold were with him. Alfred seemed always to include the two of them, no matter how small the rest of his entourage might be. Athelwold was flattered by the honor. Erlend was beginning to wonder if the reason was that Alfred did not trust them out from under his eye.

One afternoon, some three weeks into their stay at Southampton, Athelwold came seeking Erlend, who was cleaning and oiling his bridle on a bench in the manor hall.

"I have just unearthed a very interesting piece of information," Athelwold said, sitting beside Erlend and regarding the harper with an air of suppressed excitement.

"Oh?" Erlend looked up from polishing his bit. "And what is that?"

"Alfred has a mistress in the neighborhood."

Erlend was conscious of a nasty shock of surprise. "A mistress? Alfred? Someone is fooling you."

Athelwold's pale blue eyes, lashed by reddish lashes lighter than his hair, were blazing with triumph. "Not so. I learned it from Brand. She is the lady of a small manor near to here, and Alfred lived with her for a full two years before his marriage."

Erlend felt a surge of relief. "Oh. *Before* his marriage." He gave Athelwold a scornful look. "What news is that?"

Athelwold scowled at this lack of enthusiasm. "She is very beautiful, this Roswitha. *Very* beautiful. Brand told me so." The pale eyes narrowed. "I wonder if Elswyth knows about her." He spoke Elswyth's name as if it were some noxious poison.

Erlend straightened the brow band on his bridle and looked thoughtfully at his companion. Elswyth did not like Athelwold, and when the king's wife did not like someone, that someone knew it. Unlike Alfred, one was never in doubt as to Elswyth's feelings. Those she liked, she treated as brothers; those she did not like, she disdained. Whatever else she was, Elswyth was not lukewarm.

Erlend looked now at Athelwold's excited face and knew that Athelwold would very much enjoy causing trouble between Alfred and his wife. Erlend ran his finger up and down the smooth leather of his bridle and thought that although he too would enjoy seeing the confident king made uncomfortable, he did not want Elswyth to be hurt. So he said to Athelwold sharply, "Be careful you do not make a fool of yourself, Athelwold. Elswyth will never believe ill of Alfred."

The pale eyes regarded him unblinkingly. Then he said, "I forgot for the moment that you are one of her champions." The king's nephew pushed his long lanky form up from the bench and strolled away to the fire. Erlend watched him go, a frown between his triangular dark brows.

Alfred was thoroughly enjoying his stay at Southampton. The shipbuilding was progressing satisfactorily, and it seemed every day he learned something new about sailing and the sea. Alfred was always happy when he was learning, and the beautiful weather, and the smell of fresh salty air added zest to his enjoyment. If only Elswyth were at Southampton, he thought as he rode from the harbor through the town late one particularly fine afternoon, then would life be perfect. It would be extremely pleasant not to be retiring every night to a lonely bed.

He walked into his hall as he had every other afternoon for the past three weeks, sunburned and hungry, looking forward to his dinner. He was surprised when Athelwold came up to him and said, "My lord, a visitor arrived for you this afternoon."

Alfred thought that a ship from France had docked. The books! he thought with pleasure. One could always trust Judith to find what one wanted. "What visitor?" he asked Athelstan's son, looking around the hall for a strange face.

"My lord, the visitor is awaiting you in your sleeping chamber," Athelwold said respectfully. "Shall I go—?"

"No." Alfred gave his nephew an absentminded smile. "I shall go myself." And he strode across the hall to push open the door to his private room.

When he saw who was awaiting him, he stopped as if he had walked into a wall. "*Roswitha!*" The thanes in the hall could clearly hear the surprise in that shocked exclamation. Then Alfred turned and closed the door behind him.

Roswitha had heard the surprise too, and she looked at him out of huge frightened gray eyes. "My lord . . ." She paused in confusion. "Did . . . did you not send for me?"

Alfred leaned against the closed door. "No," he said. "I did not send for you."

She went very pale.

"Sit down," he said, and watched as she sank a little shakily into the chair near the brazier.

"Indeed, my lord . . ." She faltered, looking up at him and biting her full underlip. "I would not have come had I not been told you had sent for me. I do not understand . . ."

"No, of course you would not have come otherwise," he answered. He stepped away from the door and forced a smile. She was looking absolutely terrified. "Come, there is no need to look so frightened. You are making me feel like an ogre."

A little color came back into her cheeks. "You could never be an ogre, my lord," she said.

He crossed the room to the bed and sat on its edge, facing her. "Who told you I had sent for you?" he asked.

"I . . . The thane."

"Which thane?" he asked patiently.

"He said his name was Athelwold. He said you wanted to see me, that I was to come with him to Southampton manor."

"Athelwold," he said. "I see."

Silence fell. It had been four years since last they met, and much had happened during that time. They looked at each other, curious and assessing, each taking the other's measure.

She had not changed at all, Alfred thought. She had ever been one of the most beautiful women he knew, and the years had not changed that. Her beauty still spoke to him of calm and serenity and peace. He thought, suddenly, that it was good to see her, good to know that she was well.

Roswitha thought: How he has changed. Not so much in appearance, she thought as she took in the familiar catlike walk, the darkly gold hair confined by its ubiquitous headband. Though he did look stronger than she remembered, tougher. He was not eighteen anymore.

He had changed in a way that was more subtle, yet even more noticeable. There had always been a sense of authority about Alfred, she thought, even when she had first met him when he was but a boy of sixteen. But now . . . now that air of authority was much stronger. She had felt it as soon as he opened the door. This was a king who was in the room with her now, a king who was looking at her out of Alfred's familiar golden eyes. She remembered suddenly, vividly, achingly, the day he had bidden her farewell. And bent her head to hide the tears that stung behind her eyes.

"Have you not married?" he was asking, and now his voice was the gentle voice she so loved.

She shook her head.

He looked at that bent golden head and frowned in concern. "Is it that you could not marry, Roswitha? Or that you would not?"

At that she looked up and smiled at him with glittering eyes. "Would not," she said. Then, softly: "You spoiled me for the rest, Alfred."

It was the first time she had said his name. She saw it make an impact on him. He said, "Nonsense," in a clipped, abrupt voice.

She shook her head again.

He looked at her at she sat there, passive and acquiescent in her great beauty, asking him no questions, making no demands. He thought of Elswyth in the same position and immediately banished the thought. Elswyth would never be in the same position. She would have knifed him years ago.

"My dear," he said gently, "I greatly fear that someone has been playing an unkind trick on us both."

She nodded and kept looking at him out of those shimmering gray eyes.

"I do not want your reputation to suffer," he said, and felt like a fool in saying it.

"I do not care about my reputation, Alfred," she said with the great and genuine sweetness he had once found so entrancing.

What he felt now was a flicker of annoyance. She was not helping him at all. "Roswitha," he said in a crisper voice, "I am going to have you escorted home." And watched her cheeks grow pale again.

"My lord . . ." She bit her lip. Her features were pure and perfect. Her nose was small and straight. Alfred thought of the haughty thin-bridged nose that waited for him at Wilton and cursed Athelwold under his breath. Roswitha rose to her feet and began to cross the room toward him. He hastily stood up himself. "I do not understand the motive of this thane," she said in her childishly pretty voice, "but I am very glad to see you again." She came quite close to him before she stopped and looked up into his face.

The smell of her was instantly familiar. He knew he had but to make one small move and she would be in his arms. His senses were responding to her nearness, but his brain was saying coldly and clearly: *No*.

"Roswitha,'" he said, "come into the hall and let me order you some food. You must be hungry after your ride. Then I will have Wilfred take you home."

He did not want to be cruel. In fact, he was feeling rather wretchedly guilty. Why could she not be happily married? He had settled enough money on her, surely. He would see what he could do about finding her a husband, he thought as he put his hand on her arm and marched her to the door of his sleeping room.

The first person he saw as he opened the door was Athelwold. He gave his nephew a look that wiped the smile right off his face, and called to Wilfred to take Roswitha off his hands.

Chapter 26

*B*RAND was furious when he realized what his careless revelation to Athelwold had precipitated. Athelwold protested innocence, saying that he had wished only to do Alfred a good turn. But all the thanes knew of the antagonism between Athelwold and Elswyth, and none of them harbored any doubt as to Athelwold's true motives in introducing Alfred's former mistress into his bedroom.

Erlend thought that he alone understood that the true target of Athelwold's prank had not been the king's wife at all, but Alfred himself. It was Alfred's honor Athelwold had been after, not Elswyth's betrayal. Erlend was sure of it.

How impossible it would be to explain such a thing to Guthrum, Erlend thought as he lay awake on his bench later in the evening after all else had gone to sleep. The idea that a king could lose the respect of his men because he had lain with a woman other than his wife! How Guthrum would laugh at such a notion.

Erlend put his arms behind his head, stared up at the raftered ceiling, and thought about this.

His father had had other women. Indeed, Erlend had left several bastard brothers behind in the serving hall at Nasgaard when he had taken ship for England. Asmund, too, was known to sleep with one of the serving girls. That was the way of men, or so Erlend had been reared to think. It was not until he had come to Alfred's court that he had seen otherwise.

Was it this Christianity? he wondered. But Alfred's thanes were no celibates, that was for certain. When Brand had spoken of the plenitude of whores in the towns, he had spoken from experience. And Brand considered himself a good Christian. Even those thanes who were married and who had left their wives to manage at home while they took service with the king—even those thanes took advantage of whatever willing women might come their way.

Why should they expect Alfred to be different?

For there could be no doubt about it, they did expect him to be different from themselves. If he had taken Roswitha to his bed, Alfred would have lost some of the almost fanatical respect with which most of his thanes regarded him. Erlend knew this to be true, because, oddly enough, it was how he would feel himself. Which was impossible, of course, since he had none of that kind of regard for Alfred at all.

It must be Elswyth who was causing him to feel this way, Erlend thought as he stared through the dimly lit darkness of the hall. It was because he was so fond of Elswyth that he had felt that nasty shock when Athelwold hinted of Alfred's infidelity. His discomposure could have nothing at all to do with his feelings for the king.

Yet, Erlend thought further, he had nothing to reproach himself for in his fondness for Elswyth. True, he thought her beautiful. True, he found her company enjoyable. But he had never once thought of her as aught but Alfred's wife. He was not lusting after Elswyth in his heart. He was quite comfortably certain of that.

The drone of snoring in the hall was making Erlend feel sleepy himself. It was so nice and warm under his wool blanket. He yawned. Such deep thinking at so late an hour was too much of a strain. He reached down automatically to touch the harp that was tucked under his bench, closed his eyes, and went to sleep.

Erlend was not the only one who lay thinking that night, nor was he the only one to apprehend Athelwold's true motives in introducing Roswitha into Southampton manor. Alfred had never fully trusted this nephew who was so close to him in age, who had challenged his right to be king, and now Alfred lay awake in his solitary bed and contemplated what he ought to do about Athelwold.

He could most probably placate his nephew by naming him as secondarius. Athelwold was not unjustified in asking for that, Alfred knew, and might well be satisfied to know that should Alfred fall in battle, he would be the recognized next-in-line.

But Alfred also knew that he would not name Athelwold as his heir. It would be better to let things fall as they would, he thought, lying with his arm flung across his forehead, listening to the snoring of the hound that slept with its head on his feet. Should something happen to him before Edward was grown, let the witan decide who was most fit to rule.

In his heart, Alfred knew he wanted to pass the kingship down to his son. It was a primitive feeling, not based on reason at all, but when he looked into Edward's brilliant blue-green eyes, he felt that he had made a king.

So he would not name Athelwold as his heir, would do nothing to placate the injured vanity of this importunate nephew, and consequently he had to face the fact that Athelwold most probably hated him. And would do everything he could to undermine Alfred's authority.

Elswyth did not help matters either, her husband thought now, by showing her dislike of Athelwold so openly. No hope to change that, though. Elswyth was incapable of dissimulation, was clear as water always.

Alfred put his hand out to touch the cold and empty bed beside him. God, but he missed her!

What would she say when she learned about Roswitha? For learn she would, Alfred was certain. Either Athelwold or Erlend would be sure to tell her. He would wager the entire royal treasury on that.

The hound shifted his position at Alfred's feet and snorted in his sleep. Alfred grinned at the sound. Chasing deer in his sleep, he thought. Then: No need to linger here in Southampton any longer. The ships were coming along splendidly. It was time for him to return to his wife.

He closed his eyes and went to sleep.

In his reflections, Alfred had done Erlend an injustice. But the king and his following had not been back at Wilton for above an hour before Athelwold told Elswyth his own version of the tale.

Alfred was roughhousing with his children and his dogs before the hearth in the great hall when Elswyth stalked into the room. Athelwold had caught her as she was going to the kitchens to see the cook about supper, and she had turned back to the hall immediately. She stalked—there was no other word for it, Alfred thought ruefully, watching her come—to the hearth, looked down her nose at him, and said through her teeth, "I should like to speak to you, my lord. Alone."

Every ear in the vicinity was turned their way. Of course every thane in the room would know what this was about. Those who had not been at Southampton would have been informed by their friends within the first ten minutes of their arrival.

"Certainly, my love," Alfred said mildly. "Shall we go into our chamber?"

"Me too!" said Flavia, jumping to her feet and grasping her father's hand.

"No," said Elswyth in the rare voice that meant she expected absolute obedience. Both children stared openmouthed at their mother and subsided back into the pack of dogs. Elswyth stalked across the silent hall to the bedchamber door. Alfred followed, torn between amusement and annoyance. Why did Elswyth have to be so dramatic? And so publicly dramatic, at that.

He closed the bedroom door behind him and said, "What did Athelwold tell you?"

She spun around to face him, her blue eyes glittering, her thin nostrils pinched tight. "He told me Roswitha came to Southampton. He said you spoke to her in your sleeping chamber."

He nodded thoughtfully. "And did he also tell you that he was the one who had sent for her? That he did it to try to make trouble between you and me?"

"I told you once Alfred"—she was still speaking through her teeth—"I told you that if you ever went near her again, I would kill her."

He stretched his shoulders and advanced further into the room. He looked from his wife to his bed, then back again to his wife. They had been parted for nearly a month. "It was not her fault," he said. "Athelwold told her that I had sent for her."

"You were alone with her." Now she was directly accusing him.

"Elswyth, what are you so angry about?" He made a great effort to sound calm and reasonable. He did not want to quarrel with her. "Do you think I went to bed with her?"

She didn't, of course. They both knew that. She glared at him, and he went on, still in the same reasonable voice, "If you show yourself upset, you will only give Athelwold the reaction he hoped for."

His reasonableness was not having the effect he had hoped. Her chin came up. "Do not talk to me as if I were Flavia!" Her voice was beginning to rise.

"Then stop acting like Flavia." He was starting to get annoyed. This was certainly not the homecoming he had hoped for. "Athelwold played a stupid trick, that is all. Do not try to make more of it than it is."

She was quivering all over with temper. And all for no reason, Alfred thought, his own temper beginning to rise.

"I want to know why that woman is still living at Southampton," Elswyth said furiously.

Alfred looked at his wife's clenched fists. Small chance of getting her to bed in this mood, he thought. Best to leave her before things went from bad to worse.

"I will speak to you later, when you have had a chance to recover yourself," he said curtly, and turned to walk to the door.

"Don't you dare walk away from me!" she shouted at him in fury.

He swung around. "You are behaving worse than Flavia," he retorted, his own voice considerably louder than usual, and she grabbed a silver goblet from the small table by the brazier and threw it at his head. He ducked and it crashed into the door behind him, in the exact place where his head had been. They stared at each other, the only sound in the room their quickened breathing. Alfred didn't know which of them was more astonished by her gesture, himself or Elswyth.

He said, "Your aim is excellent."

She said, "Thank you."

Then, at the very same moment, they both began to laugh.

"You are a shrew," he said, leaving the door and crossing the room toward her. "I don't know why I love you so much."

Still laughing, she moved also, her arms extended, her face upraised. They met in the middle of the room and kissed passionately. A few minutes later found them where Alfred had hoped to be all along. In bed.

*   *   *

Like the rest of the men in the hall, Erlend sat in utter silence as Alfred closed his sleeping-room door behind him. Silence still reigned as all ears remained pricked in one direction only. Even the children were quiet, quenched for the moment by their mother's unusually severe reprimand.

For the first few minutes, nothing could be heard. Then, distinctly, came the sound of Elswyth's raised voice. Next, astonishingly, they heard Alfred. He appeared to be shouting back. Then came sound of something crashing into the door. Finally came silence.

The minutes ticked by. The dogs went to sleep. Flavia stood up and began to walk toward her parents' bedroom door. Edward followed, saying, "Mama. I want Mama."

"Holy Mother," said Edgar, and he swooped forward to stand before the determined duo. "Not now, sweeting," he said to Flavia. "Your mother and father are . . . um . . . talking. They need to be alone. Come and watch me carve you a new animal."

Flavia's small, extremely beautiful face set in an expression they were all too familiar with. "No," she said. Her favorite word. Edward, faithful follower that he was, echoed her sentiments.

"Where in hell are these children's nursemaids?" Edgar growled, looking around the hallful of grinning thanes.

"I'll go look," one offered, and left the room.

Flavia had resumed her march toward the forbidden door. Erlend heard himself saying, "If you like, Flavia, you can play my harp."

The little girl stopped. "Your harp? I can touch it?"

"Yes," said Erlend.

The small face lit with a radiant smile. Flavia had been itching to get her busy little hands on his harp for weeks. "Oh, Erlend!" she said. "Thank you!" And came running.

Edward hesitated, clearly torn between the two great loves of his life, his mother and his sister. "You can touch it too, Edward," Erlend said coaxingly, and that decided it.

"Those children are spoiled rotten," Erlend heard Athelwold complaining further down the hall.

They were, of course, Erlend thought as he held his harp for Flavia to pluck its strings. She was very careful, and when the clear sound rang out, her blue-green eyes glowed with delight. Spoiled with love. Perhaps, he thought, as Edward's too-familiar "Me too me too" rang in his ear, it was none so bad a thing.

The king's household did not remain long at Wilton, but moved north to the royal manor of Chippenham, which lay on the River Avon to the east of the Fosse Way. Chippenham looked very like Wantage manor, only bigger, Erlend thought as the king's thanes rode into the courtyard through the stockade gate late on a chill spring afternoon.

A young man Erlend did not recognize was waiting on the steps of the great hall to greet Alfred.

"Great God," said Edgar, who was sitting his horse beside Erlend. "What has happened now?"

"Who is that?" Erlend asked.

"Ceolwulf. Elswyth's brother." Edgar swung down from his saddle, his blue eyes worried. "He must have ridden down the Fosse Way from Tamworth. I doubt that he bears good news."

Astonishingly, however, Ceolwulf's news from Mercia was good. The Northumbrians had risen in revolt against the puppet king the Danes had installed in York and driven him forth from the kingdom. King Egbert, along with Wulfhere, Archbishop of York, had taken refuge in Mercia with Burgred.

"And Burgred is sheltering them?" Elswyth asked her brother incredulously as they talked before the fire in the hall amidst the bustle of arrival.

"Did you expect him to turn away the archbishop?" Ceolwulf replied in a like tone of voice.

"Perhaps not the archbishop," she replied, "but certainly that traitor Egbert."

"I would not call him a traitor," Ceolwulf said. The cleft in his chin, his only resemblance to his sister, dented deeper as he set his jaw. "He did what he thought best to bring peace to his country, Elswyth. Did not Christ say, 'Blessed are the peacemakers'?"

Elswyth opened her mouth to reply, but before she could speak, Alfred said impatiently, "Enough quarreling, you two. Ceolwulf, do you know who is leading the rebellion in Northumbria?"

"A thane by the name of Ricsige. Apparently he has managed to unite the Northumbrians fairly effectively. They drove Egbert out of York with little trouble. Wulfhere was one of Egbert's supporters and did not feel safe in remaining, so he accompanied the king to Mercia."

"What of the Danes?" Alfred asked.

Ceolwulf shrugged. "We can hardly expect that they will be pleased."

"No," Alfred replied slowly. "We cannot."

The Danes, in fact, were so displeased by the rebellion in Northumbria that in June they withdrew from the comforts of London and marched north to York. Erlend, who had no means of reaching his own people, learned this when Alfred did, and not before.

Summer came and the royal household returned to Wantage. It was July when Judith's messenger finally reached Alfred bearing the books he had requested her to obtain for him. Along with the Xenophon for Elswyth there were quarto copies of Boethius' *Consolation of Philosophy* and Saint Gregory's *Pastoral Care*.

The summer weather was glorious but Alfred disappeared into his room with his books for two uninterrupted weeks. Erlend was amazed. He had known the king could read, had known the king even liked to read, but this . . . fanaticism was almost beyond belief.

"He is trying to translate the Xenophon into Anglo-Saxon, you see," Elswyth explained to Erlend one day as they went together toward Copper's pasture, where Elswyth was planning to ride. Erlend was bearing her bridle and saddle for her. "He says it would be too difficult for him to try to translate out loud as he reads. His Latin is not that good. So you see, that is what is taking him so long." She cast a rueful look in Erlend's direction. "I must confess, I am almost sorry I asked him to send for the wretched book. New books always make Alfred so glum."

"Glum?" Erlend echoed. "If they do not make him happy, then why does he spend so much time . . . ?"

Elswyth shrugged slim shoulders. "It is a little complicated, Erlend. You see, there is a part of Alfred that would be perfectly happy sitting in a monastery all day reading books. That part of him is very frustrated by the lack of learning in the country at large. It infuriates him even to think of all the libraries, 'those precious repositories of learning and culture'—here she comically imitated her husband's distinctive pronunciation, and Erlend laughed—"that the Danes have burned." She sighed and became perfectly sober. "He hates the thought that he is the king of a people who have lost their claim to be considered truly civilized. And in truth, learning in Wessex has been more devastated than learning in Mercia. I cannot read myself, but I can understand how important it is to pass the collected wisdom of mankind down from one generation to the next." She looked at him, faintly raising her brows. "How else can this be done save by books?"

This was not a line of thought that Erlend had ever heard expressed before, and he did not know how to reply to it. He said instead, "I find it difficult to imagine the king as a monk."

At that Elswyth grinned. "I said that was only a part of him. But every time Judith sends him a new book, it begins again. He works himself into a h . . . he makes himself ill," she corrected herself smoothly, "trying to read the wretched thing, then he frets about the ignorance of the country. He cannot help it. It is just the way he is."

Erlend did not reply, and they walked for a while in silence, enjoying the feel of the warm sun beating down on their heads. Erlend thought about the information Elswyth had almost let slip from her briefly unguarded tongue.

"He works himself into a h . . ." What was the word she had almost used?

Erlend knew Alfred was occasionally ill. It had happened twice since the harper joined the king's court. Both times Alfred had kept his room for a day, seeing no one except his wife and Brand and Edgar. The rest of the household had been subdued but not overly concerned. It happened every few months or so, Edgar had told Erlend. The king took sick. He would be better the following day. And, both times, Alfred had in fact appeared the next day, a little pale perhaps, but otherwise perfectly normal.

No one would ever tell Erlend what the illness was. He thought that most of the thanes probably did not know. Brand certainly knew, however, and Edgar, but they would never say. Erlend had guessed it to be a stomach complaint; certainly Alfred's careful diet would lead one to suspect that the king's digestion was not overstrong. But Elswyth's words would seem to suggest otherwise, would suggest that it was a nervous illness he worked himself into. . . . Erlend walked on in silence, his brow furrowed in thought.

They were approaching the mare's pasture now and Elswyth whistled. From over the little rise of ground there came an answering whinny, then the sound of drumming hooves as Copper Queen came galloping to the sound of a beloved call.

Erlend leaned against the wattle fence and watched as Elswyth greeted her horse. The chestnut mare, he thought once again, was surely the most beautiful creature he had ever beheld. The perfection of her native conformation had only been enhanced by the kind of work that Elswyth was doing with her, and the muscles in her rump rippled under the gleaming golden chestnut hide. She was highly bred and highly strung, but to watch her go under saddle was to watch pride and power and intelligence transformed into such smooth and elegant grace that it could actually bring tears to the eyes.

For a long time now, whenever Erlend had watched Copper Queen, he had been reminded of something, or someone, but he could never quite manage to pin the resemblance down. As soon as he focused his mind on the problem, the elusive memory would flee. It was irritating, but there seemed nothing he could do to force his reluctant mind to bring forth the image he sought.

It was growing hot by the time Elswyth had finished with the mare, and Erlend shouldered her saddle and looked at her pink face with a flicker of concern. She looked too flushed, he thought. "Would you like to sit under that tree for a few minutes, my lady?" he asked. "You look a little warm."

She surprised him by agreeing. They took shelter from the sun under the full summer canopy of an ancient oak and Elswyth leaned back on her saddle and closed her eyes.

Erlend scanned her face worriedly. He was genuinely fond of Elswyth. If ever he had a sister, he often thought, he would like her to be like Elswyth: brave and fiery and loyal. He frowned as he studied her relaxed face. The hollows below the high cheekbones seemed deeper than usual, he thought. "Are you well, my lady?" he asked hesitantly.

Midnight-blue eyes opened and looked at him with a glint of amusement. "I am with child," she said. "I shall be all right directly, Erlend, I assure you."

He felt his own eyes stretch wide. She was with child! Name of the Raven, what was Alfred thinking of to let her go on riding? She might miscarry. He spoke before he thought, "You should not be riding if you are with child, my lady. I am surprised that the king allows it."

The amusement in her eyes died. "I am perfectly healthy, Harper. I have several months yet before I must curtail my riding."

Several months! "The king should not let you ride, my lady," he repeated. "Suppose Copper should come down with you?"

Elswyth's eyes were like blue ice and Erlend suddenly realized that he had made a grave mistake. It was all right to criticize Elswyth, but she would never tolerate anyone but herself criticizing Alfred. She got to her feet and looked down her haughty nose. "Bring my saddle," she said, her voice as cold as her eyes, and walked off briskly across the fields.

Alfred's intense scholarship was interrupted in early August by a minor crisis in Surrey. A delegation of men from one of the folk moots near to Dorking arrived at Wantage complaining to the king that the chief nobles in their area were fighting among each other and trampling the peasants' cornfields underfoot in the process. Ulfric, the ealdorman whose charge it was to keep the nobles of his shire from breaking the peace, was doing nothing to stop the feud. The following day Alfred took a contingent of his own thanes and rode for Surrey. Erlend and Athelwold, as ever, went along.

They were gone for three weeks. Not only did Alfred settle the feud and assess the necessary wergilds from all parties, but he dismissed Ulfric from his position and settled another in his stead. They remained in Surrey long enough to ascertain that Eadred, the new ealdorman, would have sufficient power to carry out his charge. It was late mid-August by the time they returned to Berkshire, and by then the household had removed to Lambourn.

Erlend's first thought when he saw Elswyth was that she looked well. Her cheeks were the creamy peach color which was the darkest her fair skin ever turned. The children had turned as deep a golden brown as Alfred, even Edward, whose pale hair would seem to indicate a skin more likely to burn than tan. Alfred disappeared with his family in the direction of the private king's hall and Erlend and the rest of the thanes took their gear into the main hall and found their usual benches.

The following day Alfred and Elswyth went riding together. Erlend could not understand it. In Denmark, when a woman was expecting a child she retired to the house and did not show herself beyond. Peasants were different, of course. Peasant women worked up to the very end, gave birth, then went back to work again. But peasants were strong as horses. Noblewomen were something different.

Erlend was scandalized by Elswyth's behavior, true, but his deepest feeling was not disapproval but genuine fear. He simply could not understand Alfred at all. True, the king was fond of his wife, and inclined to give her her way. But it could not be that Alfred was incapable of ruling her. Erlend had seen the efficient way he had dealt with the unruly nobles in Surrey. The king's justice had been both swift and effective. When Alfred had left Surrey there had been none in doubt as to what would happen to them should they stir up the old feuds again.

All Erlend could think was that Alfred did not understand the danger in which he was placing his wife by allowing her to continue to ride horses.

The weather turned rainy and the men took advantage of the cooler temperatures to hunt. Erlend began to fret for news of his own people, but there was little he could do. He knew his best chance of learning something was to remain where he was.

In September the royal household always removed to Winchester. Erlend was appalled when he learned that Elswyth was planning to ride the entire way. He was so horrified, in fact, that when a chance arose for him to speak to Alfred privately, he took it.

It was late afternoon, the servants were setting up the trestle tables for supper, and for a brief moment Erlend saw that Alfred was alone. He approached the king's high seat, and Alfred, who had been staring rather abstractedly at the smoldering fire on the hearth, looked up at him and raised an eyebrow.

"My lord," Erlend said hurriedly, before he had a chance to reconsider the wisdom of his words, "I am concerned for the Lady Elswyth. I do not think it is a good idea for her to ride to Winchester. Surely it would be wiser for her to take a litter."

He gritted his teeth. He had been impertinent and importunate. He knew it. But still, he was glad he had spoken. He stared at Elswyth's husband defiantly and waited.

The golden eyes looked surprised at first; then they turned not angry but thoughtful. "You are worried about her health?" Alfred inquired. His voice was quiet, pitched for Erlend's ears alone.

"Yes." Erlend drew a deep breath. He was only five years younger than Alfred, but the king always made him feel like a child. "My lord, when women miscarry, they can die." Alfred's expression did not change. Erlend said, "I know. That is how I lost my foster mother." He clenched his teeth to try to control the emotion that had so unexpectedly flared in his raw voice.

There was a stupefying silence while Erlend waited for the king to order him to leave. He did not. Alfred said instead, slowly and soberly, "Erlend, if it were my choice alone, I would wrap her in cloth of gold and tuck her away someplace safe until it was all over and she was safe. But Elswyth would hate that, would be like a caught wild creature in a cage. Surely you know her well enough to see that."

"But it would be for her own good!" Erlend said. Then, as Alfred merely smiled a little crookedly: "You are her husband. She must listen to you."

"I am her husband," Alfred said, "not her jailer." He looked for a considering minute into Erlend's confused face, and then, patiently, he tried to explain. "If you want someone's love, Erlend, you must allow that person the freedom to love. The surest way to kill love is to constrain it."

"I don't understand you," Erlend said. He had quite forgotten he was talking to a king. "She is a woman. Your wife. It is your duty to guard her, to keep her from harm."

A muscle twitched in Alfred's cheek. Erlend stared. He had never reached Alfred like that before. The king said in his most clipped voice, "The best way to keep her from harm was not to get her with child in the first place."

Erlend felt perfectly bewildered, did not know what to answer to such an . . . unusual point of view.

Alfred rubbed his temple, then gave Erlend a tired smile. "As you say, she is a woman," he said, "and so she must face the lot of women. Because she is Elswyth, she faces it bravely. I cannot gainsay her that choice, Erlend." He rubbed his temple again. "*I* risk my life," he said. "How do you think she feels every time I go out to battle? Does she tell me to be careful? Not to stand at the forefront of my men? To consider my life above all, because it is precious to her?" The king's eyes were burning bright, seemed to bore into Erlend's very brain as if seeking for an answer.

"Of course you must lead your men in battle," Erlend said. "You are the king."

"Yes." And all of a sudden, just like that, the strain left Alfred's face. He said in his normal voice, "We all live on borrowed time, Erlend. Man or woman, we all must do what tasks God sets for us, and we must do them with the best that is in us. A time will come when we shall be together with none of these worldly cares to shadow our joy, but that time is not now." Alfred leaned forward and put his hand on Erlend's shoulder. "She likes you too," he said. And rose to his feet and went to talk to his reeve, who had just come in the door looking worried.

Erlend turned and watched the king walk across the crowded hall. And it was then that he realized who it was that Copper reminded him of.

Chapter 27

*T*HE Danes did not remain in Northumberland for above a month. Alfred and his men were surprised by this; Erlend was not. Halfdan had wasted the area around York most thoroughly but a short time before; he would deem little to be gained in taking up battle for a land already plundered.

In early December word came to Winchester that the Danes had in fact moved to Torksey on the Trent and settled into winter quarters.

"Mercia," Alfred said. "This time, I fear Burgred will not escape so easily as he did at Nottingham."

Burgred, however, resorted to his usual method of dealing with the Danes and once again levied a Danegeld upon the country. Spring came, and still the Danes remained at Torksey. On an early-May dawn Erlend slipped away from Wantage manor in order to return to his own people. He did not want to go, which was why he knew that he must. In this last year he had become dangerously comfortable among these enemies of his, dangerously at home. He had almost forgotten to remember what would happen to him should they ever discover who he truly was.

"He was too much a wanderer ever to stay in one place for long," was Edgar's explanation for Erlend's departure. Elswyth was hurt by the harper's disappearance, but her life was too full for Erlend's loss to affect it overmuch. Alfred said nothing, although his thoughts did not follow the same path as did Edgar's.

In August Alfred and Elswyth's new baby son contracted summer fever and died. Elswyth, who had not slept for nearly a week, came down with the fever herself and almost died as well. It was October before she was feeling truly well again, and the necessity of being a mother to the two children left to her helped the aching wound of loss begin to close. The scar would remain, she knew, but she would go on.

In November the Danes moved down the Trent to Repton, the heart of ancient Mercia, the center of the bishopric and favorite home of Mercian kings.

* * *

In Wessex the work of shipbuilding and horse training went on. By the spring of 874 Alfred knew he could move his supplies either by river or by horse-drawn wagon. Being able to dispense with the slow-moving oxen would give him considerably greater mobility in the field when the Danes returned.

News from Mercia was sporadic. Alfred knew that Ethelred and Athulf were trying to organize a resistance against the Danish occupation of Repton, but from what they heard in Wessex, the Danes were apparently ravaging the country about Repton unchecked.

Alfred's household was at Wantage for the summer when Ethelred of Mercia came riding into the royal manor one July afternoon. Accompanying Ethelred was Alfred's sister, Ethelswith, Queen of Mercia. Alfred and his thanes were out hunting, so it fell to Elswyth to greet her countryman and her sister-by-marriage and bring them into the cool darkness of the hall.

Ethelred stood spread-legged on the rush-strewn floor and stared at the great tapestry of the white horse that hung over the high seat whilst Elswyth settled Alfred's sister. Ethelswith was looking gray with heat and exhaustion, and she dropped into a high-backed chair with undisguised relief. Elswyth sent the serving maids running for ale and cool damp cloths. Ethelswith thankfully wiped the sweat and dirt from her face and hands and then the ale arrived. Ethelred drank thirstily and looked over the rim of his cup at Alfred's beautiful black-haired wife.

Elswyth had grown up, he thought. The girl he used to know would have been hounding him for explanations the minute he set his foot to the ground. This Elswyth was putting the needs of the obviously exhausted Ethelswith before her own impetuous desire for information. As he watched the two women, he saw Ethelswith smile, and for the first time Elswyth herself took a chair. She looked up at Ethelred, who preferred to stand after so many hours in the saddle, and said, "What happened?"

God, Ethelred thought. How was he to tell her?

"Ethelred," she said through her teeth, and now she sounded much more like the Elswyth he remembered, "if you don't say something soon, I shall scream."

He smiled wearily and rubbed his hand across his forehead. "Burgred has given up," he said. "He sailed a week ago for Rome."

"What?"

"He was worn out," Ethelswith said dully. "The Danes bled the kingdom dry, and then, when there was no more geld to squeeze from us, they attacked the monasteries."

Elswyth's eyes began to blaze. She stared at Ethelred. "But did you not try to fight?"

His milk-white skin flushed with color. "We tried. At least, Athulf and I tried. But we had only our own men, Elswyth. We were too few."

"None of the other Mercian nobles would follow you?"

The color receded from his cheeks. "No," he said. It was not so difficult to tell her; Elswyth was Mercian also. His shame was her shame. But how was he to tell Alfred?

Elswyth swore. Ethelswith stared at her in shock, but Ethelred said, "Yes. I agree."

Elswyth drew a deep breath and her narrow nostrils quivered. Then she asked the question that Ethelred had been dreading: "But if Burgred has fled, who is now the king?"

All the way from Tamworth, Ethelred had rehearsed in his mind how he would say this. "Let me explain how all of this came about," he said now, his voice very quiet, very calm. "The Danes sent a messenger to Burgred saying that they would leave the country of Mercia alone if Burgred would swear allegiance to them, would hold the kingdom at their disposal for whensoever they might wish to occupy it, and would come when called upon to serve them with his own following of thanes."

Elswyth's face was very white, her eyes glittering slits of midnight blue. She said nothing. Ethelred went on, "As my lady Ethelswith has said, Burgred was worn out. He could not face having to deal further with the Danes, and so he decided to take refuge in Rome. Before he left, however, he appointed another to rule in his stead. It is the new . . . king who is dealing with the Danes."

"But who is this new king?" she asked.

Ethelred looked at her with pity. "Elswyth, I am so sorry. It is Ceolwulf."

She went even paler than she already was. "Oh, no! It cannot be! Not even Ceolwulf . . ."

A little silence fell. "I am sorry," Ethelred said again. Then, when her pale-faced silence began to grow too long: "You know how he is, Elswyth. He thinks he is doing the right thing. He honestly believes that peace is worth any price. He always has believed that."

"And what of Athulf?" Her voice sounded distinctly odd.

This was the worst part of all. Ethelred looked away from her. "The Danes demanded hostages to secure Mercia's promises," he said. "One of the hostages they demanded was Ceolwulf's brother."

"No!"

It was on that cry of anguish that Alfred entered the hall. He actually broke into a run in his haste to get to their part of the room. "What has happened?" he asked, his eyes on his wife. "Are you all right, Elswyth?" When she merely nodded and refused to look at him, he turned to Ethelred and demanded, "What has happened? Is it Athulf? Ceolwulf?" Clearly he thought that the visitors were bringing Elswyth news of a brother's death.

Ethelred's jaw clenched as he looked back into Alfred's worried face. The King of the West Saxons was but twenty-five years old, yet he had rallied his kingdom to oppose the Danes as no other English king had managed to do. Mercia was defeated; nay, not even defeated, given over. Ethelred's cheeks burned with humiliation as he recounted his tale to Alfred in a carefully expressionless voice.

"My God," Alfred said when he had finished. Then, to his sister: "I am glad you have come to me, Ethelswith."

"I would not flee with him," said Ethelswith of Mercia, and the scorn in her voice caused the color to burn ever brighter in Ethelred's cheeks.

Alfred looked again at his wife. Then he said to his guests: "You must both be dusty and tired. I shall have you shown to one of the guest halls, where you can rest."

Ethelswith smiled gratefully and allowed Ethelred to help her rise. Elswyth sat upright in her chair and did not even seem to notice that the queen was standing. Ethelswith glanced at her with compassion, looked to her brother, and found him watching his wife also. A spasm of some emotion she did not recognize twisted painfully in Ethelswith's stomach. In all her life, she thought bitterly, she doubted that anyone had ever looked at her the way Alfred was looking at Elswyth now. Then Ethelred was taking her arm and they were leaving the hall she had not seen since she was a small child, since before she had been banished to Mercia to marry a cowardly king.

"Elswyth," Alfred said as the door closed behind his sister and Ethelred. He put his hand upon his wife's arm. "Come with me."

She followed the guidance of his hand like a sleepwalker, rose from her chair, and went with him to their sleeping-room door. Once through the door, however, she pulled away from him and went to stand beside the bed, staring down at the red wool cover spread upon it. "Athulf will be safe," he said from behind her. "Ceolwulf would never do anything to endanger him. You know that."

"I know that." Her voice was deeply bitter. "Ceolwulf will be a good little puppet king, of that we can all be certain."

Alfred let out his breath. "We should not be so very surprised," he said. "We all know Ceolwulf. It is not that he is a coward, Elswyth. He is just . . . a peacemaker."

"He is a fool," Elswyth said, still in the same bitter voice. At last she swung around to face him. "I would like to kill him!" she said through gritted teeth.

He did not reply, just looked at her out of grave and worried eyes. "The rest of them did nothing either," she said. "You led the men of Wessex against the Danes for almost a full season, yet my countrymen did nothing!"

"Athulf tried. Ethelred tried."

"No one followed, save their own sworn men."

"That is what happens to a country," he said, "when the king is weak."

There was the glitter of tears in her eyes. "I don't know why I am angry with you," she said. "This is certainly none of your doing."

He held out his arms and with a rush of soft linen she was in them, her arms tight about his waist, her face pressed against his shoulder. "Oh, God, Alfred," she said. "How *could* he?"

"I do not know," he answered. "My father gave over his throne, Elswyth. Did you know that? My brother Ethelbald raised a rebellion when my father married Judith, and my father resigned the throne to him rather than fight. Wessex has its history of weary kings too, my love."

"It is not the same thing at all," she said. "But thank you."

He laid his cheek against her hair. "God," he said, "if Mercia is gone . . ."

He felt the stiffening of her spine and opened his hands to let her step away from him. "I know." She looked up into his face. "Wessex is all that is left."

"There is Northumbria," he said. "The north has rallied behind this Ricsige."

"Yes." Her nostrils were pinched-looking. "Northumbria has at least fought. East Anglia fought. Wessex is still fighting. It is only Mercia . . ."

"We must set up a government in opposition to Ceolwulf," Alfred said, evaluating the situation facing him. "He will make a Danish Mercia, but we must keep the possibility of an English Mercia open to the country."

Elswyth stared at him. He was never defeated, she thought. He never would be. She said, "Do you mean to set up another king?"

He gave her an odd look. "Not another king. Kings have not been overly successful in Mercia of late. Let us say rather a protector. Someone to serve as a rallying point for all of those who are in opposition to this capitulation to the Danes."

Her eyes scanned his face. "Yes," she said. "That is a good idea. With Athulf taken hostage, it will have to be Ethelred."

"If only," Alfred said, "he were not so young."

She smiled, the first smile she had managed since she had heard about Ceolwulf. "He is the same age you were when you were made king," she said.

He smiled back. Ruefully. "I often wish *I* were not so young."

She sighed. "I don't feel young at all, and I am four years behind you."

"Don't say that!" One fierce lithe movement and he had caught her fast in his arms once again. "I cannot bear to hear you speak thus."

She sighed and rested her cheek against his shoulder. "It is one year," she said. "In two more days it will be exactly one year since he died."

"I know." His lips were pressed against her hair.

"I want another baby, Alfred," she said.

"Are you sure?" His voice was husky.

She closed her eyes. "You have been so good to me," she said. "So patient."

"Elswyth . . ."

She shook her head, wanting to finish what she had to say. "You see, I kept thinking that having another baby would be like a betrayal. And I didn't *want* another baby. I wanted Cedric." She opened her eyes. "But now I do."

He didn't answer, but his arms about her tightened.

"Oh, God," she said. "I never thought it would be so hard to lose a child!"

By autumn the capitulation of Mercia was complete. Ceolwulf had been recognized as king by most of the Mercian bishops and ealdormen and the country was technically at peace. The Danish leaders at Repton were well-pleased with their achievement in Mercia and turned their attention to the two English kingdoms they had not yet successfully conquered: Northumbria and Wessex.

"We have been in the field here in England for nigh on ten years now," Guthrum said to Erlend as they sat together one September night before the fire in the royal hall of Repton that had once housed Mercia's kings. "The men grow weary. They have gold enough. It is land they want now. They wish to settle down, farm their own land, have their own sons. It is time to finish this war."

"Easy to say," Erlend murmured. "Perhaps not so easy to do. The moment you turn your back upon either Northumbria or Wessex, you are like to have a rebellion on your hands."

"We are going to split the army," Guthrum said. "Halfdan will reconquer Northumbria and begin to settle our people there. It should not prove too difficult."

"Split the army!" Erlend's eyes were wide and very green. "Who will take the other half?"

He knew the answer before ever he saw Guthrum's white smile. "I will," said his uncle. "And once the rest of the kingdoms are secure, then I will deal with Wessex."

Chapter 28

*I*N 875 the Danes reconquered Northumbria. The half of the army that had gone north with Halfdan wasted all the lands of Bernicia and fought also against the Picts and the Strathclyde Welsh. Then, when Halfdan had deemed the borders of Deira secure, he parceled out to his men the lands in the area of York, and Danish soldiers began to plow and to till the soil which once had been farmed by Englishmen.

It was also in 875 that Guthrum, after robbing as much of Mercia's wealth as was humanly possible, moved his army to Cambridge and settled there to finish the rape of East Anglia. By the end of the year East Anglia was also under the rule of a puppet king.

By the start of 876 there was but one independent English kingdom left in all the island, and that kingdom was Wessex.

"Papa is back!" Two children on almost identical fat gray ponies watched as a line of fifty or so men came into view. The top of the Down made an excellent viewing post for the road that led to Wantage, and Flavia and Edward had no doubt as to the identity of the party traveling along at such a steady, even trot.

"I thought he was never coming home," Flavia complained. "My new tooth will be in before ever he sees the hole where the old one came out."

Edward flashed his sister a grin. "Race you?" he challenged, and before she could reply, he had kicked his pony into a gallop and charged down the sloping hill at full speed. Flavia was after him in an instant.

Alfred recognized a landmark clump of beeches and thought with pleasure that he would be at Wantage within the half-hour. He had been gone nearly six weeks, and the closer he got to Elswyth, the more he let himself think about how much he had missed her.

He stretched his tired back, then stood a little in his stirrups to stretch his legs as well. He turned his head to say something to Brand, who was riding beside him, and saw his children tearing toward him down the grassy hill that sloped to the road. He put up a hand to halt the men behind him, and said to Brand, "I hope they can stop those ponies before they come crashing right into us."

Brand brought his bay to a halt beside Alfred's stallion and turned to look toward the flying gray ponies. "Holy God," he said.

"Papa! Papa!" Edward glanced up long enough to wave, and in that second Flavia caught him. Her pony came tearing up to the edge of the road and stopped so abruptly that he almost came to his knees. Flavia's little rear end stayed glued to the saddle and she leaned back to help the pony recover his balance. Then she looked to her father with a triumphant smile. Alfred noticed immediately that she was missing one front tooth.

"I won!" she said. Then, in quite unnecessary explanation: "We were having a race, Papa. I am glad you are back."

"No fair!" Edward cried heatedly, having arrived but two seconds after his sister. "I would have won if I had not waved to Papa."

"You had a head start," Flavia said. "*That* was unfair."

"Greetings, Papa," Edward said, ignoring his sister and giving his father a pleased smile. "Did you kill any Danes?"

"No, Edward, I did not even see any Danes," Alfred replied. He looked from Flavia's untidy golden head to Edward's equally tangled silver mop. "I think the both of you had better fall in here with me. It is getting late."

The two fat ponies came down onto the road and Brand dropped back to let the children have the place beside Alfred. The cavalcade began to move forward once more, this time at a walk. Alfred said to his daughter, "You appear to be missing something, Flavia."

She grinned hugely, showing off the gap in her teeth. "It fell out, Papa. And a new one is growing in. Look!" She stood in her stirrups and held her small face up to his.

Alfred leaned down from his stallion to examine her mouth. Sure enough, there was a little razor-sharp white tooth pushing up from beneath the pink gum. He ruffled her hair and said, "You are growing up, Flavia."

"Me too!" Edward said from Flavia's other side. "My tooth is wobbly too."

"It really isn't, Papa," Flavia said in a lowered voice.

"It is too!" came the indignant howl from her brother.

Alfred said, "How did you two come to be out on the Downs by yourselves? I thought I told you always to have an adult with you when you go out riding."

"One of your thanes did come with us, Papa," Flavia said with the guileless face that always meant she was up to mischief. "But he fell into the stream and got all wet. We told him to go home. You would not have wished us to keep him out in the cold wind in wet clothing, would you?"

Alfred looked down into his daughter's brilliant blue-green eyes. Then he looked at his son. Identical eyes, identical innocent expression. He decided not to ask how the thane had come to fall into the stream.

"That was most thoughtful of you, Flavia," he said instead, his face grave. "What poor thane fell into the stream?"

"Athelwold," she said triumphantly.

Edward gave a wicked chuckle. "Mama will be so pleased," he said, and behind Alfred, Brand began to cough.

"How is Mama?" Alfred asked, ignoring the convulsions of his companion thane.

"Very well," Flavia said.

"She spends too much time with that baby." This was Edward. He was finding it difficult to relinquish his five-year-old position as privileged younger to his three-month-old sister.

Alfred looked thoughtfully at his small son's indignant face. "Babies are time-consuming," he agreed. "But when you were a baby, Edward, you also took a great deal of Mama's time."

"I think we should give the baby back," Edward announced. "She is funny-looking and she cries too much."

"You can't give a baby back!" Flavia cried, horrified. "That is just stupid, Edward."

"I am not stupid!" Edward shouted. "You are stupid. You and Mama. Stupid stupid stupid over that baby!" His face was becoming brick red.

"That is quite enough, Edward," said Alfred in the clipped voice both his children knew. "The baby is your sister and she is most certainly staying. I am ashamed of you. Flavia was nice to you when you were a baby. She did not ask us to send you back."

Edward's mouth dropped open. "Send *me* back?" he said. "You can't send me back. I'm a boy."

"You are a boy," Alfred agreed, "and as a boy it is your duty to be kind and generous to girls. That includes your baby sister."

"Edward is just jealous because Mama is not paying so much attention to him now that the baby is here," Flavia said, accurately if not very tactfully.

"Am not jealous!" Edward shouted, beginning to get red again.

"Edward," said Alfred.

Edward swallowed. "Yes, Papa," he said after a minute. Then, heroically: "I will try to be nice to the baby."

"I like the baby," said Flavia with a sunny smile. "I think she is sweet."

Alfred was conscious of a desire to gag his daughter. Edward was jealous not only of Elswyth's attention but also of Flavia's. "That is nice," he said dryly to Flavia. Then, deeming it best to change the subject: "How are your studies with Father Erwald progressing?"

"I have learned all my letters, Papa!" Edward said proudly. "And so has Flavia."

Alfred smiled at his children. "That is the best news I could hear," he said, and two small complacent faces beamed back.

"Ethelred told me that Athulf is still a hostage with the Danes," Alfred said to Elswyth two hours later when they were in their sleeping chamber, alone save for the baby sleeping in her basket. "But he is safe. Apparently Ceolwulf has assured Ethelred of that."

"He has been prisoner for near two years now," Elswyth said. She was sitting on the side of the bed watching him sort through his charter chest. "It is too long, Alfred. I am afraid for him."

He gave up seeking in the chest, closed it, and turned to look at her. He sighed. "I know, my love. But there is naught I can do. He is being held to keep Ceolwulf loyal. This Guthrum who leads the Danes now will not give him up to me."

She made no reply, just looked at her lap. After a minute she asked, "Ethelred is still in London?"

"Yes. The Danes have been busy securing the valley of the Trent, and for the moment Ethelred has command of London. And command of the Thames." Alfred thought of the plans he and Ethelred had laid for the barricading of the river and permitted himself a small smile of satisfaction. Then, when Elswyth said nothing: "Some of the Mercian clergy have declared for Ethelred, Elswyth, and one other of the ealdormen. So you see, all is not lost."

At last she looked up. Her eyes glittered. "I will never forgive Ceolwulf, Alfred," she said through her teeth. "Never!"

"None of us will," he agreed. He watched her white, tense face, frowned, and sought to change the subject. "I see Edward is still jealous of the baby," he said.

"He will get over it." The look on her face had not altered.

His frown deepened. He knew she was worried about Athulf. One of the reasons Alfred had ridden all the way to London from Southampton had been to secure news of Athulf for Elswyth. But there was nothing he or anyone could do for Athulf. It was this very helplessness, of course, that was so frustrating Elswyth.

Alfred went to look into the baby's basket. His new little daughter was sleeping peacefully, her long black lashes lying quietly against the translucent skin of her cheeks. He thought she looked as if she would be quiet for some time yet.

He turned back to his wife. "It was bad enough that Ceolwulf should betray Mercia," she said. "But to betray Athulf!"

They had been through this endless times before, and Alfred had other things on his mind just now. He tried once again to change the subject. "I was not pleased to see Flavia and Edward riding unattended today, Elswyth. I do not think it is safe."

He watched her face as his words registered. "Nonsense," she said. "Those ponies are perfectly reliable."

"The ponies may be reliable. The children are not. God knows what mischief they might get into if there is no adult present with sense enough to hold them back." He was careful to keep his voice low so as not to wake the baby.

"I did send someone with them, Alfred," she began a little defensively, but he cut in.

"I said an adult with sense. Athelwold is not such a person."

A smile of unholy delight lit her face. He had known the thought of Athelwold's fate would cheer her. "They dumped him into a stream," she said. "He was furious."

"I am sure he was," Alfred replied. He moved away from the baby's basket in the direction of the bed. "I do not like Athelwold either," he said, "but take care how you antagonize him, Elswyth. He has yet some power in Dorset, and I need my kingdom united if I am to face the Danes once more."

"Don't be ridiculous, Alfred," his wife said. "I cannot conceive of any man stupid enough to choose to follow Athelwold over you. And I think the children were splendid to dump him into the stream."

He sat down beside her and looked into her eyes. "How did they do it?" he asked.

She told him.

"Poor Athelwold," he said, and his lips twitched.

Elswyth grinned. "Flavia and Edward are such fun," she said. "I hope little Elgiva turns out as well."

"She is going to look like you, and she will probably be the worst terror of them all," he replied promptly.

"That would be nice."

He put his hand on her shoulder and gently rubbed a finger against her slender white neck. "I missed you," he said softly. "Did you miss me?"

"Sometimes," she replied, looking at him out of the side of her eyes. The corners of her mouth curled faintly downward.

"When did you miss me?" His hand slid down her shoulder to her arm, and then he was pressing her backward, his own body coming over hers. She let him lay her on the bed. He bent over her, bracing himself with both hands on either side of her shoulders. "When, Elswyth?" he asked again, his voice much huskier than usual.

"Hmm." She looked up into the face that was now so close to hers. They had not made love since the birth of the baby. At first she had been too sore, and then he had been away seeing to his ships. She looked at him now and saw the naked desire staring at her from his narrowed eyes. Her lips parted slightly and all thoughts of Athulf and her children fled. "At night," she murmured.

He bent his head closer and then his mouth was on hers. His hair swung forward and tickled her cheeks. She put up her arms and pulled him down on top of her. He rolled to take his weight off her, and they lay together, locked in each other's arms, kissing hungrily. Elswyth's blood caught fire. It had been so long since she felt this way . . . his hand was moving up and down her body. . . . All these clothes, she thought, pressing against him and arching her throat so he could kiss her bare neck. She could not feel him through all these clothes.

From without the door there came the sound of dogs barking and then a man's voice.

"Alfred," said Elswyth very huskily, "you had better bolt the door."

He raised his head and looked down at her. His eyes were burning gold. "I already have," he said, and began to untie the strings on his shirt.

Athelwold stared at the king's closed door, and the line of his lips thinned. They had been in there for close on an hour now, and there was no one in the hall in any doubt as to what they were doing.

I'd like to have her under me, Athelwold thought savagely. I'd treat her as she deserves, the she-cat. Alfred was too soft with her. Athelwold would show her what it was like to be at the mercy of a man.

She had put her brats up to pushing him into that stream. He knew it.

God, how he hated her. And Alfred too. The king pretended to honor him, but that's all it was. Pretense. Quite suddenly Athelwold was absolutely certain that Alfred would never name him as secondarius. He wanted his own brat to succeed him as king, not Athelwold.

Which meant that if Athelwold was ever to be king, he would have to act on his own. And the best place to do that was Dorset. He had been more than two years in Alfred's household and he knew by now that there was no hope of winning allies. Everyone here thought the king was only a little less perfect than God. But in Dorset there were men who still remembered Athelwold's father. Cenwulf would remain loyal to him, and his mother's family also.

He must give over this futile hope of winning Alfred's approval and return to his manor in Dorset. The peace between Alfred and the Danes could not last for much longer now. All the rest of England had been laid low. The Danes would turn to Wessex next.

Ceolwulf was doing well for himself in Mercia, Athelwold thought. According to Brand, he had even minted some coins engraved with his name and portrait. Alfred's men had seen such coins in London. King Ceolwulf.

What the Danes could do for a mere king's thane in Mercia, they could do also for a prince of the blood in Wessex. Athelwold would willingly take a kingship under the overrule of the Danes. It would not be any worse than when Wessex was ruled under a Mercian or Northumbrian Bretwalda. So he told himself.

Alfred would have to die first, of course, but Athelwold would shed no tears over that. Another thought suddenly struck, causing his lips to draw away from his teeth with pleasure. How he would love to see Elswyth in the hands of the Danes. *That* would knock the scornful look from her face fast enough. Athelwold thought of what the Danes were likely to do to

Alfred's proud wife, and his breath began to come fast and the flesh to rise between his legs.

"Athelwold!" It was Edgar calling his name. Athelwold blinked and looked at Alfred's thane.

"Yes?"

"One of the grooms has come to tell you your horse is lame."

Athelwold looked at the groom standing before him. He had not even seen the boy approach. "Lame?"

"Yes, my lord. A bruised hoof, we think. Do you want to come and look at it?"

Athelwold swore and rose to his feet. It was the fault of those cursed brats, he thought, swore again, and strode to the hall door, followed by the groom.

Edgar watched him go, a thoughtful look on his face.

Two days before the royal household was scheduled to remove from Wantage to Wilton for Easter, Alfred and Elswyth went for a ride on the Downs with their two elder children. The spring weather was beautiful and Alfred felt he had good cause to be pleased with his world.

It seemed that Wessex would be safe from the Danes for yet another season. Guthrum was still entrenched at Cambridge, deep in the fens of East Anglia and watched by a selected guard of Alfred's thanes. Alfred's ships were sailing proudly up and down the coasts of Sussex and Kent, keeping watch for any Viking long ships that might venture into West Saxon waters. They had actually had an encounter with a small fleet of Viking ships the previous year, and the West Saxon ships, manned by a mixture of West Saxon thanes and Frisian sailors, had successfully driven off the invaders.

Alfred himself had been on board the largest of Wessex' ships during the fight, and it had been one of the most thrilling experiences of his life. Over the four-year course of this peace, the king had come ever more firmly to believe that the only way to successfully defend against the Danes would be to challenge them on the element they had so dominated for this last century of warfare with western Europe. If he could neutralize the Danes on the sea, then he thought he could beat them on land.

Next to him Elswyth said, "You are thinking about your ships again."

He turned to her, too accustomed to her reading his thoughts to find the remark surprising. "How did you know?" was all he asked.

"You get a certain look on your face."

"What kind of look?" He was genuinely curious.

"I don't know. Salty . . ."

"Salty?" He squinted a little in the sun. "Elswyth, how can a look be salty?"

She chuckled, the dark, rich sound that meant she was perfectly happy.

He smiled at her. She had ceased to hover so frantically over the new baby and was more relaxed than he had seen her in a long time.

Thank God I bought this peace, Alfred thought. No matter what may happen in the future, at least we had this time of respite. All of us.

The sound of his children's laughter floated through the air. Flavia and Edward were riding before them, talking together busily. Those two always had something to say to each other, Alfred thought, looking at his children's blue-clad backs. Edward was now slightly the taller and his sturdy back was distinctly broader than Flavia's.

"It is nice that they are such good friends," Elswyth said.

Alfred thought of Ethelred. "Yes," he said. "I think they will always be each other's best friends."

They rode into the courtyard of Wantage, happy and content, and found the household in an uproar.

"My lord," said Brand, running to hold Alfred's bridle, "the guards you had posted in East Anglia have just come in. The Danish army rode out of Cambridge three days since!"

Alfred swung down from his saddle. "Where have they gone?"

"My lord, they went first to London, but did not stay. They took the Roman road to Silchester and then continued to the west." Brand swallowed. "Toward Wilton, my lord."

"The entire army?" Alfred asked.

"Yes, my lord. All mounted and riding hard."

"Bring these guards to me," Alfred said, and strode off without a backward glance at his family, who sat as if paralyzed on their horses and watched him go.

The Danes had invaded Wessex. The peace was over.

IV

THE CRISIS
A.D. 876–878

Chapter 29

*T*HE Danes did not stop at Wilton, but continued down the Roman road almost to Dorchester before veering to the east and finally lighting at Wareham. Wareham was Erlend's idea. He had been there before while in disguise as Alfred's harper, and he had thought at the time that the site might have its uses for the Danes. Wareham had been a castellum, or fortified town, during the days of the Romans, and the old stone walls still stood. The Danes were always eager to make use of an already-well-fortified position, and Roman Wareham, situated as it was on a narrow spit of land betwixt the rivers Frome and Tarrant, was extremely well-sheltered from any attack that might be mounted from the land.

The aspect of Wareham that made it particularly attractive to Guthrum, however, was its nearness to the sea. The Danes' main tactical problem in Wessex during the campaign of four years since had lain in supplying their army. For this upcoming campaign Guthrum planned to rely upon the Vikings' age-old ally. He would use the sea this time, supply his own army from ships, and thus not be dependent solely upon pillaging the countryside. Wareham was situated on the Frome just before the river emptied into Poole harbor, and its admirable anchorage would give the Danes a perfect opportunity to bring in supplies by sea.

When Guthrum actually saw Wareham, he pronounced it perfect. The Danes took over the town, threw up some earthen walls to reinforce the Roman stone walls already there, and prepared to gather as much food and plunder from the surrounding country as possible before Alfred arrived. They began operations with the sack of a local nunnery.

It was five days before the West Saxon fyrd made its appearance at Wareham. Erlend stood on the heights of the old Roman wall and watched as the men of Wessex made camp on the far side of the Frome.

"There are fewer foot soldiers this time," he commented to the man standing beside him. "At least half of them appear to be horsed."

"Yes," Athulf replied. "And they are in far better case than you to find fodder for their horses. Not to mention food for their men."

Erlend's eyes were on the banner of the Golden Dragon, flying so bravely in the breeze from the river. Athulf knew nothing of the hundred and fifty Viking ships that were by now sailing to Wareham, bearing supplies and additional men for the relief of Guthrum's land force. Nor did Erlend say aught of the ships to Athulf now. Instead he let his eyes move across the impressive array of men in the West Saxon camp and said, "Alfred has the fyrds out in force. They must number five thousand at the least."

"More than you have," Athulf said. And smiled with grim satisfaction.

A strange sort of friendship had developed over the past two years between the hostage Mercian and Guthrum's nephew. When first Athulf had come to the Danish camp, Erlend had found himself feeling inexplicably responsible for the well-being of Elswyth's brother. He had volunteered to act as Athulf's interpreter, and Athulf had soon found himself dependent on the young Dane for the only companionship he was likely to get in his exile in a heathen world.

"My uncle will not risk an open battle," Erlend answered Elswyth's brother now. "Guthrum can show patience when patience is necessary. He knows it will take time to wear the West Saxons down."

"There!" Athulf's voice was suddenly sharp with excitement, his head lifting like a hound's that has scented its master. "There is Alfred now!"

But Erlend had already seen the man on the big gray stallion. The king was riding among his men, threading his way through the litter of the camp, giving a word of encouragement to some, a command to be followed to others. As Erlend watched, Alfred halted his horse, raised his head, and looked toward the walls of Wareham.

The brilliant spring sun gilded Alfred's face and the sea wind blew his hair, and Erlend felt as if someone had punched him in the stomach. Hard. Alfred was too far away for his features to be distinct, yet the mere sight of his distant figure on horseback had been enough to produce this breathless cramping in Erlend's stomach. The Dane was furious with himself for such a reaction, and he scowled as Athulf said, "He is a fighter, this husband of my sister. You will not get Wessex the way you got Mercia."

"We know that." Erlend sounded as angry as he felt. "I can assure you we have not underestimated Alfred," he snapped.

"I wish to God I was out there with them!" The words sounded as if they had been ripped from Athulf's throat.

So do I. The words formed in Erlend's mind before he could do aught to stop them. His right hand flew up to his mouth, pressing hard against his teeth, forcing the treacherous syllables back before he could say them out loud to Athulf.

Name of the Raven, what was wrong with him? How could he think such a thing? He was a Dane!

On the other side of the river, the man on the great gray stallion removed his gaze from the walls of Wareham and turned away. Athulf's hands clenched together into tight fists. "*There* goes my true brother," he said bitterly, turned, and walked away. A white-faced Erlend stood alone on the wall, his hooded eyes on the retreating figure of a man on a large gray horse.

"The West Saxons must number five thousand at the least," Erlend said to his uncle later in the day when he met Guthrum at the horse lines.

"I can count, Nephew," Guthrum replied. He patted his great bay stallion on its shoulder and turned to stare at Erlend. "Nor is it my intention just now to engage their full force in open battle. When once my ships arrive with our extra men, then we shall see."

Erlend looked up into his uncle's face, seeing the familiar features as if after a long absence. Guthrum's brilliant blue eyes were slightly narrowed against the sun, and faint squint wrinkles fanned out on either side of them. Those wrinkles were perhaps a little deeper than they had been five years before, when Erlend had first arrived at Thetford, but otherwise Guthrum had not changed at all. The fair hair was as yellow, the hard cheekbones and sensual mouth as reckless-looking as ever.

Guthrum added, "This is just the start of the campaign. He can collect a large army, true, but can he keep it? He could not the last time, and I do not think he will this time either. All we need do is wait him out."

He. Guthrum rarely used Alfred's name. It was always "he." Erlend said nothing, just looked away from Guthrum toward the West Saxon camp. Guthrum spoke again. "I can hold this site against any force he might gather to throw against me. You chose well, Nephew. Wareham is as near impregnable a location as we could hope to find."

"Alfred"—Erlend made it a point to use the name—"Alfred may not be able to get in, Uncle, but neither can we get out."

"We have food and fodder enough for a month," Guthrum said. "The ships will be here before then, bringing not only supplies but also several thousand more men. And in a month's time his men will have slipped away home to put in the corn. Then we will have him."

"The West Saxons have ships also." Erlend had pointed this out numerous times to Guthrum, but the Danish leader would never accept the idea that any nation could be a serious threat to the Vikings on the sea.

Guthrum's reaction now was the same as always. He shrugged his big shoulders and smiled mockingly. "You overestimate the talents of this king, Erlend. I think sometimes he must have put a spell on you. If you remember, the last time we set foot in his kingdom, he had to buy a peace from us. Yet you persist in speaking as if he were invincible." The blue eyes glittered bright as the sun-lit sea. "I think sometimes you were more comfortable among the West Saxons than you are among your own people."

"I am a Dane, Uncle," Erlend replied stiffly. He could feel the flags of color flying in his cheeks. "I am Erlend Olafson of Nasgaard, nor am I like to forget that."

There was a moment of tense silence as uncle and nephew stared at each other with barely concealed hostility. Then Guthrum said, "You do not have Nasgaard yet, Erlend."

Erlend quirked an eyebrow in unconscious imitation of one of Alfred's characteristic gestures. "That is because you have not yet taken Wessex, my lord," he answered drawlingly. "Did not Halfdan say you would lend me the strength of your arm when once you have finished your work here? And did not Halfdan also say that he himself would stand my friend?"

Blue eyes and green met and locked in silent combat. Guthrum had not been overly pleased by that promise of Halfdan's. Then he said, "We will be finished here shortly, Erlend, I promise you that." Guthrum took two steps closer to Erlend, so that he seemed to tower over the younger man. "And when that time comes, I shall sacrifice this West Saxon king to Odin." His teeth bared in his white wolf smile, he looked down at the nephew whose eyes were so far below the level of his own and added with palpable pleasure, "And you shall watch me do it."

One week later a fleet of long ships sailed into Poole harbor. At first the cry from the Danish camp was one of triumph. Then they saw the Wessex banner of the Golden Dragon.

"There must be a hundred ships out there!" Guthrum said in astonishment. "Name of the Raven, where did he get a hundred ships?"

"I told you, Uncle," Erlend replied. "He built them."

"You never told me he was building so many!"

"It has been three years since I left Wessex. He has had plenty of time to enlarge his fleet."

Guthrum squinted into the sun. "But they are long ships. Big ships. Name of the Raven, they are bigger than ours!"

"I told you that too. He brought in the Frisians to build them. And there are Frisians sailing them too, not just West Saxon farmers."

"Our fleet numbers near one hundred and fifty," Guthrum said. But his face was grim. He added, "And no Frisian yet has been able to outsail a Dane."

"True. But if there is a fight, we are like to lose some of our supplies."

Guthrum did not reply, only turned on his heel and strode away.

One month went by and still there was no sign of the Danish fleet. Nor did there appear to be any lessening in the numbers of the West Saxon fyrd.

Guthrum gave orders for raiding parties to go out from Wareham to bring in food from the countryside.

"Destroy whatever you can put to the torch," he said to his men. "Rape their women. We must begin to make our presence felt here if we are not to find ourselves in a trap."

Some of the Danish raiders got through, and pillars of smoke were seen in the surrounding countryside. The weeks passed and it seemed to Erlend's searching eyes that the West Saxons were fewer in number than they had been before.

"The sheep will need shearing," Erlend said to his uncle. "That is not a job that can be left for the women. Alfred will have trouble holding his men come sheep-shearing month."

"Where in the name of Odin are our ships? They were to come up the Thames, around the Dover Narrows, and thence to Wareham. What has happened to delay them so? Harald Bjornson knows I am depending upon him for supplies. He would not tarry unless something has happened to disable his fleet."

Erlend could not answer. No one in the Danish camp could. But one fact was clear to all: without their ships they would not have enough food and fodder to survive. They would have to break out of Wareham, and to do that they would have to face a battle with the West Saxon army.

"If we can hold out but a few weeks more," Guthrum said now to Erlend, the squint lines about his eyes graven deep in the tanned skin. "In a few weeks we must see our ships. And his army will be gravely depleted. A few more weeks, then can we face them in open battle." It was an implicit admission that in order to be assured of victory, the Danes needed to have the numbers on their side.

"We can eat the horses if we must," said Erlend, who knew what store his uncle set by his horses.

Guthrum swore viciously and went off to stare once more toward the sea.

Brand asked Alfred, "How much longer do you think he can hold out?" The two were standing together looking across the Frome toward the walls of Wareham.

"He has already held out long enough," Alfred answered. His hair gleamed in the bright June sun. "We are down to less than half our original number of men. We have disguised our lack of numbers well, else would he have attacked by now, but I dare not wait any longer. Ethelred did nobly in his blockade of the river at London, but the Danes are about to get their ships through. I can wait no longer."

"What are you going to do, my lord?" Brand asked.

"Sue for peace," said Alfred.

Brand looked at the expression on his king's face and prudently made no reply.

Erlend and Guthrum stood on the walls of Wareham and watched as the four West Saxons swam their horses across the river. The horses touched bottom, and then dry land. The four men paused to align themselves abreast and then began to trot slowly toward the walls of Wareham.

The two men on the outside carried banners. One was the Golden Dragon banner of Wessex, the other was plain and white. The West Saxons halted outside the range of arrowshot and waited.

"What can they want?" Guthrum asked Erlend.

"I do not know. They want to talk, that much at least is clear. You had better send someone to find out, Uncle."

Guthrum grunted, turned, and shouted for one of the men who spoke a little Saxon to ride out with an escort to see what it was the West Saxons wanted.

Five minutes passed. Erlend, staring intently at the West Saxons, thought he recognized Edgar. Then the gates of Wareham opened and four Danes came trotting out. The West Saxons waited where they were. In a minute the two groups had come together.

More minutes passed. "Ivor does not speak Saxon all that well," Erlend muttered, and did not notice the sharp look Guthrum cast his way.

Finally the Danes turned back toward the walls of Wareham and the West Saxon thanes wheeled to return to their own camp on the far side of the river. Guthrum scrambled down from the wall and strode off to his booth. Erlend did not hesitate to follow.

"They want a peace. That much I understood," Ivor, the man who was reporting to Guthrum, said. "If we agree, we are to show a white banner from our western wall."

"A peace?" Guthrum began to pace up and down the floor of his booth. "He must have lost more men than we thought."

"Or knows he will lose them," Erlend said.

"What has he offered?" said Guthrum.

"My lord, I do not know. We could not speak together very well. I have only a few words of Saxon." Ivor grinned. "And they are not the words of peace."

Guthrum's thick blond brows were drawn together. "Name of the Raven, how are we to make peace if neither speaks the other's language? The few men we had who knew Saxon have gone north with Halfdan."

"There is Lord Erlend, my lord," one of the men suggested. "He and the Mercian speak together all the time."

Erlend felt Guthrum's bright blue eyes resting on his face. He strove to keep his expression unreadable. "Or there is Athulf himself," Erlend said. "After two years among us, he speaks Danish with a fairly ready tongue."

"I would not trust the Mercian," Guthrum said. "It will have to be you, Nephew."

Erlend felt sweat break out on his forehead. "Once my identity is known to the West Saxons, I will be useless as a spy."

Guthrum shrugged. "It cannot be helped. Nor does it seem that we will need you in that guise anyway, Erlend. You have not returned to the West Saxon camp in almost four years' time. You will be more useful to me as an interpreter. I need to know what he wants."

Guthrum hung the white banner from the walls of Wareham and watched for Alfred's reply. The evening sky was still bright with summer sun when the four West Saxons once more crossed the river and waited for the Danish delegation to meet them.

Erlend's face was impassive as he rode his black stallion across the open space that separated him from Alfred's men. He had often wondered what Alfred would say if he discovered the truth about the wandering harper he had welcomed into his household. It had been a clever disguise, and thoroughly successful. Erlend ought to be feeling amused and superior now that he was going to confront the men he had so completely fooled.

He was not feeling amused and superior, however. He was feeling ashamed and humiliated. He did not want to be exposed as a fraud in front of the West Saxon thanes.

Elswyth would be hurt when she found out. And Alfred . . .

It *was* Edgar. Hell.

"My lords," Erlend said formally in the excellent Saxon that had acquired the touch of a Mercian drawl after two years of conversing only with Athulf, "the Lord Guthrum has sent me to treat with you about a peace."

Edgar smiled with relief to hear the Saxon. He had not yet recognized the young man on the glossy black stallion. Erlend had taken care with his appearance this day, taken care to look as different from the poor little harper as he possibly could. His brown hair was cut short, Viking-style, and hung in long thick bangs to the tips of his triangular eyebrows. He wore a golden collar about his throat, and great golden rings twisted like serpents on his naked arms above the elbows. His stallion was over sixteen hands in height, enabling him to look down on the men before him.

Edgar said, "I am the voice of the West Saxon king. Alfred has empowered me to treat for a peace."

The breeze from the river blew the hair on Erlend's forehead. He said, "If you wish a peace, you must pay for it."

Edgar was staring at him now, his blue eyes widening in dawning recognition. "Who are you?" the West Saxon demanded abruptly in a suddenly hard voice.

Erlend's stomach clenched, but outwardly he kept his face impassive. "I am Erlend Olafson of Nasgaard," he said. "Nephew to the Lord Guthrum."

"*Erlend!*"

Now the three thanes with Edgar were staring also. Erlend clenched his jaw, hating them all. "How are you, Edgar?" he said. "It has been a long time since last we met."

"*You* are nephew to the Danish leader? You are a Dane?"

"Yes."

"God in heaven."

"What does Alfred offer for a peace?" Erlend said, and now the drawl was quite gone from his voice.

Edgar's eyes narrowed. They did not leave Erlend's face as he answered, "If the Lord Guthrum will swear a sacred oath to leave the country, the West Saxon king will give him free passage out of Wessex. To further secure this oath, Alfred demands that Guthrum give hostages into his hand, five men of rank in your own army. And the West Saxon king demands the return of the Lord Athulf."

Erlend showed his teeth in imitation of Guthrum's smile. "Alfred *demands*?" he said.

"Yes." Edgar's face was grim. "You are in a bad case, my lord Erlend." There was the faintest trace of scorn in the title Edgar bestowed on him. "We have you trapped into Wareham as neatly as ever a fox was trapped in a hole. Four thousand men must eat. Your horses must eat as well. If you do not accept the terms of this peace, we will starve you to your deaths."

"You will not have the men to keep us penned into Wareham," Erlend said. "It is sheep-shearing month, Edgar. I know well what happens to the West Saxon fyrds at such a time." He patted the gleaming satin neck of his stallion. "All the men Alfred will have left to him will be the thanes of his hearthband, and perhaps the hearthbands of some of the ealdormen. And we will still have our four thousand."

Edgar was looking furious. Erlend glanced up at the Raven banner flying over the heads of the Danish negotiators, then back to Edgar. "Guthrum has sent to be relieved by way of the sea," he added softly. "You look to lose your fleet as well as your army, Edgar, if you do not make a peace."

Edgar's smile was as wolflike as ever Guthrum's got. "Ethelred of Mercia barricaded the Thames," he said. "The whole river, for a stretch of five miles, was mined with traps. Your fleet has not been able to get through."

Erlend's eyes widened. Then he looked across the Frome to the West Saxon camp. "So that is what has happened to the ships." He smiled, this time in reluctant admiration. "Alfred is rarely at a loss."

"Nor is he at a loss now," Edgar replied. "There will be no peace without the hostages. Or Athulf."

Erlend thought. In the west the sun was beginning to grow pink. The horses sidled a little and snorted at each other. Erlend's stallion did not like grays and was objecting to the presence of Edgar's powerful-looking gelding. Finally Erlend said, "Alfred will have to pay a geld, Edgar. My uncle will never accept his terms without some sort of payment."

The two men looked at each other. Finally Edgar nodded. "I will tell that to my king."

Erlend nodded also.

"How much?" Edgar asked.

Erlend thought again, then named a sum that he thought would be acceptable to Guthrum yet reasonable for Alfred. Edgar nodded again. "But we must have the hostages," he said.

"You shall have your hostages. And Athulf as well. But we must have the geld."

"I shall tell Alfred," Edgar said again.

"And I shall tell Guthrum," Erlend replied. "If we fly the white banner from the walls tomorrow morning, you will know that we have accepted your offer."

Edgar nodded and lifted his reins to turn his horse.

"Athulf is well," Erlend heard himself saying. "You may assure Alfred of that."

Edgar stared at him, nodded again, then galloped his horse back toward the river, followed by the three other thanes of Alfred's escort. Head high, Erlend himself turned back toward the gates of Wareham.

Chapter 30

"*H*E has barricaded the Thames," Erlend told Guthrum. "That is what has happened to our ships."

Guthrum swore a vicious oath.

"He will pay you geld to leave Wessex, Uncle. We have always accepted a geld payment. You will be the victor in this engagement if you force Alfred to pay a geld." Erlend knew how prickly was Guthrum's pride and how essential it was for his uncle to feel the victor if any kind of peace were to be fixed.

"How much?" Guthrum asked.

Erlend told him.

"The Mercians paid six times that!" Guthrum roared.

"It is only a little less than Alfred paid you the last time," Erlend said.

"It is considerably less!"

"My lord, our position does not allow us to ask for more," Erlend said flatly.

Guthrum's blue eyes flashed. "He cannot keep our ships penned up forever. They could be here at any time now."

"True. But first they must get through the West Saxon ships, Uncle. We are certain to lose large numbers of men and supplies in such a fight."

Guthrum swore again. Then: "He wants hostages?"

"Yes. Five of our highborn men. And Athulf."

"He can have Athulf." Guthrum waved his hand in dismissal. "The Mercians are safe enough whether or not I have Athulf."

Erlend nodded.

They were standing together near the door of Guthrum's booth. The room was dim save for the dying daylight that came in through the open door. Guthrum's expression had become thoughtful. He said, "He will accept my oath? Will agree to give our army free passage out of Wessex?"

"Yes."

"And he will pay a geld."

"Yes," Erlend said again.

Guthrum smiled. "Very well. I shall accept his terms. I shall send him

Athulf and five of my nobles, and I shall swear an oath on the sacred ring of
Odin that I will honor my word."

Erlend was conscious of deep surprise. He had not thought this would
be so easy. "What men will you give Alfred?" he asked warily.

Guthrum reeled off the names of five jarls' sons, and Erlend had to agree
their rank would meet with Alfred's requirements.

"I think the terms are fair," Erlend said, still speaking with caution.
"Both armies have come to impasse. This peace will be a way out for both."

"I will want the geld before I leave Wareham," Guthrum said. "Tell
them that, Erlend."

"Yes, my lord."

"And my ships are to be allowed into the harbor."

"Uncle. Alfred is not a fool. He is not like to agree to that."

"I must be able to communicate with my ships. How else are they to
know where to rejoin us?"

Erlend thought. "I think we can convince Alfred to allow some of your
ships into the harbor to victual the army, but not the entire fleet."

Guthrum shrugged, a characteristic gesture that served to draw attention
to the muscles in his upper arms. The June day had been warm and
Guthrum's arms, like Erlend's, were bare save for the twisted golden rings
both wore above their elbows. "Very well, Nephew. Just make certain that
at least some of the ships are given access to Wareham."

"Yes, Uncle," Erlend replied. "In the morning, when Edgar returns, I
will tell him."

"What is happening?" Athulf leapt to his feet as soon as Erlend walked
into the room. The two were sharing one of the wooden booths the Danes
had built at Wareham for shelter during the first days of their arrival.

It was growing dark outside now and Athulf had lit a candle. Erlend
walked slowly to the pile of straw that was serving as his bed, sat down
cross-legged, and looked at Elswyth's brother.

He had known who Athulf was the instant he had seen him. The same
black hair, the same high-bred facial bones, the same thin and haughty
nose. He would miss the Mercian, Erlend realized. Miss hearing that
drawling Saxon voice. He said now, simply, "Alfred wants to cry a peace,
and one of his stipulations is your return."

He saw the hope flare in Athulf's blue eyes. Not Elswyth's eyes. No one
else had eyes quite like Elswyth's. "Will Guthrum agree?" Athulf said
tensely.

"Yes."

"Thanks be to God." Athulf sat down on his own straw and bowed his
head. Erlend was silent, letting the Mercian collect himself. Then, when
Athulf raised his face once more, Erlend told him the terms of the peace.

"It is an honorable way out for both sides," Athulf said when Erlend had once more fallen silent.

"Yes."

"Who are to be the hostages?"

Erlend named them.

"That is fair," Athulf said. "Jarls' sons all."

"Yes." Erlend looked at his knees. "Athulf, I have something I must tell you. You will find out when you go to Alfred's camp, and I would rather tell you first myself."

"What is is, Erlend?" The Mercian's voice was both puzzled and curious.

"You know me as Erlend Olafson, nephew of Guthrum, heir to Nasgaard. And that is who I am. But Alfred . . . Alfred knew me as someone else."

Silence from Athulf. Erlend glanced up fleetingly, then looked back at his knee.

"Five years since," he continued doggedly, "I went in disguise to the West Saxon royal household. I lived there one year. Alfred and your sister thought I was a Frankish harper. I was there to spy, you see." He looked up again, and this time he met Athulf's eyes. "Halfdan sent me. To spy out, if I could, the weaknesses of the West Saxons."

Athulf's eyes were steady. He said nothing.

"When our army quitted Wessex, I left Alfred's household. I have never returned. They never knew who I was. Until today, when I had to speak to Edgar about the peace."

Silence fell again. Then, to Erlend's utter stupefaction, Athulf began to grin. "I wish I could have seen Edgar's face when he saw you today."

Erlend stared at the Mercian in astonishment. "I was a spy, Athulf. I took Alfred's hospitality and repaid him by spying."

"I'll wager you found out little of use to you." Athulf's voice was suddenly dry.

Erlend slowly raised his knees and rested his chin on them. "You say true," he answered, and his own voice was rueful.

"There are few men more widely liked than my brother-by-marriage," Athulf said. "And no man more capable of keeping himself to himself. I do not know how he does it, but you can be perfectly comfortable in Alfred's company without having any feeling of knowing him at all."

Erlend's eyes were on Athulf, but they held an odd, blind look that told the Mercian that Erlend was not seeing him at all. After a minute: "That is very true." Erlend's voice was slow, thoughtful. His green eyes focused. "He and your sister are very close," he said.

"Did you ever hear the story of how that marriage came to pass?" Athulf asked. When Erlend shook his head, the Mercian settled himself more comfortably and launched into the tale of Elswyth's proposal.

Erlend laughed as he had not laughed in months.

"I thought it would be a mistake," Athulf said. "Elswyth was a wildcat when she was a child. But they have grown into each other with the years. Indeed, their roots have so entangled that it is sometimes hard to know where one begins and the other leaves off. I think that is why Alfred has no need to find companionship among his men. He gets what he needs from Elswyth."

Erlend thought of how he had once confronted Alfred about his allowing Elswyth to ride while she was pregnant. He remembered the king's words. Indeed, he had never forgotten them, had often mulled them over in his mind. If you love someone, Alfred had said, then you must leave that person free to love you back.

He said now to Athulf, "He does not think of women the way most men do."

"Nor is Elswyth like most women," Athulf replied humorously. "I can speak from experience. I was the one who had the rearing of her."

Erlend felt a strange, almost illicit pleasure in discussing the West Saxon king and his wife like this. "I was never certain what Alfred thought of me," he said next. "Elswyth is clear as water, but Alfred . . . one is never certain what Alfred is thinking."

"No. And that, I suspect, is part of his fascination." Erlend lifted skeptical triangular brows, but Athulf only smiled. "Admit it, Erlend. He is a fascinating devil." When Erlend still did not agree, he added, "Watch other men when he is around. They are always alert to the least little thing he might say, to the faintest change of expression that might cross his face. It was so even when he was but a boy, before he became king." Athulf suddenly grinned. "Half the time, when you are wondering what he is thinking of you, he is probably translating Latin in his head."

At that they both laughed. Athulf sobered quickly, however, and said with forceful gravity, "I shall tell both Alfred and my sister how kind you have been to me, Erlend Olafson. If it were not for you, I do not know how I would have borne these years of exile."

Erlend felt his cheeks grow hot. "It has been a pleasure for me to have your companionship, Athulf."

There was a little silence. Then Athulf said, "You are nothing like your uncle, you know."

This was a sore point, and Erlend responded instantly. "I am a Dane!"

"You are a Dane with a conscience, my friend," said Athulf of Mercia, spreading his blanket in preparation for lying down to sleep. "Take care, for in this Guthrum has the advantage of you. I would not trust him out of my sight."

"I know that. I am not a fool. One of the reasons I agreed to act the spy was to gain the favor of Halfdan. If I am to claim Nasgaard for my own again, I do not want to be forced to rely solely upon Guthrum."

"No, by God," said Athulf feelingly. "Nor would I trust my back to him if I were you, Erlend."

But Erlend shook his head. "He would not harm me, Athulf. He is too much a Dane ever to incur that sort of blood guilt. I would not trust Guthrum with Nasgaard, but I would trust him with my life." Erlend leaned over the candle to blow it out. He said, "I have trusted him these last five years and, see, I am still here." He blew out the candle and lay down himself. "Good night," he said. "Within a short time you will be sleeping in the camp of the West Saxons."

"Please God," said Athulf, and crossed himself with fervor.

Erlend pulled his blanket over his shoulder and fell instantly asleep.

It took Alfred nearly two months to collect the geld. One-third he paid himself from the royal treasury, and two-thirds he collected from his ealdorman, who in turn collected their share from the thanes of their shires. During these summer months the West Saxons allowed ten of Guthrum's ships into Poole harbor, and thus the Danes were provisioned by their own supplies.

The swearing ceremony and the exchange of hostages for geld took place toward the end of August. A truce place had been designated near the banks of the Frome between two spears flying white banners, and there the delegations from the Danish and West Saxon camps met.

Erlend was accompanying Guthrum in order to translate. With Guthrum and his nephew were Athulf, five unhappy Danish hostages, and an escort of men from Guthrum's personal hird. Guthrum and Erlend stood between the planted spears and watched the West Saxons swim their horses across the river. There was a small boat keeping pace with them. The chest within the boat was clear for all to see.

Erlend had eyes for only one figure in the West Saxon party. Alfred's long hair was bound today by the circlet of gold that signified his kingship, and he wore a sleeveless linen tunic of the purest white. His tanned arms were bare of bracelets, but his finger rings flashed in the August sun. The gray stallion he was riding touched ground and Alfred put up his hand to halt his men at the river's edge.

The Danes watched in silence as the West Saxon king dismounted and gave his reins into the hands of one of his followers. Then, accompanied by Brand on one side and Edgar on the other, Alfred approached Guthrum and his surrounding ring of Danes. Erlend saw his eyes flick quickly toward Athulf.

Erlend's heart was hammering so hard he was sure Guthrum must hear it. Name of the Raven, he thought in suppressed fury, why was he feeling this way? Why should he care what Alfred of Wessex thought of him?

The remembered golden eyes, fringed by long gold-tipped lashes, were looking at him now. "Erlend Olafson of Nasgaard," Alfred sid. His voice was completely expressionless. "Are you here to interpret?"

"Yes, my lord." Thank the gods, his voice was steady. He filled his lungs, inclined his head toward Guthrum, and said, "Here is the Danish leader, Jarl Guthrum. He has come to give over his hostages and to collect his geld."

The two enemy leaders looked at each other and Erlend looked at them both. Guthrum was the taller by half a head, and by far the more massively built. But Alfred had the slimly muscled grace of a cat, and the face framed by the helmet of dark gold hair was wearing its hunter's look.

Guthrum said in Danish, "So, Alfred of Wessex, I meet you at last." He spoke as to an equal.

Erlend translated.

Alfred said to Erlend, his eyes still on Erlend's uncle, "I have come to see Jarl Guthrum swear a sacred oath to leave my kingdom. Is he prepared to do this?"

Erlend answered without consulting Guthrum, "Yes."

"What oath?" Alfred asked.

Erlend brought forth a heavy golden ring, set all over with huge garnets and graven with runes. "This is the sacred ring of Odin," he said. "It lies on the god's altar and is part of all his sacrifices. Lord Guthrum will swear on this ring to leave Wessex when you have paid him his geld."

Guthrum's eyes, blue as the August sky, moved from Alfred's face to Erlend's, then back again to Alfred's. Guthrum had enough Saxon to follow the exchange in general.

Alfred said, "I do not know what such an oath would mean to a pagan. To a Christian, an oath is words sworn to God. Sacred. Never to be broken without loss of all honor and faith before both men and God."

Erlend translated.

Guthrum smiled, and a shiver ran down Erlend's back. "Tell him that it is the same for us," said his uncle.

Erlend turned back to Alfred and repeated Guthrum's words in Saxon. Alfred nodded gravely. Then he said to Brand, "Tell them to bring the geld."

There were gulls flying low over the Frome, crying to each other in the bright August air. The river sparkled in the sun. It was a perfect day, Erlend thought as the heavy chest was hauled before the Danes and opened for inspection. Then Guthrum put his hand upon Odin's ring and swore an oath.

Erlend translated the words. They were straightforward and clear. He could find no fault with them. He saw from Alfred's eyes that the West Saxon king too was satisfied. Alfred nodded his golden head and Guthrum said, "He may take the hostages."

Athulf stepped forward promptly, followed more reluctantly by the five other men. Alfred smiled at Athulf and held out his arms to embrace the Mercian. "You look well, my brother," the king said then. "Elswyth has been worried about you."

Athulf laughed shakily. His eyes looked suspiciously bright as he stepped away from the king. "God, Alfred," he said. "You don't know how happy I am to see you!"

Guthrum folded his arms and watched the two Saxons, a mocking smile on his sensual mouth. Alfred looked over and saw it. He patted Athulf's shoulder, gestured him toward the boat, then spoke directly to Guthrum without glancing toward Erlend at all. "I shall treat your hostages as well as you have treated my brother, Lord Guthrum," he said evenly. "But if you break your word, I will kill them."

His eyes on Guthrum's face were steady. Erlend began to translate, but Guthrum waved him still. "We understand each other," he said to Alfred in his own heavily accented Saxon.

"Good." Alfred nodded to Edgar, who started to herd the Danish hostages toward the boat. Alfred himself began to turn away, then stopped and looked at Erlend. "I always wondered about you," he said. His face was unreadable.

"I know." Erlend tried hard for a rueful smile. "The harp. And then the horses."

Alfred's voice was as quiet and as impossible to read as his face. He said, "Nor do peasant boys have foster mothers for whom they grieve."

Erlend's eyes widened in surprise. Then he remembered the occasion upon which he had mentioned his foster mother, and he flushed. "How clumsy you must have thought me," he said, and the bitterness in his own voice gave his feelings away all too clearly.

"Not clumsy," Alfred said. "You have a ready tongue and your explanations were always plausible. It was something else that gave you away."

"And what was that, my lord?"

Alfred looked Erlend up and down. Then: "You do not bear yourself like a man of low birth, Erlend Olafson. The very carriage of your head gives you away. Remember that the next time you go harping in an enemy's camp."

Erlend stared at Alfred with barely suppressed hostility. "If you knew I was a fraud, why did you keep me?"

A slow smile came across Alfred's eyes and brows, though his mouth remained perfectly grave. "You are a good harper." He then turned to follow his men to the river, and Brand moved instantly behind the king to cover his back.

Erlend stood in silence next to his uncle as the West Saxons mounted their horses and waded once more into the Frome. The boat, empty now of geld but full of Danish hostages, pushed off into the river as well. Guthrum said flatly, "He is not afraid of us."

"No." Erlend's voice came out like a croak.

"That is a mistake."

Erlend turned to stare up at his uncle. "You have sworn an oath, my lord," he said.

Guthrum flicked him a very blue look, turned, vaulted onto the horse one of his men was holding for him, and galloped back to the walls of Wareham.

Elswyth was at Wilton, and it was to Wilton that Alfred sent Athulf the day after his recovery from the Danes. Alfred himself remained one more week at Wareham, watching the Danes make preparation to depart. Then, during the second week in September, he moved most of his remaining men, including the Danish hostages, to Wilton, leaving only a guard to watch the Danes at Wareham. It would be far easier to feed his men at Wilton than it was at Wareham.

"Do you think he will keep his oath, my lord?" Brand had asked when the order to leave Wareham was given.

"Yes." Alfred was confident of that. "If he believes in his pagan gods, he will not dare risk their wrath by breaking such an oath. In any case, he will have to take the Roman road that leads by Wilton on his way out of the country, and we can keep watch on him from there. I do not trust him to keep his men from plunder as they evacuate."

Elswyth was still at Wilton when Alfred arrived. At the beginning of the siege of Wareham she had sent Flavia and Edward and the dogs to Chippenham in Wiltshire, but she herself had remained at Wilton with the baby. Elswyth had originally thought to wean Elgiva and send her to Chippenham with the others, but Alfred had objected. He loved his children, she knew, but he did not love the months when she was bearing them. Well, nor did she, and since she was not yet twenty-two, she looked to have many years of childbearing yet ahead. It was best to keep little Elgiva at the breast as long as possible, and so the baby remained with her at Wilton, close enough to Wareham to keep in touch with what was happening, yet far enough away to flee to safety should it become necessary.

Elswyth had been delighted to see Athulf, but the news that Alfred had taken hostages of his own disturbed her. "What are we to do with these Danes?" she asked her husband shortly after his arrival at Wilton. She had watched as the hostages were marched to one of the smaller halls, and the obvious youth of the Danes bothered her.

"We keep them," Alfred answered. "The way Guthrum kept Athulf. But we need to find an Erlend to interpret for them."

"Athulf told me about Erlend," she said, diverted for the moment onto another subject. "I cannot believe it, Alfred. He was a Danish spy. And I liked him!"

Alfred smiled at her. "He found out little of importance, my love. Be sure of that."

Her eyes narrowed like a cat's. "Do you mean to say you suspected him?" she demanded, ready to be furious that he had not confided such doubts to her.

"I did not think he was a Dane," Alfred answered. "But I did not think he was what he said he was, either." He shrugged. "I thought perhaps he was the son of a noble house who had got himself into trouble at home and been forced to run away."

"I never suspected aught." Clearly she was disgusted with herself. "And he was so good with horses!"

A slow smile wrinkled the corners of his eyes. "That was one of the things that gave him away. No peasant boy learns to ride like Erlend rides."

Elswyth surveyed the faint amusement on her husband's face. "At least I hope you were angry when you saw him," she remarked.

At that his fair brows drew together in puzzlement. "Why should you hope that?"

"You are terrifying when you are angry. Erlend deserves a fright after the trick he pulled on us."

The line between his brows smoothed away and the smile came back to his eyes. "I am rarely angry."

"I know," she replied candidly. "That is why it is so scary when you are."

At that he laughed. Next he looked around the crowded hall. Serving men were carrying baggage in from the courtyard, and the door to their sleeping room was open wide for ease of passage. "Come out with me for a ride," he suggested. "It is too noisy here to talk, and we shall have light for several hours yet."

Her face brightened. "All right. But I must feed the baby first."

In half an hour they were riding out through the gates of Wilton, the September sun still warm on their heads. "Why has Guthrum not left Wareham yet?" she asked as they followed a path that wound through the woods toward the river.

"He has four thousand men in Wareham, Elswyth. It takes time to move that large an army."

"You are certain he will keep to this oath?"

"I am certain." His face was serene in the late-afternoon light.

"I wouldn't be," Elswyth muttered. "What is an oath to a pagan? Why, there are even Christian men who do not honor an oath as they should."

But Alfred was unperturbed. "Do not forget. I have his hostages. They are jarls' sons all. Athulf has confirmed that. What would happen to the trust Guthrum's army has in him if he should break his oath and sacrifice such men?"

A little silence fell. They were among the trees now, and had to proceed single file. Alfred held back to let Elswyth go first.

"I do not like this taking of hostages," she said, turning in her saddle to look back at him. "What are we to do with these men? They are so young,

Alfred! Scarcely more than boys. We cannot keep them chained like wild beasts."

"I have no intention of chaining them." Alfred gestured to a small clearing that parted the trees to their right. "Here is a nice place," he said. "Let's dismount for a while."

Elswyth turned off the path, halted, swung herself to the ground without help, and began to loosen her horse's girth. She was riding Silken today, Copper having been left behind at Lambourn. "Well?" she said over her shoulder to Alfred as he followed her. "What are we going to do with them? They cannot even speak our language!"

"I shall send them to Cheddar, with a guard of men to keep watch on them." He too had dismounted and was loosening his horse's girth. "Do not fret so, Elswyth. They shall be fed and housed and given all that they need. Guthrum did not abuse Athulf, and I have no intention of abusing these boys. They are merely here as pledges of Guthrum's good conduct."

"But, Alfred," she said unhappily, "what will happen if Guthrum breaks his word?"

"Elswyth . . ." Cat-footed, he had come up to stand behind her right shoulder. "I did not bring you out here to talk about the hostages." He took her hand and began to lead her away from the horses, toward the flat stretch of dried pine needles he had spied from the saddle.

She halted, tugged at his hand to free herself, and spoke the words that were really worrying her. "Alfred, if he breaks his word, you will have to kill them. And that will make you miserable."

"He won't break his word." He let her pull her hand away, but then curved both his own hands about her waist. "Elswyth . . ." he said. Softly. Coaxingly.

There was a tree behind her and she leaned against it and stared up at him. "I want to talk," she said.

"Later." He bent his head to hers. His kiss was deep, searching, erotic. After a moment her mouth opened and she swayed away from the tree toward him, as if suddenly caught in the path of a strong wind. "I missed you," he whispered, and moved his mouth to the arch of her throat, kissing the beating pulse he found there.

All thought of the hostages fled in the trail of fire left by his mouth. She reached her arms around his waist, spread her hands flat against his back, and felt him pull her closer, so that the whole length of her body was pressed against his. The September sunlight was filtered by the leafy branches of the birch tree they stood under. She felt the strength of his legs as they pressed against hers. Then he swung her up into his arms and carried her to the bed of pine needles in the clearing.

The sun was stronger here, not filtered by the tree, and she looked up from where he had laid her into a haze of late-summer light. He was stripping off his clothes, his smoothly muscled skin glowing in the sun, his hair a helmet of shining gold. Then he was beside her again and she reached up to cup his face between her hands. "I missed you too," she said softly, smoothing her thumbs along the clean hard line of his cheekbones.

He began to unbutton the front of her gown, his lips following his fingers as he laid her bare to the warm sun. "I like this kind of gown," he murmured, his lips against the pale silken skin of her waist.

"It is for the convenience of the baby, not for you." There was a soft breeze blowing, and it brought the smells of the deep woods to their small and sunny glade. The pine needles beneath her were prickly and fragrant. He slipped the gown from her shoulders and tugged it downward. She raised her hips to help him, and then, swift and sure, he rid her of all the rest of her clothing.

"How I have longed for you. All those lonely nights . . ." And he was bending over her again. He kissed her throat, her breasts, his mouth moving ever lower down her body.

"I too." The words were a mere breathless whisper. She buried her hands in his hair and gave a little sob deep down in her throat. At that, he slid his hands below her hips, lifted, and thrust within. She arched her back to meet him.

His back under her hands was warm with the sun, his flesh smooth and hard under her fingertips. He said her name. "I love you," she whispered, answering to his words, to his body sheathed within hers, the both of them building and building to a place where the world would crash and splinter and nothing would matter save the two of them.

It was not until much later, when they were dressed and once more on their horses, that Elswyth thought again of the hostages. She opened her mouth to speak, looked at Alfred's profile, and closed her mouth again. After all, what was to be said? He needed hostages to guarantee Guthrum's word. She understood that perfectly. What happened in the future would be up to the Danish leader, not to Alfred.

Guthrum would not break the oath, she thought to herself. Alfred was a good judge of men. The Dane had taken their geld and given hostages, and Wessex would be safe for a few more years.

Chapter 31

*I*T was the dark night of October 17 when the Danish force under Guthrum rode out of Wareham and headed, not north toward Mercia, as expected, but westward and deeper into Wessex. Erlend had not believed even Guthrum capable of such treachery, but when he protested, his uncle had bared his teeth and told him he had been too long among the Christians, that his stomach had gone weak.

"But our hostages!" Erlend had persisted. "Alfred said he would kill them if you broke your word."

"Men die in war," came the brutal reply. "Besides, this Christian king may find it more difficult than he thinks, to slay men in cold blood rather than hot. I think the hostages will be safe with Alfred of Wessex, no matter what I do."

And so nearly four thousand Danes thundered out of Wareham, past the watching West Saxon guard, and onto the coast road that led to Exeter. It had been Harald Bjornson, the captain of Guthrum's fleet, who had known of the old Roman site of Exeter, protected still by the original walls and accessible to the sea via the estuary of the River Exe.

It was the strategic position of the Danish fleet that had been the deciding factor in Guthrum's decision to ride for Exeter. Alfred's ships were still in Poole harbor, blockading Wareham, hence there was nothing between the Viking ships and Exeter save the waters of the southern channel. The Danish fleet, with its cargo of three thousand men, would be in the estuary of the Exe before the West Saxon ships could do aught to stop them. Once the ship army had landed, Guthrum would have seven thousand men under his command. Wessex would be his.

Four men from the guard at Wareham galloped through the night to bring word to Alfred at Wilton of what had happened. They arrived at the royal manor to find the household at breakfast. Within minutes of hearing the news, Alfred had the thanes flying for their horses, scattering rushes as they raced across the floor of the great hall, stuffing the last of their bread into their mouths as they ran.

"The supply wagons?" Elswyth asked as she watched Alfred putting on his byrnie in their sleeping chamber.

"To come after us. The reeve will see to them. Check the horses before they are harnessed, Elswyth, to make sure all are sound."

"All right." She swallowed. "Do you think you can catch them?"

"It depends upon how far they are going. If they are aiming for Exeter, which has the best land defense for them, then perhaps. It depends upon whether or not they stop for rest."

"Why Exeter?" She came to help him belt his sword.

"There are still Roman walls around the town, and then there are the estuary and the river." He stood still and let her buckle his swordbelt. "There will be nothing to hinder Guthrum from landing his ships to disembark his men and unload his supplies." She finished with the belt and looked up at him. The line of his mouth was very grim. He said, "That is where I would go were I Guthrum. He may be a treacherous bastard, but he is clever. I think he is heading for Exeter."

"My lord, we are ready." It was Brand from the door.

"All right. You have the hostages horsed?"

"Yes, my lord."

"I shall be right there, Brand," Alfred said, and waited while the thane closed the door behind him. Then he looked once more at his wife. She said, "You are taking the hostages?"

"Yes."

"I suppose you must."

"Yes," he said again.

She looked up into strange eyes that were fierce and pitiless as the eyes of a hawk. Her mouth felt dry as dust. "Godspeed," she said. "I love you."

He bent his head, kissed her on the mouth, quick and hard, and then was gone.

Alfred had over two thousand horsemen pounding after him as they galloped down the Roman road that would take them first to Dorchester, and then, if the Danes were not there, west along the coast toward Exeter. They stopped only when it was necessary to rest the horses.

The Danes were not at Dorchester, but the folk there told the king that they had been through many hours before, riding west. Alfred exchanged some of the more exhausted of his horses for fresh mounts and then turned toward the west himself to follow. As the day progressed, the sky had turned an ominous gray, and as night came on, the rain began to fall.

The wind whipped up and the lightning bolts shot from the sky and the rain fell in driving sheets. Alfred was forced to halt for several hours; both horses and men were exhausted, the weather was making a muddy morass of the road, and it was too dark to see beyond the length of an arm. The West Saxons found what shelter they could and waited out the worst of the storm, many of the men wrapped in their sodden cloaks and sleeping on the wet ground, oblivious to the storm that raged about them.

On the sea, Alfred's fleet sought shelter within the protective wings of Poole harbor. Guthrum's ships were not so lucky. They were off the cliffs of Swanage in Dorset, on their way westward to Exeter, when the storm caught them. There was no safe harbor. They fought the sea for hours, with the heavy winds driving them back against the cliffs and the heavy seas rushing over the low sides of their shield-lined long ships. When the dawn came, gray and wet, and the seas began to subside, Guthrum's captain was finally able to assess the extent of the damage.

One hundred and twenty Danish ships had gone down in the seas off Swanage that night. Nearly three thousand men had been drowned. After a futile search for survivors, a grim-faced Harald Bjornson turned his remaining thirty ships and sailed west and south. Not to Exeter in Devon, as previously planned, but to Cornwall, to the land of the West Welsh.

Part of Guthrum's plan for this autumn's campaign had been to approach the West Welsh, and perhaps win them to a Danish alliance. Harald at least hoped to accomplish this mission for Guthrum. Then the remnants of the Danish fleet would sail even further west, in search of Ubbe, brother of Halfdan, whose ships should be sailing the seas between Dublin and the coast of Wales. It was necessary for Harald to gather another fleet if he hoped to relieve the Danish army at Exeter. He dispatched one of his remaining ships to bring the news of shipwreck and of his revised plan to Guthrum at Exeter, and then set sail himself for Cornwall.

The decisive blow of the campaign had been struck off Swanage, but neither Alfred nor Guthrum would learn of it for several days. It was very late in the evening when an exhausted West Saxon army finally came to rest before Exeter and saw the Raven banner flying from the Roman walls of the old city.

Alfred pulled up his men on the plain to the east of the city and bade them make camp for the night. Then he called for Brand. "I want a scaffold built within full sight of the walls," he said. "Make sure it is out of range of arrowshot. See to it first thing in the morning."

Brand looked at the king's face, then looked away. "Yes, my lord."

The West Saxon army ate the provisions they had left in their saddlebags and settled down for the night. The following morning the first reinforcements from the Devon fyrd, led by their ealdorman, Odda, came riding into camp. They were just in time to see Alfred hang his five Danish hostages, one after the other, in full view of the Danes who lined the walls of Exeter, watching in grim silence.

The West Saxon thanes looked after their king as he strode away once the last Dane had been cut down, and respect and admiration could be plainly read on all their faces.

"Thus does Alfred deal with oath-breakers," said one of Alfred's hearthband to a shire thane from the Devon fyrd. "The king knows well how to answer a treacherous enemy."

Brand stood beside Edgar, and the two of them also watched Alfred stride away. "I hope to God he will not have a headache on the morrow," Brand muttered in a low voice to his friend.

Edgar's face was grim. The Danish boys had died bravely, but it had not been an edifying spectacle. "He will," said Edgar in reply. "I would wager you my sword upon it."

To the satisfaction of neither thane, they both proved to be in the right. Alfred was incapacitated for the whole of the following day by a headache. It was the day after that that the West Saxons learned of the disaster off Swanage.

It was Wareham all over again, Erlend thought as he stood on the walls of Exeter and watched the West Saxon camp. Alfred's ships lay in the estuary blockading the entrance to the river, and Alfred's fyrds lay outside the gates, guarding against any raiding parties Guthrum might send out for food and fodder. And the winter was coming on.

"Our only hope lies in rousing the West Welsh," Erlend said to Guthrum, who was standing beside him. "That was your original plan, to win a Danish base in Dumnonia. Perhaps Harald Bjornson will be successful among the Celts."

"I do not see how he can fail to be," Guthrum said. "All of Europe does know how the Saxons did drive the Welsh from their lands, did push them back into Wales and into Cornwall. The Welsh would be fools not to take advantage of the chance to turn on their ancient enemies."

"One would think so," Erlend murmured.

Guthrum scowled. "You are the one who is always singing those Saxon songs of victories over the Welsh."

"I know." Erlend shaded his eyes with his hand to screen the glare of the sun. "And if it were the Welsh in Wales and the Mercians, I should have little doubt as to the outcome. But the West Saxons have ever been more generous toward their Celtic neighbors, Uncle. There were Celts serving in Alfred's hearthband when I was with him, and Celts are recognized under law as having a wergild half as great as that of a Saxon thane. This is not true in Mercia, but it is true in Wessex. The West Welsh may not be so disaffected as we would like."

"Name of the Raven!" Guthrum swore. "Who could have predicted such a storm in October? It has ruined all my well-laid plans."

Erlend could not resist saying, "Perhaps Odin did not like the way you broke your oath."

Guthrum swung around, violence flickering across his face like summer lightning. "Odin loves the strong," Guthrum said, and his voice was like the lash of a whip. "Not the weak of stomach. Yon Alfred is no lily-liver, Nephew. He hanged our men without a qualm." Then, grudgingly: "I did not think he had it in him."

"He is no lily-liver," Erlend agreed, and his own voice was cold as ice, "nor do I think he will trust you a second time."

Guthrum looked back toward the West Saxon camp. "How many men do you judge that he has?"

"He will have his own household thanes as well as the fyrds of Somerset, Dorset, and Devon," Erlend answered. "At the least. With the men of Wiltshire ready to come at his call. Equal numbers to us, I should think. At the least."

"It is too chancy," Guthrum said. "They are good fighters, these West Saxons." Then, grimly: "We shall have to wait them out. He has never yet managed to keep such a large force in the field. We shall wait until his numbers are low, and then we shall press for a fight."

There was silence as both men trained their eyes on the moving figures in the West Saxon camp. "Yes," said Erlend at last. "That will be the best."

But the time of year was not in the Danes' favor. The harvest was already in, and Alfred offered good geld to the men who would stay with him at Exeter. For most of the squire thanes and the ceorls, the geld would more than compensate them for the work time they might lose at home. A month went by and the West Saxon army kept its numbers. Nor was there any news of the West Welsh.

The cold of winter set in. Guthrum sent his raiding parties out at night, when it was easy to get over the wall unseen by the watching West Saxons. Sometimes the raiding parties got back with food, sometimes they did not. By the end of January the Danes had stripped the surrounding area of all the food and fodder that was easily come by. And wagonloads of supplies were rolling in for the West Saxons.

"I can hold out here no longer," Guthrum said to his council of jarls one day in early February. "We desire to obtain land to settle upon in Wessex and to win security for all Danes on this island by eliminating the threat posed by Alfred of Wessex. I can do neither of these things by starving my army to death in Exeter."

Grunts of agreement came from all the men seated around the fire. Then Jarl Svein asked, "What will you do, Guthrum?"

"Sue for a peace and remove into Mercia. The plan we had here was not at fault. It was the wreckage of our ships in the storm that was our undoing."

Louder grunts of agreement.

A muscle jumped in Guthrum's cheek. He said, "I have heard of the discontent among my men. I have heard it said that those who went with Halfdan are masters of their own lands by now, sitting at warm hearths with willing wives to warm their beds by night, while we are still in the field."

A faint rustle went around the circle. Erlend had heard some of the jarls say much the same thing. Guthrum's eyes began to smolder. "I shall divide up the lands of Mercia," he said. "Let those who are weary of war take up their plows. I lead no man who does not wish to follow me."

There was an uncomfortable silence. "That will be best," said Jarl Svein finally. "You are right when you say our men are weary of war, have lost their hunger for gold and for blood. It is land they want, Guthrum."

"I will give them land." Guthrum rose to his feet and looked down at the circle of men seated before him. He added scornfully, "No good to have such as they at your back in battle."

Another silence, this one even more uncomfortable than the first. Few of the jarls were able to meet Guthrum's eyes.

"Will Alfred agree to a peace?" It was Erlend's voice for the first time in the council.

Guthrum hooked his thumbs into his belt and stared through the smoke of the fire at his nephew. "I think so. We are not so ill-matched that we cannot break out of Exeter by force of arms if we must. We would lose many men in so doing, but so would he. He cannot afford to throw away his men, this Alfred of Wessex. I think he will make a peace."

"Send Erlend to the Saxon camp," said Svein, "and we will find out." The rest of the council grunted their approval.

Guthrum had read Alfred's situation with some accuracy. Much as the West Saxon king would have liked to finish forever the Danish army at Exeter, he knew he did not have the numbers of men to enable him to do so. In fact, Alfred had considerably fewer men than had Guthrum, though thus far he had managed to disguise this lack successfully. It was best for all to make a peace.

The making of the peace, however, did not proceed as smoothly as had such negotiations in the past. To begin with, while Alfred agreed to allow the Danes free passage from his kingdom, he refused to pay a geld, even the modest geld that Erlend had suggested.

"It is a question of pride, my lord," Erlend tried to explain to Alfred when he met with the West Saxon king to discuss the terms of the peace. "It will not look well for Guthrum if he must leave the kingdom without having taken a geld."

"Wessex has its pride as well," came Alfred's cold reply. They were meeting in the West Saxon camp, within the king's tent, and they were alone. Erlend was completely disarmed; Alfred wore a small dagger thrust through his belt beneath his cloak. The day was heavy with fog and it was cold.

"You have paid Danegeld before," Erlend said.

"This time the Danes are under more compulsion than are we." Alfred's breath hung white in the chill air. "I will agree to let you go because it will be easier thus for my men, but if you insist upon a geld, then I will fight."

Erlend had prepared himself for this meeting, had armored himself with all the ancient grudges he bore against Alfred, had determined to be as objective and unemotional in his dealings with Alfred as the king was in his dealings with him. So now he looked Alfred in the face steadily and assessed what he saw there.

Alfred had changed in these last five years, he thought. Or perhaps not changed . . . perhaps just grown more completely into what he had always been. All the delicacy of boyhood was gone from that clean-shaven face, had been hammered into a fine-drawn, purely masculine beauty. Well, Alfred was . . . twenty-seven, it must be. Five years older than Erlend himself. Fifteen years younger than Guthrum.

"And I want hostages," Alfred said.

Erlend let out the breath he had unconsciously been holding. "Why?" he asked.

Alfred smiled. It was not a smile of amusement. "I realize that Guthrum's word is as reliable as is the sky in spring," he said. "Nor does he appear to care overmuch about the men he gives away as hostages. But I must have some guarantee that it will cost him to break his word. I will take fifty hostages this time, Erlend. And I want one of them to be a jarl."

Guthrum had been furious when Erlend returned to Exeter with Alfred's demands. It had taken Erlend nearly an hour to calm his uncle enough to enable them to speak sensibly.

"He is right, my lord," Erlend said. "We are under more constraint than are they. If you were in Alfred's position, you would not pay a geld either."

Guthrum ignored this insulting observation. Danes took gelds, they did not pay them. Instead, "How many men do you think he has in his camp?" Guthrum was pacing up and down the room, as he had been for the last hour. "Did you get a good look around?"

"I tried, but they took me to the king's tent immediately. The point is, however, that even if he has not our equal number in camp just now, he has his ships still in the estuary. If they are filled with fighting men, then could they come in on our rear and catch us between."

Guthrum cursed.

"Nor are our men in the best of heart," Erlend continued remorselessly. "We have been besieged for too many months, first in Wareham and now here. It is not a way of life to the liking of a Dane."

Guthrum cursed again.

"About these hostages . . ." Erlend said.

Guthrum sat down. "I cannot send him a jarl."

"No."

"Name of the Raven, I cannot send him anyone of rank!"

"Not after what happened to the last hostages," Erlend agreed smoothly.

"I will keep to my word this time," Now Guthrum was sounding aggrieved. "I have every intention of removing into Mercia. If he will agree to return the hostages when once I have left Wessex, then perhaps—"

"I do not think that is what Alfred had in mind."

Guthrum gave Erlend a piercing blue look. "What is it that *you* have in mind, Nephew?" he asked. "I can see from your face that you have something to say."

"I think I might have a solution," Erlend admitted.

"Tell me," Guthrum said.

It took the better part of the night to convince the Danish leader to accede to the proposal Erlend put forth. On the following morning, Erlend rode once more into the West Saxon camp.

Alfred's answer to Erlend's first question was simple. "I shall keep the hostages," he said, "as guarantees that Guthrum stays out of Wessex. The moment a Danish army sets its foot over my borders, I shall kill them all."

"Fifty is a large number, my lord," Erlend countered. "To have to feed and house and guard fifty men for an indefinite period of time will be a burden to you. Wessex is not a prison, nor are your thanes or reeves prison guards."

Alfred's face did not change, but Erlend could see from the way the king lowered his lashes to screen his eyes that this thought was not new to him. But, "I must have a guarantee," Alfred repeated.

They were meeting once more in Alfred's tent, but this morning the sun was shining and the flap door was open to let in the light. "Guthrum will send you the hostages you require, plus one man of high rank," Erlend said. "If you swear to return the fifty when once the Danish army has passed over your borders, you may keep the man of rank indefinitely as guarantee of Guthrum's word."

Alfred raised his eyes and looked once again at the Dane. Now that Erlend had reached his full growth, there was but an inch between the two of them. "Who is this man of rank whom Guthrum can so dispense with?" Alfred asked.

"Me."

There was a surprised silence. After it had gone on for too long, Erlend added, "Nor would you have to keep me under close guard, Alfred of Wessex. I will give you my word not to try to escape. Unlike Guthrum's"—and here spots of color flamed in his usually pale cheeks—"my word is good."

Alfred's face remained unreadable. He said, "From what Athulf has told me, there is little love between you and your uncle. Athulf says in fact that Guthrum has some reason to wish you dead. If this is so, you are no good to me as hostage for Guthrum's word, Erlend."

The king's voice was its most clipped. The spots of color faded from Erlend's face and he replied in equally crisp tones, "It is true that Guthrum has no great love for me. If I were dead, then would my uncle be the proper heir to Nasgaard, and Nasgaard is a great prize indeed. But if Guthrum truly covets Nasgaard, my lord, he cannot betray me to my death. There is no Dane would follow him if he bore bloodguilt for a nephew upon his hands." Erlend raised his eyebrows in Alfred's own gesture. "I am in fact the safest hostage you could hold. It would please Guthrum to see me fall in battle, but he will not cause my death himself."

"Was it Guthrum's idea to propose you as hostage?" Alfred asked.

"No." Erlend met those unreadable eyes and held them. "The idea was mine. Guthrum did not like it. It took me near half the night to convince him that this was the best way." Erlend smiled wryly. "It would prove a little difficult to find a jarl to send in my stead, you see."

"I can imagine that is so." Alfred's voice was bleak.

"My uncle did not think you would have the stomach to kill our hostages in cold blood," Erlend said candidly. "He knows differently now, and so does our army."

A shadow seemed to cross Alfred's face, a bruising under the eyes which had not been there before. "Yes," he said. "Now you know."

"Let us go safely into Mercia, my lord," Erlend said. "It will be best for all."

With a quick, lithe movement, Alfred suddenly stepped forward so that he was but a hairbreadth away from Erlend. In an abrupt, harsh voice, he asked, "What does Guthrum plan to do in Mercia?"

Erlend looked into the narrowed golden eyes. He had never before been so close to Alfred of Wessex. All his detached calm fled and his heart began to slam within his chest.

What is the matter with me? he thought frantically. He wet his lips with his tongue and answered, "He will parcel out the country to those of his men who desire land, my lord. There are those among us who are weary of war, who would settle down to the farm and the plow. It is the reason many Danes came to England, to find the land they could not get at home."

"And what of the Mercian king?" Alfred demanded. "What of Ceolwulf?"

Erlend was so close to Alfred that he could feel the heat from the king's body, see the golden stubble of beard under the skin of his face. Erlend said, in a voice that was not as steady as he wished, "Ceolwulf will have his share, a part of the kingdom to keep for himself and his people. The rest will Guthrum take for the Danes."

There was a silence. Alfred's body did not move, but Alfred himself seemed to withdraw. It was a trick of the king's Erlend had seen before, this withdrawal of his spirit deep within while he made a decision.

Then, after nearly a full minute had passed, "So be it," Alfred said. "If the Mercians object, then must they join with Ethelred. My charge is Wessex."

Erlend said nothing, was incapable of saying anything, just stood there before the king and waited. He feared that Alfred must be able to hear the hammering of his heart, it beat so loudly in his own ears. Alfred said, "You may tell Guthrum that I accept his offer. I will return his hostages once he is over the Mercian border. But you, Erlend Olafson, you I will keep."

"Yes, my lord," said Erlend. He began to step back, away from Alfred, but the king put a hand upon his upper arm to hold him.

"You will give me your solemn word not to escape?"

"Yes," said Erlend. "I will."

Hawk eyes searched his face. Then, slowly: "*Your* word I will take."

"Why?" It was suddenly the most important thing in the world to know why Alfred would trust him.

"For the same reason I let you stay five years ago," Alfred answered.

"And what is that, my lord?"

Alfred smiled. "Elswyth likes you," he said, "and I have never known her to be wrong about a man yet."

Erlend stared into the face that was so close to his. Alfred was not jesting, he thought incredulously. He truly was basing his trust upon the judgment of a woman.

Alfred finally released his arm, but Erlend did not immediately step away. The king said grimly, "Your uncle, on the other hand, I would not trust beyond the range of my sight. I will take those fifty hostages, Erlend, and Guthrum will not get them back until he is well into Mercia and away from my borders."

Erlend took one step back. "I will deliver your message," he answered, "and tomorrow I will come with fifty other hostages to your camp."

Two pairs of eyes, almost on a level, met and held. Alfred nodded, turned away, and went to call for Erlend's escort.

Chapter 32

ALFRED took no chances this time, but gathered all the men still left to him and followed the Danish army as it went up the Fosse Way and into Mercia. Only when Guthrum was reported safely in Repton did Alfred release his hostages and send them in the wake of their retreating army. Then he himself, along with his companion thanes, returned to Chippenham, where his family awaited him. Erlend Olafson rode to Chippenham in Alfred's train.

Erlend knew Chippenham from his previous sojourn in the West Saxon royal household. Chippenham had ever been a favorite manor of Alfred's for hunting; the forests in the area were very fine. It was a good time of year for hunting too, Erlend thought as the high stockade fence of Chippenham rose up under the ever-changing March sky. He thought the chances were good he would be allowed to join the royal hunting parties; Alfred's companion thanes seemed disposed to treat him more as guest than as enemy hostage. They would not be behaving thus if they had not had their directions from the king.

The king's party had been sighted and the great gate of Chippenham was swinging open. Then the royal guard was riding into the courtyard, one hundred strong, with Erlend riding directly behind the king, Edgar on one side of him, Brand on the other.

The courtyard filled with running groomsmen, ready to take the horses. Erlend looked toward the great hall and saw two children standing on the step, jumping up and down in their excitement. Erlend could hear the high childish voices even over the jangle of stirrup and bridle and the deeper rumble of male chatter in the yard. "Papa! Papa!"

Erlend swung himself to the ground like those around him and stared in astonishment as Alfred went forward to be enveloped in a rush of arms and legs. "Name of the Raven," he said. "That can't be Flavia and Edward!"

Brand had come to stand beside him, and now the West Saxon grinned. "No one else," he said.

"But they have grown so big."

"Children will do that." Brand looked down at the Dane. "I do not know

299

if they will remember you," he said, "but I am quite certain the Lady Elswyth will."

Erlend looked up into the green eyes that were so oddly similar to his own. "What think you she will do to me?" he asked Alfred's thane with mock apprehension.

"God knows," said Brand. "But you had better come along and see for yourself." He put a big hand upon Erlend's shoulder, and Erlend recognized that its touch was for comfort rather than compulsion. Brand had guessed that the apprehension was not entirely pretense after all.

It was dark inside after the brightness of the day. Even for a royal manor, the great hall at Chippenham was extremely large, with a double hearth in its center to give the warmth of two fires to those who clustered within. A trestle table was standing before the hearth this day, with a tapestry laid out upon it. The women who had been working there had gone, however, and only Elswyth remained in the room, with her husband, her children, and four deliriously happy dogs. The men were beginning to come in to claim their sleeping spaces on the benches along the wall. Alfred was holding a very young child in his arms, and all the royal family, with the exception of the baby in her father's arms, turned to watch Erlend as he slowly crossed the floor toward them. The dogs ran up to sniff at him, then raced back to crowd around Alfred's legs once more, their tails creating a breeze, they wagged so hard.

Then Erlend was before them. He stopped.

"Elswyth," Alfred said, and Erlend could distinctly hear the amusement in his voice, "here is Erlend Olafson, hostage for the good word of the Danish leader."

"My lady," Erlend said, stood there in his twisted bracelets and his golden collar, and looked at her with wary eyes.

Dark blue eyes looked back, looked him up and looked him down. He had almost forgotten how beautiful Elswyth was. Erlend added with absolute sincerity, "It is good to see you again."

"I should be furious with you," Elswyth said, and her husky drawling voice was suddenly welcome to his ears. "We treated you with kindness and you spied on us."

"Not very well, I am afraid," Erlend answered immediately. The tips of his triangular brows rose higher. "It was I told Guthrum that Alfred was sure to defend Wilton, I who enabled the West Saxons to come in on us unawares and steal our horses."

"Harper," said Flavia suddenly from where she stood between her parents.

Erlend looked at Alfred's daughter. Dark gold hair in two long braids, those startling not-to-be forgotten blue-green eyes. "Yes," he said with a faint smile. "I used to be your harper, Flavia."

"You are a Dane," said Edward. "Danes dress like you." Edward's eyes were on Erlend's arm bracelets; he did not sound friendly.

Elswyth put a hand on her son's sturdy shoulder. "Lord Erlend is a special Dane, Edward," she said. "He was kind to my brother Athulf when Athulf was made hostage. We owe him kindness in return."

Edward turned his eyes, the same color as his sister's, toward Alfred. Flavia looked like her father, Erlend thought, but not this one. Edward was already two full inches over Flavia, and the thick fair hair framing his rosy childish face was more silver than gold. "We do not like the Danes, Papa, do we?" he demanded.

Alfred shifted his younger daughter from one arm to the other in an effort to evade the fingers that were grasping at his hair. "No, Edward," he answered, "we do not like the Danes. But as your mother said, Erlend is our guest, and we like him."

Despite his efforts, the baby had managed to get a fistful of Alfred's hair, and now she began to pull. His brows knit with the pain and he reached up to untangle the little fingers. Erlend smiled at the expression on Alfred's face and said to Elswyth, "How is Copper Queen?"

The haughty look left Elswyth's face and she almost smiled back at him. "Wait until you see her," she said. "She is splendid."

Alfred had managed to detach his hair from his daughter's grasp, and now he handed the baby over to Elswyth's waiting arms. "It takes having children to understand why it is that married women bundle their hair off their faces," he remarked to Erlend, and then bent to scratch the ears of his oldest hound. "Erlend has given me his oath not to escape," he said over his shoulder to his wife. "He is to do as he likes. You will have to find him a place to sleep."

The hound was quivering all over with ecstasy at Alfred's touch. The other dogs gathered around, anxiously awaiting their turns.

"Will you harp for us, Erlend?" Flavia asked, looking up at him with wide and innocent eyes.

Erlend looked down into the beautiful little face of Alfred's daughter. "I should be happy to harp for you, my lady," he said, and did not realize himself how tender his voice suddenly sounded.

Elswyth heard the note, however, and for one brief moment her eyes met with her husband's. "Your accent is more Mercian than West Saxon these days," she said. "Athulf's influence?"

Erlend nodded. "I suppose so, my lady." He asked with genuine interest, "How is your brother?"

Elswyth kissed the fat little hand that was so enthusiastically patting her lips. "As well as can be expected." She tried to speak around a fist that had abruptly been inserted into her mouth. "He is visiting Queen Ethelswith at present. She resides on one of Alfred's manors in Surrey."

Erlend, prudently, said nothing.

"Where is your harp?" Flavia asked.

Alfred looked up from his dogs and grinned. "She is just like her mother," he said. "Relentless. You had better go and get your harp, Erlend, or we will have no peace."

"Oh, good," said Flavia, came forward to stand beside Erlend, and put her small hand into his. She gave him a sunny smile. "I'll go with you."

"Wouldn't you like to go too, Edward?" Elswyth asked, having transferred the baby to her hip.

"No," said Edward in a tone that made it perfectly clear he still did not like Danes.

"All these men," said Elswyth, looking around the hall. "I had better go and check with the reeve about the supper."

"I will stay with Papa," was the last thing Erlend heard from Edward as Flavia tugged him toward the door, toward his baggage and his harp.

Elswyth was already in bed when Alfred came into their sleeping room later in the evening. "I am glad you were nice to Erlend," he said to her as he began to strip off his clothes. "He was nervous of meeting you again."

She shrugged. "I could do nothing else. He was very good to Athulf." She sat up against her pillow and watched him piling his clothes on the chest. "You are always so neat," she said with amusement. "Do you fold your garments so neatly every night when you are in the field?"

"I scarcely ever get *out* of my clothes when I am in the field," he retorted. "That bath I had today was the first good washing I have had in a month."

She grinned. "If ever you write a book about the hardships of war, chief among them will be listed the lack of proper baths."

He pulled off his last bit of clothing, his headband, ran his fingers through the hair at his brow, then shook his head like a dog. Elswyth said, only half-humorously, "How I have missed all your little rituals, Alfred."

He turned and came toward the bed, moving with the springy grace that was so much a part of him. The single lamp shone with a golden light on his bare skin. He got into the bed beside Elswyth, leaned over her, and said, his clipped voice very soft, "I have missed one ritual in particular. Can you guess what it is?"

"I fear you have picked the wrong time of the month for your homecoming, my love," she said. Her blue eyes were full of sympathy. "I have my courses."

At that he groaned, flopped down beside her on his back, and stared up at the roof. It was her turn to lean over him. "I am sorry," she said.

Golden eyes gazed up at her. "It could be worse." Then: "Safe for another month."

"Listening to you, one would never think you were so loving a father," she said. Her loose hair had fallen forward and was hanging down now, enveloping him in a lavender-scented curtain of soft black silk. "You adore the children, you know you do."

He didn't move. "Once they are here, they are fine," he said. "It is the waiting for them to arrive that is so hard."

"Father Erwald would say it is a sin to put your carnal pleasure before the getting of children."

His eyes did not waver. "It is not just my carnal pleasure," he said. His mouth quirked. "Though I admit that is part of it."

She bent her head closer and kissed him on the mouth. "I know," she said, then nestled against him, her head pillowed on his shoulder. "Wouldn't it be lovely if we were the only two people in all the world?" she said dreamily. "No children, no thanes, no Danes to threaten our peace. Just you and I alone together."

"And the horses and the dogs," he added, his arm curving to hold her close.

"And the horses and the dogs. Of course."

He touched his lips to the top of her head. "It would be like paradise," he said. "I could do without the dogs even, if I had you."

She snorted. "Nor would I be a fool like Eve, to let a devilish snake betray my joy."

"I have no doubt that you would send Satan about his business with little delay," Alfred agreed, amusement warming his voice. "No fallen angel would have a chance against you."

"Very true," she replied complacently.

He laughed, deep and soft.

"Tell me," she said. "How did you come to take Erlend as a hostage?"

They talked for over an hour, and then Elswyth fell asleep, her head still nestled against his shoulder. Alfred had blown out the lamp earlier, and he lay now in the dark and listened to the soft breathing of his wife lying at his side.

It was true, he thought, that he did not welcome the news that he was to have a new child as joyfully as he should. It was true also that a child was a gift from God, that it was a sin to place one's own carnal pleasure above the Lord's command to be fruitful and multiply.

But . . . It was not that he did not love his children. Nor was it only the continence that advanced pregnancy and childbirth imposed upon him. It was this feeling he had that in giving Elswyth so many children he was burdening her, chaining her, who was always meant to be free as air.

Sometimes he would look at her as she went about the manor, a child in her arms and children at her skirts, and he would feel so guilty.

She had grieved sorely for the little son who died. He too had sorrowed for the child, but it had been far worse for Elswyth. And, too, with every new child came the added fear for her own safety. Women died in childbirth far too often for any man to rest secure that his woman would be safe.

"Wouldn't it be lovely if we were the only two people in the world?" she had said to him tonight. No children, no thanes . . . no Danes to threaten their peace.

It would be paradise, he had answered.

But this was not paradise, this was the world. And to each of them who lived in this world had God given duties. Alfred's duty was to be king, to bear the burden of the safety of his people, to protect them and, in better times, to educate them so that they might come to a better light of understanding of the ways of God. His duty was to educate his children so that they too could lead their people in the way God most desired.

These were the burdens God had laid upon him, and he accepted them. It was not for himself he minded the fetters of this world; it was for Elswyth.

Sometimes he looked at her, and his heart would catch, and he would think: What have I done to deserve that God should have given me Elswyth?

He could smell the lavender from the soap with which she washed her hair. Put him blindfold into a room anywhere in the world, and he would know if Elswyth was there. As she would know him.

Well, at least they looked to get a time of peace from the Vikings. The last time he had made a peace with the Danes, they had stayed away for nearly five years. Surely he could expect at least half that much of a respite this time. If Guthrum were to settle his men in Mercia, the Danish leader would be well-occupied.

The fyrds could be sent home, the corn put into the fields, the sheep sheared, and all the work of the land go forward as it should.

Thank God for his ships. He did not think that Guthrum would have made a peace if it were not for the ships.

A picture of the Viking leader came before his mind: the brilliant, violent blue eyes; the short-cut yellow hair; the mocking sensual mouth. He was a predator, this uncle of Erlend's; and he was a leader. Alfred did not think Guthrum was finished in Wessex. He would try again. But they would be safe for a while.

Elswyth stirred, as if his thoughts were disturbing her, and Alfred turned on his side and settled her so that her body fitted into the curve of his. The scent of lavender drifted to his nostrils, and he fell asleep.

Shortly after Guthrum moved to Repton, he sent to Denmark for new recruits. Then he began to parcel out to those of his followers who wished to settle, the lands of Mercia in the areas around Derby, Nottingham, Lincoln, Stamford, and Leicester. Tamworth he left to Ceolwulf, who was forced to shelter those Mercians who had been dispossessed by the land-hungry Danes.

Ethelred of Mercia was still in London, and Guthrum knew from his scouts that he had been joined by Guthrum's former hostage, Athulf. For the time being, however, Guthrum was content to leave London to the Mercians. Guthrum's major intent was to replenish his army, nor was it the recapture of London that was the aim of his present strategy.

Guthrum had no intention of allowing himself to be bested by Alfred of Wessex. The humiliation he had suffered at being forced to retreat from Wessex without a geld still burned in his heart. All through the spring he sat in the royal Mercian hall at Repton and plotted his revenge.

He knew, none better, the problem that beset the leader of any Viking army attempting to take Wessex. His weakness was that once established in a secure base, he had to forage for food and for fodder in the surrounding countryside. The West Saxons were adept at intercepting such foraging parties, and the resulting loss of men and of supplies was crippling to the Danes. It was lack of supplies that had forced Halfdan to withdraw from Reading six years ago, and it was lack of supplies that had forced Guthrum out of Wareham and Exeter just recently.

Supplies, then, were the main problem Guthrum must solve if he were successfully to take Wessex.

On the other hand, the main advantage of the Viking army was its mobility. Even though Alfred had mounted large numbers of his men, still the West Saxons were not accustomed to moving as swiftly as could the Danes.

The main advantage of the West Saxons was their unity. In no other Saxon kingdom had the men of all classes so stood together. No other country had been able to mobilize to fight, again and again, and still keep coming back in spite of defeat. And the reason for the West Saxons' unity had become quite clear to Guthrum during this last campaign. It was their king.

Without Alfred to lead, the West Saxon defense would likely crumble. Guthrum was too much a leader himself to underestimate the importance of the man at the top. And now that he had met this Alfred face-to-face, he knew beyond a doubt that *there* was the heart and the brain behind Wessex' success.

Men would follow Alfred. Even Erlend—Guthrum had seen the look in his nephew's eyes when he gazed at Alfred. And for all his irritating ways, Erlend was no fool. If his enemy thought Alfred of Wessex was a hero, then what must his own people think?

In the face of all these facts, there was only one sensible conclusion that Guthrum could reach. Eliminate Alfred.

Eliminate Alfred, and the defense of Wessex would shatter. Eliminate Alfred, set a puppet king up in his stead, and the land would lie open before the Danes as willingly as any whore would lie for the man with the power to buy her.

Guthrum did not have to defeat the entire West Saxon fyrd. He just had to kill the West Saxon king.

Once he had settled on the goal, the plan to achieve it came easily.

Chapter 33

IN October 877 Alfred was holding a King's Justice in Winchester when word came that the Danes had moved from Repton to Gloucester.

"Gloucester," Alfred said that night as he discussed the situation with the ealdormen and thanes who were in attendance at Winchester for the court. "Gloucester is in Mercia, true, but it is overclose to the Wessex border for me to be comfortable."

"The Danes have finished giving away the lands of eastern Mercia," said Cenwulf, shire thane of Dorset. "Perhaps Guthrum now looks to do the same with the lands of the west. The soil about Gloucester is rich and fertile, and the Severn flows wide and deep there toward the sea. The Danes are never happy far from the sea."

There was the faintest of lines between Alfred's fair brows. "My understanding was that Guthrum was to leave the west of Mercia to Ceolwulf," he said.

Ethelnoth of Somerset snorted. "Who can put faith in the word of a Dane?"

"No Saxon can, that is certain," said the Ealdorman of Hampshire.

Alfred had decided. "We had better keep a troop of men at Cirencester," he said. "From Cirencester, scouts can keep watch on the road out of Gloucester, can give us fair warning if the Danes look to be thinking of invasion."

"Keeping men at Cirencester would be wise, my lord," agreed Godfred of Dorset. "We ealdormen can go by turn in sending men to keep the watch. No need to lay the burden on your own household."

Ethelnoth of Somerset said, "If you desire, my lord king, I can send a troop of my fastest-riding men to Cirencester in the morning. They can keep a close watch on Gloucester, observe if there seems to be any suspicious gathering of an army."

Alfred thought for a long moment, then slowly nodded. "All right," he said. "I do not need a fighting force, you understand, just good men with fast horses. And if there is any news, they are to come to me, not to you, Ethelnoth."

"Yes, my lord," said Ethelnoth of Somerset. "I understand."

The royal household did not go to Dorchester to hold Christmas that year. There was sickness reported among the resident household at Dorchester, and so Alfred decided to break with tradition and celebrate the Christmas holidays at Chippenham.

Thus far the Danes in Gloucester had remained quiet. At the beginning of December the men of Somerset had been replaced in Cirencester by the men of Dorset, and with winter settling in, Alfred thought it highly unlikely that the Danes would attempt to move out of their Gloucester base.

Erlend, who had slipped as unobtrusively as he could manage it into Alfred's household, accompanied the royal family to Chippenham, and watched the Christmas festivities with a thoughtful eye. In some ways, he thought, this Christian feast of Christmas was like to the Norse winter feast of Yule. There was a Yule log laid upon the fire, in the old Norse way; the hall was decorated with evergreens from the forest; and a pig was roasted for the festival banquet. But the religious aspects of this Christmas were foreign to him.

Erlend had not been free to ask questions about Christianity when last he had been at Alfred's court, as he had been masquerading as a Christian himself. But in his present situation he could ask as many questions as he liked. And the person he found himself questioning the most was the king.

Alfred truly believed in this religion of his. The more Erlend questioned him, the clearer that fact became. Alfred believed in this Father-God, in this Christ who was God's son, and he believed that this God actually intervened in the lives of men.

"It is divine providence that rules our lives, Erlend," Alfred said to him. "Not fate, as you would have it. Always within us, God is working. It is our fault if we do not listen and hear."

This belief was at the very core of the man that was Alfred; Erlend could see that. He tried to comprehend what Alfred meant by this "divine providence" of his, but it was difficult. Fate was a concept any Dane understood thoroughly. This other was somewhat more complicated.

The royal household gathered at Chippenham that Christmas was considerably smaller than was usual. The king's companion thanes had been in the field for a large part of two years; many of them had not seen their kin during all that time. Now, at Christmas, with the Danes quiescent in Gloucester for the winter, Alfred had allowed those men who so desired to go home for the feast. About sixty of the hundred thanes who comprised the king's personal guard had chosen to do so.

There were many West Saxons who rendered up thanks to God that Christmastide for the peace that reigned in Wessex. The thanes and ceorls who comprised the various shire fyrds knew heartfelt gratitude to be at home this Christmas with their families. The men of Wessex had been in the field against the Danes for almost two years, but there had been no battles, and few West Saxons had been killed. The Danes were in Mercia; Wessex was at peace.

God's blessing on the king. It was a toast heard again and again throughout the land that Christmastide. *God bless King Alfred.* Because of Alfred, because of his courage and his resolution, they had defeated the Danes. Thanks be to God, Wessex was at peace.

The feast of the Epiphany, the twelfth day of Christmas, was celebrated at Chippenham with a great hunt and a great feast. A small amount of snow had fallen the day before, just enough to dust the world with purest white and make it sparkle in the winter sun. Elswyth had ridden out with the men and brought down her own hart.

The following day dawned gray and bitter. Elswyth awoke to find Alfred pacing up and down the floor of their sleeping room, fully dressed and wrapped in a warm cloak. One look at his face was enough to tell her that he had a headache.

There was nothing to be done, of course. That was the worst part of it all, that there was nothing to be done. At least, she thought, the feasting was over. He could keep to his room for the day without fear of disappointing anyone.

He did not want cold cloths for his head, he just wanted to be left alone, so she dressed and went out into the hall to have her breakfast.

"The king is ill today," she said quietly to the thanes. "You will have to go hunting without him."

No one wanted to go hunting if the king was ill. Consequently, most of the thanes were in the hall when Cedric, shire thane of Wiltshire, came galloping into the courtyard demanding to see the king.

"You cannot," he was told at first. Then, when he blurted his news out to all the hall, Elswyth ran to get Alfred.

Erlend could tell immediately that Alfred was in pain. It was there in the set of his mouth, in the shadows under his eyes, in the way he held his head.

"My lord king," said Cedric of Wiltshire, "you must flee from here. The Danes are coming down the Fosse Way. Hundreds of them, my lord! All on horse! They are making straight for Chippenham. And they are but five miles away!"

There was a moment of appalled silence. Everyone was looking to Alfred. Erlend felt sick to his stomach. He said, "Guthrum is seeking to capture you, my lord. He must know you are here at Chippenham. It is not an invasion, not with only a few hundred men. He is seeking you." Now everyone was staring at Erlend. "You must get away from here, Alfred!" Erlend said urgently, meeting the shadowed eyes of the king. "You must save yourself!"

The door to the hall opened and Flavia and Edward came in from the outside. Erlend saw Alfred look to the door, then to Elswyth, who was standing beside him. "Saddle the horses," he said, and his clipped voice sounded perfectly normal. "We must all get away from Chippenham. We cannot risk being caught here with the children."

"Where shall we go, my lord?" It was Brand speaking as the men began to run for the doors. "To Selwood?"

There was a moment's silence. "No," said Alfred. "We will ride for Somerset. It was the men of Dorset let the Danes go by; I will not trust my family to Dorset." He looked past Brand. "Where is my reeve? He had better send the serving girls out to nearby farmhouses. I do not want any women left here at Chippenham when the Danes ride in."

"I am here, my lord," said the reeve of Chippenham, stepping forward to receive his orders.

Elswyth said, "Flavia, Edward, go and put on your warmest clothing." It was the voice her children never disobeyed. "Tell Tordis to dress Elgiva warmly also. Quickly, now!" As the children ran for their sleeping room, Elswyth turned toward her own room to dress herself in warm clothes for riding.

It took only ten minutes before the horses were saddled and the whole of the party that would ride out of Chippenham was mounted and in the courtyard. Edward and Flavia were perched before two of the thanes, while Elgiva had been given into the charge of Edgar. The dogs ran underfoot; Alfred had refused to leave his dogs for the Danes. The day was damp and bitter cold; the wind smelled of snow. Finally the royal party cantered out of Chippenham and turned south and west, toward Somerset and Ealdorman Ethelnoth, whose loyalty to Alfred was not to be questioned.

The steady three-beat stride of his cantering horse was an agony for Alfred. There was grayness all about him; his senses had almost completely gone. All that was left was a furnace of pain in his head. He heard Elswyth say, "Give me your reins, Alfred," and he let her take them. He couldn't see well enough to steer. It was a monumental effort just to stay in the saddle.

It had always been one of his greatest fears, that a headache would strike at a time when he was desperately needed. Before every battle he had prayed, "Not now, dear God. Please, not now."

He set his teeth against the blinding agony in his head. Just breathe, he thought. Breathe in, breathe out. In. Out. One and two and one and two. The pain would stop. Another few hours and it would stop.

He would stay in the saddle. If it killed him, he would stay in the saddle.

"Where are we?" he asked.

"A few miles west of the Fosse Way," he heard Elswyth's voice reply.

"No main roads," he said. "Keep to the smaller roads. Keep going southwest, toward Cheddar."

"All right," she said. "We will."

Breathe in. Breathe out. One and two. His body was staying in the saddle from instinct alone. He wrapped his fingers in his horse's gray mane. God, if only he could see!

After two hours of riding, they halted to rest the horses and to give the children a respite. A number of the men went into the forest to relieve themselves, and Elswyth gave her children some bread and cheese.

Alfred did not dismount. He sat on his stallion, his face as gray as his horse's coat, his eyes half-closed, his teeth set in his lower lip, and it was plain to Erlend that only the force of his will was keeping the king in the saddle.

"I want to ride with Erlend!" It was Flavia's voice, and he looked down to see the child standing before him.

"Flavia . . ." Elswyth started to reprimand, but Erlend put in, "I will be glad to take her, my lady. My horse is strong yet, and I am lighter to carry than most of the thanes."

"He is a Dane." Erlend did not recognize the voice but it came from the ranks of the thanes.

"Flavia may ride with Erlend." It was Alfred's voice, a little hollow-sounding but still clear. "Let us go," he added. The thanes began to swing up into their saddles.

They rode more slowly now, not to strain the horses. Flavia leaned against Erlend's chest and dozed. Erlend looked down at the small golden head nestled so trustingly against him, and felt his heart contract. He spread his cloak so that it covered her more closely.

What would have happened to Alfred's children, Alfred's wife, had Guthrum caught them at Chippenham?

Erlend had no doubt at all of what would have happened to Alfred.

He looked up from Flavia to the man who was riding now directly before him. Elswyth still had Alfred's reins, Erlend saw. No one had volunteered to take them from her; Silken was the only horse that Alfred's gray would tolerate so close to him. They were going single file along a narrow forest path, with Brand and a few other thanes leading the way. Great snow-dusted trees enclosed the track on both sides, and the dogs ran steadily and faithfully at the heels of Alfred's stallion. They had long since ceased to chase into the woods on a stray scent.

The men of Dorset had been on guard at Cirencester. Dorset, Erlend thought, Dorset was the home shire of Alfred's nephew Athelwold. Guthrum knew about Athelwold. Erlend himself had told his uncle about the dissatisfied son of Athelstan and his hatred of Alfred.

Name of the Raven, could it be that Guthrum had managed to approach Athelwold? Some sort of treachery was involved in this move of Guthrum's out of Mercia—of that Erlend was certain. Several hundred mounted men could not have moved onto the Fosse Way without being spied by the scouts Alfred had posted at Cirencester. But if those scouts were Athelwold's men . . . then perhaps they had been told not to report Guthrum's move to the king.

It occurred to Erlend, as his horse stepped over the twigs and small branches that the wind and the snow had brought down onto the forest track, that Guthrum had broken his word again, a word that Erlend's life had been pledged to secure. But at the moment Erlend could feel no care for his own safety. He was too full of horror at the thought of what would have happened had Guthrum managed to catch Alfred at Chippenham.

The blood eagle. He had never seen it done, but he had heard enough about it to know what a torture it could be if the executioner was minded to draw it out. He looked at the man in front of him, at the flexible back moving in rhythm to the motion of his horse's slow trot.

That perfect-looking body of Alfred's, he thought, was no stranger to pain. He was blind right now from the pain in his head. He must be, else he would never have allowed Elswyth to take his reins.

It was headaches he suffered from, then. And he had lived with them since he was a child.

Elswyth turned in her saddle to look at her husband. The sting of cold air had brought a rosy glow to her usually creamy skin. Erlend had never seen such an expression on her haughty high-bred face. She said nothing, but in a moment had faced front again.

The expression on Elswyth's face matched the feeling in Erlend's stomach. And it was at that moment that the Dane finally understood that he did not dislike Alfred of Wessex at all. If anything, the feeling he had for the West Saxon king was quite the opposite of dislike, was in fact far more nearly akin to love.

"I'm hungry." The voice came from the horse behind Erlend and was distinctively Edward's.

"We will stop soon, Prince," Erlend heard the thane who was riding with him say. "You are being a very brave boy. Just a little longer, and we will stop."

"You don't have to stop for me." The child-voice was clear and proud. "When my papa is ready to stop, then I will eat."

Erlend felt a tightness in the back of his throat. Seven years old was Alfred's son, he thought. They had been in the saddle for above five hours, and it was freezing. Erlend thought, and it was the first time that such a thought had ever come his way, he thought that someday he would like to have a son like Edward.

He looked ahead, and it seemed to him that Alfred was sitting more erect in his saddle. Then Erlend heard the king ask, "Where are we?"

Elswyth turned, looked at her husband again, and her face lighted with a sudden radiant smile. "Near enough to Cheddar," she said. "Are you all right? Do you want your reins back?"

"Yes."

"Another hour or so, and we should be at Cheddar," Elswyth said as Alfred looped the reins back over his horse's neck.

"Good. I think it will be safe to stay the night at Cheddar." Alfred turned in his saddle to look back over the line of horses following behind him. They were coming into the Mendip hills now, and the forest lay all around them. The royal manor of Cheddar lay in the heart of the hills, surrounded by the steep escarpments and the ravines of limestone that Erlend remembered from a previous visit.

The wind had whipped up, and it was beginning to snow. Flavia whimpered a little, and Erlend held her closer, trying to impart some of his own scant warmth to the child. "We are almost there, sweeting," he said to her softly. "Just a little longer."

Alfred must have heard him, for he called, "Are you all right, Flavia? Do you want to ride with me?"

"Oh, yes, Papa!" came the immediate answer.

Alfred pulled his horse to the side of the path and waited while Erlend came up beside him. They transferred the child from one pair of arms to the other, and as Flavia looked up at her father, Erlend could see the relief glowing in her blue-green eyes. "Are you better, Papa?"

"All better, love. You try to go to sleep. I'll hold you safe enough." Alfred nodded at Erlend, then moved his gray back onto the path behind Elswyth, his daughter hidden from sight beneath the folds of his cloak.

It was growing dark by the time they reached Cheddar. This manor was more a hunting lodge than a full royal estate, and the main hall was a small one. The reeve was dismayed to see them; the king did not usually descend upon a manor without giving his reeve ample time to provision it. At this time of year Cheddar was provisioned only for the staff who lived there, as the reeve explained unhappily to Elswyth.

Elwyth paid him little mind, just commanded him to set food upon the tables within the hour, then went to see to her exhausted children, whose nurses had been left behind in a ceorl's cottage at Chippenham. The reeve bustled off, muttering beneath his breath, but within an hour the trestle tables had been set up and some sort of repast was ready to be served. None of the thanes was in a mood to be fussy about his food, and they all fell to with dedicated concentration.

Erlend had nearly finished eating when he became aware that he was being watched. He did not have to look to know instantly whose eyes were upon him. He licked his fingers clean, then slowly turned his head toward the high seat.

"If you are finished eating, Erlend," Alfred said, "you may come with me."

"Yes, my lord." Erlend's voice was commendably steady and he rose from his bench with equally commendable calm and followed Alfred into the single private room in the hall, the king's sleeping chamber. He could feel the eyes of all the men in the hall following him as he left.

Alfred had brought a candle with him, and now he lit the room's single lamp. "Sit," he said to Erlend, gesturing to a stool while he himself prowled up and down the room's whole length. Erlend sat, folded his hands in his lap, and waited.

"It seems your uncle is not so careful for your life as you said he would be," Alfred said at last, halting for a moment in his prowling and fixing Erlend with hooded eyes. "He broke his word to me. He broke it knowing full well what happened to the last hostages he betrayed in like fashion. Is he relying on my fondness for you, perhaps, to stay my hand?"

Erlend's green eyes did not waver, nor did his voice falter in reply. "He would not expect you to have any fondness for me, my lord. Nor, if you did, for it to stay your hand."

Alfred's eye remained hooded, the long lashes screening them from any chance of being read. "And what of you, Erlend Olafson? You do not look very apprehensive for a man who knows his life is forfeit."

"If you were going to kill me, my lord," Erlend answered, "you would have done it at Chippenham, and left my body there for Guthrum to find."

Alfred resumed his pacing of the room. "I was not thinking with full clarity at Chippenham," he said, "or that is what I might have done."

"I do not think so," said Erlend. And watched as Alfred swung around to stare at him once more. "Guthrum was not planning to send me to my death, you know," Erlend continued conversationally. "He was looking to capture you. You personally, Alfred of Wessex. If he had been able to catch you in Chippenham, you would not have had a chance to put me to my death. Then would Guthrum have been my rescuer. I do not think he will be happy to find that you have me still. He will be even less happy if you put me to death."

"Is that why I should stay my hand?" Alfred asked. "Because it will make Guthrum unhappy?"

"No." Erlend looked into the king's face. Alfred looked weary, he thought. Bitterly weary. This night he looked every minute of his twenty-eight years. "Alfred," said Erlend, for the second time unconsciously calling the king by his given name, "I do not think Cheddar will be safe for you, or any other of the royal manors either. Guthrum has managed to catch you unprepared, and he is too much of a general not to follow up his advantage. He will be after you. He will not give you time to settle in at one of your manors and call up your fyrds."

"I know." At last Alfred came to rest, sitting on the edge of the bed with his feet braced against the floor. "Erlend," he said, "how do you think Guthrum got through the Dorset guard in Cirencester?"

"I think he suborned them," Erlend replied. His pale face was bleak. "Your nephew Athelwold is of Dorset, my lord, and Athelwold hates you. He hates you for refusing to name him *secondarius*." Erlend dropped his eyes, then bravely raised them again. "Guthrum knows about Athelwold," he said. "I told him when I left your household during the time of the first peace."

Two pairs of eyes met and held. For a long moment neither spoke. Then Erlend asked, "Who was the thane in command in Cirencester?"

"Cenwulf," Alfred replied. And Erlend's breath exploded in his lungs.

"I knew it. Then that is how Guthrum got around the Dorset guard. Cenwulf has ever been Athelwold's staunchest supporter."

"Yes. That is what I thought might have happened."

Erlend leaned a little forward on his stool, urgent to make the king understand. "Guthrum wants *you*, my lord. He knows what would happen to the West Saxon defense once you were gone. There is no one else who can lead your people as you can, no one else who can command the loyal following of all of Wessex. If he can kill you, then this war will be over."

"Did you tell him that also, Erlend Olafson?" Alfred's voice was very soft.

Erlend went, if possible, even paler. "No, my lord, I did not. But my uncle is clever enough to figure that out for himself."

Alfred did not reply, but pushed away from the bed and began to pace the floor once more. He spoke over his shoulder. "What will Guthrum have offered Athelwold in exchange for his cooperation in Cirencester? A kingship such as Ceolwulf has in Mercia?"

"Probably," Erlend said in a muffled voice. "One of Wessex' strongest defenses is its unity. My people have ever found it effective to split the loyalties of a country by setting up a nominal king."

"What of the sea? Is Guthrum like to have recruited a new sea army?"

Erlend shrugged. "I have not been in a position to find out, my lord." There fell a small silence as Alfred came to a halt before the Dane and looked down.

"Would you tell me if you knew?" Alfred asked.

Erlend slowly rose to his feet. They were very close, their eyes almost on a level. "If our positions were reversed, would you?" he asked the king in return.

There was a long silence. Finally Alfred broke it. "No," he said, "I probably would not."

Erlend could see the faint lines of weariness at the corners of Alfred's eyes, could sense the effort it was costing the king to stay on his feet. "Nor would I," he said. Then, urgently, as if it were all that mattered now in the world: "Get you to bed, my lord. You must be fit to ride tomorrow, and you will not be unless you get a good night's sleep."

There was a white line about Alfred's mouth. "Do I still have your oath not to try to escape?"

"Yes."

There was another silence. "Very well, Erlend," the king said. "You may go."

Erlend was putting his hand on the door latch when Alfred spoke once more from behind him. "You could have stayed behind at Chippenham. We had no time to spare to look for you."

Erlend turned his head. Even from a distance of ten feet, the strains of weariness were evident on the king's face. "I keep my promises, Alfred of Wessex," Erlend answered. "I will not escape from you until you give me leave."

"Why?" Alfred asked in his most clipped voice.

"I like your children," Erlend answered, grinned, lifted the latch, and went out into the hall.

Chapter 34

ALL the West Saxons at Cheddar bedded down immediately after the trestle tables had been cleared away. Outside, the snow was still falling, light but steady. Flavia balked at being put to bed in the small hall that the children ordinarily used at Chippenham, and so this night the big bed in the king's sleeping room held not only Alfred and Elswyth but also their three children.

"Let them come in here," Alfred had said when he heard Flavia's tearful voice. "Not even a crowded bed will keep me awake this night."

Elswyth was exhausted as well, and all five in the king's bed fell asleep as soon as Alfred pulled up the blankets. Elswyth awoke at dawn with Flavia's rump stuck into her side. Elswyth and Alfred were on either end of the bed, with the three children wedged between them. Elswyth raised herself on her elbow and regarded her brood. All were sleeping soundly.

She shut her eyes. Dear God in heaven, she prayed fervently, keep my children safe.

"I am thinking of sending them into Kent." Alfred's soft voice came from the other side of the bed, and Elswyth opened her eyes once again and looked at him.

"Is that where you are going?" she asked, keeping her voice equally quiet.

He was lying on his back, his face turned toward her, his hair spilled on the pillow like a saint's halo. "No. I cannot leave the west entirely open to Guthrum, Elswyth. I will stay here for as long as I can."

"At Cheddar?"

One eyebrow rose. "Elswyth, I have forty men in my guard. I cannot stay here at Cheddar, or at any of the royal manors. Not until I have raised more men."

"Send out a call for the fyrds. They will rise to your aid."

"I am not sure if they will."

"What?"

"Shh. You will wake the children." Alfred sat up a little, keeping the blankets pulled up around his shoulders against the chill January morning.

"Erlend thinks that Guthrum will offer the kingship of Wessex to Athelwold."
His breath hung white in the cold air of the sleeping chamber.

Elswyth sat up also. Her stomach heaved a little at the motion; she beat
the nauseous feeling down by sheer force of will. "The men of Dorset were
the ones keeping guard at Circencester," she said.

"Yes."

"Treachery." Her expressive mouth looked set and stern.

"I fear so," Alfred replied.

"We will keep the children with us," she said.

"Listen, love." He reached a hand up from under the blankets to brush
the hair away from his brow. "I am going to have to go into hiding for a
while until I can gather more men. Guthrum caught me unawares, and at
the moment I do not have the men to mount any kind of defense. The rest
of my companion thanes will find their way to me. Of them I can be
certain. But if Wessex goes the way of Mercia . . ."

"It will not." Her voice was utterly certain. "Wessex will rally to you,
Alfred. But you are right. You must be careful, wait to see who is friend
and who is foe."

"I cannot drag you and the children along with me through the swamps
of Somerset."

"Why not?"

"Elswyth . . ." Now he sounded impatient. "For once in your life, will
you please be reasonable? It is the depths of the winter, for God's sake!"

"I am being reasonable." Her dark blue eyes were perfectly sober. "I
will not trust my children to someone whose loyalty may prove question-
able, Alfred. Nor will I send them on a dangerous journey across the width
of Wessex while the Danes are free in the land."

He looked back at her, and his own eyes were dark and troubled. The
children were a weight on him; she could see that. "Let us take them to the
monastery at Glastonbury, Alfred," she said. "Glastonbury is safely in
the midst of the Somerset fen country. In the winter it is an island. They will
be perfectly safe there, and they will be close enough for us to put our
hand on them if we must."

There was silence as he considered her words. "If you will stay at
Glastonbury with them, Elswyth."

Her answer was instantaneous. "I would rather be with you."

"I know you would. But the children will be frightened if they are left
alone at Glastonbury."

This was true. She knew it, yet still all her being longed to be with him.
"You don't want me," she said, and her voice was bitter.

"I always want you." His eyes searched her face. Then he frowned a
little as he thought. "I cannot leave the children at Glastonbury unless I
know someone is there to get them away to safety should such action
become necessary," he said. "Someone I can trust to react quickly." He

pushed at his hair once more. "I could leave Brand, I suppose. Or Edgar."

"You cannot afford to lose the services of Brand or Edgar." She inhaled, then let out her breath in a short explosive sigh. "All right, Alfred. I shall stay at Glastonbury with the children."

Their eyes met over the three small heads, gold, silver, and ebony, that lay between them.

Edward opened his eyes and whined, "Elgiva is kicking me!"

Alfred said, "Everyone must wake up now anyway. We ride in half an hour."

Guthrum had hoped to catch Alfred at Chippenham, and he had hoped to retrieve his nephew Erlend as well. The failure of both these schemes was infuriating, but the rest of his plan for the taking of Wessex looked promising indeed.

Chippenham had proved to be an ideal location for a base camp. The town was situated in a strong defensive position, protected by the Avon on three sides and by a ditch and palisade on the fourth, blocking off the promontory. The sort of defenses a Viking leader most loved. The royal manor had been provisioned for the king's Christmas visit, and so the Danes were further pleased by the food stores of salted meat, eels, bread, honey, and unhopped beer that they found waiting for them in the manor storehouses.

And so, on the night of January 7, while Alfred lay a fugitive at Cheddar, Guthrum sat in the royal hall at Chippenham and found himself well-pleased. He had a secure base here, close to two main roads by which he could probe ever deeper into Wessex. This part of Wiltshire had as yet been untouched by previous Viking raids, so the local inhabitants were ripe to be squeezed for more food, fodder, horses and, possibly, geld. Supplies would be no problem this time. Guthrum would easily be able to feed the four thousand men who were following him to Chippenham on the morrow.

It was a nuisance that he had been unable to catch Alfred. Someone had evidently seen the Danish vanguard coming down the Fosse Way and had managed to warn Alfred in time. Guthrum had decided against setting out in pursuit of the West Saxon king. It would have been eminently satisfying to have that hawk-eyed West Saxon in his power, but it was more important to consolidate his base of power first.

It was Alfred's kingdom that Guthrum wanted, and the Dane had no intention of letting slip the advantage he had won. He knew from Athelwold of Alfred's present shortage of men. It was the first time Guthrum could remember that the West Saxon king had so let down his guard. The Dane had every intention of striking hard while Wessex' king was yet vulnerable.

As all Vikings knew, terror was always the most effective weapon. Thus far, Wessex had managed to stay remarkably clear of the devastation that the Danes had visited on the other English kingdoms of Northumbria, East Anglia, and Mercia. Well, Wessex would learn. So Guthrum thought, with deep satisfaction, as he sat this winter's night in Alfred's high seat, in Alfred's royal hall, and contemplated the destruction of Alfred's kingdom.

This time, Guthrum's plans would not fail. As before, he had reinforcements coming by sea in the spring, and the additional thousands of men would make the Danish army invincible. But even with the numbers he had presently, Guthrum was still safe. The men of Alfred's fyrds would be too busy at home, with their own burning barns, to answer this time to the call of their king. They might rally to defend their own shires, but such a fragmented defense would play right into Guthrum's hands.

This time, thought Guthrum, raising his drinking cup and draining it in one long swallow, this time nothing could go wrong. By the summer, he should have put his hand upon Alfred himself.

Within days, raiding parties of Danish horsemen were galloping down the Fosse Way and along the Roman road to Winchester, looting, raping, and burning as they went. Toward the end of January, Athelwold rode to Chippenham to see Guthrum and to protest the harshness of the Danish occupation.

Guthrum laughed.

"You promised to make me king!" Athelwold said in fury through the medium of the interpreter Guthrum had brought from Repton. "King, as Ceolwulf is king in Mercia."

"Exactly as Ceolwulf is king in Mercia," Guthrum agreed derisively. "King by my pleasure, king at my command. When once Wessex is subdued, my lord Athelwold, then will I name you king. But if you wish the people to forsake Alfred and turn to you for salvation, then first must they feel the power of my fist."

Athelwold thought about this, and it made sense.

"Alfred is in Somerset," he told the Danish leader, his voice more conciliatory than it had been at first. "He has taken refuge in the fens, where he hides himself and his few followers from your vengeance."

"I know where Alfred is," Guthrum replied, his blue eyes glittering dangerously. "He cannot hide from me forever. Once his kingdom is delivered over to my yoke, then will I worry about taking Alfred."

"The marshes are easier of access in the summer," Athelwold said. His pale reddish lashes flickered as he blinked nervously. "In winter half the land is covered with water, and you must know the tracks and trails, else you will never get through, but in the summer it is dry."

"You are most helpful, my lord," said Guthrum, and his eyes were now as derisive as his voice.

Athelwold flushed as red as his hair. "He does not deserve any pity from me," he said angrily. "He would rob me of what is mine by right."

"Go home," said Guthrum. "I will send for you when I want you."
After a fractional hesitation, Athelwold obeyed.

It was the worst winter in West Saxon memory. The Danes swarmed over the land, burning and pillaging. Wiltshire, wherein lay Chippenham, was struck particularly hard. Churches were desecrated, monasteries destroyed, West Saxon boys and girls taken and sold for slaves. The Ealdorman of Wiltshire, Wulfhere, newly appointed by Alfred the previous year on the death of the faithful Ethelm, followed the example of Burgred of Mercia and fled overseas to escape the vengeance of the Danes.

The Welsh suffered as well that winter, from the depredations of Ubbe, brother of Halfdan, who was wintering in Wales before sailing to Wessex in the spring to bring his ship army to reinforce Guthrum.

Like an Old Testament plague of locusts, the Danes also swarmed out from Wiltshire over the rest of the land: to Somerset, in hopes of capturing Alfred; to Dorset, against the protests of Athelwold; as far south and east as Hampshire, where many Saxons fled overseas before the Danes, as centuries before the Britons had fled before the Saxons.

The long cold winter dragged on. The only thing that kept any hope alive in West Saxon breasts all through that drear and horror-filled time was the thought that Alfred was yet free. The Danes had made numerous attempts to penetrate into the Somerset swamps, but none had been successful. The king was yet free, and while Alfred lived, hope of deliverance could not entirely die in the hearts and minds of those who had once fought under the banner of the Golden Dragon.

"I will never give up." Such was the promise Alfred had made to his country when he had taken the kingship seven long years before. During the winter months of 878, the nadir of all the years of the Danish wars, it was a promise that he kept.

The west of Somerset was mainly fenland, enclosed in an irregular horseshoe of forested hills. The marshes stretched inland from the coast for about twenty miles, changing from swamp to lagoon according to the rainfall and the tides. It was in these marshes, unapproachable in winter either by water or by land, safe only for those who knew their ways, that Alfred found shelter from the Danish juggernaut that was riding over Wessex.

The winter was hard going. January and February were bitter months, with the king and his small band of companion thanes sheltering in peasant huts, forced to rely upon the poorest of the poor for safety and sustenance. As the winter went on, the men of Alfred's guard who had not been at Chippenham for Christmas began to find their way into the king's camp. Alfred's companion thanes had stayed loyal, but the news they brought from the rest of the country was disheartening.

Over all the shires of Wessex, the West Saxon thane class was capitulating to the Danish overlords. In order to save its land and its families, the nobility of Wessex was giving in. Not one shire had organized a stand against Guthrum. Not one ealdorman had risen to defy the Danish jarl, who now was styling himself as king. Unbelievably, it seemed as if Wessex would go the way of Mercia after all.

By the end of February the mood in Alfred's camp was as dark and gloomy as the news that trickled in from the outside world. One particularly bitter day, Erlend, who knew better than anyone the ruthless efficiency of his uncle, decided that the time had come for someone to speak frankly with Alfred.

"He must save himself," Erlend said to Brand as they stood side by side rubbing down their horses after a long day's hunt. "Once these swamps become accessible to the outside world, Guthrum will come after him. Alfred must get away to France while still he can."

"You tell him that if you like," Brand returned with forthright vigor. "I don't have that sort of nerve, Erlend."

"Very well,' said Erlend. "I will."

At the moment Alfred and his men were encamped at the royal hunting lodge of Athelney, which lay deep in the Somerset marshes. In the summer Athelney was a part of the surrounding countryside, but in winter the waters of the Parret rose and it became an island of some twenty-four acres of dry land rising above the surrounding swamps.

The living at Athelney had always been rough; one small sleeping hall and several outbuildings were all the shelter available on the island. It had been kept as a hunting lodge for the royal princes, not the king, hence the accommodations were geared for no more than forty men. There were seventy thanes now in Alfred's guard, and quarters were very tight for both men and horses.

Alfred and his men were presently living chiefly off the food they themselves brought in from the hunt. They got other staples such as bread and ale, as well as some fodder for their horses, either from loyal local farmers or from the baggage of Danish raiding parties who had ventured too close to the swamps. Upon these occasions the hunted turned into the hunter, and during the last months the Danes had learned to go warily in western Somerset.

The winter sun was beginning to set when Erlend turned his back upon Brand and went in search of the king. Alfred was not in the small hall, nor was he yet at the stable. Erlend happened upon his quarry totally by accident, after he had given up the search and gone down to the spring for a drink of water. There he found Alfred, sitting on the trunk of a fallen alder in a lingering patch of sunlight, reading from his book of personal devotions.

The book was a small one that the king had carried ever since they had been forced to flee into Somerset. It was bound in such a way that he could easily suspend it from his belt; the outer leather cover folded over in front, and it was elongated at the top, forming a kind of hanging bag. According to Brand, it was a book of Alfred's own making, containing passages from various authors that the king found particularly inspiring. Alfred looked utterly absorbed at the moment, his head bent, his eyes on the pages spread before him.

Erlend stopped, hesitating to interrupt what was obviously a private moment. Alfred had precious little chance of those in the close quarters they were all forced to share these days. But then, just as Erlend was thinking he had better go, the king looked up from his book and saw him.

"My lord." Erlend spoke from the edge of the clearing. "If it is not too troublesome, I would speak to you."

Alfred folded his book and put it on the log beside him. "It is not too troublesome," he answered pleasantly. "Speak what you will, Erlend."

Erlend raked his fingers through his dirty hair and began to walk toward the king. They were all dirty these days, he thought as he crossed the clearing, the mud squelching under his feet. Dirty, bearded, ragged. The king's companion thanes, reduced to this. Alfred himself was in no better case. How scornful Guthrum would be, Erlend thought, if he could see them now.

Erlend stopped before the King of Wessex and looked down. Alfred sat there on his rotting log, as dirty and ragged-looking as Erlend, and seemed utterly unperturbed by the indignity of his situation. He met Erlend's eyes and raised one finely drawn, inquiring eyebrow.

Erlend hesitated, not certain, now that he was facing Alfred, that he would have any more nerve than Brand had had. "It is about the news from Wales," he began uncertainly.

The news he was referring to had come in just that morning. A Somerset thane with a Welsh wife had told the king that his wife's relations said that the Danish fleet was devastating Dyfed quite as thoroughly as Guthrum had been plundering Wessex. "My lord," Erlend said, at last deciding on the approach he should take, "I am as certain as I can be of anything that come spring, Ubbe will be sailing to Wessex."

Alfred did not answer, just continued to look up at him, that single eyebrow still asking its question. "Guthrum spent the early winter in Gloucester," Erlend continued, spreading his legs and planting himself more firmly upon the muddy ground. "It is easy to communicate with Wales from Gloucester. And Ubbe is Halfdan's brother, cousin to Harald Bjornson, who had the command of Guthrum's ships that went down off Swanage. Above all else, my uncle is a Viking. He will ever look to reinforce himself from the sea."

Alfred's eyebrow returned to its normal arch. He looked thoughtful. "Where do you think they will land?" the king asked.

"I cannot say, my lord. Somewhere along the Bristol Channel, I would guess." Then, with more intensity as he came near to the point of his discourse: "Guthrum will never turn his back on the west so long as you are free, my lord. Come spring, he will make a serious effort to flush you out of hiding. I would wager he will have Ubbe land as close to Somerset as possible."

No flicker of alarm crossed Alfred's politely interested face. He said only, "I will send word to the Ealdorman of Devon to keep watch on the coast."

Erlend set his teeth and came to the point. "The men of Devon cannot stop Ubbe," he said, blunt and brutal. "The time has come for you to face the facts, my lord king. The West Saxon defenses have crumbled as surely as did the defenses of Mercia, East Anglia, and Northumbria. Nor is Guthrum the man to let his advantage slip." Erlend took a step closer to the rock whereupon sat the ragged king. Without his realizing it, his voice had begun to rise. "By spring he will have a noose around Wessex, and there will be naught you can do to remove it. The time has come, my lord, to save yourself. If you wait much longer, it will be too late."

Alfred's dogs, hearing the raised voice, came racing out of the trees and clustered around the figure on the log. Alfred murmured a few words and scratched a few ears, and Erlend watched him, an expression of angry frustration on his face. When the king did not reply to him, just continued to soothe his dogs, Erlend said with unforgivable rudeness, "Did you hear what I just said to you?"

In one easy fluid movement Alfred was on his feet. "I heard you," he replied mildly. He bent to pick up his book. "And how do you propose I go about saving myself?" he asked as he straightened up again.

"You must take ship to France," Erlend said. "Collect your wife and your children and get you to safety, my lord, before Guthrum cuts your back open and spreads your ribs in an eagle's span for Odin."

It was brutal, Erlend thought, but brutal measures were called for.

"No," Alfred said. His voice was perfectly quiet and perfectly final.

Erlend's anger grew hotter as he stared at the man standing before him. Alfred was bearded now, like the rest of them, and the golden whiskers disguised somewhat the leanness of his cheeks. His hair was dirty and matted, his clothes were mud-stained and ripped from the narrow paths they rode through the marshes. The long fingers that held the leather-covered book had broken nails and were blistered with chilblains. He looked tired and dirty and cold; but somehow, Erlend did not know how, he yet managed to look like a king.

"I never before thought you were stupid," Erlend said furiously. "Are you incapable of assessing the situation? Then let me assess it for you. You have been deserted, my lord. Which of your thanes has come flocking to your call? Which shire fyrd has even tried to rally to meet my uncle's army in the field? Wessex is finished, my lord king! There is no need for you to die with it."

"There are worse things than death," Alfred said, still in that same quiet, final voice.

"Yes," Erlend flashed in instant agreement. "Torture is worse than death. And that is what Guthrum will have waiting for you!" The golden eyes looking at him were unclouded and perfectly fearless. Erlend felt a fury such as he had never before known rip through him. "You are beaten, Alfred of Wessex," he said viciously. "I know the sagas. There is no king who has ever been able to wrest victory from a defeat as thorough as this one."

"I am not beaten until I am dead," Alfred said. "And I am not dead yet, Erlend Olafson." He turned his head away from Erlend to look toward the small spring from which they got their water, and the setting sun cast a red glow upon his bearded face. The dogs left Alfred's feet and ran down to the spring to search out what might be there.

Erlend said, aiming for the one place he knew Alfred was vulnerable, "If you will not think of yourself, think of Elswyth and your children."

For a long moment Alfred did not answer. Erlend suddenly thought that the king looked very alone, silhouetted there between the bleak muddy earth and the blazing red sky. Then Alfred said, "They are safe at present with the monks. If it becomes necessary, I shall get the children away to Judith in Flanders. You can rely on that."

"And your wife?" Erlend asked tightly.

"Elswyth will never leave me. You know her well enough to know that." Alfred's still profile was unreadable. Then he turned. "Should something happen to me," he said, "I want you to promise me you will see her safe. Will you do that, Erlend Olafson?"

"I . . ."

"I can face whatever Guthrum may have in mind for me," Alfred said. His face was stark. "But not Elswyth. Erlend, promise me you will see her safe."

"Nothing will happen to Elswyth," Erlend said. "I would die for her. You know that."

Alfred nodded and turned away, hiding the naked emotion that had been exposed much too clearly on his face.

"You will not leave yourself." It was a statement, not a question, but Alfred answered it anyway.

"I cannot." Alfred was intently watching his dogs. Then, clearly feeling he owed the Dane more of an explanation: "You see, I am not just a king, Erlend. I am a Christian king. And to me Guthrum represents the darkness." Still Alfred watched his dogs as his voice went on evenly and firmly, "He is the darkness of ignorance, of cruelty, of wealth abused and power misused. He represents everything my Christian faith tells me to abhor."

Finally Alfred turned his head and looked once more at Erlend. "I must oppose him," he said. "While there is breath left in my body, I must oppose him."

Erlend looked back into those steady eyes and suddenly found he did not have enough air in his lungs to speak. Silence fell while he struggled with himself. Finally: "You have nothing to oppose him with."

He watched in stupefaction as Alfred smiled. "I have just been reading some words of the apostle Paul," the king said. His voice was quiet. "It is a passage I have read and reread many times in these last months. Would you like to hear it?"

Erlend looked at the book in Alfred's work-stained, ringless hands. "All right," he said grudgingly.

The king opened the worn leather pouch, spread the page, and, after the briefest of pauses, began to read. " 'If you are to resist the Evil One, you must put on the armor of God. Do all that your duty requires, and hold your ground. Stand fast, with the truth as the swordbelt around your waist, justice as your coat of mail, and zeal to propagate the gospel of peace as your footgear. In all circumstances, hold Faith up before you as your shield. It will help you extinguish the fiery darts of the Evil One.' " Alfred began to close up the book, still reciting, obviously by heart, " 'Take up the helmet of salvation and the sword of the spirit, which is the Word of God.' "

Erlend said harshly, "The East Anglian king, Edmund, he whom Guthrum spitted for the kill like an eagle, he thought the same."

"Edmund died a martyr for Christ," Alfred replied. He finished folding the book and looked toward Erlend. His eyes were wide and clear and absolutely dedicated. "If I must die, so be it. I will go to God, where we shall all find peace at last."

"You are very sure of this god of yours," Erlend said. For some reason, his whole body was beginning to shake.

"Very sure." Alfred attached his book to his belt, and then his hand came up to touch Erlend's shoulder. He said, "Christ came for the Danes also, Erlend. Think you of that sometimes."

The strong thin fingers closed briefly in a gesture of encouragement and friendship, and then Alfred took his hand away. Without another word or a backward look, the king strode off in the direction of the camp.

Erlend stood stock-still and watched until the shabby figure that yet moved with such light-footed elegance was lost in the trees. Then, slowly, he put his hand on his own shoulder, over the exact place that Alfred's fingers had touched. He was shivering all over, like a leaf in a high wind. Abruptly he sat down on the deserted log and buried his face in his shaking hands.

Chapter 35

FEBRUARY was going out in a relentless deluge of icy winter rain. Balked of their day's hunting, the thanes at Athelney clustered within the single small hall to pass the cold wet afternoon. Men lined the wall benches, feet thrust toward the warmth of the fire, fingers busy mending leather gear and tools and carving in wood. The deep rumble of male voices drowned out the sound of the rain.

The king sat among his men this afternoon, Edgar on one side of him and Brand on the other. There was no high seat in the hall at Athelney, just the simple benches. The weather had forced them to close the smoke hole in the roof, and consequently the air in the crowded room was thick with smoke.

Alfred had been sitting in silence for some time when Brand finally turned to speak to him. The king returned only an absent nod and continued to stare unseeing at the deer roasting on the fire. Nor did Alfred see the worried look Brand gave him before the thane turned back to his conversation with Erlend, who was seated on his other side.

Alfred's preoccupation did not lift even when the dogs came in from the wet yard and shook themselves all over two of the thanes seated by the door. He did not even hear the laughter. He saw only how dirty and ragged were the men who jammed the benches, how filthy and muddy were the rushes that covered the hall floor. The stink of wet wool and leather and unwashed human flesh, of wood smoke and roasting meat, assaulted his nose.

God in heaven, he thought as his nostrils quivered in involuntary disgust, what am I going to do?

Erlend had been right yesterday, Alfred thought with deep and unusual bitterness. He was beaten. Only a fool would not be able to recognize that. Guthrum was King of Wessex. Alfred was king of twenty-four acres of swamp.

He shifted restlessly on his seat. That conversation with Erlend had kept him awake for most of the previous night, had forced him to confront his present situation squarely and evaluate it. For months now he had been living from day to day, concentrating on survival alone, with little thought of the future beyond the morrow.

Well, he had survived. The question was, for what?

The words that had kept him from sleep all night sounded once more in his brain. "Let me assess the situation for you," Erlend had said. "You have been deserted."

Suddenly Alfred could bear the smells of the hall no longer. He said to Brand, "I am going outside for some air," almost leapt to his feet, and began to walk toward the hall's single door. He was so accustomed to being watched that he scarcely noticed all the eyes that followed him as he crossed the filthy rush-strewn floor.

He closed the heavy door behind him and stood for a moment in the shelter of the wooden porch that fronted the hall. Out here the sound of the rain was clearly audible. Alfred could hear it beating like pellets onto the roof of the porch and into the mud of the courtyard. The front of the porch was not enclosed and the wind blew drops of heavy stinging rain into Alfred's face. He threw back his head and inhaled, long and deep. The wet and icy air felt good to his suffocated lungs.

His mind went back to its bitter conversation with itself. He had spoken fine words to Erlend yesterday, he thought. Fighting words, words of fire. But words were no good unless they were backed by deeds.

I am not beaten until I am dead.

Brave words, but empty. He was beaten, all right, and this bleak desolate February afternoon, as he stood before the miserable accommodation wherein he had packed his men, he knew it.

Let me assess the situation for you. You have been deserted.

Ubbe would land on the coast, bringing new recruits to the aid of Guthrum's already-victorious army. Thus reinforced, the Danes would be invincible.

The yard looked to be knee-deep in mud. If the weather turned cold enough to freeze, the footing would be treacherous.

Let me assess the situation for you. You have been deserted.

Where in the name of God were his ealdormen? Where were the shire fyrds? How had it been possible for Guthrum to quell Wessex without even one single battle?

Alfred frowned and moved to the very edge of the porch. There looked to be movement in the courtyard. Then, suddenly, horses appeared like ghosts out of the thick rain and mist. It took Alfred but a second to recognize one of the riders, and his heart leapt in his chest with fear and with joy. "Elswyth!" he said out loud, and jumped off the porch to run into the rain and mud of the courtyard to meet his wife.

"Is everything all right?" he asked as he set his hands about her waist to lift her down from Silken's back. "The children?"

"Everything is fine," she assured him, and at the sound of her husky voice his heart leapt again, this time from joy alone. They remained thus for the briefest of moments, he with his hands about her waist, she still seated on her horse, looking down into his face. She reached out to touch him briefly on his wet cheek. "I just decided I wanted to see you. So I came."

He lifted her into his arms, and instead of setting her down in the yard, he waded back through the mud to the porch. "You are drenched," he said as he put her on her feet. "It was mad to ride out in such weather as this."

"I am wearing a lot of clothes," she replied. For the first time she smiled. "Aren't you pleased to see me?"

He stared hungrily into her rain-streaked face. There were raindrops hanging off her long black lashes and dripping from the tip of her haughty nose. Her translucent skin was flushed with rose from the cold. He bent his head and kissed her cold wet lips. Hard. "I am very glad to see you," he said fiercely.

She smiled again and said, "You had better tell my men where to put the horses."

He did so, and then he took her into the hall. All talking stopped as the thanes looked to see who it was coming in with the king. Then, from almost all the throats in the hall, there rose a loud shout of welcome.

Elswyth looked around the packed benches and grinned. "You stink," she informed the hallful of her husband's men, and they roared with delighted laughter.

The bleak and desolate afternoon was suddenly transformed. Alfred took his wife into the small cluttered bedchamber so she could remove her wet outer clothing, and ordered a measure of carefully hoarded ale for everyone in the hall.

The ale had been poured by the time the king and his wife returned to the hall, and a place had been made for Elswyth on the bench next to Alfred. Then Erlend brought out his harp.

"What would you like to hear, my lady?" he asked, running his fingers enticingly over the strings.

Alfred looked at his wife, seated so close beside him on the bench. Her damp hair was plaited into a single braid as thick as his wrist, and her cheeks were still flushed with color from her ride. She smiled at Erlend and said definitely, "*The Battle of Deorham.*"

Erlend nodded, and a sigh of satisfaction went up from around the hall. The harp sounded again; then Erlend's clear voice began to chant the words all West Saxons learned in babyhood:

> Ceawlin the King
> Lord among Earls
> Bracelet-Bestower and
> Giver of Gifts,
> He with his son

> Crida the Aetheling
> Gaining a lifelong
> Glory in battle
> Slew with the sword-edge
> There at Deorham
> Brake the shield-wall,
> Hewed the lindenwood,
> Hacked the battleshield,
> Coinmail, Condidan, Farinmail
> Lords of the Welsh

Alfred looked around the hall as Erlend sang this song of one of the greatest of his ancestors' most famous victories. The firelight flickered on the intent faces of his thanes, bright now from within as well as from without. The song continued:

> Many a carcass they left to be carrion,
> Many a livid one, many a sallow-skin—
> Left for the white-tailed eagle to tear it, and
> Left for the horny-nibbed raven to rend it, and
> Gave to the garbaging war-hawk to gorge it, and
> That gray beast, the wolf of the weald.

Alfred thought: Wessex gone, without even a fight. How could it have happened? What would his ancestor Ceawlin have thought, if he learned of such a shameful capitulation?

The song was soaring high now, Erlend's voice thrilling out above the ringing notes of the harp:

> We the West Saxons,
> Long as the daylight
> Lasted, in companies
> Troubled the track of the host that we hated,
> Grimly with swords that were sharp from the grindstone,
> Fiercely we hacked at the fliers before us.

Alfred had spoken yesterday to Erlend of his Christian faith, but right now what he felt thrilling in his veins was the warrior blood of his pagan ancestors.

He looked around the hall once more, at the blazing faces of his men. His loyal men. *We the West Saxons*, he thought. We are not beaten. Not these men ringing his hall this day, nor the thanes of his shires, nor his ealdormen. We have lost a battle, he thought. Well, we have lost battles before. And risen to fight again.

The song was ended and the men began to stamp their feet and to call for another. Alfred stretched his legs out before him, leaned his shoulders against the wall, picked up Elswyth's hand, and rested their linked fingers on his thigh. He could feel her arm pressing against his.

How had she known to come? He had seen her only once since he had left her and the children at Glastonbury nearly two months before, and that was when he had ridden to the monastery to see them. She had never before tried to visit him in any of his fugitive camps.

He bent his head until his mouth was near her ear. "How did you know to come?" he asked.

Her mouth curled down at the corner. "I don't know," she replied, her voice so low only he could hear. "When I woke up this morning I just felt you needed me. So I came."

The grip of his fingers tightened on hers, but otherwise he did not reply.

Erlend sang, ate, then sang again until he was hoarse. Even the thanes who did not like Elswyth had to admit that they were glad she had come. No one could remember the last time they had seen the king as light-hearted as he was this night.

"He will be all right now," Brand remarked to Erlend as the men prepared to bed down for the night. "There is no one who can cheer Alfred so well as Elswyth can."

Erlend was spreading his blanket upon the bench and just grunted in reply.

Brand checked the sword that lay under his bench beside his shield and his byrnie. "It must be a grand thing to have a marriage like that," he said, sitting down to pull off his shoes now that he had made sure his sword was safe.

"You could marry, Brand," Erlend said. "Alfred is a generous lord. You have won enough treasure to buy a manor of your own and settle down."

"Perhaps, but I have no wish to do so, Harper. I like my life the way it is, thank you."

"You would not have to leave Alfred's service. There are some married thanes among the king's hearthband."

Brand bunched up his cloak to make a pillow for his head, then settled himself on the hard bench, pulling a blanket up over him for warmth. Erlend did the same. The two of them were lucky to have the bench; half of the men were sleeping on the floor or in the lofts over the barns.

"A woman is fine in your bed at night," Brand said. "In fact, I would not mind one here right now. But marriage . . . that is another thing altogether."

"Just one minute ago you were singing the praises of marriage," Erlend protested.

"A marriage such as Alfred has," Brand said.

Erlend put his hands behind his head and stared upward into the darkness of the hall. "There is not another like Elswyth in all the world," he said, his voice very quiet.

The reply to that was prompt. "Even if there was, she would not be the wife for me." Brand gave a sleepy chuckle. "If I were married to Elswyth, she would end up doing my breathing for me. A situation neither of us would like overmuch." There came the distinct sound of a yawn. Then, drowsily: "In truth, I doubt if it is in me to feel strongly for any woman."

"I know." Erlend's voice was perfectly awake, perfectly sober. "Why is that, do you think, Brand?"

"All our love is spent on Alfred," came the devastatingly simple reply. A minute crept past and Brand began to snore.

Erlend lay awake for a long time, listening to the sound of the rain on the roof.

The single bedchamber at Athelney had never been planned to accommodate a king and his appurtenances. There was little floor space, and what was there was now taken up by the chests that contained the West Saxon treasury. The treasury always traveled with the king, a custom that had proved its wisdom when Guthrum had almost caught Alfred at Chippenham. The king might be a fugitive, but at least he was not a penniless fugitive.

Elswyth sat on the quilt in the middle of the bed, combing her hair. Alfred stood in the narrow space at the bed's foot watching her. One of her hands held the comb; the other hand held a strand of her hair near to the scalp so that the comb would not hurt when it pulled. The long ebony tresses flowed around her like a mantle, shining like silk in the flickering light of the bedside candle. She finished with the lock she was working on and lifted her eyes to Alfred's face.

"You look so strange in a beard," she said. "I shall have to get used to it."

A faint look of disgust crossed his face. "I hate it," he said. "I have always hated the feel of a beard. That is why I never grew one." He shrugged. "I have little choice these days, however. The niceties of good grooming are not precisely a matter of prime concern."

She put the comb down beside her on the quilt. "What happened?" she asked.

For a long moment he did not answer, just looked back into the unveiled blue of her eyes. *I just felt you needed me,* she had said. He ought not to be surprised. He had always known that when it came to him, Elswyth understood with her blood and her bones and her flesh. She did not need words to know how he was feeling.

At last he said quietly, "It was Erlend. He wanted me to flee the country."

"You won't." It was not a question.

A faint smile glimmered in his eyes.

She said, "You must do something, though, Alfred. From what we hear at Glastonbury, the country is simply lying down in front of this Dane." Her lips curled in scorn. "Like Mercia," she added.

He came to sit beside her on the bed. "Erlend said I have been deserted."

She looked at him in thoughtful silence. Slowly she shook her head. The shining black hair rippled with the movement. "I do not think that."

"What do you think, Elswyth?" he asked curiously.

"I think the West Saxons are like most men. They are simply waiting for someone to tell them what to do."

His look was somber. "I have begun to think that also."

"Men are like horses, Alfred," she told him seriously. "They are herd animals, miserable when they are alone, happiest when they have an acknowledged leader to order them about. Put six strange horses out into a pasture together, and by the end of the day they all know who the leader is. When the leader comes, they come. When he goes, they go. Men are the same. Deprive them of their leader, and they mill around aimlessly, waiting for someone to tell them what to do."

His mouth was looking a little grim. "I thought that was what I had ealdormen for."

"The ealdormen are not Alfred," she said. "There is only one man whom the West Saxons will rise to follow now. And that is you."

He picked up her comb and held it balanced between his two hands. It was a simple bone comb, not set with jewels or inlaid with enamel. He said, "So it seems." He sounded resigned.

"It is up to you to herd them together, my love," she said. "No one else can do it."

He put the comb down and picked up a lock of her hair. "Do you have any suggestions as to how I might go about such a task?" he inquired, watching the shining black strands run through his fingers.

"No."

"That is what I was afraid of." He quirked an eyebrow at her.

"You will think of something. You always do."

He looked down at the strand of hair he still held between his fingers. "Every other woman in the world would be begging me to save myself," he said. "And you are thrusting my sword into my hand."

"You could not run away," she said. "I would never ask you to so betray yourself as to do that."

A silence fell. The candle flickered on the small bedside stand. He rubbed the strand of clean silky ebony between his thumb and his forefinger, feeling its texture, raised his eyes, and said, "I look at you, Elswyth, and I ask myself how ever I came to be so lucky."

"You didn't have yellow teeth."

He threw back his head and shouted with laughter. Then, when he had got his breath: "You must be exhausted." He leaned around her to pull back the quilt. "Get under the covers. It is cold in this room."

"I am not that exhausted," she said.

"Elswyth." Imperceptibly he increased the space between them. "This is not the time to get another child. If aught goes amiss, you might have to take the children and go to Flanders. I do not want to burden you with more than is necessary."

"I admire your nobility, Alfred," she said. His eyes narrowed at her tone. "But you are a trifle late with it."

His breath hissed in his throat. His eyes raked her figure. "When?" he asked. There was a white line about his mouth.

"It was a Christmas present," she said. Then, impatiently: "Don't look like that. I do not try to live your life for you."

He put his thumb and forefinger under her chin and turned her face to the light of the candle. Her skin was translucently pure as always, with a faint flush of rose along the cheekbones, but there was an indefinable, fine-drawn, great-eyed look that he had missed earlier and recognized now. He felt his heart contract. He dropped his hand and looked away from her. The white line about his mouth grew even more pronounced.

"I wasn't going to tell you," she said. "I knew you would not be pleased."

At that he turned back and met her dark blue gaze. He muttered something under his breath, then took her into his arms. "I am sorry, love," he said. As she pressed against him, his arms tightened. "I am an ungrateful wretch."

"Sometimes."

His mouth was buried in her hair. "I am filthy. I shouldn't come near you."

"I am so glad I rode through the rain to see you," she said. Her voice was a little muffled as her mouth was being pressed into his shoulder. "You have given me a lovely welcome."

"What do you want from me?" He sounded fierce.

She pulled her head away from his shoulder and raised her face to his. "I want you to kiss me."

His head bent instantly and his mouth covered hers. After a minute they slowly toppled sideways until they were lying together on the bed. "Like that?" he asked at last, and now his voice was husky with desire.

"Hmmm. Now, *that* was worth the riding twelve miles in the rain."

"I have a few other things I could do."

Her mouth curled. "I have never made love to a man with a beard."

He had one hand wound into her unbound hair. "You are about to."

"Always promises," she said. And he growled, pressed her back, and kissed her again.

Chapter 36

ALFRED slept deeply and dreamlessly, and in the morning when he woke he knew what he had to do.

"I must talk to Ethelnoth," he said, referring to the Ealdorman of Somerset. "There is no reason why he cannot rally the Somerset fyrd to me immediately."

"Ethelnoth is a good man," Elswyth approved. They were still in bed, huddled together like children, with the quilt pulled up around them for warmth. "Did I tell you he came to see me at Glastonbury?"

"No." Alfred looked both surprised and pleased. "Did he?"

"Yes. He assured me that he would be at my service if ever I needed help."

"You will be safe at Glastonbury until the waters begin to go down," Alfred said. "Guthrum cannot know you are there. But once the swamps begin to dry, Elswyth, you will be safe no longer. Then, if the Danes still hold sway in Wessex, you must get the children away to Judith in Flanders."

"I will," she said.

"You must go also."

"That I do not promise."

He gave her his hawk stare. Her own eyes did not waver. "I will not leave if you are in danger."

His nostrils dilated. "The Danes are not known for their kindly treatment of women."

"They are not known either for their kindly treatment of kings."

"I do not intend to become the object of Guthrum's butchery."

"Good. Nor do I intend to become the object of Guthrum's lust."

She was adamant. He had known she would be. He brought up his alternative plan. "If it becomes necessary, Erlend will shelter you," he said.

She drew her knees up under the quilt and propped her chin on them. "Clearly, Alfred, the wisest course is to throw the Danes out of Wessex."

He scratched his head. "Thank you for the advice."

"What will you do with Ethelnoth and the Somersetshire fyrd?"

"We must start to take the offensive," he said. "It is the only way to begin to put heart back into my people. The combination of woodland and fenland here in Somerset makes it ideal country for strike-and-run raiding. We have done that somewhat this winter, when we robbed the Danes for food and for fodder. I mean to increase those attacks, make it clear to both Danes and West Saxons that I am still a power to be reckoned with."

"Splendid," she said. He twitched his shoulders and she leaned over to scratch between his shoulder blades.

"Perdition, Elswyth, but I am so itchy!" Nothing could make Alfred so fretful as lack of washing.

"I hope you have not given me bugs," she said.

"I don't have bugs!" He stared at her in outrage.

She grinned.

"God knows what I have," he said.

"You have the heart of a lion." Her hand moved up his back and began to rub his neck. His eyes half-closed with pleasure. "Have you not seen Ethelnoth?" she asked.

"I saw him when first I came into Somerset. He sought me out and assured me of his loyalty. I have not sent for him since." He sighed. "I kept waiting to hear that my other ealdormen had rallied their men."

"No news of that rat Athelwold?"

"None that I have heard."

"I wish Flavia and Edward had drowned him."

"How are the imps? Are they behaving themselves at the monastery?"

"What do you think?"

He shifted a little so she could rub the muscles between neck and shoulder. "They both send you their love," she added. "Edward wants me to bring him back a sword."

He snorted. "And Elgiva?"

"Elgiva is such a sweet-natured child. I have no idea where we got her from, Alfred." He chuckled. "Flavia and Edward will never include her in their games. I think it is a very good thing we are to have another child. Elgiva needs a friend."

He sighed. "I suppose." He did not sound convinced.

She said, "What is that I see crawling around in your hair?"

"What?"

Her voice brimmed with laughter. "I am sorry. I could not help it. You are so funny in that beard. . . ."

He stared at her and slowly his face began to change. "Elswyth," he said, pronouncing her name with the clipped accent she so loved. He ran his forefinger along her cheek, tracing the high sharp bone in a light, yet utterly possessive caress. She stared up into eyes that were suddenly narrowed and intent. Hunting eyes. "You are so beautiful," he murmured, and now his clipped voice was low and husky. "I have missed you so much." Then his shoulders were coming over hers and he was sliding her down toward the center of the bed, so that she lay on her back under him, her hair spread out above her head like a long ebony ribbon. He began to kiss her all over, her slender throat, her proud breasts, her faintly swollen belly.

Liquid fire ignited in her veins. The quilt was still pulled above them, enclosing them in a warm, dark tent of private passion. She felt the hardness of his fingers as they caressed her breasts, her waist, her thighs. They were hard and callused, but their touch was the touch of a lover. At last he was sliding his hands under her hips, and she arched her back for him, offering up all her warm moistness for him to sheath himself in.

Giving and taking, giving and taking, they brought each other first to joy and then to heartfelt peace.

Chapter 37

*E*THELNOTH was sought and found, and he and Alfred consulted for long hours in the small hall at Athelney. As a result of the discussion, Alfred informed his thanes that they would begin to build a fort right in the clearing at Athelney where the hunting lodge was located. The few buildings on the island were not protected by a palisade and ditch, nor would they hold more men than the number already jammed within. They needed shelter for the men of the Somerset fyrd, Alfred said. And stockade walls for protection should an enemy penetrate into their fastness.

It was the work of a month to throw up walls, dig a ditch, and build shelters to accommodate nearly five hundred more men at Athelney. All of Alfred's thanes, including Erlend, worked on the job. The king himself was not above shoveling earth or hauling logs cut from the dense forest of alders that grew all over the island. "Lenten penance," he called it, and would not let anyone else do his share of the labor.

Alfred had heeded Erlend's warning about Ubbe and had sent word to the Ealdorman of Devon that there was likely to be a Viking landing on his coast. Ealdorman Odda had promised to do what he might to beat back such an attempt, and on March 20, Holy Thursday, Odda sent word to Alfred at Athelney that Halfdan's brother had indeed landed in Devon.

The news was brought by a thane from the Devon fyrd, Bevan by name. It was growing dark when the Devon man crossed the narrow plank bridge Alfred's men had thrown up across the Parret, and he found the king and most of his followers at dinner in the hall.

Alfred did not take the messenger aside into his private chamber, but instead bade him speak before all the assembled men. The hall fell very quiet as Bevan began to deliver his message. It seemed to Erlend, who was among those listening so intently, that even the dogs had ceased to chew.

"Twenty-three ships landed, my lord," Bevan began. "Twenty-three ships and twelve hundred men. All the Danes who ravaged Dyfed so fiercely during the winter months." The boy, for Erlend thought he could not be above the age of twenty, was looking only at Alfred, but the clear pitch of his voice betrayed his awareness of the hall of listening men behind him.

Bevan, whose looks as well as his name betokened British blood, continued, "Once we learned of their coming, Odda, our ealdorman, gathered the fyrd and occupied the old fortress of Countisbury." Slight pause. Then, "Do you know Countisbury, my lord king?"

Alfred nodded. Bevan said, "Its ramparts are in ill repair, but its situation gives it protection on every side save the east, and Lord Odda deemed it would be the easiest fort to hold against the Danes."

The Devon man raised his black head high. "The Danes followed us, my lord," he said, "and we prepared for them to storm the fortress. But days went by and they did not move." Bevan paused and Erlend thought, with a mixture of amusement and irritation, that the boy ought to be a harper, his sense of the dramatic was so sure.

Alfred waited, and the thought flashed through Erlend's mind that it was like Alfred to allow the boy his moment in the sun. Finally Bevan spoke again. "They were going to do to us what you did to Guthrum at Exeter, my lord. Starve us out. As they would have, since Countisbury has no supply of water within its defenses."

The hall was breathlessly silent. Alfred's face was politely attentive, but something in it must have reached Bevan, for he hurried on with his tale. "Ealdorman Odda spoke to us, my lord, said there were but eight hundred of us to oppose twelve hundred of them, but battle with the hope of victory was preferable to slow starvation. We all agreed. On Monday of Holy Week, as the dawn was breaking, we rushed out of the fortress and fell on the Danish camp."

Alfred was leaning forward a little in his chair. There was a faint line between his fair brows. "Yes?" he prompted as the boy paused once more.

The answer came with a ring of triumph. "We took them by surprise, my lord king. It was a complete rout. We killed their leader, Halfdan's brother, eight hundred of his men, and forty of his personal guard. And then . . ." With another dramatic pause the boy reached inside his cloak. "We captured this!"

A hissing intake of breath ran all round the hall. What the Devon thane was holding, spread wide in his hands, was the feared and hated Raven banner of the Danes.

Alfred's face was no longer unreadable. It blazed now with the same triumph that had sounded in Bevan's voice. "Good lad!" he said. Bevan's dark face glowed back at him.

Alfred took the banner from the Devonman's hands and turned to face his men, who had leapt to their feet at the sight of it.

"Did you hear the news, my friends?" Alfred cried, holding the Raven banner outstretched above his head.

"We did, my lord!" his thanes roared back.

"And are we to do any less than the thanes of Devon?"

"No, my lord!" came the joyful thunder.

"In three days' time at the church in Aller we celebrate Easter," Alfred said, his voice a little quieter. "The feast of the resurrection of our Lord Jesus Christ. And so too will we celebrate the resurrection of Wessex from the ashes of defeat." He paused as his eyes moved from face to face around the room. "On Easter Monday, the men of Wessex go on the attack!"

The hall was pandemonium. Erlend watched as Alfred moved to stand next to the young Devon thane, and then the king signaled to Edgar.

The resurrection of Wessex, Erlend thought, watching as Edgar came to Alfred's side. The king said something and then Edgar put a hand on the boy's arm and began to lead him toward a bench. Alfred swung around and caught Erlend looking at him. Irresistibly, Alfred grinned.

Erlend shrugged his shoulders; then, unable to stop himself, he grinned back. Guthrum would be livid when he discovered his sea army had been thwarted once more, he thought. And quite suddenly, as he and Alfred shared that brief and private smile amidst the uproarious hall, all the conflicting loyalties that had been rending Erlend's heart for so many long years fell quiet.

Admit it, he thought to himself. You are glad that the men of Devon have beaten Ubbe.

It was not an easy admission for him to make, but on that wet and blowy Holy Thursday afternoon, it was inescapable. He, Erlend Olafson, born a Dane, heir to one of the greatest of Danish jarldoms, was unarguably happy to learn of a Danish defeat.

Erlend had been but eighteen when first he joined the West Saxons at their camp near Wilton; today he was twenty-four. Six years it had taken for him to allow his brain to recognize what his heart had known all along.

He loved Alfred of Wessex. Loved him as a brother, a friend, a king. On this momentous afternoon, Erlend stood alone in the midst of the noisy and crowded hall, and his eyes followed Alfred as the king went among his boisterous thanes.

Never, Erlend thought, his eyes on the rough golden head as it moved from group to group, never would Alfred fail or betray the people or the kingdom that had been given into his charge. Never would he put his own needs and desires before the wants of those who stood beneath him.

Guthrum stood for an age of axes, an age of wolves. Conqueror and predator, he was Viking to his fingertips.

Alfred stood for all the things Guthrum had never honored and would never understand.

Erlend did not understand them fully either. But he was beginning to realize that he would like to learn.

*　　*　　*

On Easter Monday, Ethelnoth of Somerset came to Athelney with fifty of the thanes of his hearthband. As the day progressed, more and more thanes from the Somersetshire fyrd, along with some ceorls, crossed the rough bridge that Alfred's men had flung up over the River Parret to give access to the island. By nightfall, nearly three hundred men were within the stockade enclosure of the fort. The king had the beginnings of his army.

To look at, Alfred's fort at Athelney was a desolate place. The hastily erected huts of rough timber and wattle were barely adequate, and outside the ditched and palisaded defenses was a bleak landscape of swamp and mud and alder forest. The clouds had a tendency to brood low and dark over the island, and the spring rain to fall heavy and hard.

But the spirits of the men encamped within Athelney were high. There was the victory of the men of Devon at Countisbury to cheer them. And, too, this time of year, food was abundant. There were deer and game in the forest, and on the clearings and islands amidst the swamps were countless farms and pastures. This fen country was the deepest heart of Wessex, untouched as yet by the Danes, and the loyal folk of the farmsteads willingly brought wheat and milk and eggs to their ark of salvation, the king's fort at Athelney.

Indeed, hearts all over Wessex were beginning to rise, for their king was abroad in the land. Time and again, Alfred and his men would emerge from their swamp, fall upon a party of unsuspecting Danes, slay the men and steal their horses, then withdraw back into the watery wilderness where the Danes were not able to follow.

Guthrum sat in Alfred's royal hall at Chippenham and raged. He had spent the winter feasting at Chippenham and watching his raiding parties return laden with the booty of the rich countryside. Guthrum had thought to have Wessex pinned firmly beneath his fist. He had even begun to give some thought to portioning out the rich farmland of the country among his followers. And then, when all seemed to be accomplished, Ubbe was killed by the men of Devon, and eight hundred of his men along with him.

Guthrum had already made plans for Ubbe and his men. He had decided that when the ship army landed, he would launch a combined land-sea attack upon Alfred in Somerset. Consequently, the loss of Ubbe and his men had been a heavy blow. Further increasing Guthrum's displeasure was the fact that once Alfred learned of the defeat of Ubbe, he had greatly increased his attacks upon Danish war bands. Alfred must guess, Guthrum thought bitterly, that without Ubbe, the Danes would not have the necessary manpower to confine the West Saxons to the marshes.

As the spring advanced, it became clearer and clearer to Guthrum that it was absolutely essential for him to capture Alfred. Time after time Guthrum sent parties into the fens of Somerset to track down the fox who was harrying his war bands, and time after time he lost men and horses in the reeds and the lagoons.

"You will have to wait until the water goes down," Athelwold told the Danish leader one April afternoon in the hall at Chippenham. Athelwold had come to the royal manor as an uninvited visitor, to find Guthrum distinctly out of temper. "In winter and spring, the marshes are impenetrable to all but those who know them," Alfred's traitor nephew concluded.

"Name of the Raven," Guthrum swore. "He has control of the whole of western Wessex from those cursed swamps. And we never know where next he will emerge! I cannot wait until the summer. Already I sense a change in the mood of the country."

"Name me king," Athelwold demanded eagerly, bringing up the object of his visit. "Name me king, as you promised, and you will see a change. The West Saxons will follow one of their own where they will not follow a foreigner, a Dane."

"They bow to me because of the strength of my fist." Guthrum's face and voice were brutal. "You they will never follow, not while Alfred lives. Once he is dead, then I may name you king. Not before."

Athelwold raged, but he raged in private. Like the rest of his countrymen, he went in terror of this Danish conqueror who knew little of mercy and even less of fear.

It was the fourth week after Easter when Alfred sent out from Athelney several parties of his thanes dressed in peasant garb, traveling on foot. Their mission was to find the ealdormen of Wiltshire and Hampshire and give them a message.

The memorized command they bore was simple: SEND WORD TO THE MEN OF THE SHIRE FYRD TO MEET ME AT EGBERT'S STONE ON THE DAY OF WHIT-SUNDAY. ALFRED THE KING.

The king was calling out three fyrds only: the men of Somerset, who were with him at Athelney; the men of Wiltshire, whose ealdorman had fled to France and who consequently must be led by a new replacement; and the men of Hampshire west of Southampton, those who had held firm to their land and refused to flee with those of their shire who were less hardy.

Three shire fyrds out in full force, together with the hearthbands of their ealdormen, would give Alfred perhaps twenty-five hundred men. Ethelnoth had suggested that the king call up the men of the more easterly shires also, but Alfred had refused. The whole key to his plan lay in surprise. The fyrds were not to gather; each man was to make his way to Egbert's Stone on his own. Alfred did not want Guthrum to know what was afoot until the men of the three shires were gathered together.

He explained this to Ethelnoth. "It would be too long a march for the men of Sussex and Kent. It is too long even for the men of Berkshire. I do not want Guthrum to know we are abroad until we have joined together at Egbert's Stone. For now, I want only the shires I can collect quickly."

Ethelnoth had acquiesced in the king's reasoning, and had ceased to protest.

The one flaw in Alfred's plan was obvious: the way Alfred had arranged for the fyrds to be notified meant that he would not know until he got to Egbert's Stone whether or not his summons had been answered.

No one suggested that Alfred send word of his undertaking to Dorset, home shire of Athelwold.

Chapter 38

*I*MMEDIATELY after dawn Mass on Sunday, the eleventh day of May 878, Alfred and his followers rode out from the marshes of Somerset to meet with the men of Wiltshire and Hampshire at Egbert's Stone. This famous landmark, associated in folk memory with Alfred's grandfather, lay on the eastern edge of Selwood, and could be reached in a day's march by most of the men Alfred had summoned.

Erlend rode with Alfred. "I will not fight," he had said. "Not for Guthrum, not for you. But you may need me to interpret." He did not say the other thing that was in his mind: You may need me to bargain for your life.

Alfred had prepared for this venture by going during the week to see Elswyth and his children at Glastonbury. He had come back clean-shaven and with his hair looking several shades lighter than it had been when he left.

"I see your wife washed you up, my lord," Erlend had said when Alfred first arrived back at Athelney.

Alfred grinned. He looked younger without the beard. Or perhaps it was just the glow that being with Elswyth always gave him.

"She said none of my men would recognize me if I arrived at Egbert's Stone looking as I was."

Erlend's eyes measured him, from the top of his now-shining hair to the tip of his muddy boots. The Dane shook his head. "They would recognize you, my lord," he said. "No matter how you disguised yourself, they would recognize you."

Alfred rubbed his bare cheek. "Erlend," he said fervently, "I cannot tell you how good it feels to be rid of that itchy beard!"

Erlend had laughed.

He remembered that conversation this morning as he mounted his black stallion and prepared to follow behind Alfred and Ethelnoth, who were riding side by side in front of their men. With Erlend marched the men of Alfred's hearthband and the men of the Somersetshire fyrd who had been with them at Athelney.

There would be more Somersetshire men at Egbert's Stone, so Ethelnoth had assured Alfred. The ealdorman had sent word around the shire. All those who had not been able to leave their farms to join the king at Athelney were to meet with him at Egbert's Stone on Whitsunday. Ethelnoth seemed quite certain that a minimum of a hundred more men would answer this call.

What if they did not? It was the thought that had been preying on Erlend's peace of mind for the last two weeks. Alfred was putting his life into jeopardy with this open-ended summons of his. The king had no assurances at all that the fyrds of Wiltshire and Hampshire would rise. Neither shire had as yet made any attempt to rise in its own defense. Wiltshire's ealdorman had even fled over the sea, and Alfred's summons had been sent around by a new appointee. Who was to say the men of the shire would answer him? And Hampshire . . . Many men of Hampshire had fled overseas also. Where were those remaining to get the courage with which to answer the call of their king?

Name of the Raven, what if there was no one at Egbert's Stone? Or only a few hundred?

Alfred would be left standing alone on Salisbury Plain, with no marshes to escape to, no refuge to shelter him from Guthrum's vengeful knife.

Erlend looked once more at the too-vulnerable back of the man riding before him. So slim Alfred seemed, yet he was stronger than you would think. He had lifted logs at Athelney with the best of them.

Erlend ran a hand through the brown hair that was blowing forward across his cheek. Name of the Raven, he thought furiously, this whole plan was madness!

They were passing out of the fen country now, following the River Brue as it wound eastward toward Salisbury Plain. It was a magnificent spring day—a light breeze was blowing, bluebells dotted the grass, and cuckoos called in the oak trees—but Erlend found he could not appreciate it. His apprehension about what awaited them at journey's end was too great.

The Brue began to slant to the north, and Alfred's troop forded it and went instead directly east, on into the ancient forest of Selwood. Here, within the protection of the thick trees, Erlend felt safer. A forest such as Selwood could function similarly to the fens of Somerset. If necessary, he thought, appraising his surroundings as they rode along a fairly well-traveled forest track, at least Alfred could find shelter in Selwood should his plans come to naught.

The miles passed and the day waned.

MEET ME AT EGBERT'S STONE ON THE DAY OF WHITSUNDAY. The message had been sent. The king was staking his life, and the lives of those who followed him, on his blind faith that the men he had called would answer him.

"What is Egbert's Stone?" Erlend had asked Brand when first he learned of Alfred's plan.

"Legend says it is the place where Alfred's grandfather, before being driven out of Wessex by Beorhtric, swore a great oath to return and one day claim his kingdom," had come the reply. "It stands near the borders of three shires—Somerset, Wiltshire, and Dorset—and is a good gathering place, as it is centrally located and well-known."

Erlend thought now: What if only the two ealdormen and their hearthbands await Alfred at Egbert's Stone? Two ealdormen's hearthbands would yield only two hundred men. Not enough, Erlend thought, despairing. Not nearly enough. Guthrum had four thousand men in Wessex. Alfred could not fight if he were outnumbered over four-to-one.

Even if the full number of men turned out, still would they be outnumbered nearly two-to-one. Alfred was calling up only three shires.

The miles passed slowly by. Alfred's companion thanes were horsed, but many of the men of the Somersetshire fyrd were not. The horses Elswyth had trained so painstakingly were all in their pastures at Wantage and Lambourn. Guthrum had no doubt acquired them by now.

Finally the trees began to thin and the ground began to rise. Erlend looked toward the sky and reckoned it to be about four in the afternoon. Beside him Brand said, and his voice betrayed his tension. "The Stone is just over the rise of yonder hill."

At that moment Alfred turned in his saddle to survey the men who followed him. Seeing Erlend and Brand staring at him, he gave them an encouraging smile, then turned back to face ahead.

The day was very quiet. Too quiet, Erlend thought as their horses began the ascent of the gently sloping hill. If there was an army on the other side, surely they would be hearing the sound of voices.

He began to feel sick to his stomach. Name of the Raven, he thought, for perhaps the twentieth time that day, this is madness!

Then the king, with Ethelnoth beside him, was on the summit of the hill. Erlend, watching closely, saw how Alfred checked his horse. The sick feeling in Erlend's stomach became acute. Ignoring it, ignoring all protocol, he pushed his horse forward to bring him to Alfred's other side. Then he looked down into the valley.

It was filled with men.

Without a word, Alfred pressed his horse forward. Ethelnoth let him go alone, and fell in behind with Erlend and Brand and Edgar.

A single sharp cry came from the massed men below them. Then a general stir, as men faced toward the west, raising their hands to shield their eyes as they squinted into the sun.

The late-afternoon sun shone behind Alfred's head like a heavenly halo. A roar went up from thousands of throats, a sound such as Erlend had never before heard. There was no word, no cry of "The king!" or "Alfred!" Only this mighty roar of bellowing joy.

They had come, Erlend thought, trying to swallow around the lump in his throat. Alfred had asked, and the men of Wessex had answered. They had trusted him, as he had trusted them. And the note that sounded loudest in their joyful thunder of welcome was the note of love.

It was not merely the men from the fyrds who had answered Alfred's call to come to Egbert's Stone this Whitsunday afternoon. A thousand men had come from Hampshire alone. "Every man left in the west of my shire old enough to hold a spear," said Osric, Ealdorman of Hampshire, with pardonable pride.

The men of Wiltshire had done as well. Fifteen hundred men of that shire stood with their swords and their spears at the gathering place of Egbert's Stone this bright Whitsunday afternoon.

And Ethelnoth of Somerset found he had underestimated the number of men from Somersetshire who would answer his call. Six hundred men had found their way to Egbert's Stone to join with their fellows who were already under arms in the king's train.

Thirty-five hundred men in all were gathered together this day on the high ground to the east of Selwood, in the place where three shires met.

The scouts Alfred had sent out days before also awaited him at Egbert's Stone. The news they brought was that Guthrum had moved from Chippenham to the royal manor of Ethandun on the chalk hills to the north of Salisbury Plain.

This was good news to Alfred. As in all the royal manors, the hall at Ethandun was protected by a palisade fence, but the manor itself was more a hunting lodge than it was a main residence, and its defenses were token. Ethandun would be much easier than Chippenham to take by assault, if that was the path Guthrum should choose to go.

On the other hand, should Guthrum choose open battle, Alfred had hunted from Ethandun many a time, and he knew all the tracks and local landmarks. It would not be difficult for the king to take his stand on ground favorable to the West Saxons.

On the whole, Alfred thought as he listened to his scouts report and watched the men in his camp gathering around the cookfires for their suppers, things could not have fallen out better.

"At dawn tomorrow we march for Iley Oak," he said to the ealdormen who were gathered around him.

Eadulf of Wiltshire grunted his approval. Iley Oak lay some ten miles to the northeast of Egbert's Stone, in Eastleigh Woods. It would make an ideal camp for Alfred's men, as there was an old Celtic fort in the area whose earthworks were still intact. Both woods and earthworks would provide the army with protection should Guthrum decide to take the offensive and mount an attack.

"The Danes will know we are out," said Osric of Hampshire. "Thirty-five hundred men cannot march through the countryside unnoticed."

"I do not desire to surprise Guthrum," Alfred replied soberly. "I desire to force him to do battle. We are of almost equal numbers. Our men are hot for Danish blood. Now is the time to strike, before the fire in their hearts has time to cool."

"The king is right." It was Ethelnoth speaking. "I for one have had enough of these games of cat-and-mouse."

"What if Guthrum chooses to hold siege within Ethandun? Or retreats to Chippenham to hold siege there?" asked Eadulf of Wiltshire.

"Then we besiege him," Alfred said grimly. "I will not make a truce with him again. I have learned that lesson at last."

"Aye," agreed Ethelnoth. "There is no faith in a Dane."

"Not unless there is also a knife held to his throat," the king said. "And I intend to be that knife."

Within an hour after the food had been eaten, the men of Wessex had lain down wrapped in their cloaks to sleep. They had marched far this day, and would be up again at dawn to march tomorrow. To Iley Oak, in the Eastleigh Woods, seven miles from the royal manor of Ethandun, wherein lay the Danish army and its leader, Guthrum.

It was midmorning on the Monday of May 12 when Guthrum first learned of the West Saxon advance.

"*How* many men?" he asked the leader of the troop who had ridden into Ethandun with the news.

"Nigh on four thousand, my lord. All marching under the banner of the Golden Dragon."

"Alfred is with them?"

"Yes, my lord. I have seen him before. He is not a man you can mistake."

"Coming toward Ethandun, you say?"

"Yes, my lord. But slowly, as most of them are on foot."

Guthrum felt a flash of satisfaction as he thought of all of Alfred's horses penned uselessly at Wantage. "You shall have a reward for this, Erik. You did well to bring me this news."

The man's face creased into a pleased smile, and when Guthrum dismissed him he went immediately to tell his fellows of his good fortune.

Left alone in the single private chamber of Ethandun's hall, Guthrum paced up and down.

Name of the Raven, how had Alfred done it? How had he gathered four thousand men under Guthrum's very nose?

Coming toward Ethandun, Erik had said. Guthrum thrust a hand through the short hair on his forehead and continued his pacing. He had two choices, he thought. No, three choices. He could remain here at Ethandun and hold siege. He could remove to Chippenham and hold siege. Or he could meet Alfred in the open and fight.

The first choice he dismissed almost immediately. Ethandun was not well-enough-fortified to hold out under intense attack. Chippenham was better situated if Guthrum wanted to hold siege.

Name of the Raven, but he would not do it! He was sick unto death of being penned within walls while Alfred played captor from without. The time had come to meet these West Saxons on the battlefield.

The Dane's long legs continued to pace as his brain mulled over his chances. One battle only had the West Saxons won from the Danes. The battle of Ashdown. In all the other engagements in which the two armies had fought, the honors had gone to the Danes.

Guthrum, who was usually honest with himself, if not always so scrupulous with others, forced himself to face the fact that in all the battles in which the West Saxons had been defeated, they had also been greatly outnumbered. The single battle they had fought with equal numbers had been Ashdown. And that battle the West Saxons had won.

No matter, he thought now grimly as he laid his plans for the morrow. The time had come for this struggle between himself and Alfred of Wessex to be decided. Like all his race, Guthrum was a fatalist, and he felt now that it was time for fate to take a hand. He would go out to do battle with the West Saxon king. The odds were nearly even, and what was fated to be would be.

Having made his decision, Guthrum threw back his yellow head, squared his big shoulders, and went off to give orders to his men.

The scouts Alfred had posted to keep watch on Ethandun returned to the king at Iley Oak with word that the Danes looked to be preparing for battle.

"Thanks be to God," Alfred said fervently. Like Guthrum, he was sick of sieges. And he gave the order for his men to prepare to fight.

To the north of Iley Oak rose the steep chalk hills of the northwestern promontory of Salisbury Plain. There was a track Alfred knew well that ran across the plain to the hills and the ancient fort of Bratton. Cut into the turf of the hillside at Bratton was the figure of a chalky white horse. A symbol, folklore said, of the victory of one of Alfred's ancestors hundreds of years before. The White Horse had been the emblem of the royal house of Wessex until Alfred's grandfather, Egbert, had changed it to the Golden Dragon.

At dawn tomorrow, Alfred thought, he would make for Bratton Fort and there take up his battle stance. He would fight this, the ultimate battle for Wessex, under the symbols of both the White Horse and the Golden Dragon. And with God's help, the West Saxons would triumph.

The men encamped at Iley Oak spent the evening in confession and in prayer. Alfred would not let them fast. They would need all their strength on the morrow, he told the priest who reprimanded him for issuing supper rations.

"The Lord will be your strength," the priest who was attached to Osric of Hampshire's household said with exemplary piety.

"The Lord will do his part but he expects us also to do ours," Alfred replied bluntly. And his men ate.

At the first light of dawn, about five-thirty in the morning this time of year, the West Saxons broke camp. With the mounted men in the vanguard, they pushed on over the Wylye and up the old white track that led up the steep chalk ledge onto Salisbury plain. They halted on the down of Ethandun, which hill had given its name to the royal manor situated nearby. There, under the sun-bright symbol of the White Horse, they took up their battle position.

Erlend had come to Ethandun with Alfred's army, but as the West Saxons began to form their shield wall, he separated himself, and, leaving his horse behind, climbed up the hillside, all the way to the figure of the white horse that had been cut into the chalk so many centuries before. From this vantage point, a wide vista of Wiltshire landscape lay spread out below him.

From the heights of his hill, Erlend could see northwest across the Vale of Pewsey all the way to the Marlborough Downs. The old West Saxons had fought many a battle on those Downs, mainly against the Britons whose country it had been before their coming. Erlend himself often sang *The Battle of Beranbyrg*, a tale of Alfred's ancestors Cynric and Ceawlin. He would be able to see Beranbyrg from here, he thought now, if only he knew precisely where to look.

A movement to the north caught his eye, and Erlend looked in the direction of Ethandun manor and saw the advancing army of the Danes.

Their helmets and shields glittered in the morning sun. Nearly four thousand men on horseback, coming from the manor of Ethandun, swords and spears at the ready, to join in a battle whose victory prize would be the ownership of a country.

There was a tightness in Erlend's chest as he saw them come, the Raven banner flying bravely, the colored banners of the jarls fluttering in the early-morning breeze. There were good men in Guthrum's army; men he knew well; men he had counted as friends. Slowly then he let his eyes move to the army positioned directly below him.

Alfred's hair gleamed as brightly as any Viking helmet as he went among his men inspecting their shield wall, giving encouragement and advice.

It was spring. Wildflowers colored the turf and chaffinches sang in the trees. Pewits flew through in the air, crying and wheeling, crying and wheeling. Then the two armies saw each other, and the sound of the birds was drowned in their screams of defiance.

The traditional beginning of every battle was now under way. Swords clashed on shields. Insults were shouted, each side trying to intimidate the other by its warlike posture. Nearly eight thousand throats set up a roar that frightened the birds and sent them wheeling off to the safety of the plain.

Erlend stood, a solitary figure silhouetted against the white chalk of the horse, and watched as the Danes dismounted to take up their positions. Without consciously realizing what he was doing, he began to compose a song in his head. "At break of dawn," he improvised, "the shields rang, resounded loudly. The lean wolf in the wood rejoiced, and the dark raven, greedy for slaughter . . ."

The shouts were becoming more threatening and now the West Saxon archers were coming to the fore of their lines. From his post high up on the hill Erlend could see the deadly shower begin to fly toward the Danish lines.

"Then keenly they shot forth showers of arrows, adders of war, from their bows of horn." Erlend could hear the words in his mind as clearly as if he were saying them out loud. Then his breath caught and the poetry stopped forming in his brain. A slender golden-haired man had stepped forward from the West Saxon lines, sword raised. Then he began to run forward. With a deafening shout, the fyrds of Wessex poured after their king.

There was an answering shower of arrows from the Danish ranks; then the Danes too were advancing, shield and sword and spear at the ready. Erlend thought he could see his uncle standing under the banner of the Raven. Then, with a noise greater than all that had gone before, the two armies came together with a resounding crash.

The carefully formed shield walls did not hold for long. Within minutes it seemed that the whole field had become a heaving sea of man-to-man combat. Erlend watched, transfixed, all poetry vanished from his mind.

For a very long time neither side had the advantage. Erlend tried to keep watch on the two great banners of the leaders, but it was impossible to single out individuals among the shifting mass of men who milled around them. The sky shone a brilliant blue and the taunting cries of prebattle bravado were replaced by the bloodcurdling screams of the wounded.

For over two hours the armies remained locked together in bitter combat. From his vantage point above the action, Erlend could see how the turf underfoot was trampled and stained with blood. Men climbed over the wounded and dead to get at each other. Then, as Erlend watched, the banner of the Golden Dragon faltered as the thane holding it aloft slowly crumpled to his knees.

Edgar! Erlend spoke the name aloud, even took two steps down the hill, as if to go to his friend's assistance.

Then someone else had lifted the banner. Erlend could not see who it was, but all at once, in the circle of men around the fallen standard-bearer, he could see the king. Alfred had been bending over the man crumpled on the ground, and now he straightened, stepped away, cut through the protective ring of his men, and engaged the enemy, his sword slicing through the Danes swarming over him, his shield raised to catch the ax blows that were aimed at his vulnerable, unhelmeted head. The men of Alfred's hearthband abandoned their fallen comrade and surged after their king.

The battle raged on. Slowly at first, then with ever-increasing urgency, the Danes began to give ground. Back and back and back they were driven. Erlend's eyes sought the Raven banner and his uncle.

Guthrum was fighting like a madman. The Raven banner was in the fore of the Danish lines, and now the West Saxons were beginning to surround it. Foremost in the West Saxon van was the banner of the Golden Dragon, symbol of the presence of Alfred, the king.

It happened a little at a time, not all at once as in the past. The Danes began to break ranks, turn, and flee from the field toward the horses picketed in their rear.

Erlend knew instantly that this was not a false retreat designed to lure the enemy into pursuit. This was the real thing. Danes were flinging themselves onto horseback and heading toward the road north, the road that would take them back to Ethandun manor, or, thirteen miles beyond, to Chippenham.

Guthrum was one of the last Danes to leave the field. The West Saxons were already running for their own horses to ride in pursuit when Guthrum finally gave way and, leaving a shield wall of his personal retainers to hold back the intense press of Alfred's attack, found his own horse and galloped away to the north.

Those West Saxons who had come to the field of Ethandun mounted rode swiftly in pursuit of the fleeing enemy. Those who had not been mounted sought the horses that had belonged to the Danes now lying dead or wounded on the battlefield. Within minutes the field of Ethandun was deserted, save for the parties of men Alfred had left behind to tend to the wounded and to collect the dead.

Slowly Erlend descended from his hill, to lend a hand with the gory work of separating the injured from the slain. He had marked carefully the place where he had seen Edgar fall, and it was to that part of the battlefield that he went first.

He saw immediately that Edgar was dead. A spear had penetrated his ringed mail byrnie right in the place where his heart was. It must have been a ferocious blow, Erlend thought. But then, the mail had probably been damaged by earlier blows. The king's standard-bearer was always a prime target for the enemy, but Edgar would never hear of relinquishing his post to any other.

Gently Erlend closed the blue eyes that were staring sightlessly up at the beautiful spring sky. Edgar was not yet stiff, and Erlend managed to lift the weight of the dead thane in his arms and stagger with him off the reeking field. Alfred would not want Edgar thrown in a common grave with the rest of the West Saxon dead.

As he lowered to the ground the body of one of the kindest men he had ever known, Erlend thought of the song he had started to compose as he watched the beginning of the battle from the top of his hill that morning. Edgar is gone, he thought, his hand lightly smoothing the rumpled hair of the dead man away from his forehead, but in going, he has won glory for himself in battle.

The traditional comfort of his people came into Erlend's mind, the watchword of the Viking warrior. "One thing will never die, the reputation we each leave behind at our death."

Erlend would do that for his friend. He would write a song about Edgar and the battle of Ethandun, would see to it that the reputation of Edgar the Saxon would be honored for as long as harpers sang.

Somehow, the thought did not bring the comfort he needed.

Alfred would say that Edgar had gone to God. As Erlend looked down at the still face of his friend, he found himself hoping that Alfred was right.

Chapter 39

THE Danes bypassed Ethandun and galloped for the more strongly fortified Chippenham, with the West Saxons hard on their heels. As soon as Guthrum was within its walls, the Danes closed the gates of Chippenham, leaving those of their number still without to the mercy of the enemy.

Alfred was in no mood to show mercy. He knew well he had to strike a killing blow in order to win back Wessex, and without hesitation he gave the order that all Danes caught outside the gates of Chippenham were to be killed. The West Saxons fell to with a vengeance and soon the earth was running red with Danish blood.

Once the Danes were dispatched, Alfred next gave orders that all the cattle and sheep that were in the pastures at Chippenham be taken to Ethandun. "I do not want to leave any hope in Guthrum's heart that he might be able to mount a quick raid for food," the king said to Brand when he gave the order about the animals.

"Yes, my lord," Brand replied, and promptly went to collect a party of men to do as Alfred commanded.

Alfred next ordered his men to pitch camp on the fields of Chippenham, far enough from the walls to be out of the range of arrowshot. Then he settled down to starve Guthrum out.

Guthrum stood on the walls of Chippenham and watched the West Saxons digging a huge trench wherein to bury the Danish dead.

He could scarcely believe what had happened to him. But two weeks ago Alfred had been a landless fugitive skulking in the marshes of Somerset in fear of his life. Today he sat with his army outside the gates of Chippenham, the conqueror. And Guthrum, trapped within, was the conquered.

Name of the Raven! How had it happened? How had Alfred managed to gather the fyrds of Wessex under Guthrum's very nose? Not only had he gathered them, he had hurled them into battle. And they had won!

The West Saxons had finished digging the trench. It was very deep and they had put a rope ladder down to the bottom of it in order to climb out.

Guthrum looked broodingly at the scene before him, his brow furrowed in thought.

He had strong magic, this Alfred of Wessex. He was a fine battle leader, true; but so too was Guthrum. The difference between them lay somewhere else.

Always before this, Guthrum had thought of Christianity as the religion of the weak. Perhaps he had been wrong. Perhaps this crucified god called the Christ was indeed stronger than the gods of the northmen. Stronger even than Odin, who had been hanged once himself.

There was no other way Guthrum could account for the fact that he was trapped here within Chippenham and Alfred was without. Alfred had been as thoroughly defeated as ever man could be. Yet today . . .

It was magic, Guthrum thought as he watched the bodies of his men being slung into the gaping hole the West Saxons had dug. Nothing else could explain such a catastrophic reversal of fortune.

It took two weeks for the Danes within Chippenham to run through the available food supplies. Then Guthrum did what he had known he would do all along; he sued for a peace.

The Dane was not surprised when Alfred sent Erlend to do the negotiating. Erlend came to Chippenham alone, which did surprise Guthrum, a fact he mentioned as he met with his nephew within the king's bedchamber in the royal hall.

"He will take your word for what transpired between us two?" Guthrum asked, his thick blond eyebrows raised in surprise. "I would not have thought Alfred to be so trusting."

"He knows I will speak truth to him," Erlend said. "But I cannot say that he has the same confidence in you. After all, you have broken your word to him twice already, Uncle."

Guthrum did not look at all discomfited. In fact, he even smiled. "I am glad he did not kill you, Nephew, as he did the other hostages."

Erlend stared in astonishment into his uncle's bold blue eyes. The man had no conscience at all, he thought, and did not realize what an odd thought that was for a Viking to have.

"If you had any care for my well-being, you would have kept your word," he said tartly to that shameless face.

Guthrum shrugged. "I thought I could capture Alfred. If I had, then you would have been perfectly safe."

"The possibility that you might fail never crossed your mind?" Erlend's voice was heavy with sarcasm.

Guthrum gave him a familiar wolf grin. "It was worth taking the chance," he said. "I almost succeeded."

Erlend slowly shook his head, amused in spite of himself. Then Guthrum asked, "Why did he not kill you, Nephew? He was quick enough to hang my first hostages. Yet here you are, healthy as ever."

"He hanged those first hostages to teach you a lesson. Doubtless he came to realize that you are unteachable. Hanging me would have had no effect on you, and would have deprived him of a harper."

Guthrum grunted. "What terms does Alfred offer me?"

"To begin with, the usual ones," Erlend replied. "You must swear to leave Wessex, and give Alfred hostages to secure your word."

Guthrum's eyes narrowed and he regarded Erlend with patient skepticism. "And that is all?"

Erlend looked at the rush-strewn floor. It was filthy, a part of his mind noticed. The rushes did not look to have been changed for months. Elswyth would be furious to see what Guthrum had done to her lovely room.

"No," he said. "That is not all."

Guthrum grunted. He had not expected that to be all. "Well?" he prompted as Erlend remained silent. "What else?"

"You are to be baptized a Christian," Erlend said, and waited for the storm to erupt.

Instead, there was silence. After what seemed like an age, Erlend tore his eyes away from the floor and raised them to his uncle's face. To his astonishment, he found there an expression that he had never expected to see in a response to Alfred's condition. Guthrum looked interested.

"He wishes me to become a Christian?"

"Yes," Erlend replied, his voice faint with surprise. "Will you do it?"

Guthrum grinned. "Why not?"

Erlend's jaw dropped. *"Why not?"*

Guthrum stroked his close-clipped blond beard. For the first time, Erlend noticed streaks of gray among the blond. "You object?" Guthrum asked. "You have observed the worship of this Christian god more closely than I. Is there aught in it that would shame me?"

"No, nothing would shame you." Erlend thought for a moment before he went on carefully. "You realize that the god of the Christians is very different from our gods, Uncle?"

"I think he is more powerful," Guthrum said. "Statues of this hanging god are in all of Alfred's manors, Erlend. I have seen them myself. Alfred worships this god with great faithfulness, and the god repays him with victory."

An arrested look had come over Erlend's face. "I see," he said on a drawn-out note. Then, cautiously: "So you will become a Christian to share in the favor of the Christian god?"

Guthrum answered simply, "Yes."

"Very well." Erlend swallowed. "I will tell Alfred."

*   *   *

"He will accept your terms," Erlend said to the king some twenty minutes later as they met within Alfred's tent in the West Saxon camp outside Chippenham.

Alfred's eyebrow quirked. "He has little choice."

"True. But I expected him to object to the baptism."

"And he did not?"

"He seemed almost to welcome it! At first I did not understand, but then it came clear. I hope you realize, my lord, that Guthrum's idea of Christianity is not your own."

"What is his idea?" Alfred asked curiously.

"He thinks your god is more powerful than his. And, being Guthrum, he is anxious to get upon the winning side."

Alfred's white teeth flashed. "Perfectly understandable."

"But what is the point of baptizing him?" Erlend cried in bewilderment. "He has no understanding of what he is doing, of what your religion really means."

"I know that," Alfred replied, and now his face was grave. "But if his own religion is not sufficient to bind him to his word, perhaps a new and more powerful religion will be."

Erlend's triangular brows drew together. "What do you mean?"

The reply was blunt. "I mean to scare Guthrum so badly with what will happen to him if he breaks his oath to Christ that he will keep out of Wessex forever."

Erlend could feel his eyes stretching wide. "Scare him?"

"That is right." Alfred's mouth was grim, his voice harsh. "Honor means nothing to Guthrum. It is self-interest alone that drives him. I mean to make it seem very much in his self-interest that he keep his word to me."

There was a moment of silence as Erlend digested these words. "Why don't you just kill him?" he asked curiously.

"If I had caught him in battle, I would have killed him," came the sober reply. "But he has sued for peace. If I kill him now, I shall probably find myself involved in a blood feud with the Danes who have settled to the north. They will feel obligated to avenge him. I do not want to involve Wessex in a blood feud, Erlend, so it is best if I can arrange matters in such a way that Guthrum and I cease to be enemies and become neighbors instead."

"You will let him have Mercia, then?"

"He can have whatever part of England he chooses, but he cannot have Wessex."

"What hostages will you take?"

Alfred smiled. "Not you, my friend. You have served your time in that capacity, I think."

Erlend did not reply.

"What will you do, Erlend?" It was Alfred's turn to ask a question. "Will you sail home to claim Nasgaard, as you said you would?"

"Home," Erlend said. His smile was crooked. "I don't know where home is anymore, my lord. I have been from Denmark for so long . . . have dwelled for so many years among your people . . . I am like a creature caught between two worlds."

"You will always have a place in my household," Alfred said, and Erlend felt his heart begin to accelerate.

"As your harper?" he asked.

Alfred shook his head. "As my friend."

Erlend bent his head so his hair would swing forward to hide his face. "I don't know. I don't know what I am going to do." His voice sounded oddly muffled.

"Become a Christian with Guthrum," Alfred said.

Erlend's head came up slowly. His nostrils were dilated and he was breathing as if he had been running. He found Alfred's grave eyes waiting for him. "You understand what Guthrum does not," Alfred said softly. When Erlend still did not answer, he said, "Think about it, Erlend." The king's hand rested for a brief moment on his shoulder; then Alfred went out into the sun, leaving Erlend alone in the tent.

The baptism ceremony for the Danes was held at Aller, the church where Alfred and his men had worshiped during their time at Athelney. Receiving baptism along with Guthrum would be twenty-nine of his chief men, and Erlend Olafson, his nephew.

Like Athelney, Aller was deep in the marshes of Somerset. Guthrum looked around with interest as his horse followed Alfred's through the perilous reeds; there was no way of telling to the untutored eye where lay dry land and where lay water. All Guthrum could see for miles around was this vast sea of reeds.

Guthrum looked from his surroundings to the back of the man riding before him. These marshes had been the saving of Alfred of Wessex, he thought. Had it not been for them, and the protection they had afforded . . .

Alfred's head suddenly swung around, as if he had heard Guthrum's thought, and the two men looked at each other. Guthrum said in his thick Saxon, "You . . . lucky . . ." and he gestured to indicate he meant the swamps.

Alfred grinned. "Yes," he replied. "I know."

Guthrum understood him. He found Alfred's crisp diction surprisingly easy to follow. "How long . . ." he said. "To church."

"Not long now," came the reply. "We are almost there."

And indeed in less than half an hour they had come to the church at Aller. Aller was like Athelney and Glastonbury, an island when the waters were high in spring, but in the summer its moat dried up and it was left accessible on all sides. At this time of year they still had to cross by the narrow planked bridge that gave access to the church to the people of the surrounding area.

The church at Aller was a small narrow stone structure with high narrow windows cut into the stone on both long sides. There were many churches in Wessex that were more impressive. Indeed, the church at Wedmore, not too far distant, would have seemed a more likely place to hold these auspicious baptisms. Wedmore not only had a large church but also was a royal residence and could provide comfortable accommodations for all of the party.

But it was at Aller that Alfred had prayed during the most bitter hours of his exile in Somerset, and it was to the baptismal font at Aller that he was bringing his Viking king and all his followers. It was Alfred's thanksgiving for the way his prayers had been answered.

Guthrum had been in Christian churches before, but only to sack them. Today he was here to profess allegiance to the Christian god he had so often defamed, and he found himself impressed. Aller was not nearly as large as many of the monasteries Guthrum had previously passed time in, but there was power breathing in the air here. Guthrum could feel it; it prickled the hair on the back of his neck. This was the well from which Alfred drew his strength, Guthrum thought as his eyes went searchingly to the grave face of the man who was his sponsor.

Alfred was not weak, nor was he the man to worship a god who was weak. Alfred was a leader, strong, ruthless, and, thanks to his god, blessed with luck.

Guthrum's eyes moved from the golden-skinned face of his godfather to the crucifix that hung over the altar. This hanging god expected faithfulness from his worshipers. Guthrum had been made to understand that. When he swore an oath on the statue of the hanging god, he must keep it. If he did not, ill luck would plague him all his life, and in the afterlife he would burn in a place called hell.

He had been a fool all these years to think Christianity a religion of weakness, Guthrum thought now as the white linen headband was bound over the chrism on his forehead. This Christ was a god of battles, a god of vengeance. Guthrum could understand power like that. Gladly would he pledge his allegiance to such a god.

A god was in the air. Erlend felt this as well as Guthrum as he knelt before Alfred's priest and felt the coolness of the chrism being placed on his forehead. Light was slanting in through the high narrow windows cut into the stone and falling on the tapestried hangings, on the golden altar vessels, and on the two fair heads of Alfred and Guthrum. The diffused scent of balsam hung in the air, the scent of the god. Father Erwald was chanting words in Latin as he bound the white linen headband around

Guthrum's forehead to keep the precious chrism in place. Then the priest was advancing to do the same for Erlend.

Erlend had not yet decided what he would do when this christening tide was over. He could take the men that Guthrum had promised him and sail for Denmark to reclaim his inheritance. Or he could go with his uncle and settle the lands of East Anglia, which was what Guthrum planned to do. Guthrum was no more for Denmark. He liked it in England, he said. He liked the climate and he had come to like the women. He would stay here and rule as king over the lands of East Anglia and Mercia. Erlend was welcome to join him.

Or he could stay in Wessex. At Alfred's court, as Alfred's friend. Heart-whole at last, no longer playing a role, pretending to be that which he was not.

The priest was now going down the line of Danes, binding the linen around all their foreheads. The linen must remain for a week, Alfred had told Erlend; then it would be removed in a chrism-loosing ceremony. That ceremony would be held at the royal manor of Wedmore, whence the party was headed on the morrow.

A beam of light slanted in the window and fell on Alfred's face. The king was looking at Guthrum, and he wore an expression that Erlend had not expected to see in this particular place, at this particular moment. There was no trace of triumph, of exultation, of joy, on Alfred's face. Instead the king looked almost grim.

A shiver ran down Erlend's back. Guthrum, he thought, had better honor his word this time.

Then Guthrum's head turned, and for a brief moment the eyes of the two kings met. Erlend was certain that his uncle read in Alfred's face the same message he had. For a moment his breath held as he watched Guthrum's vivid violent eyes locking with Alfred's ruthless golden gaze. Then a corner of Guthrum's mouth flew upward in a crooked smile, and the Viking sketched a gesture of almost courtly submission with one of his hands. Alfred's hawk eyes veiled themselves and he gave the Dane the faintest of nods. Then both kings were once again turning to the priest, who had finished with the linen and was returning once more to the altar.

The sun was hiding behind a cloud when the baptismal party issued out of the church. As they stood together near the small cemetery beside the church, waiting for their horses to be brought so they could continue on to Glastonbury, where they were to spend the night, the cloud passed over and the sun came out full strength.

An omen, Erlend thought, lifting his face to the warmth of the sky. He heard his uncle's deep bellow of laughter and felt an unaccustomed stirring of affection.

. The old pirate, he thought. He's met his match at last, and he has the grace to acknowledge it. One has to admire him.

"You look very noble in your chrism linen, Erlend." It was Brand's voice, and Erlend turned to look into the familiar greenish eyes of his friend. Before he could reply, Brand said, "It was good of you to take his name for your own."

Each of the Danes had had to take a Christian name along with the holy chrism. The name Erlend had chosen was Edgar.

"I miss him," Erlend said simply.

"We all do." Brand sighed. "I dread the thought of facing Flavia. She was so fond of him."

"I know."

They stood together in silence, each busy with his own thoughts; then there was a stir as the groomsmen who were holding the horses began to bring them up. Within ten minutes the whole party was on the way to Glastonbury.

Chapter 40

AFTER passing one night in the guesthouses in Glastonbury, the entire christening party, with the addition of Elswyth and her children, proceeded on to Wedmore to spend the following weeks. The royal manor of Wedmore was situated on the edge of the Somerset marshes, near the foot of the Mendip hills. Its remoteness had saved it from being raided by the Danes during the recent invasion, and now it stood, well-stocked with food by its reeve, ready to play host to the king's new-baptized guests.

The reeve was not alone in waiting to welcome Alfred and his party. Standing beside the small round man Erlend remembered from a previous visit was a tall thin red-haired thane with a distinctly nervous expression on his face. With a shock of disbelief, Erlend recognized Athelwold.

"Name of the Raven," he said, "how had he the nerve to show his face here?"

"Alfred sent for him," came Brand's laconic reply. "As you can see from the look on his face, it was not Athelwold's idea."

Erlend turned to stare at Brand. "What does Alfred mean to do with him?"

Brand shrugged. "He has not confided in me."

As the two men watched, Athelwold came forward to hold his uncle's bridle. Alfred spoke to him briefly, dismounted, then turned to lift his wife from her horse.

Erlend looked at Elswyth. Her eyes were on her husband's nephew, and Erlend shivered at the look he saw in that inimical dark blue stare.

"Athelwold had better keep his distance from Elswyth." It was Brand, as discerning an observer as Erlend was. "From the look in her eye, she would put a dagger in him as soon as not."

"She might do even worse," Erlend said. "She might put him in the path of Flavia and Edward."

Brand grinned, and shivered dramatically. "I might like to put a knife into Athelwold myself, but I have never been a man for torture," he said.

Both men laughed and swung down from their saddles.

Athelwold had disappeared into the hall. Elswyth's voice came clear. "I would like to tear his eyes out!" she was saying to her husband.

Alfred put an arm about her shoulders and began to walk her toward the hall, his head bent to hers, his voice pitched for only her ears to hear.

Erlend sighed with profound satisfaction. He was home.

"He is the son of my brother, Elswyth," Alfred said to his wife much later that evening when they were alone together in their bedchamber. Elswyth had retired from the feast early, but she was still awake when at last Alfred parted from his guests and came into their room.

"I do not care whose son he is," Elswyth returned now fiercely. She was sitting up in bed, propped against some pillows. Even by the dim light of a single candle, Alfred could see how her eyes were flashing. "He is a traitor! Were he anyone else, you would have him hanged. You know you would."

He replied pacifically, "I do not deny that. But he is not anyone else. He is Athelstan's son, and I cannot harm him." He was undressing, laying his clothes with his usual methodical neatness in a folded pile on the garment chest.

"He would have harmed you! He would have you killed in the most vile and bloody way—"

"I know. I know. I am not excusing him." He pulled his tunic over his head, emerging with ruffled flyaway hair. "Nor am I saying I will ever trust him. I am simply saying that I cannot hang him, thirsty though you may be for his blood."

Her mouth curled downward. "You are making a mistake."

"Perhaps I am. But I cannot do otherwise. I would never rest easy knowing I had taken the life of my father's grandson. No matter what he may have done."

Mutinous silence came from the bed.

He was down to his headband, which he untied and laid carefully on top of the pile of clothes. "If you could get your hands on Ceolwulf, would you hang him?"

"It is not the same thing," came her impatient reply. "Ceolwulf is not worth the hanging."

"Neither is Athelwold."

Elswyth let out an explosive breath. "I hate to argue with you, Alfred! You always turn things about so it seems that you are in the right!"

Alfred grinned. "Guthrum admires you," he said to change the subject. "He told me he thought you were very beautiful." He began to walk toward the bed.

Elswyth snorted, not impressed by the Dane's compliment.

"He also said he'd wager you were good in bed."

"*What!*"

"But what impressed him most of all," Alfred continued, ignoring her seething outrage and climbing in beside her, "was when I told him you had personally trained all the horses we robbed from him at Wilton. He was much taken with the improvement in them when he reannexed them at Wantage."

"It seems to me you are getting much too friendly with that disreputable Viking," Elswyth said severely. "Don't forget, Alfred. That is the man who almost stole your kingdom."

"I am not like to forget that, my love."

He held out an arm and she nestled cozily into the hollow of his shoulder. "Do you really think you can trust him this time?" she asked.

The teasing note had quite left his voice when he answered, "I think so, but I promise you I have no intention of relaxing my vigilance. Wessex must be put into a perpetual state of readiness. I doubt we shall see real peace in my lifetime, Elswyth."

She pressed her cheek against the warm bare skin of his shoulder. "So Guthrum will continue to be King of Mercia and East Anglia," she said.

His arm around her tightened. "I am sorry, love. There is naught I can do for Mercia now. Our task is to hold out here in Wessex. For the moment we must leave it to Ethelred to lead the Mercian resistance. Ethelred and your brother Athulf. And perhaps someday Edward, who is half Mercian himself, will be able to take a more effective stand than I can."

A little silence fell as she considered this thought. Then she asked, "What will you do here in Wessex?"

"I will build the fortified burghs we have talked about before. And I must work out a system that will enable me to keep an army in the field at all seasons. This coming and going of the fyrd is disastrous."

"Mmm." He felt the tickle of her long lashes as they brushed against his bare skin. He moved his hand up and down her shoulder in a slow, deliberate caress and touched his lips to the satin smoothness of her crown.

He said lazily, "And I must begin to seek out men of learning, teachers who will come to Wessex to help restore the civilization we have lost during these many years of struggle."

"I knew we would get down to the books eventually," came Elswyth's husky voice.

He chuckled. "You know me too well."

"What will Erlend do now?" she murmured. "Will he return to Denmark?"

He dropped a soft kiss on her hair. "I don't know what he will do. Poor boy. He said to me the other day that he had been in England for so long that he was like a creature torn between two worlds."

"I don't think he would be happy in Denmark," Elswyth said. "Of all that fierce crew you have had baptized, Erlend is the only one with the soul of a Christian."

"I know. I invited him to remain in Wessex if he wished."

"That was nice."

"Elswyth . . ."

"Mmm?" She tilted her face up to look at him, and her long hair streamed across his arm like an ebony mantle.

"I told Guthrum you were *very* good in bed," he said.

Her eyes narrowed to mere slits. Even half-hidden and dimly lit, they still looked blue. "You didn't," she returned.

A faint smile came across his eyebrows and eyes. "How do you know?"

"You are only saying that to pay me back for telling you you had bugs in your hair."

He grinned.

"But I love you anyway," she said, her voice at its huskiest, her long slim fingers running now over his torso, loving the lean-muscled feel of him, loving the smoothness of his skin, its lovely golden color.

"God, Elswyth. I missed you so much." He slid down in the bed, carefully drawing her with him, conscious always of the child she carried within.

"I missed you too," she whispered.

He turned on his side and drew her against him, not wanting to put his weight on her in any way. She wound her arms about his neck and responded with a torrid kiss. He made love to her with his own special mixture of fierceness and gentleness and they went to sleep wrapped in each other's arms.

For twelve days the Danes remained feasting with Alfred at Wedmore. The king spared no expense to honor his guests. As an Anglo-Saxon, Alfred understood well the heroic dimensions of kingship that would impress the Danes. The king must be generous, a bracelet-giver, a sword-giver, a praise-giver. The king must entertain his followers with hunting by day and feasting and harping in his hall by night. The king's band of retainers must offer comradeship and faithfulness to the brave and the true of heart.

All these things Alfred understood; indeed, they were as much a part of his heritage as was his Christian faith. So he knew well how to entertain Guthrum and his followers, how to bind the Danes to him with ties of friendship and respect. Alfred did not waste his time or his money during the twelve days he kept the Danes with him at Wedmore.

Such were Erlend's thoughts as he sat at the supper board on the last night of the Danes' stay at Wedmore, pretending to listen to one of Guthrum's jarls reliving the day's hunt. The serving folk were clearing away the supper dishes and Erlend's eyes followed a particularly pretty girl as she piled platters on top of each other and then went toward the door. The girl went out and Erlend next turned his eyes toward the high seat, even as he made noises of acknowledgment to the garrulous jarl beside him.

Guthrum and Alfred sat side by side on the high seat this night, as they had on every other night of Guthrum's stay at Wedmore. Elswyth sat at the trestle table directly to Alfred's left, having gracefully relinquished her accustomed place to the Dane.

Guthrum and Alfred were talking together. Guthrum's Saxon had greatly improved during his stay at Wedmore, and the two kings seemed to be conversing with little difficulty.

It amused and somewhat awed Erlend to see his powerful uncle so under the sway of Alfred of Wessex. Guthrum was convinced that the West Saxon king possessed strong magic. Perhaps he did, Erlend thought now. Alfred certainly cast a spell on men. He had cast one on Erlend, that was for certain.

The serving folk had finished with the supper dishes and now the hum of talk in the hall began to die down as Alfred rose to his feet. Erlend looked around the crowded hall, blazingly lit by torches burning every few feet along the tapestry-hung walls. The smell of food still lingered in the air, rising with the smoke toward the smoke hole in the roof. The fire was burning steadily in the central hearth, throwing light from the center of the room to meet with the light from the torches on the walls.

The king began to speak, and Erlend's eyes swung instantly back toward the high seat.

Alfred began by honoring Guthrum's prowess in the hunt that day and expressing his belief in the friendship that now bound the two kings together as brothers. A small sound from the door drew Erlend's attention, and he turned to see the serving girl he had noticed earlier slipping back into the hall to listen to the king. Nor was she alone; a crowd of serving folk had come with her and they all clustered quietly by the door.

She was really very pretty, Erlend thought, noticing the burnished copper of her hair. She had no eyes for him, however. All of her attention was on the king. Slowly Erlend turned his eyes back to Alfred.

"When all is well in the land," Alfred was saying, "praise for that goes to the king. But no man can show any skill, or exercise or control any power, without tools and materials. I will tell you now what are a king's materials, the tools with which he must govern. They are a land well-peopled with men of prayer"—here Alfred looked toward his priest—"men of war"—the golden eyes went around the circle of thanes—"and men of work" —now the king looked gravely at the cluster of serving folk at the door. Erlend had thought he was the only one to notice them come in.

The room was perfectly quiet, as it always was when Alfred spoke. The copper-haired serving girl's face was lit as brightly as one of the torches that flamed on the walls. How was it, Erlend wondered, that no matter how large the group, when you listened to Alfred you always had the distinct feeling that he was speaking directly to you?

"Without these tools," Alfred was continuing, "no king can do his work.

Furthermore, besides these tools, the king must have material. By that I mean he must have provision for the three classes to live on: land, gifts, weapons, meat, ale, clothes, and whatever else they may need. Without these the king cannot preserve the tools, and without the tools he cannot accomplish anything that he ought to do."

This is why I love him, Erlend thought as he watched Alfred standing there before his people. Easy to be generous with gifts of gold. All good leaders knew how to do that. Gold was one thing, but sharing fame, sharing credit, that was something else. That was the test of true generosity. And to go so far as to include the lowest minions in the land! Men of work.

Erlend looked once again toward the serving folk at the door. Some of the men there might even have been at Ethandun, he thought. It had not been just the upper class or the landed ceorls who had filled the valley near Egbert's Stone on that auspicious Whitsunday afternoon. Large numbers of working folk from the various manors had come as well, carrying their borrowed spears, ready to give their lives for Alfred, their king.

Alfred had finished his remarks and now was turning to ask Guthrum something.

Wessex would survive, Erlend thought, suddenly knowing it in his blood and in his bones. This single English kingdom had managed to stand alone against the Danes; and it would continue to do so in the future. The men of prayer, the men of war, and the men of work, united under one great king, would keep Wessex, and hence England, free, and Christian, and Anglo-Saxon for future generations to know.

Guthrum was getting to his feet. Erlend felt a flash of surprise. His uncle must indeed be growing confident of his Saxon.

The Dane stood there for a moment, as silence fell once again around the hall.

He looked splendid, Erlend thought as he beheld his uncle's tall, broad-shouldered form. The yellow hair, still thick, though now lightly touched with gray, gleamed in the light of the wall torches. The sensuous mouth was unusually grave. In the absolute silence, Guthrum raised his cup.

"To Alfred," he said in perfectly comprehensible Saxon, "the most feared by his enemies and loved by his friends of any man in England."

There was a moment of stunned silence.

Good for you, Uncle, Erlend thought.

Then the hall erupted with cheers.

Before she retired to bed, Elswyth sought out Erlend.

"We go to Wantage within the next few days," she said to the Dane. "I hope you are coming with us."

Erlend looked into Elswyth's haughty face. Guthrum, he knew, had not known what to make of Alfred's beautiful wife. She fitted into no category of woman that the Viking had ever come across before.

"I do not know, my lady," he returned now. He added honestly, "I do not know what I should do."

"You think you should return to Denmark," said Elswyth. "But think you, Erlend, what will you do if once you win back Nasgaard?"

"Find me a wife like you and settle down to live like a lord," he replied promptly.

"You would be miserable with a wife like me," Elswyth said. "You need a nice sweet girl who will let you protect her."

Erlend was half-annoyed and half-amused. "You think you would be too much of a handful for me to hold on my rein?"

"I would lead you around as if you had a ring through your nose," Elswyth replied bluntly. "You would not enjoy that at all."

Erlend recalled that Brand had once said much the same thing. He said now to Alfred's strong-minded wife, "Then I will live like a lord in Nasgaard with a sweet and biddable wife to smile at me by day and warm my bed by night."

"Better find a nice West Saxon girl and stay with us," Elswyth recommended. "You will be lonesome in Denmark. No one there thinks like you do."

Erlend stared at her. "How do you mean that?"

"I mean that you have been too long with Alfred. You have become too Christian, Erlend. Stay in Wessex, and Alfred will give you a manor of your own."

"I don't know . . ." Erlend said again.

"I do," came the arrogant reply. Then she bit her lip. "It is bad enough that Edgar is gone. It will be horrible if you go too."

Erlend's heart, which had lain heavy in his breast all week, miraculously began to lighten. "You would miss me?"

"I would miss you. Flavia would miss you. Alfred would miss you most of all. And what is more, Erlend"—her blue eyes met his straight on—"you would miss us."

"I know I would," he replied.

"Your returning to Denmark would be like my returning to Mercia," Elswyth said. "There is nothing there for me anymore. My heart is here in Wessex. As is yours."

Erlend's face was very pale, his green eyes very bright. He said nothing.

The haughty Mercian nose lifted. The midnight eyes glittered. "Do not be a fool, Erlend," said Elswyth, Lady of Wessex. "Stay here with those who love you."

Erlend's face suddenly split into a radiant smile. "Well, yes," he said, "I suppose I will."

Elswyth nodded her black head and gave him an approving smile.

"Thank God," she said. "Now I will have someone to help me with the horses."

Erlend threw back his head and shouted with laughter.

Erlend of Wessex, he thought as he watched Alfred's wife walking back across the floor to the high seat. It had a nice sound to it.

He wondered if the copper-haired serving girl was married.

Afterword

I suppose it was inevitable that I should end my trilogy of Dark Ages England, which began with Arthur, with a book about Alfred the Great. For Alfred holds in real history the place which romance gives to Arthur. Indeed, if one is a true believer in the myth that Arthur will return when England needs him most, then one might even say that Alfred is Arthur reincarnated.

In eleven centuries of English monarchy, only one king has ever been called "the great," and that king is Alfred. The main events of the story I have told in this novel are true. Alone among English kingdoms, Wessex was successful in resisting the Danes. The years that followed Guthrum's treaty with Alfred at Wedmore saw more fighting, true, but no Danish army ever successfully invaded Wessex again. It is because of Alfred, and his courageous leadership, that England did not become a mere colony of Denmark, but preserved its Anglo-Saxon culture and its Anglo-Saxon tongue.

But it is not just as a war leader that Alfred is remembered. In the years of sporadic peace that followed the Treaty of Wedmore, Alfred struggled to bring back a remnant of learning to his devastated land. The educational system of Anglo-Saxon England had been founded on the great monasteries, and these had been devastated by the Danes, leaving Wessex in a state of absolute poverty in regard to learning.

Latin was known only to a few, and the samples we have of it from Alfred's time are of poor quality. Most priests probably knew only the rote words of the Mass. As Alfred himself wrote in the preface to his translation of the *Pastoral Care*: "So general was its decay in England that there were very few on this side of the Humber who could understand their rituals in English or translate a letter from Latin into English; and I believe there were not many beyond the Humber. There were so few that I cannot remember a single one south of the Thames when I came to the throne."

When you consider the state of Wessex at this period of history, in constant readiness for war, tackling the building of a series of fortified burghs that would be the foundation of many future cities, it is nothing short of astonishing that the king should turn his mind and his energies to something as seemingly unimportant as the circulation of books.

That he did so is one of the things that makes Alfred so extraordinary. He understood that a nation needs more than mere freedom; it needs a soul as well. And so he embarked upon his great series of translations from the Latin, transcribing into Anglo-Saxon that handful of books that he felt it was "most needful for men to know."

In the words of Michael Wood, "To embark on such a systematic program of instruction at such a time was the act of a remarkable man, practical, resolute, and ruthless: he took on himself not only the strain of defense but also concern for the future lives of his subjects. That is why, alone among English kings, he is 'the Great,' and why he has rightly never lost the esteem of the English-speaking world."

The bare facts of Alfred's struggle against the Danes are recounted both in *The Anglo-Saxon Chronicle* and in *Bishop Asser's Life of King Alfred*. Little is known of his personal life, save that he suffered extremely from some mysterious illness (which I have made migraine headaches). Asser says nothing about Alfred's wife, Ealhswith, except for giving the date of their marriage. Alfred's will, however, gives a clue as to the king's feelings for his wife.

The king begins his bequests, as is proper, with those to "Edward, my elder son." The will continues with the list of property he wishes to go to, "My younger son . . . my eldest daughter . . . my middle daughter . . . my youngest daughter." Then comes, "And to Ealhswith the estate at Lambourn and at Wantage and at Ethandun."

Not "my wife," but the very personal use of her name. And to her he gave his favorite estates: Wantage, where he was born; Lambourn, the estate nearest to Ashdown, where he had his first great victory over the Danes; and Ethandun, where he triumphed over Guthrum and in so doing saved Wessex.

England was also fortunate in Alfred's successors. His daughter Ethelflaed (Flavia) married Ethelred of Mercia and, upon his death, ruled that country as the Lady of the Mercians. She, working hand-in-glove with her brother Edward, brought to completion Alfred's great plan of fortified burghs. By 916 a line of fortresses from Essex to the Mersey, eleven of them built or repaired by Ethelflaed, sixteen by Edward, menaced the Danes, who hurled themselves against them in vain. History has probably never seen a more successful brother-and-sister act than the one performed between 911 and 918 by Alfred's two eldest children.

Upon Ethelflaed's death, Edward effectively added Mercia to the crown of Wessex. Edward, known to history as "the Elder," was an extraordinarily competent king, and at his death in 924, Scandinavian England was once again under English rule as far north as the Humber.

It was Edward's son, however, who truly brought all the Danish-occupied lands of England under the rule of the Wessex monarchy. At the battle of Brunanburgh, Athelstan defeated Olaf the Dane and became effectively the first true King of England.

One further note on Alfred's children. One of his daughters married Baldwin, Count of Flanders, thus cementing a friendship between England and Flanders that would last for many years. This Baldwin was the son of Judith of France and Baldwin "Iron-Arm," the warrior she eloped with from her father's palace of Senlis.

One of the main difficulties I encountered in the writing of this book was the names. Half of all Anglo-Saxon names seem to start with the preface "Ethel," and to a modern reader it can get very confusing. I helped the reader as best I could by modernizing Ealhswith to Elswyth, calling Alfred's eldest daughter Flavia instead of Ethelflaed, and changing some of the historical Ethelreds and Ethelwulfs to other, more recognizable names. I also provided a list of characters at the beginning of the book to assist readers who may have lost their way.

The poem *The Battle of Deorham* is a reworking of Tennyson's rendition of *The Battle of Brunanburh*. Other poetry in the book is from the Anglo-Saxon poems *Judith, The Voyage of Saint Andrew*, and, of course, *Beowulf*.

I am appending a list of the sources I used to write this book for any readers who may be interested.

Sources Consulted

Original Sources

Asser's Life of King Alfred, ed. W.H. Stevenson, Oxford, 1959.
The Anglo-Saxon Chronicle, ed. J.A. Giles, London, 1912.

Secondary Sources

Burne, A. H. *Battlefields of England*, London, 1950.
Duckett, Eleanor S. *Alfred the Great and His England*, London, 1957.
Finberg, H.P.R. *The Formation of England 550–1042*, London, 1974.
Helm, P. J. *Alfred the Great*, New York, 1965.
Hodgkin, R. H. *A History of the Anglo-Saxons*, Vol. II, London, 1935.
Kirby, D. P. *The Making of Early England*, New York, 1967.
Plummer, Charles. *The Life and Times of Alfred the Great*, Oxford, 1902.
Stenton, Sir Frank. *Anglo-Saxon England*, Oxford, 1947.
Wood, Michael. *In Search of the Dark Ages*, New York, 1987.